WITCHING AFTER FORTY

VOLUME FOUR

A LIFE AFTER MAGIC MYSTERY

L.A. BORUFF

LIA DAVIS

An Inherited Midlife

© Copyright 2024 Lia Davis & L.A. Boruff

Published by The Phantom Pen

PO Box 224

Middleburg, FL 32050

Cover by Glowing Moon Designs

Formatting by The Phantom Pen

All rights reserved under the International and Pan-American Copyright Conventions. No part of this book may be reproduced or transmitted in any form or by any means, electronic or mechanical, including photocopying, recording, or by any information storage and retrieval system, without permission in writing from the publisher.

This is a work of fiction. Names, places, characters and incidents are either the product of the author's imagination or are used fictitiously, and any resemblance to any actual persons, living or dead, organizations, events or locales is entirely coincidental.

Warning: the unauthorized reproduction or distribution of this copyrighted work is illegal. Criminal copyright infringement, including infringement without monetary gain, is investigated by the FBI and is punishable by up to 5 years in prison and a fine of $250,000.

A FIENDISH MIDLIFE

WITCHING AFTER FORTY BOOK 15

LIA DAVIS

1
LUCY-FUR
THE CAT, NOT THE DEVIL

"I GUESS I'm sorry I haven't been in to see you." I paused and studied Alfred's prone form on the bed. He was so still that if I hadn't noticed his chest rising and falling, I'd dismissed him as being dead. Hell, he wasn't undead anymore. Whatever that meant. "To be frank, I've only just missed you today."

With a sniff, I inspected my right foot. The first claw there felt like it was loosening. Ugh, so annoying. I'd asked Ava several times to schedule someone to come give me pedicures, but each time I'd asked, she'd shaken her head and rolled her eyes.

As if I were *amusing* to her.

Pfft. She didn't know the struggle. Besides, there were plenty of cat owners who gave their cats petties.

"Ava said you've been in here since November." I nibbled at the loose claw and considered the date. "I think we're in March now, so it's not like you've been missing all that long." Ava was so dramatic sometimes, seriously. "Four months? That's nothing.

How am I supposed to keep track of everyone all the time, anyway?"

Alfred didn't respond, which I tried to ignore. It wasn't exactly fair to be annoyed at a sleeping man, even if I was halfway sure he was a big fat faker. Seriously, if he needed a vacation from all of Ava's craziness, he just had to say so.

See? I'm a good cat. I do *try* to be nice, and at least twenty percent of the time, I succeed. Maybe fifteen...

For a cat, that's excellent, right?

It doesn't really matter if you think it's excellent or not. *I* think it is, and my opinion is the one that matters.

"Anyway, it's been such a boring few months since you've been snoozing away up here. The man named after me, Luci, with an I, has been running around like a maniac. I've never seen him look so frazzled and, ugh, sweaty."

It'd been disgusting. I mean, come on, was it too much to ask to blot his ugly hairless face once in a while? Maybe take one of those water baths humans were so attached to.

Alfred didn't even snore in response, but that was okay. When I spoke, people listened. No doubt he was processing and absorbing my words.

A muffled sound, like a grunt or something, came from somewhere in the room. I paused in the grooming of my tail and listened. "Is someone in here?" With a long stretch, I stood and cocked my head to hear better. "Hello?" It almost sounded like someone was whispering to me. "Am I on camera?"

If someone was pranking me, I'd scratch their face off.

The volume of the whispering increased. I squinted as if that could help me hear better, and Alfred's voice differentiated itself from the whispers. *"Tell Ava it's the..."* It faded out. I knew it was him because he sounded like a squirrel on helium even from wherever he was talking to me.

"What?" I yelled. "Alfred, is that you? Why are you whispering? Can't you speak up? Just wake up for fuc—"

"Shut up!" he whisper-yelled.

How rude!

"Tell Ava it's the necromancers!"

"Okay, okay, you don't have to be so rude about it, geez."

I hopped off of the side of his bed. "Anything else, your majesty?"

The whispers had disappeared, along with Alfred's annoying high-pitched voice.

What a whiner.

I strolled out of his bedroom and down the hall.

"Hey, Lucy," Ava said as she passed me going toward Alfred's room.

With a massive sigh, I replied, "Hey." Ugh, why did she always have to talk to me? Was talking *that* important?

At the top of the stairs, something bugged me, so I looked back at Ava in time to see her enter Alfred's room. Seemed like there was something I was supposed to have told her.

Oh, well.

2
AVA

"ALFRED," I whispered near his ear right before placing a soft kiss on his forehead. "I'm so sorry it took me so long to get up here. I hate leaving you alone in here."

Although he wasn't really ever alone for long because Winnie refused to leave his side unless one of us made her take a break. Sitting on the rocking chair beside the bed, I glanced over at Alfred's still form. "I trust you won't rat me out to Winnie." I snorted, but then the snort nearly turned into tears. "I'm sorry. I want more than anything to get you up and about. I hope you know that."

He didn't respond, but I hadn't expected him to. "I doubt you can even hear me, but on the off chance you can, I want to keep you up to date on our lives."

Not that they'd been particularly riveting over the last four months. Once Alfred conked out, we'd pretty much gone on hiatus, spending all our spare time trying to find a cure for him or trying to help Luci with his little problem of being locked out of Hell.

Trying being the operative word there. Nothing had worked. I was beginning to think that there was a bigger issue at work. What that could be, I hadn't a clue.

"Luci still hasn't come back." I pulled a blanket over my lap and grabbed my latest release. I'd actually had time to finish it in between the failures of helping Alfred and Luci. "He is so freaked out." He'd been MIA for a couple of weeks now. Olivia was getting really worried.

Rocking the chair, I tried to remember the last thing I'd told Alfred. "Did I tell you Luci got this little statue from a shaman in the Amazon? Um, he's been carrying it around like a security blanket." He had been the last time I'd seen him, anyway. I rolled my eyes and laughed. "The last time I saw him, it was tied around his neck, but he either didn't want to try or couldn't get a hole in it, so he'd weaved a leather string-thing around it, then tied it around his neck. It looked ridiculous. I'm still trying to figure out if he was actually trying to channel the shaman's magic or being a weirdo." I snorted again.

"Anyway, none of that matters right now." I stopped the rocking chair and grabbed Alfred's hand. It was cold, but I held it anyway. "What matters is..." What mattered was that we'd hit a dead end in helping him. We'd tried everything we could think of and everything anyone we knew could think of. I didn't want to tell him that, so I said, "...that Winnie's coming up in a few minutes. I made her take a long lunch and an hour's nap."

Setting his chilly hand back on the blanket, I tried for the thousandth time to heal him.

For the thousandth time, it didn't work. "Yeah, okay, so—" I was trying to think of something to tell him that I hadn't said, probably twice already, when Winnie stuck her head in the door.

A flash of pain crossed her face when she saw Alfred. She'd been completely, utterly wretched the last four months without Alfred. "Hey," she called, her voice soft and sad. "Just letting you know I'm grabbing a sandwich, then I'll be in here."

"Take your time." I waved my novel at her. "I haven't even started reading yet."

She nodded once, then ducked out.

I sighed and got myself together before I tried to read, taking a moment to make sure my voice wouldn't shake. "Chapter Three." I read loudly and steadily and made it through the chapter without looking at one of my favorite people in the whole world in what amounted to a coma beside me.

When I turned the page to chapter four, I glanced up to find Drew leaning against the doorway. "Hey, you." I smiled as he walked toward me. My breath caught as I drank him in. How did I get lucky twice in a lifetime in the husband department? "I was focusing so hard on the chapter," and on not crying, "I didn't hear or feel you come up." We were bonded, which meant I generally knew where he was at all times. It wasn't an exact science, but it sure was handy to see whether he was safe or not. As an officer's wife, worry was my job while he was busy at his.

"It's a good chapter," Drew said, sitting in the second chair we'd brought it in weeks ago. His presence was like a tiny wave of calm in this storm.

I smiled at him, then back at Alfred. "It's taking too long."

Drew reached over and put his hand on my knee. "We don't need to talk about that now."

He was right, of course, but I was upset and growing more so every single day.

"I do have some news." The smile on his face made me hopeful for a distraction.

"Oh, yeah?"

He rocked his chair and squinted at me. "Ian's coming."

His words had said good news, but his tone now said dread and woe. "Why doesn't that sound like you're happy about it?"

"No, no, I am, of course. I'm the one who invited him here."

He needed to inform his face of said happiness. "This is about the job opening? Not a visit?"

Oh, there went his face again. "Yes, he uh." Drew sighed. "He says he's getting tired of the instability of the hunter lifestyle. He wants to settle in one place like Lily did."

Drew's sister Lily had taken a permanent hunter job in Florida, kind of close to her step-grandchildren. To my great luck, Drew had retired here to Shipton Harbor many years ago. He still took the occasional hunter job when they really needed him, but they were few and far between.

"Why here?" I asked and stood to retuck Alfred's blankets around him. My constant healings had kept him from wasting away here in the bed, even though they did absolutely nothing toward waking him up. Even so, Winnie did exercises with him three or four times a day, keeping his body moving. She didn't want him to get sore lying there in the bed. After all, he was completely human now, so we had to worry about blood clots and stuff like that.

"I guess because I invited him." Drew helped me, lifting Alfred so I could fluff the pillows under him. We adjusted him slightly on one side rather than flat on his back, using a few spare pillows.

"I'm glad," I said, smiling at Drew when we were done. "It'll be great for you to have your brother here."

Drew grimaced a smile that brought a giggle to my lips. "What's that face about?"

"I love my brother. You know I do."

After I folded the blanket that had been on my lap, we settled back in our rocking chairs. "I do know."

"The thing is, Ian and I work best in small doses. The occasional hunt, sometimes hanging out. That's how we're at our absolute top brotherly shape."

I could understand that, sort of. I didn't really have anyone in my life like that, but I could imagine. "If he lives here full time, you're afraid you'll get sick of each other?"

He shrugged. "It's not forever. Once he's fully trained at the police department, I can focus on retiring and leave him to it."

"That is a good point." I grabbed his hand and grinned. "After that, you can drive me crazy."

He squeezed my fingers. "That's the goal."

"You feel good about Ian being voted in as sheriff?" I asked.

He nodded and shrugged at the same time. "He's definitely competent, and now that Sam's a vampire, there's nobody else who is the right age or has the right qualifications. Or who isn't an idiot."

I chuckled as I imagined the deputy who had prompted that statement. The poor man was a bit more Barney Fife than Andy Griffith. A total sweetheart, but not so much in the common sense department.

Drew stood and leaned over me, caging me in my chair. A

spark of desire fluttered through my insides. "Sorry, my love. I have to go to work. Ian isn't here and working yet."

"Which means you're still pulling extra shifts." I sighed and held my face up for his smooch. "I'll miss you."

"You, too," he whispered.

"Oh, Alfred," I said softly once Drew left. "Would you please just wake up?"

I stared at him for a few seconds before a loud noise outside the door pulled me from my seat.

"I'm going to *kill* you!"

Uh-oh. That was Zoey's voice, and she only ever got that tone when she was furious with Lucy-Fur, our sassy white cat. I opened the door in time to see a streak of white go by. *Lucy*.

Quickly behind her came Zoey, my nineteen-year-old semi-adopted tiger-shifter ghoul daughter.

Her boyfriend and my semi-adopted ghoul son, Larry, hurried soon after, holding onto his head. He was fully fleshed out, but his head never had properly reattached when I'd accidentally animated him. He'd been a skeleton back then, and his head had an unfortunate habit of falling off. It couldn't fall off now that he was fully human-looking again, with skin and all, but it did like to flop over on him. It was disturbing.

"Puke on the bed," he called.

Ew. Not again. Lucy really had to stop doing that.

I turned to the right to watch him run down the stairs after the two cats and found Winnie pressed against the wall, waiting for the chaos to pass before she came into the room.

She came in with a big ball of yarn and a partially knitted...something... in a big canvas bag. "Blanket?" I nodded toward the bag.

"Scarf."

Erm. "For who?"

"Winston." She said it so matter-of-factly that I nearly accepted her words at face value.

"Winston, the *house*?" I asked.

She rolled her eyes. "It's a blanket, Ava. I thought you sold all those books because they were funny?"

Hmph. I *was* funny, thanks very much. "You're cranky."

She shot me an apologetic glance. "Sorry. I am cranky. I miss Alfred."

I squeezed her shoulder. "I know you do." My phone pinged from my back pocket with Olivia's custom tone. "And I'm so sorry, but I have to go."

She waved me off. "Go. Me 'n Alfie have catching up to do. I haven't talked to him in several hours."

At the door, I looked back at my aunt. She looked completely different from how she'd looked as I grew up, but that was because she had a brand new body. One with spectacular boobs.

Over the last four months, she hadn't flaunted them, not once. Even now, she wore an oversized sweatshirt. She'd lost interest in her excitement of her new body.

Who would've thought that would be disappointing?

3
OLIVIA

"HELLO?"

Ava's voice floated up the stairs from the foyer of Luci's house. Oh, good, I'd been hoping she'd get here sooner than later. "Coming!"

I rushed out of my bedroom and grabbed the bag full of notes and things I'd been accumulating to take to the school. "Coming, coming."

Descending the stairs, I watched every step because it didn't matter how many stairs I'd come down successfully, that one time I'd fallen down the stairs at school, bouncing like a freaking bouncy ball ass over teakettle was the only thing that stuck in my head.

Once safely at the bottom of the stairs, I ran through the living room and down the hall that seemed longer than it had yesterday, and why wouldn't it? This house was nuts. Finally, I burst into the kitchen to find my best friend Ava looking at a nasty burn on my biological father's arm.

My father, Lucifer.

What are you, new here? My dad is the devil. Move on.

"Where have you been?" I fixed Luci with a glare and marched forward to put my stuff down on the table, then round it and snatch his arm out of Ava's hands. "Why are you hurt? I didn't even realize you could get hurt like this." To be completely honest, I didn't have the foggiest clue what would or would not hurt the man. Any time I attempted to bring the subject up or anything else personal, he got cagey and changed the subject.

Not suspicious at all.

"It was my own dumb fault."

Ava pulled his arm back and worked her magic to heal it. "You're lucky I can do this," she muttered. "My magic still isn't working right."

Luci studied her as she bent over his arm. "Indeed. I still can't see why. If I weren't so focused on getting back into my domain, I might be able to figure it out." She glanced up at him, and he smiled fondly down at her. Aw, my dad liked my bestie. How sweet.

Another way to look at it: The devil was fond of his necromancer.

Potayto, potahto.

"How did you say this happened?" I asked pointedly. "And more importantly, where in the world have you been?"

"Oh, that. I found a weakness in the barrier between here and Hell and tried to exploit it."

"I see that worked out really well for you," I said dryly.

With a wink, he continued, "As for where I've been, you know where. I've been trying to get through the barrier. I spent a week or so trying to bribe Cerberus, but he's too well-trained." He rolled his eyes. "He should be. I trained him myself."

"Who's Cerberus?" Ava asked.

"He's the three-headed hound that guards the gate to Hell," I answered, then directed my next statement at Luci. "You've disappeared for extended periods before," I said as the burn slowly began to disappear. "But not weeks. Please don't do that again."

"You were worried?" He reached over with his good hand and tweaked my nose. "My sweet girl."

"Yeah, yeah. Phira was worried, not me." Big, fat lie. I'd been absolutely bothered. "Why is it taking so long?"

Ava shot me an exasperated look. "You're in a mood. My powers suck, and I'm trying to heal a minor god here."

Luci gasped dramatically. "Ex*cuse* me? *Minor*?"

Ava dropped her hands and stared at him. "Do you want me to heal, or do you want to lecture me?" She crossed her arms. "Actually, I'm intensely curious about what kind of god you are, so go ahead. Lecture."

He pursed his lips and sniffed, then held the now-smaller burn out. "Fine."

Ava got back to work on the burn while I tried not to let my nostrils flare too much. "As soon as you're healed, you go find Phira, you hear me?"

Luci held up his other hand and saluted me. "Yes, ma'am."

Ugh. There was only about a seventy percent chance he'd do as I said.

"You're an incredibly lucky man, you know." I pointed at him. "If Phira weren't so independent, you'd be all alone."

"You think I don't know that?" His gaze left me as he winced down at Ava. "We were made for each other, but, dear daughter, don't worry about your mother. She'd been with me on most of my trips. She's been helping me try to get into Hell, and still, I have not been able to get in."

I stared at him for a long moment. "She has? Why hadn't you kept me up to date? I haven't seen much of either of you lately, and no one stops to update me on if you're alive or not."

He nodded with a frown. "I know, and I'm sorry. You're right. I'll try to keep you updated."

Ava released his arm, and he stood, stretching for a moment. "Thank you, my dear."

She smiled up at him and waved away the thanks. "I'm just glad I could *do* it."

"I didn't manage to get into Hell," Luci said as he inspected his perfect-looking arm. "However, that doesn't mean I was wholly unsuccessful. I managed to lock *this* world. Nobody can get in or out without my permission. No more monsters appearing for us to fight over." He grinned. "That hunter friend of yours in Florida, Blair?"

Ava nodded. "Yeah, she's Drew's friend. I haven't actually met her. Well, more Lily's friend now, but Drew knows her from his hunter days."

Luci beamed at Ava. "Well, she had the key to Earth. Can you believe it? We thought it was lost centuries ago. How it ended up in a little shop in St. Harmony, Florida, I'll never know." He turned to me again, his expression serious. "I promise I won't disappear like that again without checking in with you or at least leaving you a note. You have my word."

I gave him a long look, then sighed and forgave him. "Thank you."

He nodded and set off into the house, leaving Ava and me in the kitchen.

"Never in a million years could I have said I'd be here healing the devil." Ava chuckled and looked at the back door when someone knocked on it. "That should be Mom and Dad."

Ava's parents were heading to the school with us. They'd been involved, especially her dad, from the get-go. The Howe family home, a real-life castle tucked in the mountains of West Virginia, had been sitting empty for decades. The only reason it hadn't crumbled while vacant was *magic*. When we'd been trying to figure out where to put the school, John had immediately volunteered the castle.

We'd been working on renovations and getting everything set up since then, and I'd learned one thing.

I did *not* want to be a full-time headmistress.

Teach a class? Sure.

Help them get the school off the ground? Absolutely.

Play substitute when needed? Heck, yes.

Five days a week run the whole shebang?

Ew. Not a fan.

Opening the door, I smiled at Ava's parents. Her dad, John, we'd thought was dead for most of her life—turned out he'd been captured by evil vampires for thirty-some-odd years.

Her mother really had been dead since she was ten, but once she knew how to use her powers, she raised her; then when Winnie found a new body to jump into, Beth had as well.

"Great, the gang's all here," I said brightly. "Everyone ready?"

John wore a big backpack, and Beth had a messenger bag slung over her shoulder. "Ready," she chirped. She looked as excited as she could be.

"You guys really should run this school together," I said. "I'll stick around until we find an appropriate replacement, but I still think it's you two."

Beth looked at John and smiled. "We've been talking about it, and as long as you can get us a portal from the house to the school, we're in. We want to be around a lot for the new baby."

Ava beamed at them. "Of course you'll be around for the baby. She's going to need her great-grandparents."

Ava's son, Wallie, was having a baby soon. Well, his girlfriend, Michelle, was. We loved her.

"I can't tell you how happy I am to hear that." I couldn't help myself. I gave Beth a big hug. "Let's go see your school." It was such an immense relief to know I wouldn't have to do this all the time. Beth had just made my day times ten.

"I'm really excited," Ava said as we stepped into the pantry Luci had created to be a portal room to the school. "I haven't been here since you started renovating."

Didn't I know it? I'd been *dying* to show her. We stepped through the portal into a small closet near the administration offices.

My enthusiasm only increased when Ava stepped out of the closet and into the hallway. She gasped, her mouth dropping open in awe. The hallway was grand, with marble floors and a bright red runner leading through the building. Every window had been filled with stained glass depicting various magical scenes and creatures.

"Come on. Quick tour?"

Ava nodded eagerly. John and Beth had been here lots, but they tagged along anyway.

"When are we set to open?" Ava asked.

"If all continues to go this well, and we get enough teachers hired, we might be able to do a few summer classes, but the official first term will be in September." Five or so months to go.

The classrooms were all decked out with the newest technology. Just because we were all magical and stuff didn't mean we could do without Wi-Fi or television.

Nobody should have to miss watching Jensen.

I stopped in a doorway and turned on the lights. "Potions classroom."

With a sharp intake of breath, Ava looked around with stars in her eyes. "I've never seen anything like it."

The room was filled with cauldrons waiting for bubbling ingredients, shelves full of said ingredients, and a long smartboard. We'd thought about doing whiteboards but ultimately wanted to use the latest technology. That was the most modern thing in there, though. The stone walls gave the room a sense of history.

"We're going to have so much fun here," Ava said, and I couldn't help but agree.

We were going to make something amazing.

I was certain of it.

"Come on, let me show you the dorms."

We were almost sure to have a few live-in students. We'd considered making it a daytime-only thing, but between us, we'd been able to name three children who would probably love to stay here. If Zoey were a few years younger, she might've wanted to as well.

"We just finished the eight to twelve wing." I opened the door to the spiraling staircase that went up the tower to the girls' side.

Ava looked around in admiration. The spaces were open

and sunny, the top the brightest, with a skylight at the top of the staircase. The walls were stone, like pretty much everywhere else, and in each bedroom was a bed, desk, and dresser.

"There was enough room in this gigantic tower to put a three-bedroom dorm on each floor. Each dorm has its own common area, kitchen, and bathroom."

"This is amazing." Ava peeked into the bathroom and sighed. "Can we live here, too?"

"Winston would revolt," Beth said as she opened the fridge. Empty.

"We're working on stocking it." I grinned sheepishly.

Ava just shook her head. "This place is going to be amazing for the kids. I'm so happy for them."

My heart swelled with pride. We had something special here and were about to open the doors for some lucky magical children. It was going to be fantastic.

"Let's go check out the grounds before we go," I said. "There's a wonderful place for the gardens, which—"

Beth clapped her hands and practically jumped up and down. "John and I are starting the garden today." She hurried out of the room, dragging John behind her.

Ava and I exchanged a glance. I smiled and shrugged. The two of them would be thrilled to work outdoors. Beth liked gardening and growing herbs more than Ava.

We stepped outside and were immediately surrounded by beautiful trees, flowers, and a stream flowing right through the middle of the grounds. I pointed out the spot Beth had in mind for the garden, and Ava's face lit up.

"Perfect." She beamed at me as her parents walked away and

started pointing at the garden and talking about what should grow where. "Are you sure you don't want to do this full-time?"

"Don't get me wrong. I've loved getting the castle ready." I really had. It'd been a blast. "But I miss my kids and my husband. I even miss my parents, both sets."

"Well, thanks. Mom and Dad, once they made the decision to take you up on the job, have spoken of nothing else."

She looked up at the castle and pointed to the side. "What's going on over there?"

I swung around to see what she meant. "Oh, that's the wing the godmothers asked for."

"Eh?"

A giggle fought its way out of my mouth as I looked at her confused face.

"I was as surprised as you look like you are. There is a branch of fae who are fairy godmothers. They're technically the Tian, but they like the name godmothers and get this." I grabbed her hand and squeezed. "The women go by fairy godmothers, right? The men go by *sugar daddies!"* I collapsed against Ava, laughing my butt off. I'd hee-hawed about the sugar daddies from the moment the head Tian had told me about them.

We shared a good laugh but finally calmed enough for her to ask, "They're having classes here?"

"Yeah, that whole wing will be for their students to live in and their classes. Apparently, the Tian don't come into their powers until middle age. Usually forties to fifties. They have to be thoroughly trained, and their current facilities are worn down, so I offered to incorporate them here."

"Whoa," Ava said, staring up at the tarped roof of the godmother wing. "That's nuts."

"Not so nuts when you hear how much they offered to kick in of the remodel." I raised my eyebrows. "It covered seventy-five percent of the *whole* thing."

After a low whistle, Ava said, "Sugar daddy fits, then, eh?"

Indeed.

4
AVA

THE BUZZING COMING from my phone put a frown on my face. At this rate, I was never going to get this paragraph done. I turned over my phone to see who was calling. *Melody. Hm.* Why was she calling me at nearly midnight? Couldn't be a good reason.

"Hello?"

"Ava, you gotta get over here to my house." Melody's voice was panicked. As the leader of the local witch coven, she wasn't one to easily get rattled. That was partly why I'd chosen her to pass the leader mantle on to.

By her worried tone, something had spooked her.

“Umm, sure.”

"I just saw lights on in Penny's dark, empty house. Penny's on the run, isn't she? It could be her getting something from her house. I mean, it could also be a break-in, but we should check it out,” she whispered.

“Where are you?” Hopefully, she wasn’t heading over to

Penny's house without backup. Penny and her brother Bevan were dangerous.

"I'm in my kitchen, peeking out the window." Again, she whispered her words.

So, I lowered my voice and whispered back. "Why are you whispering?"

"Oh." She laughed and spoke at a normal volume. "I don't know. Can you come over?"

I hesitated for just a moment before agreeing. I'd had a busy day with Olivia at the school, helping Mom and Dad get settled in. We hadn't returned home until well after dark. I just wanted to get one little chapter done before going to bed.

Drew was still at the station, but any strange activity in our small town could mean trouble. Any strange activity at Penny's house almost definitely meant big trouble. "Stay put. We'll be right there."

If I was being dragged out at midnight, then my bestie was coming with me. No way I was going alone. Olivia and her handy-dandy portal-making ability. Luci might've been a better choice, but who knew if he was still around? He'd be in big trouble if he wasn't, but that was his problem.

I dialed Olivia's number and waited anxiously for her to pick up.

"Chello?" she said sleepily.

My heart rate quickened as I explained the situation. "We might have a real lead. If Luci is there, bring him along."

"Ten-Four. Be there as soon as possible."

I hung up the phone, slightly relieved but still a little freaked. We needed to hurry.

I texted Drew as I went downstairs. **Melody saw lights at Penny's. Olivia's coming to take me to check it out.**

His reply was quick and firm. **You WILL wait for me at Melody's before going in.**

Oookaaay. Mr. Alpha Walker was putting his foot down. Shew, I wasn't mad about it. I typed a quick reply. **Yes, sir. Can you be this commanding tonight once we're both here together?**

This time the reply took a few seconds as I stood in the kitchen doorway and waited for Olivia. Eventually, he sent back two emojis. An eggplant and a peach.

Hehehehehehe. Yessir. I was about to catch a case of the tingles.

"Mom?" Wallie walked out of the living room. I hadn't even realized he was there. "What are you giggling about?"

And there is the kid to chase away the tingle.

"Nothing, dear. You and Michelle having a movie night?" Now that I wasn't absorbed in Mr. Drew Walker's texts, I heard the sounds of some action flick or another. The kids had been spending a lot of time here when they weren't in school.

"Yeah, we have a long weekend and are out Friday." He checked his watch. "Er, we're out today, that is. It's midnight."

"It's also April Fools' Day." I winked at him. "In this family, you better be on your toes."

He drew himself up and puffed out his chest. "How about it is you who should be on your toes?"

Pushing at him, I chortled. "You better not prank your mama."

He walked back to the living room. "We'll see."

I didn't know where the other inhabitants of my house were, but Olivia and I didn't need a big entourage for this.

The front door opened a crack with a slight groan from Winston. I turned to see Olivia inching through the tight opening in the door.

"Uh, Winston?" She looked up at the ceiling. "Little help here?"

The house hadn't liked Olivia at first, but he'd since grown to be pretty fond of her. He almost always opened the door for her now.

"Winston," I scolded. "Why are you being rude to Olivia?"

Winston groaned again, and the door opened another inch or so. With a huff, I hurried forward and yanked on the door. It gave without a bit of resistance, sending me careening backward.

Air rushed past me like a strong breeze carrying the scent of some spicy cologne, and Sam caught me before I butt-planted hard on the floor. He set me firmly back on my feet.

"Thanks for the assist," I muttered, glaring around at my house. "What is the deal?"

Winston groaned again, sounding almost pitiful.

"Okay, I get it. You're sorry. If that was an accident, I forgive you. If it was intentional, you're in big trouble, mister."

The last groan he gave was barely audible and definitely felt contrite.

"Sam, are you going with us to check this out?" I asked.

He snorted. "Drew called. He got held up by a drunk and disorderly, so I'm your muscle."

"What a nice muscle you are," Olivia said, looking at her husband-slash-my lifelong best friend with starry eyes.

"Yeah, yeah, he's handsome. Let's go." I winked at her as I waited for her to open a portal to Melody's backyard. We'd portaled there more than once for various reasons. Mostly coven meetings.

As soon as we stepped through the portal, a familiar rush of energy pulsed through my body. That sometimes happened with Olivia's portals, like a zing. I glanced over at Olivia, who was already looking around with a grin on her face, and Sam adjusting his sleeve. Melody's backyard was just as beautiful as ever, with a garden that I knew was vibrant in the daylight, not so much under the new moon. A cozy patio area stretched out from the back door. We'd portaled so many times it had become second nature to us. No nerves, no worries. Just us and her portals. Simple as that.

"Hey," Melody said, rushing off of the back patio. "The light went out about ten minutes ago. I never saw anyone leave, but I think we missed the mark."

I knew we hadn't hurried enough, darn it.

"Let's still go." I started walking around Melody's house. "They could still be there, or there could be some clue or something."

"It's the cook, in the library, with the candlestick," Olivia said with a giggle.

I snorted but kept walking. Sam hurried in front of me, shooting me an exasperated look as he did. He was here to be protective, and he was going to take his job seriously.

Not that I'd expected any less.

So, I wouldn't remind him that I could control him at any moment. Not that I would do that to him.

We tiptoed across the street toward the empty house, and I couldn't stop a shiver from running down my spine. I didn't scare easily, but this place was eerie. Knowing Penny or Bevan could be there even now. They weren't powerful enough to cause me any alarm, or at least they shouldn't have been, and yet somehow, they'd evaded us for months.

Granted, Luci had been focusing more on getting into Hell than finding his two runaways, but still. I'd given considerable attention to finding them, as had Olivia, the coven, and my parents... and Winnie when she wasn't with Alfred.

As Sam pushed open the creaky door, my heart raced with anticipation. Please let this be something helpful. It would've been really nice to tick the Penny and Bevan line off of my to-do list. Crystal was presumably still trussed up in Hell. That was if whoever had taken over the reins hadn't let all of the prisoners loose.

Now that was a scary thought I tried to stay away from. If every bad soul was loose in Hell... ugh. Hopefully, that was something Luci could handle. At least they couldn't get to Earth now.

The house was dark and a bit musty, like it'd been closed up for a while. Which it had been. We hadn't been here since we'd nabbed Crystal. Melody'd been keeping an eye out, but we had no reason to come here and dust. The house definitely needed a good dusting. Cobwebs covered every corner of the place.

Dead silence itched at me, and I couldn't shake off the feeling that we were being watched.

Sam closed his eyes and inhaled. "There's nobody here," he said. "But someone was recently."

"Duh," Olivia muttered and poked him in the side. "We knew that."

He gave her a scathing look that only people in love could get away with. "I mean, my vampire senses and smells are confirming it."

"Thank you." I grinned at Sam. "I appreciate it, even if your cranky wife doesn't."

"I'm not cranky," she grumbled, then cocked her head. "Maybe a little cranky."

We started searching, but the house was just... a house. DVDs in the entertainment center, books scattered on shelves, pictures of Penny, Crystal, and Bill, her late husband who'd been killed when I first returned to Shipton. Lots of other people were pictured, too. Presumably, extended family. "Have we looked into these people?" I asked. "Penny and Bevan could be staying with them.

Pulling out her phone, Olivia typed on the screen. "I'll send Luci a note to make sure. If he hasn't, it's something we can work on."

We quickly searched the house, looking for any sign of why someone had been there. I followed Olivia, Sam, and Melody as we made our way through Penny's house.

We searched every room but found nothing until we reached the office. The lack of dust on the desk showed us exactly where something should have been. There was an outline where a book-shaped object had once rested. Someone had taken it from here not too long ago.

"I can't be positive," Olivia said, "but I think that was a day planner."

"Where this clean spot is?" The dust was perfectly outlined in a rectangle. It was the perfect size for a day planner.

"Yes, or maybe it was an address book." She shrugged. "That has to be what they came for. Nothing else has been disturbed."

Sam inhaled deeply. "I can almost smell them. Just a hint of something..." He cocked his head. "Fruity? Like berries."

I had no idea what that meant, but at least we had some idea of why they'd come.

"What's that?" Sam pointed to the area around my feet.

I bent and grabbed the small piece of paper I'd totally missed, even though I'd almost stepped on it.

"It's torn off of a bigger piece of paper." There was no way to tell what kind. "It just says June twenty-fifth."

I looked over at my friends. Olivia's eyes went wide, and Sam's nostrils flared as a growl rumbled through his chest. He'd always been so protective of me.

"June twenty-fifth?" Melody looked at the three of us. "Why do you seem so freaked out?"

With a shiver, I looked at the coven leader. "June twenty-fifth is my birthday."

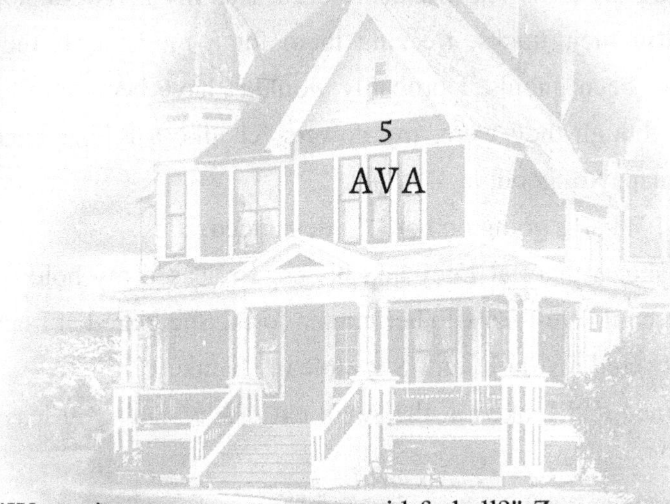

5
AVA

"WHERE'D YOU PUT IT, you stupid furball?" Zoey screeched from upstairs.

Oh, not again.

Stepping out of my office, I peered around the corner, stopped, and waited while Lucy-Fur thundered down the stairs. How did such a small cat manage to sound like such a large elephant?

Lucy streaked by as Zoey rounded the corner and came into sight upstairs. Instead of running down the stairs, Zoey leaped and shifted into her tiger form. How could one cat make a tiger so mad? I had to keep a straight face, but it was difficult.

A crash from the living room spurred me into action. I flew across the foyer and into the living room to find Zoey chasing Lucy around in circles while they batted at each other. Two cats smacking at one another wasn't usually a big deal, but Zoey was a two-hundred-pound tiger. Even though she was on the small side, she'd knocked over the end table and was dangerously close to demolishing a stack of books.

Flinging my arms out to either side, I used my magic to stop both cats in their tracks, freezing them for a moment. If they hadn't both been ghouls, I probably wouldn't have been able to, and even though they were, my powers felt like a rubber band about to snap. Not good.

"Zoey! What is going on here?" I demanded.

Zoey shot a glare at Lucy and hissed. I released my hold on her so she could shift back to her human form. She glared at Lucy as she answered my question. "She stole my blanket!"

I groaned and looked at the small cat. "Why can't you leave her alone?"

Lucy yawned, unimpressed by my reprimand.

"Fine," I said, "Lucy, give Zoey back her blanket. Now."

Lucy stared at me for a moment like she wanted to argue, then sighed and hung her head. "It's in the attic."

Zoey huffed in Lucy's face, which blew Lucy's downy white fur back. "Oh, disgusting." Lucy gagged and jumped up on the back of the couch to put some distance between Zoey and her.

Zoey retaliated by turning back into a person, then reached over and shoved Lucy off of the back of the couch. "Brat."

Lucy screeched but didn't come out from behind the sofa.

Enough of this circus and these monkeys.

As I turned toward the kitchen to go get some breakfast started, the doorbell rang. I looked around. "Uh, Winston? Can you get that, or is it a non-magical being?"

Nothing. He didn't even groan at me. So odd.

I walked over to the door and peeked out the window beside it. "Oh!" I called up the stairs. "Drew, Ian is here."

I'd completely forgotten he was coming after the eventful day we'd had yesterday. Once I'd hit the bed, I'd crashed and slept straight through until this morning. Drew had worked late again. I hadn't even realized he'd come in last night.

He thundered down the stairs with a big smile as I opened the door to find Pearl on the other side of Ian. Glancing back at Drew and his smile, which was a bit dimmer now, I bit back a chuckle.

He loved his grandmother, but her appearance never meant anything good. "Hey, hello."

Ian walked in and hugged me. "I'm glad you're here," I said warmly. "It's so nice to see you."

"You too, little sister."

I couldn't help but beam at him for that comment. He wanted me to feel welcome in the family. I didn't exactly *not* feel welcome, but his family hadn't been overly concerned with reaching out. In fact, Ian had his own concerns when we first met. It was nice to see that he got over that.

Drew said his family was just like that. They hunted, and they didn't do much else, so I didn't take it to heart.

"Grandmother," Drew said as he took Pearl's hands. "What are you doing here?"

She turned her cheek up for him to place a kiss on it, which he did dutifully.

They were about as warm as a river rock, and I shivered at the thought. "What brings you here? Please, come in."

"Family business," Pearl said in her no-nonsense tone.

"Speaking of family business," Drew said.

At the same time, I motioned toward the living room. "Please, sit down."

She shook her head at me, then looked at Drew. "Yes?"

"Why did you send us on that hunt after Scotland?" He raised his eyebrows at her. He'd been stewing on this for a while. I'd talked him out of calling her and confronting her, but he obviously was going to use her visit as the ideal time to bring it up. "Any hunter could've done that."

I wasn't sure I agreed with that assessment. That monster had nearly kicked our butts, and together we were pretty strong.

Pearl sniffed and reached into her little leather handbag. "In my considerably knowledgeable opinion, you two were the best for the job." She pulled something small out. "Here, hold this."

As she held it out to Drew and his hand rose up to take it, Ian yelled. The whole scene played out in front of me like I was watching some random comedy movie. Drew took the object as Ian hollered, "No, don't!"

Too late. Drew held up a small cat figurine. "What?" He blinked a couple of times, looking stunned. After about a second, I knew why. Through our bond, I felt a muted version of what was happening inside him. I was used to feeling the ebb and flow of magic around me. This was unreal, as though a bolt of lightning surged through our connection, igniting a fire within me. Power coursed through his veins, pulsing with a vitality that was both daunting and exhilarating. It was like the first time we had connected all over again. Our love was not just physical but mystical. Nothing would tear us apart.

While he stood there looking flummoxed, Pearl grinned from ear to ear. She plucked the cat figurine out of his hand. "Thank you." She drew out the vowels in the words, clearly pleased with herself. "I'll see myself out." She walked outside with Ian on her heels.

I rushed to Drew's side and grabbed his arm. "Are you okay?"

He looked at me with wide eyes. "I think so? What in the world was that?"

Ian returned and closed the door. "She portaled back to North Carolina."

The power moving between Drew and me began to dim. I helped him into the living room and onto the couch. By the time we sat, it was at a manageable buzz.

"What was that?" he asked again.

Ian sighed and sat across from us. "You know Lily took that job in Florida with Blair at the antique shop?"

Drew nodded. "Yeah."

"Blair has a knack for finding mystical objects. Do you remember when we were kids, something was stolen from the artifact room?" Ian arched one eyebrow as Drew smacked his face with the palm of his hand.

"The cat figurine." He moaned. "She unlocked my powers."

"*What*?" I stared at Drew, my mouth hanging open a bit. It'd been pretty clear some sort of power had been given, but I'd assumed it was temporary or a burst of energy from the cat.

He sucked in a deep breath and shuddered. "This is a power that was already within me. Thirty years ago, that object was used to unlock powers for every hunter who hit maturity. If it hadn't been stolen this would've been done years ago."

"But what is it?"

Drew furrowed his brow. “It would seem I have the ability to boost others’ magic.”

That made sense because that is exactly what it felt like.

Noise in the kitchen drew my attention, so I made my way there. I found my dad at the stove, stirring something in the stew pot. Whatever it was smelled amazing.

"Whatcha cooking?" I hadn't even known anything was cooking until I stepped into the kitchen.

He didn't look at me right away, which made me a little suspicious, but then he turned and smiled at me. "It's time to do an extra powerful spell to find Penny and Bevan. So, I'm making a stew to give us enough power to do the spell. This should help your little magic problem too."

A stew that helped boost my magic, huh? "What's in the stew?"

He waved me off and stirred the mystery stew. "A little of this and that."

I crossed my arms. He was so full of crap. "What is it?"

Dad picked up a fork, stabbed a piece of meat from the stew, and then held it out to me. "It's human. Necromancers need to eat human flesh and meat to become strong enough to perform the most powerful spells."

Oh, yeah, he was *full* of crap. "I don't think so."

Ian sauntered into the kitchen and sat at the table. "No, it's true. I researched necromancers once and ran across that and a few other weird stuff they do."

I studied my brother-in-law for a few moments, gauging whether he was telling the truth. My empathy didn't detect a lie. That meant at least he believed it.

"How come no one told me about this? Seems like I would've at least heard about it by now."

Everything I knew about being a necromancer up to this point was self-taught through trial and error. Most of the time, I made it up as I went along. So, this human meat thing could've been true. Too bad Owen wasn't here to verify it for me. Not that my dad had any reason to lie to me.

Stepping closer to Dad, I took the fork and smelled the meat. The scent wasn't unlike the animal meat we normally ate. In fact, it smelled pretty good. I brought the fork to my mouth and nearly gagged. Bile threatened to come up and out of my throat. "I can't eat human meat!"

That was when Dad and Ian burst out laughing. Dad took the fork from me and shoved the piece of meat into his mouth. After he chewed it—and chewed it, and chewed it again, gag me—to my shock, he said, "April Fools!"

Ugh, good grief. They were complete and utter buttfaces. "That is *not* funny. I almost ate that."

He grinned at me and forked up another bite. "It's pork roast."

I was *so* done with my father for the day.

Done.

6
OLIVIA

"EVERYBODY READY?" I leaned over and pressed a kiss to Sammie's forehead. "Young man, do not talk your grandmother Phira into letting you stay up late. You know she can't say no to you."

With a cheeky grin, Sammie blinked his eyes, fluttering those long eyelashes at me. "I promise, Mommy."

"Mmhmm." He was full of a bunch of hooey. "I mean it, young man. Bedtime is eight, and that's with brushed teeth and a washed face."

Suddenly I didn't want to go with Sam and Wade to interview a new bartender candidate. I wanted to snuggle up in bed with my little long-lashed boy. I pulled him into an extra tight hug. "Sleep well, babe. I'll see you in the morning."

Sam gave him a big hug, too, then held out his hand to me. Taking Sam's hand with mine, I finger-waved at Phira. "Thanks again."

"It's my pleasure." She tugged on Sammie's hair. "Come on. I think we should eat dessert and then eat dinner."

Oh, yeah. Sammie wasn't going to miss us at all.

Sam grinned and led me toward the door. "Let's go get Wade."

We didn't have to go far. He lived in a small apartment under Winston, but he was walking across the field between Ava's house and Luci's, where we'd been staying since we all manifested our powers. It was a lot easier to have us here, sort of cushioned away from society.

Wade smiled as we neared each other. He was tall and burly in a fit kind of way. His salt and pepper hair had grown out over the months since moving to Shipton, so it started to curl. "I'm more excited than I thought I would be to go interview a bartender."

Sam chuckled. "Same." They started chatting about qualifications and salaries as I created a portal into the back room of their bar. I had to admit, I was excited for them.

They'd been working so hard on this venture. I'd been trying to stay out of it mostly, but man, was it hard. My instinct was to jump in all gung-ho and help with the nitty-gritty. Cute as it was to see them so passionate, I wanted to make sure they didn't bite off more than they could chew. Hehe. Bite.

Red Lipped Mary was going to be quite the spot. They weren't just trying to attract vampires. They'd been working hard to get the information out to all of the supernational community within a couple hundred-mile radius.

"When does he get here?" I asked as we exited the office.

The bar looked amazing. The darkness engulfed us, and I relished the sensation of the dim lighting, the sultry ambiance that beckoned us to indulge in our deepest desires. The beautiful stone walls were partially lined with red velvet, and the air was thick with the scent of cinnamon and incense.

Wade reached around the bar and picked up a remote control. Soon the sound of throbbing bass music resonated throughout the room, and I couldn't help but sway to the rhythm. Sam and Wade both grinned from ear to ear, their eyes gleaming with excitement. After spending time in Faery, I was no stranger to the enchantment of a beautifully designed space, but this was different. It was dark and dangerous, a haven for creatures like us. I was ready to lose myself in it, and my husband could tell.

He pulled me close and swayed with me a bit. "I'm ready for a night off," he whispered. "Maybe we can sneak away."

Ignoring Wade, I pressed myself close to Sam and gave him a deep, passionate kiss.

"Ahem," came Wade's voice from behind us. "Our candidate will be here any minute."

Drat. It was kinda rude to make out with Sam in front of Wade anyway. I made myself behave.

Good timing, too. The door opened, and a figure stepped in. He was tall and slim, with piercing jade eyes that seemed to glow from within. His hair was slicked back, and his lips were plump and pink, contrasting the paleness of his skin. He surveyed the space before he stepped forward.

"Name's Hank," he said in a smooth voice. "I have an appointment?"

Sam and Wade both made their way around the bar and greeted him with a smile.

"Hank, it's so nice to meet you," Sam said warmly. "We're looking for someone to manage the bar. Please, sit down." He motioned toward one of the closer tables. I'd helped them get interview questions together. We didn't exactly have to follow the same HR rules and laws humans did, but we also didn't want to say something rude.

Hank nodded, his eyes never leaving Sam's face. We all took our places around the table, and Sam began to ask Hank questions.

"So, what made you interested in managing our bar?"

Hank grinned. "I'm a vampire," he said as if that should explain everything.

A smile tugged at my lips.

"I'm sure you can guess why," he continued. "The idea of a safe, welcoming place for creatures like me is attractive. I'm sure this bar will be a great success."

Sam nodded, clearly satisfied with Hank's response.

We went through the other questions, then Wade asked, "Can you tell us about yourself?"

I couldn't help but feel a bit sorry for Hank Talbert as he sat across from us, completely still. He had come so highly recommended by Jax, the vampire leader of the United States, and seemed like the perfect candidate for the head bartender position at our new club. We were set to open in a month's time, so Sam and Wade needed to get the staff trained.

Anyone with such an unfortunate backstory deserves some compassion. "I was turned by a vampire in New York City more than two hundred years ago," he began. "My family..." He shook his head. "Even after all this time, it hurts. I eventually confessed to them what happened to me. I'd hoped my wife would choose to join me, but she rejected me, as did my children." The shadows in his eyes told me he still mourned them.

"Were you turned against your will?" I asked quietly.

Sam and Wade shot me sharp glances.

"I'm sorry. Is that a rude thing to ask?" I wasn't sure at all. Sam had only been a vampire for a short time, so all these rules were completely new for us.

Hank smiled warmly. "Not really. It doesn't bother me, at least. Yes, I was turned violently." He shuddered. "The man who sired me put me through unimaginable torture before finally turning me. I was devoutly religious as a human, so turning me into a vampire was just about the worst thing he could've done to me."

My chest tightened, and I swallowed a lump in my throat. We sat in stunned silence for a moment. It was hard to hear stories like that, and there wasn't much any of us could say in response.

Finally, Sam spoke up and asked Hank to expand on his working experience. He was an experienced bartender. "This is a job that makes decent money while allowing me to work exclusively at night."

Sam and Wade exchanged glances as they read through his resume one more time before making their decision. As far as qualifications went, there was no doubt that Hank would do an excellent job behind the bar.

"One question I expected you to ask was why I hadn't accumulated a fortune." Hank looked nervous now. "I'll tell you honestly: I'm terrible with money."

A laugh bubbled up my throat. "I do admire honesty."

"I've tried investing, but I always end up investing in the wrong companies. I can't bring myself to compel anyone to give me money."

"Compel them to handle yours," I suggested. "And if they do a good job, give them a cut."

He cocked his head at me. "I never thought about it that way."

With a shrug, I grinned. "I'm a problem solver."

The look on Hank's face changed from nervousness to relief when Sam offered him the position of head bartender at our new club.

We were all confident that with Hank's help, our new bar would quickly become popular among vampires and humans alike.

Hank accepted the offered salary with enthusiasm, and an hour later, I headed home, leaving Wade and Sam there to keep working. They had far more people to hire, and it was time to start getting their first order ready.

As I climbed the stairs to the second floor and my bedroom, the sound of Sammie crying reached me. I rushed past my bedroom, past the hall closet, and into his bright blue room. "Sammie?"

He sat up and rubbed his eyes.

"What's wrong?" I asked and pulled him into my arms.

"It was so scary, Mommy," he said, his voice trembling as he tried to fight back tears. "A woman was coming after Daddy."

I hugged him tightly. "It's ok, sweetie, it was just a dream."

"This is my fault." Phira walked in and sat on the other side of Sammie's bed. "We watched that vampire slayer TV show before bed."

"Yeah." Sammie's lip trembled. "Biffy is going to come put a wooden stake in Daddy's heart."

"She's not going to come hurt Daddy." I rocked him back and forth. "She's not real, honey."

"But I've heard you and Aunt Ava talk about how Uncle Drew

is a hunter. Is that the kind that's going to stake Daddy and make him turn into dust?"

I couldn't help my chuckle. "No, my love. The hunters don't do that sort of thing." Anymore. "They only go after evil vampires, and Daddy is certainly not evil."

"Besides," Phira added. "If she did exist, Grandpa Luci would know her."

Sammie brightened up. "That's true. He wouldn't let her hurt my daddy."

"No, he wouldn't." I pressed a kiss to the top of his head and then settled him back against his pillow. "Now, you go back to sleep, and if Biffy shows up again, tell her she can deal with Grandpa Luci."

His eyes began to drift shut almost immediately. Poor little guy. This had to be a big scary thing. He now had powers and magical grandparents. His life was certainly not going to be anything like normal.

Phira and I left the room. I pulled the door to, leaving it cracked a little.

“I'm sorry,” Phira said. “I didn't know it would give him nightmares.

I took her hand and gave it a little squeeze. “It's not your fault. I let him watch stuff like that all the time. I think it had more to do with the newness of learning about the paranormal than a TV show.”

Looking back at the door, I frowned and worried that he wasn't dealing well with his new powers. That was when Phira squeezed my hand. “He's a strong little man. He'll be okay.”

A smile tugged my lips. She must have known what I was thinking. A mother's intuition. I pulled her into a hug, and she squeezed me back. “Thanks for being here. I really couldn’t get through half this stuff without you, Luci, Sam, Ava, and everyone.”

We pulled apart, and she framed my face. “I’m so happy I found you.”

7
AVA

"WHERE'S EVERYONE AT?" Zoey asked as she plopped down beside me on the couch.

"Olivia and Sam should be here any minute. Drew is showering, and Mom and Dad are at the school."

Dad could stay his funny butt there after his little pranky-prank yesterday. Pfft. Trying to make me think I was eating a person.

"Larry is with Wallie doing something on the PlayStation," she said. "Michelle's at her mom's."

I paused and thought about who else lived here. Most days it was like I didn't even know who was staying here and who wasn't. "Ian is in his room, I think, and of course, Winnie is with Alfred." I stretched over and scratched the top of Snoozer's head. "Where's your pretty lady?" Lucy was as crazy as a soup sandwich, but she *was* gorgeous. No denying that. Snoozer didn't answer, but then I hadn't expected him to. We had no idea why

Lucy could talk, but if Snoozer was anywhere as snarky as Lucy, we didn't *want* him talking.

"Is something wrong with Winston?" Zoey asked as she picked at her fingernail.

That same question had been on my mind, but I'd kind of figured it was just a fluke. If I wasn't the only one noticing it, though... "Why do you ask?"

"Well, he always closes my window if I forget, and he hasn't the last two nights. Plus, my floors never used to creak, and all of a sudden there's a super squeaky floorboard." She shrugged. "Doesn't seem like a big deal, but it's like he's been quiet all of a sudden."

I looked around the living room and tried to reach out with my magic. I wanted to see if I could sense Winston's magic, but all I got was darkness. Winston had gone silent.

My heart sank. Winston had been a part of our family for so long I couldn't believe that something had happened to him. Something bad enough to make him go this quiet. What had happened to him? He'd stopped opening doors and hadn't been arguing with me in his creaky, moany way.

"Let's try something," I said, standing up and turning toward the kitchen. "I'll see if I can sense Winston's magic." My magic was such crap right now. Maybe Olivia could figure something out when she got here.

We walked into the kitchen, and I closed my eyes, focusing on my breathing. Nothing.

"Helloooo?" Olivia's voice came from the conservatory. "Anybody home?"

"Come in," I called as though she needed permission. "I take it the door didn't open for you?"

"No." She dangled her keys at me. "I had to let us in." She had a key to our house, just in case. Like times like this, apparently. "What's up with Winston?"

Sammie ran past his mother and straight up the stairs. "Zoey!"

"She's in the living room," I called, then looked at Olivia and Sam, who had joined her. "That's what I was hoping you might sense." I gestured around. "My magic is so unpredictable I can't tell if it's me not sensing the chasm magic or if there's no chasm magic to sense."

Drew walked down the stairs. The clomping sound of his boots gave him away.

To my surprise, it wasn't Drew who walked in. It was Ian. "Hello, there."

"Hey, what's going on?" He nodded toward Sam. "How are you out in the sun? Aren't you a vampire?"

"We don't want this information becoming public knowledge." Sam looked at Olivia with raised eyebrows.

Olivia nodded. "I think we can trust Ian."

"It boils down to it being very convenient to be a vampire married to a demigod." Sam grinned. "With her not being full god or fae, I can control myself, but something about her blood makes it so I can be in the sun."

"I don't know what I am," Olivia added. "Demi-god? Nephilim? I have no idea. What we do know is it's not my fae side, or every vampire would hunt down every fae, not just for the taste of their blood, but to be able to go in the sun."

"If you could bottle that..." Ian rubbed his hands together. "Cha-ching."

Sam and Olivia exchanged a glance. "That's why we don't

want it getting out. I can't make enough blood to sell it. I barely make enough to keep Sam in business."

"Maybe a spell could replicate it," I mused. "It's an interesting thought."

"For another day," Sam said as Drew joined us. "Are we playing cards tonight?"

"Actually..." I held up a hand. "I'm worried about Winston." Looking at Olivia, I said, "Can you sense any power coming from the chasm?"

She cocked her head and closed her eyes, then after a long minute, said, "No. Well, a little, but it's like it's being blocked."

"Should we go check it out?" Ian asked. "I've always wanted to see it, anyway."

"Sure. I was going to see if we could attempt another spell to wake Alfred, then cards." I smiled. "A trip to the chasm sounds like a good alternate plan, and then we can attempt the spell."

"Heck, yes," Ian said. "Let's go."

"I wanna go!" Sammie stood in the kitchen doorway and scrunched his eyebrows. "I like the chasm."

Zoey stuck her head in to see who was all in the kitchen, then pointed up to indicate that she was going upstairs. Most likely to hang out with Larry and Wallie while they played video games.

I looked at Olivia. There wasn't a real reason he couldn't go down there with us as long as he wasn't scared. I was half-convinced Sammie wasn't scared of anything, except maybe *Biffy*, the vampire hunter.

She shrugged. "It's okay with me."

Sammie jumped up and down. "Let's go!"

I wasn't sure who was more excited, Sammie or Ian.

"Quiet," I cautioned as we descended the stairs, mostly talking to Sammie and Ian. Everyone else knew to keep quiet in the basement during daylight hours. Wade slept until dark still and probably would for decades unless he happened to find himself a demi-god like Olivia.

That seemed unlikely.

I led the way as we tiptoed through the basement and past the door to Wade's bedroom. Sam brought up the rear.

When Sam's voice echoed through the basement hallway, I jumped and whirled around, my heart beating a mile a minute. "You know we don't have to be quiet?" he yelled at the top of his voice. "Wade wouldn't wake up if a tornado went through his bedroom."

I sighed and shook my head. Drew laughed and shrugged, used to Sam's antics by now.

Olivia swatted his arm as Sammie doubled over in laughter. "You made them jump high, Daddy!"

We continued down the hallway, less tip toey this time, and out the hidden bookshelf-door that led to the cave system underneath the house. I formed a ball of light to float ahead of us, but it almost immediately flickered and went out.

Olivia took pity on me and threw one in the air as I led the way to the cave room that held the smaller magic cache.

Sure enough, the small source of power directly under the house wasn't glowing. "Crap," I muttered. "Am I the only one who doesn't see the glow?"

"No, it's not there," Olivia said. "It's not your faulty magic."

"It looks like the power is out," Drew said. "What would make that happen?"

I had no clue, but the thought of never talking to Winston again made my heart hurt.

Drew took my hand, probably feeling my despair through the bond. "We'll figure it out."

Sam stepped forward and squinted at the small stone table that held the small, clear quartz gemstone. It had glowed white and blue all the other times I'd been here. Now it just looked like a dime-a-dozen piece of pretty rock.

"Am I the only one who sees the red?" He looked back at me as Sammie pushed forward and peered at the stone.

"No, Daddy, I see it, too."

Sam straightened and looked down at his son. "Can you describe it?"

Little Sammie scrunched his nose. "It looks like string. It goes that way." He pointed in the direction of the larger chasm."

Sam nodded. "Yep. It looks like string to me, too, but glowing. He definitely sees it."

"How?" I asked and pulled on my power and Drews to try to sense or see this glowing red threat.

Nothing.

"Well, I'm not sure," Sam said. "But it's definitely troubling. Why can my son and I see something the rest of you can't?"

"I didn't think vampires had powers like that," Ian said.

"Some do." I pulled out my phone. "No service. I was thinking I'd call Jax and ask."

"Get on Wade's Wi-Fi," Drew said. "It should work here."

After pressing a few buttons on my phone, I was able to get service. "Nice. I forgot he'd installed that."

I pulled up the contact info for Hailey, the mate to the king of the vampires, and called her. She answered after the second ring. "Hey, Ava, how are you?"

She was sweet. She'd bought my house in Philadelphia, and

we'd stayed in touch since. She and Jax even came to our wedding. Plus, Jax was a silent partner in Red Lipped Mary's.

"I'm well." I paused for a moment. "Actually, I'm kind of crappy. My powers are on the fritz, but that's not why I'm calling."

"What can I do for you? You sound like you need to get down to business."

"I guess I do. You remember Sam?" I put the phone on speaker then so everyone could hear. "I have him here with me."

Her voice brightened. "Of course. How are you doing as a vampire, Sam?"

"Great, thanks. We just wanted to ask if vampires can have magical abilities."

"Yes, as a matter of fact. I can manipulate metal, though it's extremely hard to master. Another vampire I know can sense things about people. What kind of paranormal creature they are, how they got their powers, and so on."

"Sam here is seeing some sort of magical thread. It's red," Olivia said.

"Hang on, let me ask Jax." The line went dead for a couple of minutes while we stood around and shuffled our feet. Then she came back. "That isn't something that he's familiar with. He says if you had any sort of magical ability before, or if it was in your DNA, it's possible for it to be enhanced now that you're a vampire."

"Okay, Hailey, thank you. I do appreciate your time." I grinned at the phone like a dummy, as if Hailey could see me. It wasn't a dang video chat.

"Anytime. You should invite us out sometime this summer. I'd love a Maine vacation."

That sounded nice. I liked Hailey and Jax. "You got it."

As soon as I hung up, Olivia said, "It's got to be something from before. Sammie has it too." She pointed at Sam. "Do you have any witches in your family?"

He shook his head. "No. My parents don't even know Ava is a witch. They're completely human, and as far as they know, everyone else is, too."

"I've been calling Luci from the moment you saw it," Olivia said. "He's not hearing me, or he's ignoring me."

"I'm not ignoring you."

I barely managed to keep from jumping out of my skin again as I turned to find Luci in the cave with us. "Nice of you to join us," I said with only a little bit of sarcasm in my tone.

"You rang?" He looked at his daughter expectantly.

"Can you see any sort of magical ability in Sam and Sammie?" Olivia asked. "I know you can sometimes read that on people."

Luci cleared his throat, then made a big production of squinting at Sam and Sammie as he walked slowly around them. He hemmed and hawed, looking high and looking low, circling them three or four times as Sam rolled his eyes up to the cave ceiling.

The drama this man gave us. How had we gotten through life without it before I'd accidentally summoned him?

After a solid minute of his dramatics, he stopped and clapped his hands together once. "They're psychic."

As though it was the most obvious thing in the world.

"What?" Same said, shocked.

"Yep. I can barely see it, but when I try very hard, it's there. Psychics are sort of reddish most of the time."

"Reddish?" Oliva asked. "What do you mean?"

Luci cocked his head and held up one finger. "Hold on..." He seemed to be listening to something or someone that we couldn't hear. "Yes, okay. I must go. Cheerio." With that, he disappeared.

"Damn," Ian muttered. "That dude is so weird."

Indeed.

8
AVA

WHILE OLIVIA TOOK Sammie to her adoptive parents' house for the night, we followed Sam, who was following the red thread. We ended up in the big chasm of power.

It was also dark.

"What do you see?" Ian asked Sam.

"The whole thing is wrapped in the red thread." Sam shook his head and gestured toward the gigantic quartz stone. "It goes down into the chasm in the stone, but it also wraps all the way around it."

"Anything else?" I gently prodded as Olivia walked into the cave. "That was fast," I muttered.

"Yeah, I told them I was in a hurry. Stopping to remind Sammie he can't do any magic around them took the longest."

"The thread leads up and that way." Sam pointed toward what I was pretty sure would be the main road once we got outside. "Maybe I can see it once we go out there." We traipsed out of the cave, going toward the beach instead of toward Winston.

Once out on the beach, Sam turned and peered. "I can't see it from here."

"Come on. I'll port us to the top of the cliff." Olivia opened a portal, and we walked through.

The cave was well down the beach from our house, though still on my family property. "When was the last time you were down here?" I asked Sam, who was squinting into the small copse of trees between the beach and the main road. It wasn't *quite* a forest, though I'd always thought of it as one.

He turned and looked at me, then jumped and rushed to my side. "Ava!"

I cocked an eyebrow at him. "Sam!"

"The red threads. They're all over you."

I looked down at myself, as did everyone else. "Um."

He circled me, reminiscent of how Luci had gone round and round him and Sammie. "All over you. Twined around your body. It looks like they should be constricting you to the point of knocking you over. If they were literal ropes or thread, you'd be trussed up like a mummy."

I stared at him in shock. "You're messing with me. This is another April Fools' joke, isn't it?" I glared at Drew. "Did you put him up to this?"

He held his hands up. "No, I swear I didn't. I'm as surprised as you are."

Okay, okay. I could tell through our bond that he was feeling shock and the beginnings of rage. He did *not* like the thought of me being messed with.

How I loved that man and his protectiveness.

"You have a string leading away. It meshes with the string coming from the ground." Sam jogged a few yards away and pointed to a seemingly random spot on the leafy ground. "Here."

"Let's follow it." I squared my shoulders. "I want to know who in the world could have red strings of power all over me." Drew's fury had mingled with my own. I hadn't been this mad in... I wasn't sure how long. Lightning crackled around my fingertips.

We walked until the power thread got to the main road. Sam pointed away from town. "It goes that way."

"Hang on," Olivia said. "Stay right here. I'll go get a vehicle."

"Get my SUV," Drew said and tossed her the keys. "We'll all fit."

She saluted him and then disappeared through one of her portals. I sat on the side of the road on a big rock and tried not to spontaneously combust. After a few minutes, Drew's SUV came roaring up the road. We weren't that far from home.

We climbed in, and Olivia moved so Sam could drive. "Now I can just follow it," he said.

It wasn't easy sitting still in the back seat while Sam and Drew sat up front. My bond with my husband was like boiling water rushing back and forth between us. My anger fed his, and vice versa. Both of us were careful not to trigger his new power-boosting ability.

"Why couldn't you see the threads on me before?" I asked.

Sam glanced at me in the rearview mirror. "I have no idea. I've never seen anything like this before tonight."

"Sammie obviously has," Olivia said. "And he might have seen these but maybe didn't know how to say it."

She was his mom, but my Sammie would've told me if he'd seen me being constricted by magical rope—no need to say that out loud, though.

The SUV veered right as Sam turned on a dime. "Sorry. That turn came up quickly."

Olivia peeled herself out of my lap, and I pushed away from Ian. I hadn't quite ended up in his lap, but definitely, he'd kept me from falling all the way over.

The road turned into a gravel drive until it stopped in front of a largeish RV.

It clicked. "I know who is going to walk out that door." Lightening rose to my fingertips again as we clambered out of the car.

Ian, Drew, and Sam tried to stay in front of Olivia and me, but I shoved my way forward as the door to the RV opened.

The Viking elder Arne stepped down the little metal stairs, followed by his two henchmen, who were apparently not important enough to introduce me to, as he never had. "What are you doing here?"

Sam stepped back and leaned close. "The red strings are going directly into him."

White-hot anger coursed through my veins. I tried to call my lightning, but all it would do was dance across my fingers. I wished fervently I had something besides Drew I could draw on for power to give me enough of a boost to fry these mother effers.

My truth stone appeared in my hand. Okay. That was weird. It pulsed, sending power into my palm.

A lot of power.

A whole freaking lot of power. I screamed as it filled me and danced with my fury.

Lightning rained from the sky like a freaking fireworks show. Every bit of it went directly into Arne and his two associates. Our hair stood on end, and even I had to shield my eyes from the brightness of the electricity.

When I opened them, Arne and the tweedles were nothing but greasy black tar.

My magic slammed into me like a freight train. I screamed again, but this time it was out of surprise and at least a little bit of fear. Once my magic was inside, the fear lessened as a rush of energy through my body electrified me, the feeling indescribable. It was like a door had swung open in my mind, and all of the power that had been taken from me came crashing back in an overwhelming surge. I gasped as it continued flooding through me, a feeling of electricity coursing through my veins, filling me to the brim. It was like a shock to the system, and for a moment, I was paralyzed by the sheer intensity of it all. But then, I let it wash over me, grinning widely and feeling invincible. I was myself once more, and no one would take that away from me again.

I hoped.

"Ava, it's okay." Drew had his arms around me, and warmth rushed through me. "Are you all right?"

I nodded, my mind spinning from the sudden overload of power. "I'm good. Just give me a second."

Once they knew I was okay, Olivia, Sam, and Ian went inside the trailer to search it. Drew sat me down in the passenger seat of his SUV, then stood beside me, squeezing my hand. "They were getting to my power through you," he said. "I never realized."

I took a moment to look past the storm inside me to feel our bond. Sure enough, the power I sensed there was quite a bit stronger. "We're going to be unstoppable together," I said with a grin. "Let 'em come after us now."

Ian led the way with Olivia and Sam right behind them.

"Nothing but this amulet," he said and handed it to Drew. I didn't take the time to look at it just yet. I was doing well to stay upright.

"Let's go home," I muttered. "I want to check on Alfred." The necromancers draining me and the chasm couldn't have been unrelated to Alfred's long nap. It was far too coincidental.

Drew tucked into the backseat beside me with Ian on my other side. Sam drove us back to Winston.

Halfway there, I pulled out my phone and texted Winnie. **You okay?**

She didn't answer.

"Hey," Olivia said. "It wasn't the baby."

I stared at her blankly for a second, and then my brain caught up to her words. "It wasn't the baby draining me."

"That makes me wonder how powerful the baby will be," Drew said. "With your heritage plus Michelle's water magic added in."

"We won't know for a while," I murmured as I tried texting Winnie again. I pulled the truth stone out of my pocket and prodded it with a little bit of power.

It absorbed it.

"This isn't just a truth stone," I said, my voice a bit awestruck. "It's a power reservoir. There's no telling how long the power it gave me today had been in there, waiting to be used."

"Was it fae magic?" Olivia asked. Her uncle, the king of Faery, had been the one to give it to me.

"I couldn't tell. It happened so fast, and it was so incredibly potent."

Sam drove us right up to the front door, and I was ecstatic to see the front door open. "Winston," I said happily. "You're back."

He moaned at me in his way, and the sound of the kitchen

cabinets opening and closing brought a big smile to my face. "I love you, too, Winston."

"Winnie?" I called up the stairs as everyone came in behind me. "Win? Alfred?"

I had one foot on the stairs when I realized what I was hearing.

Rhythmic thumping. From right above our heads.

Alfred's bedroom was right above our heads.

Thump. Thump. Thump.

Oh, my goodness.

"Well, then," Olivia said in a loud, too-bright voice. "How about we wait to see Alfred out on the patio?"

We practically sprinted out there to find Wade already in a chaise lounge. "It's loud in there," he said.

"Alfred?" I asked.

"Yeah. I'd just come upstairs to see where everyone was when I heard her shout that he was awake. I tried not to listen, but soon after she shouted, the, umm, other sounds began."

Sam covered his face and moaned. "I can still hear them."

Wade grimaced. "I'm trying really hard to sing the alphabet song in my head."

Suddenly I was grateful not to have vampire hearing.

9
AVA

Sam jumped up. "I'm going to go see if the chasm has its power back." He ran toward the beach.

"Wait for me," Wade yelled, then used his vampire speed to catch up to Sam.

"Well, then." I settled back into a chair, glad I wasn't a vampire.

A few moments later, Larry and Zoey walked out of the kitchen. Larry was laughing, and Zoey said, "Did you guys hear—"

"Oh, yeah," Drew cut her off. "That's why we are all out here."

"Is that Alfred and Winnie?" Larry asked around his chortles.

"We're pretty sure." Olivia grinned. "Ava killed the necromancers."

I let my friends tell the story, but they had to start it over a few minutes later when Wallie and Michelle walked outside. "Hey, um, it's really inappropriate in there," Wallie said. He nodded toward

Larry. "Thanks for the text." Then he glared at me. "Next time maybe you can tell me when Alfred wakes from a mystical sleep."

"Us too," Mom said as she and Dad followed Wallie and Michelle out. The back deck was getting crowded.

Sam and Wade walked across the yard super slow, especially for vampires. "We still hear them," Sam called. They stopped halfway across the lawn. "The chasm is back, though!"

That was a relief.

"I wonder why the chasm didn't take power from the ghouls?" Mom asked after we told her the whole story.

"I thought about that," I said. "But the stones they wear hold their own power, and it's a considerable amount. I don't think they're still connected to the quartz in the cave." They'd become self-sufficient once they'd been separated from the big stone.

Sam and Wade began to creep forward. Once on the porch, Sam said, "I think it's over."

After cocking his head, Wade nodded. "Yeah, it's safe to go in. They're dressing."

I looked at Drew in horror, then at Wade. "Can you always hear things... like *that*?"

Wade grinned. "Yes, but when in the basement, I have really good headphones. Plus, Alfred and Winnie are particularly, ah, voracious."

Ew, ew, ew.

We clambered into the kitchen in time to see Alfred and Winnie walk down the stairs.

"It is so good to see you," I said as I rushed to hug my good friend and ghoul. "So good."

He hugged me tightly. "It's so good to hug you."

My heart swelled as I clung to Alfred. I hadn't quite realized how worried I'd been. He'd become like a brother to me, and my life had been a little less colorful in the four months since I'd last heard his squeaky voice.

"Come, sit," I said, swiping at my eyes to brush away the tears. "Talk to us. Tell us what happened."

"Have you been aware?" Olivia asked as we moved into the living room, which became crowded very quickly. "Were you in pain?"

"No pain," Alfred said as he took a seat of honor in the middle of the sofa with Winnie plastered to his side. "But I was aware, yes."

After taking a deep breath, he started his story. "I was conflicted about the necromancers. Not because I was waffling about whether or not to sacrifice someone, but because I didn't want to completely lose touch with my former coven members because I wasn't willing to sacrifice a human." He shrugged. "Part of me was drawn to them. I hadn't seen anyone who could remember the things I could in so long."

Winnie squeezed his hand. "That's understandable, hon. You could've talked to us about it."

Poor Alfred. "We would've understood, yes."

I leaned forward and put my hand over his and Winnie's. "I'm sorry to tell you, in the process of getting our powers back and confronting the necromancers, I..." I grimaced. "I sort of fried them to a crisp."

"More like fried them to a sludge," Ian said, then snickered.

Drew shot him an exasperated look. "Not helping," he muttered.

Alfred sat for a second, absorbing the information. "I guess it doesn't matter now."

"As it turns out, they were draining the chasm and Ava," Drew said. "They had to be dealt with."

Alfred met his gaze. "I know. I was aware. Every time you came in and sat with me, catching me up on what was going on, I knew it. What was more, from the moment I fell into the chasm, a few bits of information were suddenly completely clarified to me. I knew the necromancers were draining Ava."

"How did you fall in?" Sam asked.

Before Alfred answered, Lucy sauntered into the room, hopped up onto the coffee table, and began licking her right front paw.

Alfred fixed her with a glare. "Four months? You didn't know I was missing for *four* months? *And* I asked you to tell Ava it's the necromancers, and you didn't."

She paused her licking for a second to say, "How am I supposed to keep up with the drama of the two-legged?" Then she resumed her licky-licking of her paw.

It would've been completely fair if Alfred had knocked her across the room, but he took the high road and turned back to Sam to answer his question. "I don't have any idea. I just went for a walk. When I got near the cave, I had the strongest urge to go in. The last thing I remember is walking in."

"Once we pulled you out, when did you wake up?" Drew asked. "We know the necromancers weren't draining the chasm then, or Sam would've seen the threads."

"No, Sam didn't go, remember?" I pointed out. "He and Wade were asleep."

"It started after that," Alfred said. I was able to go away from my body for short stints. They felt the power surge when you got me out of the chasm. Within an hour, they were there, doing their rituals to connect the power in the chasm to Arne."

"Darn," Olivia said. "Rotten luck, but why didn't you wake up?"

"I assume because the chasm needed to finish me."

Winnie grinned. "I felt a big surge of power right before he woke up."

"Wow," I whispered. "That's a series of unfortunate events."

"What about your powers?" Mom asked. "Are you human or witch?"

"Necromancer." Alfred grinned. "As far as I can tell, I'm fully myself again. As though I never died. I think I'm around thirty, though that's hard to tell." He looked down at himself. "It's the best feeling."

"Isn't it?" Mom said. "I don't know what it's like to wake up in my real body again, but waking up in this one was like... well, like coming back to life."

"This talisman was in the trailer the necromancers were staying in," Drew said, pulling it out of his pocket. It looked like a silver snake with an emerald embedded in it. A thick red ribbon hung through a hook at the top.

Alfred took it but shook his head. "I don't recognize it." He bounced it around in his hand, then closed his eyes and focused. "It doesn't have any power."

Ian stepped forward and grabbed it. "Wait, let me look at it." He held it up and studied it. "I don't sense anything either." He handed it to Drew, who did the same.

"No, if it had magical properties, I think we'd sense it. Still, let's keep it put up." He slid it back into his pocket as Alfred gave an affirming nod.

Lucy walked across the coffee table, drawing my attention. She gingerly stepped into Michelle's lap as we all watched in shock.

To our even bigger surprise, the crazy, ornery cat curled up into a ball and put her head down with a contented sigh.

What in the world?

We looked at Michelle, who shrugged. "I have no idea," she said softly.

That made two of us.

I smiled at the girl who was fast becoming a part of our family. "You should invite your parents over for dinner soon."

Alfred perked up at that. "I'd love to cook for us."

Everyone spoke at once, trying to figure out what night would be good so that Michelle's mom and dad could meet the whole crew. "Guys, they might get overwhelmed with this bunch."

As everyone spoke over everyone else, the house moaned and rumbled.

That shut everyone up in a hurry. We looked around the living room. "Winston?" I called. "You okay?"

Slowly, with much groaning and fanfare, Winston expanded the living room to double its original size. It hadn't been overly small to begin with, but we were quite the crowd.

Olivia grinned from ear to ear, waved her hand, and another couch appeared, along with a plush recliner and a couple of nice-looking end tables.

"Nice," Larry said. He and Zoey went to cuddle in the recliner as we inspected the new half of the room.

"Thanks, Winston. It's nice to see you're feeling better." I sent loving feelings out at my house.

I mean, how did one express to a sentient house that he was very loved?

Drew found a nice way. "I'll give you a good pressure washing soon. How's that sound?"

Winston clattered the kitchen cabinets in response.

Apparently, that sounded nice.

10

OLIVIA

"Aw, honey, don't be nervous." I smoothed Sam's hair behind his ear. It amazed me that it still grew when he was officially undead. He was so much the same as he had been when he was human. I forgot sometimes, but then there were times like these... I held out my hand and leaned into my wonderful husband as his fangs descended, and he sank them into my wrist. The first time he drank from me, I felt a tiny pinch and a bit of discomfort. Now, it gave me joy knowing that I provided for him. I barely felt his bite.

"Thanks," Sam whispered a few moments later. He licked the bite marks to heal them, then pulled away with a sigh. I tucked my arm back into the sleeve of my robe. We stood in silence for a moment, sharing a look that said so much without words.

We had been together for years now, and our love only seemed to grow stronger as the days went on. It was beautiful, but it also scared me at times. I felt like we both knew that if something happened to one of us, the other would never be the same. We didn't talk about it, but we both felt it.

Today was not a day for sadness though, so I smiled and put my hand on Sam's shoulder.

"Ready?" I asked, and he nodded. We had a lot of work to do today. The club's soft opening was tonight. I'd gotten Sam up in the early afternoon, thus the need for my blood.

"I am. Yes, I'm a little nervous but also confident." He beamed at me before bending to tie his shoes. "It's going to be so much fun. It's nice to feel like becoming a vampire doesn't mean everything has to stop or be ruined. There's going to be a future for us, for me."

The future was something that had been a pretty sensitive subject for a while, but now that it was clear we'd be able to spend it together, the sky was the limit.

"Let's go."

After we said goodbye to Sammie and Phira, I opened a portal directly in the back room of Red Lipped Mary.

It really was an awesome name.

"Wade's in the dark room," Sam said. "He'll be out the moment the sun goes down."

"Did he sleep here?" I peered down the hall toward the rooms in the very back: storage, the fridge, freezer, and a light-tight room for any vampires who might end up here during the day.

"Yeah, we worked until dawn the last few nights. I was able to make it home, thanks to you, but he crashed here."

"Good thing someone had the idea to include it." I looked at him out of the corner of my eye.

"Yes, Olivia, you're the best, with the best ideas, and what would I ever do without you?" He spoke with a big smile, pulling me into his arms and placing a kiss on my throat. A shiver of desire fluttered through me. The words were sarcastic, but love shone in his tone.

"What's left?" I asked. "What can I do?"

"We got the final drink delivery today. I paid the delivery guy extra to put it in the big storage bin outside. I'll bring it in if you'll get it organized behind the counter."

"Can do."

He carried box after box while I organized and stocked the shelves and refrigerator. We worked in silence for a while, just enjoying being together in our new place.

When everything was put away and the boxes broken down, I took the duster and gave the place a once-over while Sam checked out the sound system. "Are you hiring a DJ?" I asked.

"Not tonight. Just playing this playlist I made." He waved his old cell phone at me.

"Smart, using that one." I began pulling the chairs off of the tables. "Did the VIP sofa get here?" I couldn't quite see it from here.

Sam nodded and turned the music on low. "Yep, and since it was late, they gave us twenty-five percent back."

"Score."

Twenty minutes later, I stopped and shook off my hands. "Now what?"

Sam grabbed my hand and pulled me onto the dance floor. He tilted his head back, eyes closed, and we swayed to the music. I laid my head on his shoulder and enjoyed the feeling of being in our new club. It had all come together just as we'd dreamed, a real purpose for Sam. Hopefully, a bit of money, though that wasn't the biggest concern.

All of our friends were coming tonight, along with the full staff. If there were any more kinks to iron out, we'd know after the next eight hours or so.

"Hey, guys." Wade walked out of the backroom door and then rolled his eyes. "Do you do anything besides act all lovey-dovey?"

I giggled. "Yeah, but it'd be even grosser to you than our PDA."

Wade turned in a circle, looking around the bar. "I shouldn't have asked." He grinned, then stopped circling. "This place looks fantastic."

Over the next half hour, the employees came in. Hank, our new head bartender was first, he lined glasses up, then moved all the liquor bottles around to his preference.

I wasn't offended. After this was his job, and he had a lot more experience than I had.

Soon after, the servers and two more bartenders arrived. We didn't really need the bouncers with it being only our friends, but we'd asked them to come in anyway, just to make this as much like the real opening night as possible.

"Did the mailers go out?" I asked Sam as the servers tied on their aprons.

"Yep. Fifteen thousand to households who have people ages twenty-five to thirty-five. Jax sent out notifications to the leader of the North East vampires, Clinton, and he's going to send the information out to his vampires."

Ava and Drew walked in the front door, followed by pretty much their entire household, and my mother and father.

"I told you to call," I said. "I would've come and got you."

"Luci and Phira stopped by and offered," Ava said as she scoped out the place.

Wade leaned across the bar. "Olivia, if you could set up a permanent portal from the basement to the light-tight room here, that'd be great."

“You got it.” Then I walked Ava around, showing her how we'd gotten everything finished. As we rounded back to where we started, the front door opened, and Jax and Hailey walked in with Kendra, their witch friend. "Come on in," I called. "Welcome." Jax was a partial investor in the club. It was great to have his support. Plus, it was good to see Hailey. I'd met her a few times now. They'd asked me to make portals for them a time or two, which I'd been happy to do.

Hey, it's kinda cool being one of the only people in the world who could make portals.

I'm special. My daddy said so.

Said daddy is the devil, though, so grain of salt and all that.

"Where's Luke?" I asked.

Ava widened her eyes at me. Oh, crap. I'd forgotten. Luke's boyfriend and Jax's right hand man was missing. He'd been missing since November, nearly about the same amount of time we'd been dealing with the Alfred and Luci locked out of Hell fiasco. "I'm so sorry. He didn't feel like coming, I guess."

Ava shook her head with sad eyes, and Jax grimaced.

"It's been hardest on him," Kendra said. "Though none of us realized how much Jax depended on Ransom."

"Hell, I didn't realize how much I did."

"You still don't have any leads?" Ava asked.

Hailey shook her head. "We assume it's his sire who has him, but none of our efforts to find him have panned out." She shook her hair back. "I hear you finally had a breakthrough with Alfred?"

Ava pointed him out in the small crowd. Of course, Winnie was plastered to his side, but he certainly didn't look disappointed in his situation. He had one arm around her, his fingertips flirting with the side of her mostly-exposed breast.

Ewww. I loved them, but they were some next-level PDAers.

"I'd be happy to try searching for him," Ava said. "I have my powers back now."

Jax brightened up. "I rarely think of you as a witch. To me, you're the most powerful necromancer, but you do have a witch side, don't you?"

She nodded. "Sure do, and not to sound braggy, but I'm pretty good. Come on. We can scry in the office."

After making sure Sam and Wade had things covered, I headed to the back room. Jax hadn't asked me to look for Ransom either, but I would volunteer. Might as well try to help out our friends.

By the time I made it to the back, Ava was staring at a world map in frustration.

"Not working?" I asked.

She shook her head. "No, and I tried it a couple of different ways." Every witch tended to have a particular way of doing locator spells that they preferred, but there were lots of ways to try to locate someone.

A watch sat on the map. Jax motioned toward it and said, "That's Ransom's. I keep it on me, and the map, just in case I have a chance to scry for him."

"Smart," I said. "Let me try?"

Ava scooted over and squeezed Hailey's arm. "Olivia is a

special kind of witch. You never know what she might pick up." She scooted around. "I'm going to go get my son's girlfriend. She's a water elemental. She might be able to do a reflection."

Kendra popped her head in. "Any luck?"

We all shook our heads.

"We're going to try a couple of different things," I said. "It might be helpful for me to have Luke here. Do you think he'd come?"

Hailey nodded. "He might."

"I'll go get him," Kendra said brightly, then disappeared.

I picked up the watch and sat in one of the chairs so I could focus. Thinking about Ransom, I tried to picture his face, his build, his voice. I hadn't met him all that many times, and I honestly couldn't say I'd ever heard him speak. He was the polar opposite of Luke, but sometimes that was the way things worked out.

Sam and I weren't too far from that.

No matter how much magic I pushed into the watch, nothing came back to me. Time dragged as I kept trying. How cool would it have been if I could've found Ransom for them?

Eventually, I had to stop. Opening my eyes, I started as I realized the room had gotten much fuller. Luke sat across from me in the other chair, leaned forward, and nearly touched me. "Anything?" he asked hopefully.

"I'm sorry, no."

Luci and Phira stood in the doorway. "Let me try," Luci said. He looked even more exhausted than he had the last time I saw him when Ava healed his arm.

Luke jumped up and snatched the watch out of my hand.

"No, hang on," I said. Holding out one hand, I smiled at my father.

"Let's try working together." Before he'd been so distracted by trying to get into Hell, we'd been working on magic together, and both found our powers boosted by one another. I held my other hand out to Luke. "Think about him hard," I said. "Everything about him, physically."

A gleam of humor flashed in Luke's eyes, chasing away the panic for a split second.

"Everything but *that*," I said.

Everyone chuckled but quickly quieted down as we stepped forward. I did the same thing I'd been doing with the watch, but this time focused on Luke.

Nothing. Not even a tickle. Wherever Ransom was, he was extremely well-guarded. We tried for a good half hour before finally admitting defeat.

Luke stepped back with tears in his eyes. "Thank you for trying." He looked at Luci, then pursed his lips for a moment before saying, "If he were dead..."

"I'd know." Luci reached over and squeezed Luke's shoulder. "I've been locked out of Hell, but I can still sense the inhabitants. I built that realm. They can't completely sever me from it. If Ransom were there, I'd be able to sense him."

"What about... *not* Hell?" Jax asked.

Luci grinned. "You're vampires. Don't you worry. You'll be coming to hang out with me when you die."

There was a sobering thought. Hell wasn't *quite* as bad as some religions made it out to be, but I also hadn't noticed it being a walk in the park, either. "Uh, maybe don't scare them?"

Luci chuckled. "Don't worry. Your eternity is still dependent on what kind of person you are when you die. If you don't want to be tortured for all of time..." He shrugged. "Don't be a dick."

"Did someone ask to see me? Sorry it took so long. I'd just gotten back home." Michelle walked in and smiled. She was such a sweet girl.

"I'm sorry to pull you back out," Luke said. He smiled at her baby bump. "Congratulations, by the way."

Wallie followed her in and shook Luke's hand. I didn't realize they knew one another. They'd probably met at Ava and Drew's wedding.

The room was full of people now, but none of us really wanted to leave.

Wallie pulled a bowl and bottle of water out of a backpack. "Here you go."

Michelle set the items on the desk, filled up the bowl, then turned to Luke. "Do you have something of his?"

Luke handed her the watch. "Should I hold your hand or anything?"

She nodded. "That might help and definitely couldn't hurt."

Wallie pulled a chair up for her, and she perched delicately at the end of it. There wasn't any fanfare or drama, but after a minute or two, she gasped. A split second later, Luke did, too.

"It's the baby," Michelle whispered. "She's boosting my power."

The bowl began to glow, and everyone rushed forward. I caught myself trying to push to the front, then remembered this wasn't my battle and made room for Jax, Hailey, and Kendra.

Still, I *had* to see what was going on in that bowl, so I tiptoed around until I could see over Ava's shoulder.

A reflection appeared in the still water. Luke sobbed as Hailey clutched his shoulders. Jax looked choked up and said, "Luke, he's desiccated. Depending on what he's been going through, that's a good thing. He's in a dream-like state."

Luke nodded as tears streamed down his face. He reached toward the bowl as if he wanted to touch it, but Wallie gently stopped his hand.

"Don't touch," Wallie whispered. "It might sever the connection."

Instead of touching the bowl, Luke grabbed Hailey's arm and bit back his tears. He was close to breaking down.

"I can't tell where it is," Michelle said in a dreamy voice. "Can you see anything from the image?"

We took turns moving forward and studying the scene, but nobody had any insight. When it was my turn to look, I understood why. Ransom looked like a mummy. I wouldn't have recognized him if I'd been in the room with him. What I could see of the surrounding room was just stone. Stone floor, stone walls. "Maybe a castle?" I suggested. "It reminds me of an old castle."

"That doesn't narrow much down," Jax said. He sounded so defeated.

"This is still progress," Ava said. "And we can try again, join more power. Anything to try to help."

Michelle let go of the bowl and Luke with a sigh. "That was intense," she said and looked up at Ava. "This baby has got some power in her."

The party dwindled after that. The Philadelphia guests departed with the understandably shaken Luke. Luci and Phira left to get some rest, and we went out to the main part of the club to help until our other guests decided they'd had enough.

By the time we cleaned up and went home, dawn was peeking over the horizon.

Despite the setback in attempting to locate Ransom, the night had been a smashing success. The real grand opening was going to go well, I just knew it.

Sam and I collapsed into bed and snuggled into each other as sleep claimed us.

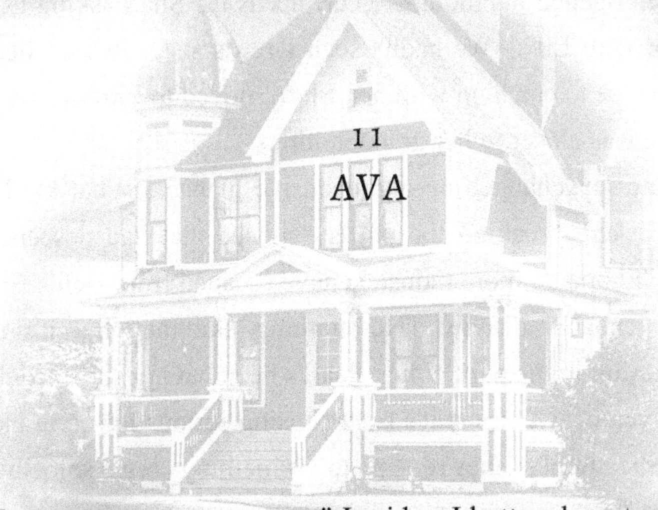

11
AVA

"THAT WAS FUN LAST NIGHT," I said as I buttered my toast. It was nearly noon, but at least it wasn't just me who'd slept in this time. Even Drew had only gotten up a few minutes before me.

"That club is going to be amazing," Winnie said. She tossed her long blonde hair over her shoulder.

"I like that robe," I said, hoping to encourage her whenever she wore something appropriate. The robe in question was pink and fuzzy.

Most importantly, it covered all the private parts.

Drew's phone buzzed loudly, startling us all. He grabbed it and grimaced. "It's Pearl."

Ian chuckled. "That's never good."

They loved their grandmother, but she wasn't their favorite person in the world, to say the least.

Drew put the phone to his ear, and though we couldn't hear what Pearl said, it was easy enough to guess from Drew's expression. His face became graver with each passing moment, and when he hung up the phone, he looked like a man who had just been given an unenviable task. I knew what was coming before Drew even opened his mouth. "Pearl needs us. She's asking us to do a hunt with Lily." We hadn't seen Drew's sister in a while. It would be nice to catch up with her. She'd moved to Florida, which meant she was closer to her grandchildren.

Ian and I exchanged an apprehensive glance. "What kind of hunt?" I asked, breaking the uneasy silence that had descended upon us. "I hope no more monsters have escaped from Hell?"

Drew exhaled heavily. "No, nothing like that, but it's not exactly a walk in the park either. Pearl's been having some trouble with a coven of witches that's been causing serious havoc in New Jersey. She thinks they're up to something big, something dangerous."

"Thus, why we're meeting up with Lily," Ian said. "Do we have any more information?"

Drew nodded. "Pearl emailed me some files." He tapped on his phone, then read us what he found. "Apparently, this coven has been performing some sort of dark ritual. She thinks they're trying to summon the Jersey Devil."

"That's real?" I asked, shocked.

With a chuckle, Drew winked at me. "Oh, yeah."

"Come on, Ava," Ian said. "Haven't you figured out by now that pretty much every legend has a root in truth if it isn't completely true?"

I rolled my eyes at Ian's comment, but I couldn't deny that he had a point. In our line of work, we had come across some pretty strange things. Summoning a legendary creature like the Jersey Devil didn't seem too far-fetched. "So, what's the plan?" I asked. "The Jersey Devil? That's just, I don't know, too surreal."

Drew shrugged. "Whether it's real or not, we have to go. Pearl wouldn't have called us if it wasn't important."

Ian nodded in agreement. "Yeah, we can't just ignore this. So, what's our next move?"

Drew pulled up a map of New Jersey on his phone. "We need to head to this town where the coven has been spotted. We can meet up with Lily there."

"All right," I said. "Let's do this. How are we getting there?"

"Yoohoo," Olivia called as the back door opened.

Nice to see Winston back to his old polite habits.

"Good timing," I said. "Care to give us a portal?"

"Sure." She leaned over and snagged a piece of toast. "I was coming to see if you wanted to spend the afternoon with me at the academy, but I can schlep you guys somewhere. Where are we going?"

"To investigate witches who are summoning the Jersey Devil." Drew watched her absorb his words with a gleam in his eyes.

"The what?" She stopped chewing and stared at my hubby.

"The Jersey Devil is real?" Olivia mumbled around her toast.

Ian chuckled. "What a newb."

As Olivia made a face at him, Ian got up and took his plate to the sink. To my amazement, he rinsed it, opened the dishwasher, slid the plate in, and closed it back.

Wow. Even Drew would only set his dishes in the sink, and he was about as perfect as a man could get. Go, Ian. He was going to make some lady very happy one day.

At least in the kitchen, which was about all I could speak to.

"Can you open a portal we can drive a car through?" Ian asked.

With a shrug, Olivia nodded. "I can."

"Great. That way, we have a way to get around in New Jersey." Drew nodded at Ian. "Good thinking."

Ian looked at Drew for a half tick, then narrowed his eyes. "Are you being sarcastic?"

"No," Drew protested. "I'm serious. That was a good idea. Plus, if we can't get ahold of Olivia later, we could drive ourselves home."

"I'll go ahead to Jersey and find a good spot for the portal," Olivia said. "Where are we going?"

"Asbury Park." Drew consulted his email, then gave her a more specific area of the town.

"Meet me in your driveway in ten." She opened a portal, stepped through, then the portal closed.

"What should we take to something like this?" I asked. "It's not like I keep a supply of Jersey Devil killing potion."

Drew chuckled. "I doubt there's such a thing as a Jersey Devil killing potion. We'll have to rely on our skills and wits for this one."

Ian nodded in agreement. "I'll grab my crossbow and some iron bolts."

I raised an eyebrow. "Iron bolts?"

He shrugged. "Iron seems to bother a lot of magical creatures."

Okay, then.

We traipsed out to the driveway and got in Drew's SUV. He turned it around, and a few minutes later, a gigantic portal opened. Drew pulled forward, then rolled his window down. Olivia climbed in the backseat with me. "I could go to the school later. Fighting a Jersey Devil sounds too fun to pass up, so I'm coming with you."

"Okay, cool." My phone pinged in my pocket. It was Wallie sending me a picture of a cute baby outfit they'd bought.

I showed the picture to Olivia, who sighed. "I love shopping for babies."

Then I showed it to Drew and Ian, but they didn't get nearly as mushy as Olivia and I did.

Men!

I texted back with a heart emoji, then pocketed my phone.

The portal spat us out into a parking lot behind an abandoned building. Drew drove around to the front of the building, and I spotted Lily leaning against a light pole. Drew parked the SUV next to the pole, and we got out.

"Hey, guys," she said with a big smile before giving each of us a hug, saving Ian for last. When he made a face at her, she punched him in the arm. "I just saw you a few months ago."

"Ready to do this?" Drew asked.

We all nodded and followed his lead as he opened the door of the building and stepped inside. The darkness was broken by a few small lights along the walls, creating an eerie atmosphere just perfect for our mission. We crept in quietly, alert to any danger that might be lurking ahead of us.

Chanting echoed down the hall that I recognized as a summoning spell. "We need to stop that spell," I said picking, up my pace.

The closer we got, the louder and more intense the chanting became. Magic rippled through the air, nipping at my awareness.

We reached a large metal door at the end of the hallway, and Drew motioned for us all to wait while he tried to open it. After a few minutes of struggling with the door, he finally managed to pry it open just enough for us to slip through.

We stepped inside to be met by a strange sight: a group of cloaked figures standing in a circle around a large pentagram drawn on the floor, their voices rising in unison as they chanted. This wasn't generally how these things were done, but they seemed to be making good progress.

"Stop!" I yelled, but it was too late. In the center of the witches' circle, a Jersey Devil appeared. I mean, I was pretty sure that was what a Jersey Devil was supposed to look like. It was a large deer-like creature with bat-like wings and stood upright. If that was a Jersey Devil, then we had one bonafide JD here in our midst.

The witches whirled around to face us, their hands shaped into claws with magic flowing from their fingertips.

Not good.

I stepped forward and raised my arms, summoning a strong gust of wind that pushed the witches and the devil back several feet. The witches scrambled to their feet as I continued to hold the Jersey Devil at bay with my magic. Oh, wait. I had access to insane amounts of power now. Pulling a little from Drew, I wrapped magic around the lot of them, freezing the witches and the devil in place. Ha. Take that bi...witches. "They can't move. Go kill the devil."

As Lily and Ian strode forward, Olivia and Drew stayed by my side. "Take all the power you need," Drew said quietly.

"Thanks, but so far, so good." I watched with a bit of revulsion as Ian lifted a machete that had appeared out of nowhere and slicked it down toward the devil's long, hairy neck.

We all froze and stared in shock as the machete froze in midair and the devil transformed with a lot of pomp and circumstance—and glitter. Why glitter? —into a—

"Aunt Evie?" Olivia gaped at the gorgeous fae now standing between us and the coven of witches. "What are you doing here?"

Now that Olivia said the name, I remembered meeting Evie right after we freed Phira from the Inbetween.

Evie smiled brightly at her niece and walked over to pull her into a hug. "I'm just having a little fun with these witches. They are up to no good and needed to be taught a lesson."

Olivia laughed. "Okay, then, but be careful, Auntie. You almost lost your head." She nodded toward the witches. "We got it from here. The hunters will take care of these fools."

Evie shrugged and waved bye before teleporting away.

"What in the world?" I asked. "Why was your aunt pretending to be the Jersey Devil?"

"The fae are a big source of the trickster mythology across the world." Olivia grinned. "They like to play." She squinted and pursed her lips. "Come to think of it, so is Luci."

Now Luci, I would've understood. If the Jersey Devil had turned into the *real* devil, there would've been no surprise here.

"That makes you…" Ian pointed at Olivia.

With a wide, mischievous grin, Olivia said, "Trouble."

Nailed it.

12
AVA

THE NEXT EVENING, in the hours before Michelle's parents' visit, I bustled around the kitchen, making sure everything was perfect. Wallie helped too, but Alfred was the one really running the show, to nobody's surprise.

Why was I so nervous? We'd agreed to have a nice dinner at our house with everyone together. This way, both families could get to know each other better.

"They're coming at six?" I asked Wallie.

He stopped wiping down the cabinets and stared at me. "For the fourteenth time, yes. Why are you freaking out?"

"Hopefully, you'll only do this once." I pointed at him. "Which means we're going to eat with these people for the foreseeable future, hopefully for a good eighty years."

He opened his mouth, no doubt to tell me I'd probably be dead before eighty years went by, but the doorbell rang.

I checked my phone. "It's five forty-five. They're early." He turned toward the door, but I held up one hand. "No, I want to answer it."

Oh, sweet ghosts, I still had an apron on. Without a second thought, I tried untying the knot behind my back. Oh, my geez. It wouldn't budge. I tugged and tugged, then gave up and grabbed the strings on the knot around my neck. To my dismay, the apron caught in my hair. As I tugged, somehow, miraculously, the lower knot unraveled.

How? I don't freaking know. That thing had been glued three seconds ago.

The strings hit the ground, and as I struggled with the knot and my hair, I tripped on the dangling cloth. Laughter bubbled up my throat as I stumbled into the kitchen table.

"Hello?"

A woman's voice made me freeze in place. Winston had opened the front door to let our guests in.

My hair was a rat's nest in the back, with my apron still tangled in it. Alfred and Drew stood near the stove, staring at me in complete shock. This wasn't like me, the clumsiness and falling over. Wallie, on the other side of the table, looked at me like he was trying to figure out a way to disown me. He was a little too old to emancipate. He was stuck with me.

Michelle rushed forward. "Are you okay?"

She was such a sweet girl. I straightened, waved my hand, and made it all better. My apron disappeared—I'd actually transported it into a volcano in Hawaii. That apron would pay for tangling me up like this. It was already lava fodder.

With the same hand sweep, I fixed my hair back to a perfect coif.

Oh, yeah. It was good having my powers back. "Come in, please." Striding forward, I held out my hands.

Michelle's mom put her hands in mine and beamed at me. "I was so happy when Michelle told me you'd invited us over."

"We're delighted to have you here." I didn't even care if that sounded fake. We were having dinner together and having a baby together. Well, not us. Our kids were having the baby. Anyway, I *was* delighted to have them here. "Please, come in."

"Official introductions," Michelle said. "Mom, this is Wallie's mom, Ava." I shook her hand again as Michelle said, "This is my mom, Kathy."

"So happy," Kathy and I said at the same time, then dissolved into giggles.

"Dad, this is Drew." Drew stepped forward to shake hands. "Drew, this is my dad, Mark."

"Nice to meet you." They shook hands and nodded. It was going to be okay. I could already tell. Drew's feelings in the bond told me his hunter senses were happy, thank goodness.

Michelle pointed at me. "Dad, Ava. Ava, Mark. Drew, Kathy. Kathy Drew."

"I'm Wallie," my dorky son said. It might've been super corny, but it worked. Everyone laughed.

We headed into the living room. "I'm going to apologize in advance, but our entire extended family is coming tonight. It might get overwhelming, but I wanted you to get a full picture of our insane life so you'd know exactly what Michelle's getting into."

Kathy laughed. "She warned us already. I'm looking forward to placing the people with the names and stories."

"Well, here they come." I grinned at my dear Aunt Winnie as

she came down the stairs. Alfred met her in the hallway, and they came into the living room.

Oh, Winnie. She'd dressed so well for the evening. Her long, blonde hair was pulled into a bun, and her beautiful blue eyes flashed. The best part was that her dress wasn't revealing at all. It was still sexy, clinging in a way that made her movements sensual, but it lacked the distinctly trashy vibe she'd been putting off for the last several months.

Something about Alfred's sleep had mellowed her. Like a reality check. If nothing else good came from it, at least we had that.

"Oh, I know this one," Kathy said happily. "Alfred and Winnie?"

They beamed and shook hands with Kathy and Mark.

Larry and Zoey came in behind them. Zoey's ears twitched on top of her head. Ah, these two would be easy for her to guess, especially since Larry's head wobbled when they stepped forward. "Larry and Zoey," Kathy said warmly. "You two we've met, of course."

"Aha, you get a pass on that one," I teased.

Alfred disappeared and returned a few moments later with a tray with a teapot and cups. I stepped forward to serve, but the sweet man waved me off.

"It's my pleasure," he said with a wink.

Over the next half hour, Kathy and Mark met Mom and Dad, Olivia and Sam, along with Sammie, who almost instantly ran upstairs to find Snoozer and Ian. I'd told them that Wade wouldn't be up until after dark.

Oh, no. I forgot to do something to distract Lucy. I'd meant to get her a movie started so she'd ignore everything downstairs.

Thinking of that little devil...The white cat herself sauntered down the stairs. "Was nobody going to tell me we had company?"

I glared at her, trying to mentally threaten her life if she said a cuss word.

She jumped onto the coffee table, then delicately stepped over into Michelle's lap, rubbed her head against Michelle's belly, and sat, staring at Kathy and Mark.

"Hello, Lucy," Kathy said. "Michelle has told us so much about you."

Michelle looked at me and winked. "I warned them," she said wryly.

Lucy sniffed, looked at Michelle's parents, then said, "I'm sure she did."

Michelle laughed. Oh, thank goodness the cat was on her best behavior.

Wallie reached over and touched the top of Lucy's head, clearly intending to pet her.

"Hey," she screamed. "Don't touch me!"

Wallie jerked back as Lucy jumped back to the coffee table. She turned and glared at him. "You son of a—"

"Lucy!" Olivia, Drew, Sam, Michelle, and I yelled at once.

She froze, then turned her narrowed eyes on us. "I'm going upstairs. Send my dinner." With that command, the hot-tempered feline jumped off of the coffee table and stalked out of the room, across the foyer, and up the stairs.

"So," Kathy said. "That was Lucy?"

Laughter spread through the group at the insane cat's antics.

"Ava, guess what we found out?" Olivia asked.

I raised my eyebrows. "What?"

Leaning forward, Sam continued, "I went to my parents' house yesterday and went through their old family records and pictures. My mom went through a whole ancestry thing a few years back, so there was a lot of good information."

I sensed some big revelation coming. "And?"

"And we have a psychic in the family." Sam smiled bigly. "She's like seven generations back, but it explains my and Sammie's newfound abilities."

Leaning over, I pushed at his shoulder. "That's awesome. Has anything else happened since the chasm thing?"

He shook his head. "No, but I'm going to try to find some psychics through the school to help Sammie and me navigate this whole thing."

"Dinner is ready," Alfred said from the doorway. We stood and shuffled to the kitchen. So many of us were here at once it seemed to take an eternity to get everyone from one room to another. I wasn't quite sure how Alfred had managed it, but the kitchen table was extra-long with plenty of chairs to accommodate us all. He was powerful, that much I could feel resonating off of him, but he didn't have the sort of powers to expand a kitchen table.

"It seems we have perfect timing," Luci said as he and Phira walked from the conservatory doorway.

“As always,” I muttered, and sat between Drew and Olivia.

Luci sent me a wink and led Phira to their seats directly in front of Olivia, which I realized was also in front of me.

We ate and laughed and told stories about the kids because there’s a rule that moms have to embarrass their kids on a regular basis to keep them on their toes. It’s not my rule. It’s in the mom book they give all new mothers in the hospital.

I don’t make the rules.

Just before Alfred brought out dessert, Wallie stood and cleared his throat. I watched my son while holding my breath. He was nervous, and I had a sneaking suspicion why. Holding in my squeal was too hard.

He pulled a small black box out of his pants pocket, and Michelle sucked in a breath as Wallie turned to her and dropped to one knee. I clutched Drew's hand in joy.

"Michelle, I've loved you from the moment I saw you in the administrative office. I'd planned to do this sooner, but we found out about the baby, and things have been crazy at school and here." He paused and glanced at me. I mouthed, "Just ask her."

Wallie took her hand and slid the ring onto her finger. "Will you marry me?"

Michelle threw her arms around Wallie. "Yes, yes, yes!"

It was the perfect ending to a wonderful evening.

13
OLIVIA

"WHAT A DAY." I looked at John and Beth and sighed. "How many more interviews?"

After consulting the list on my desk, Beth said, "Three."

"We can do this." I picked up the folder with the teachers' resumes. It turned out there was a surprisingly large number of people in the supernatural community who were either qualified to teach or interested in teaching.

There were *not*, however, many people in the supernatural community who were *both* qualified to and interested in teaching. Today had proven that.

Some of our teachers came quickly and easily. Our friend Carrie would be one of the teachers for the youngest of our children. The godmothers would provide all of their own teachers and had graciously offered up their course list for anyone interested in joining them for any classes. That was nice, though I had made them promise to send me detailed information about all of their teachers.

They'd be in a school with our children, after all. I had to vet them.

I opened Jeanne's folder and glanced over her resume. Psychic Studies? I'd never heard of that before. Still, her credentials looked impressive. After getting what I could from her resume, I opened the door. "Jeanne Maclay?"

"Welcome, come in." I offered her a chair and motioned for John and Beth to sit down as well. We'd have to make this quick. I was stinking exhausted.

Jeanne looked nervous, but she exuded an aura of confidence.

"First of all, can you tell us about yourself?" I smiled as encouragingly as I could.

Jeanne took a deep breath, obviously gathering her thoughts. "Well," she began, "I've been studying psychic abilities for the past twenty years, traveling around the world to learn from some of the best teachers in the field. I've held seminars, taught classes, and even written a few books. Most humans think it's hogwash, but everything in my books is completely true."

"May I ask what your abilities are?" John asked.

"I am telepathic, though it is something I can turn off and on. I'd never use that power inappropriately." She chuckled. "I learned long ago that breeds heartache." The pain in her eyes told me there was a big story there, one I probably wasn't allowed to ask in a job interview. "I'm also telekinetic. I can move small objects with my mind. That one is harder to master. If I'm upset or shocked, sometimes they fly without warning. From what I understand, that's very common among people with this power."

Beth leaned forward. "We'd love a demonstration if it's not too much trouble." Her kind eyes twinkled.

Jeanne smiled and held up her hands. The paperweight on my desk slowly rose, hovering in the air for a few seconds before gently settling back down.

I glanced at John and Beth and they both nodded in approval. We went through the standard questions, and she answered them perfectly. After half an hour or so of chatting, I said, "Welcome to the team, Ms. Maclay," I said. "Provided all the paperwork goes smoothly and the background check, we'll be in touch."

Jeanne grinned and shook my hand before saying her good-byes. As she left, I felt a wave of relief wash over me. We'd found our psychic studies teacher.

It had been a long day. "Two to go," I said with false cheeriness. "Who is next?"

John held up another folder. "John Eaton. He applied for Elemental Studies. This says he's best with fire but has limited abilities with all elements."

"Oh," Beth said. "That's pretty rare."

"Does he have any teaching history?" I picked up the file to glance through. "He's currently a science teacher in Vermont. Nice." Opening the door, I stuck my head out and looked at the last two people. Presumably, John and our final interview. "John?"

He came in and got settled, and I began the same questions. John had a calm, gentle air about him that was different from Jeanne but no less impressive. He told us all about his studies and experiments, showing off a few of the items he had created with fire. After asking him to demonstrate his powers on one of the plants in the corner, it was quite clear that he was a whizz of elemental studies.

"What makes you want to leave your school in Vermont?" I

asked, then glanced at his file again. "It says you've been there twenty-three years."

He sighed. "As you know, witches live longer than humans, generally. I'm seventy-seven years old, and that's not such a big deal to you. My coworkers and bosses, though, know my age, and while they think I look amazing for my age—" He did look sixty at best "—they've been pressuring me to retire. I think they're afraid I'll drop dead in front of the kids."

John snorted, then covered it with a cough. "Sorry," he muttered.

"Welcome aboard," I said after we finished, then gave the paperwork spiel again. "We'll be happy to have you here for another twenty-three years, should you choose not to retire."

John beamed on his way out.

I didn't even pull the last file, just stuck my head out the door. "Come on in."

As I sat, I glanced at her name. "Catrin Lawson, tell us about yourself."

"Well, I'm a shifter," she said. "I don't have any powers I can teach, but besides the core studies, I can teach a shifting class."

As she told us about her time as a homeschooling mom and teacher amongst her pack, I looked at her credentials. No official teaching license, but she'd seen over a dozen children through to college. "I like what I see," I said. "We have workarounds here, so the lack of license won't be a problem, though we've been doing trial runs for any unlicensed teachers."

Catrin nodded eagerly. "I'd be totally fine with that."

After twenty more minutes of chatting, I looked at John and Beth. They both nodded in approval, so I smiled and said, "Welcome to the team, Miss Lawson. I think you'll fit right in."

Catrin beamed as she shook my hand and thanked me before she left.

As the door closed behind her, I sighed in relief. We had our teachers, and now it was time to make this school a reality.

14
AVA

"LUCI?" I stepped into the kitchen and looked at the world's most confident man—demon? demigod? —in concern. "Are you okay?"

Drew closed the front door behind us and put the keys in the bowl beside the door. We'd been in town having dinner alone. Date night.

"What are you doing here?" Drew asked. "Not that you aren't welcome, but..." He trailed off as Luci looked up at us. "What is it?"

"I don't know what to do." Luci shrugged and looked down at his hands. "I can't get into Hell. I don't know what's going on in there. I can sense all the souls, of course, but not what they're doing, whether they're happy."

Drew and I exchanged a glance. "You want them to be...hap-py?" I asked.

The devil looked at me, clearly horrified. "I didn't say that.

What if they *are* happy though? That would be a travesty." He scoffed. "I can't believe this is happening."

"We're here for you," Drew said, patting a hand somewhat awkwardly on Luci's shoulder. "What do you need us to do?" It was a nice gesture on Drew's part, and Luci rose to the occasion.

Not literally. He reached back and patted Drew's hand, then pushed it away. "I'm the worst ruler of Hell ever."

"There have been more?" I asked. Not that it mattered in the current situation, but I was curious.

He shook his head with his forehead on the table. "No, but I'm still the worst."

"With that logic, you're also the best." As he moaned, I pulled out my phone and opened the group chat that had pretty much everyone local and supernatural on it, including Melody, the coven leader. **Luci's at my house. I've never seen him so low. Everyone should come. We need to put our heads together and figure this out.**

"I can hear you typing," Luci muttered as the text pinged on Drew's phone. "Was that about me?"

"Yes," I said and moved to the stove to boil water for tea. "I'm calling in reinforcements. You sit tight. Everyone will be here soon."

Thankfully, it was a Friday evening, so most of them should be off work. I hoped I didn't interrupt any important plans, but this trumped all other plans. Luci needed all the help he could get. I'd grown rather fond of the infuriating man over the last several months.

The tea kettle whistled, and I made a pot of calming chamomile tea, just what Luci needed now. I even added a little magic to Luci's cup to give him calm and clarity. We needed him focused to help solve this problem.

He was still despairing when people started to arrive. The kitchen table was still huge from our dinner with Michelle's parents, so we all gathered around it as people trickled in. Alfred soon arrived and took over the hosting duties, to my relief and only a little guilt. Winnie sat at the head of the table in an only sort of skimpy outfit. Definitely still an improvement.

After a little while, I ended up having to expand the table again. I changed it to an enormous round table, and Ben and Brandon conjured extra chairs from their B&B storeroom as more people arrived.

In the end, I stood with Drew and looked at the gathered people.

It was abso-freaking-lutely insane how many people had turned up. "Can I ask what made you all so willing to come out tonight?" It wasn't that I doubted their willingness to help, but this was *Luci,* after all. I wouldn't have thought so many would help the man downstairs.

"We owe you one." Ben and Brandon smiled at Luci appreciatively. "What you did by getting our B&B on that travel show? That made all the difference to our business. We're booked months out and talking about expanding."

Melody nodded. "I still appreciate you showing up with that turkey on Thanksgiving."

Everyone looked at her with big questions written all over their faces. She shrugged and blushed a little. "I burned mine, and my mother-in-law was there. It was the first time she'd relented and let me host Thanksgiving, so ruining dinner would've been..."

"Awful," I finished for her.

"Yes." She nodded toward Luci, who still looked dejected, even with Phira's arms around him and her head on his shoulder.

A young fae woman I hadn't met before had come with Phira. "The fae are in your debt. You found my lost child in moments. If you need warriors, they will come, and I am here to offer any magical aid I can." She bowed her head slowly and respectfully.

Wow. I had no idea Luci had helped so many people.

Zoey smiled shyly. "Luci helped me start researching my family. I was orphaned very young, and I don't know any relatives. Plus, it's not like I can do a DNA test like humans can." Her ears twitched as she spoke.

Holy crow, I hadn't realized that either. I had asked the ferret shifter couple, Dana and Rick, to ask around the shifter communities, but no one could find anything about Zoey's parents or family.

Snoozer yowled loudly from the corner. Lucy-Fur, sitting beside him, sighed. "He says he never would've met me if Luci hadn't told him where to look in the forest." She rolled her eyes and huffed. "Thanks, I guess."

Wade had come up as soon as the sun went down. He cleared his throat. "Yeah, um, he helped me with some investments, and now things are setting up nicely."

Owen, who had appeared from the conservatory with Lily, nodded his dark head. "He got me talking to the right people and even helped with a few contacts. Now the hunters hold me in higher esteem, and I've been getting better jobs, which usually pay well."

I couldn't believe it. All these people had come out of the woodwork to help Luci. My heart warmed as I listened to them talk about how Luci had helped them.

He'd helped Jess get into a different college. I'd known that she'd changed but not that the dean owed Luci a favor, so he called it in.

"Pearl sends her support," Lily said. "She couldn't come herself, but the hunters are available if you need more of us."

Luci looked at her with his face unreadable. After a few minutes, he cracked one of his signature winning smiles. "It sounds nice when you say it like that, but now you all owe me a favor."

Hank, the new manager at Sam and Wade's bar, snorted. "Yeah, and we're all paying you back right now. We like you, but we're not stupid."

Leaning back, Luci looked at him appraisingly, then roared with laughter. "That you are not. None of you. Thank you for coming, but I don't see how your being here will help me. You've all individually tried already."

We sat in silence around the big table, everyone looking in a different direction. I tapped my fingers rhythmically on the wood.

"What about a ghost?" John asked. "Have we tried to see if a ghost can get in?"

The group looked at my dad at the same time.

Luci's jaw dropped. "That is a *fantastic* idea."

"Does anyone know a ghost?" Olivia asked. "I guess we could try to get back to the Inbetween."

Phira shuddered. "Ew, no, please. Let's try to avoid that."

"We do." Dad smiled at me. "My grandfather. He's just hanging out at the family home."

"At the academy," Olivia said brightly. "That's genius."

"I can go get him," Dad offered.

"I'll go, too." Alfred stood. "I've been listening to you guys talk about getting it ready while I was asleep. I'd love to see it. Plus, I used to have the ability to command ghosts, which is rare amongst necromancers. I haven't had an opportunity to test it out since I woke."

Dad smiled. "It's my ancestral home, but it's your, uh, descended home."

Descended home didn't quite sound like a real phrase, but we all knew what he meant.

"While you're there, I'll head over to the hunter headquarters and look through our artifact room. Maybe we have something there that could help that we've overlooked," Ian said.

Luci sighed. "Thanks, everyone. Even if none of this works, it means a lot that you're willing to try."

Was that a tear I saw in his eye?

He blinked, and it disappeared. Must've been a trick of the light. The great Lucifer couldn't possibly be choked up by friendship, right?

15

OLIVIA

"Let's not waste any time," I said and stood. "Ian, I can take you to North Carolina."

He nodded eagerly. "Thanks. I didn't bring one of the portal stones with me."

Phira and I had figured out how to enchant crystals to allow people to portal to a set location. We hadn't really had time to keep messing with it so a stone could let the user portal anywhere. Right now, they had limited uses before they needed a refresh. We'd gone to North Carolina to enchant a big bowlful of stones for the hunters, all of them leading back to the Boone headquarters.

"Anybody else want to go?" I offered.

Ava, John, and Alfred were going to head to the school to see if their great-grandfather could go try to get through Hell's gates while Ian and I went to the hunter compound.

"Sure," Lily said. "I'll go. I can help go through the artifacts a little faster."

Ava held up one hand. "Everyone else, meet back here in two hours. You're welcome to stay while we're gone, or you can go and come back."

With a slight bow, Luci cleared his throat. "I appreciate you all very much." Instead of one of his normal jokes, he sat back down. Phira put her arms around him again.

"Ready?" I nodded to Ian and Lily. "Let's hurry. There's no telling how long it'll take to find whatever this artifact is."

We stepped into the conservatory, and I whipped up a quick portal. "Don't try to go inside the compound," Lily said. "It's spelled so you can't."

"Noted." I'd been there once before, so it was pretty easy to open one up right at the gates. We stepped through, and I looked up at the tall metal gates. My magic allowed me to see the huge ward covering the place. It was pretty extreme. "Don't I need some sort of charm thingy to repress my power?"

Lily shook her head as she placed her hand on a metal square on the gate. "Nope. That was before. Now, witches, shifters, fae, and anyone else are welcome here. We even have a necromancer living here." The gate swung open, and we stepped through. Power hummed in the air, a strange mix of hunter magic, protective spells, and something older.

"Hello," Pearl called as she stepped off of the front porch of the closest building. The place had several within the gates. "Welcome."

"Did you tell her we were coming?" I asked softly.

"No," Ian and Lily said in unison.

"How'd she know?" I glanced at them, but they kept their gaze on their grandmother.

"We've been asking ourselves that question for years," Lily said, barely moving her lips.

Ian glanced at me briefly, then said, "She's creepy. We know better than anybody."

Pearl moved into earshot then, and both of them smiled broadly.

"Hello," Ian said.

Lily echoed his words, then said, "Lovely to see you."

"Please, come. You're here for the artifact room?" Pearl air kissed their cheeks, then turned to me. "Olivia, lovely to see you again."

"You as well." Ugh, so awkward and formal. How did Pearl's family do it, especially those who lived here at the compound?

"Ian," Pearl said commandingly.

Seamlessly, Ian and Lily switched places. "Yes?" he responded.

"There's a necromancer we need to keep our eyes on. I fear he's going to become a problem."

Ian nodded as we stepped onto the porch. "Okay, that happens. Why don't you have Owen take the case?"

She hummed low in her throat. "Owen is busy with other matters. I would like you, your brother, and Ava to handle it."

Ian sighed. "We'll see. I can talk to Drew and Ava about it, I suppose."

Pearl's face softened. Well, it didn't look quite so icy, at least. A teensy bit less hoity, though still plenty toity. "That would be nice."

Ian walked a bit faster, leading us down a hallway. We'd only been in the building thirty seconds, and I was already lost. Pearl turned her frosty gaze on me. Oh, crap. "Olivia. Tell me how you're getting on with your newfound fae family?"

Who had told her about that? Ava and Drew wouldn't have. I shot Lily and Ian quick glares. It had to have been one of them. "It's been an adjustment," I said carefully. I didn't want to give too much away. "It's a good one, though. They've been very welcoming."

Pearl's brows creased. "Nice of them. I understand they've been helping you with your training?"

I cleared my throat to reply, but she kept going.

"We don't know much about the fae. Secretive people, aren't they?" Her tone was light but had an edge to it. She had a very specific reason for asking.

"Yes, they—"

"And you, as their kinswoman, are uniquely poised to help the hunters establish a relationship with them."

Crap! "Well, I don't know all that much about them. I learn more every time I go to Faery."

Pearl stopped short in the middle of a dim, somewhat dusty hallway. "You've been to Faery?"

Lily and Ian, still ahead of us, stopped a few feet away when they realized we weren't following.

"Yeah," I drawled. "I kind of have to."

Pearl stepped forward, just barely getting into my personal bubble. "Why?"

Oof. "Because I'm one of the heirs to the throne," I whispered. Why was I telling this woman my life story? I was a strong, confident princess. Nobody intimidated me.

Except, apparently, Pearl Walker. "You're a fae princess?" Oh, geez. Her voice had gone all low.

"I'm kind of a double princess." I looked at Lily for help, but she just widened her eyes and shook her head. Some friend. "I'm Lucifer's only daughter, so I'm the Princess of Hell, technically."

Pearl's face shut down like someone had flipped her switch. All emotion left.

Gone.

This probably wasn't a good thing...

"Come," she said briskly. "Let's see if we have any artifacts connected to Hell."

Ava

LUCI OPENED a portal for us to step through into the closet at the castle. "I'll get one set up for you here," he offered. "While you're gone."

"Thanks." I gave him a little finger wave and stepped out into the beautiful castle hallway.

Silently moving down the hall, I looked at Dad. "How do you know where to find Grandpa Lynn?" I'd taken to calling him that, even though the ghost was my great-grandfather. It was still neat to have access to a family member who remembered that far back.

"He likes to hang out in the big library," Dad said.

Alfred's facial expression caught my gaze. He walked beside and a little behind me with an astonished expression. "This place is great," he said, all high-pitched when he caught me watching him. "I would've loved living here."

"You could," I said. "Not that I'd ever want you to move out of Winston, but this is your family home as well. Plus, you and Winnie could always help with the school."

I was pretty sure this school would end up being all hands on deck. I already saw the potential for dozens of different magical studies.

"I don't know," Alfred said. He waved his hands in front of him like he was shrugging off the idea.

We turned a corner and came face to face with a huge library door. It looked like it belonged in an ancient castle, but the inside was quite modern, with all sorts of magical artifacts. Grandpa Lynn stood behind a desk and waved when we opened the door. "Hello, come in!" he said.

We stepped in, and Dad walked forward first, followed by Alfred and me.

"Grandpa, this is Alfred. Alfred, meet Lynn Howe."

Alfred shook Grandpa Lynn's hand. I wasn't totally sure if Lynn being touchable was due to our necromancer powers or him just being a particularly strong ghost. Probably both.

"Gramps, Alfred is our ancestor," Dad said.

Granda Lynn gave Dad a confused look. "So, he's a ghost, too?"

"No," Alfred said. "I was animated as a ghoul for many years, but then I fell into this chasm of power, and now I have my original body back."

"The best we can tell, he's fully human and a necromancer again," I explained.

Lynn stepped back and looked at Alfred in amazement. "How far back of an ancestor?"

"That's a long story, and we don't have a ton of time," I said. "Alfred's been wanting to come to meet you, though."

Grandpa arched an eyebrow at me. "Give me the condensed version."

"Ah, okay, um..." Alfred clasped his hands together. "I was a Viking necromancer. Came to America and went very dark. Died in a cave. Last century a local necromancer to Shipton Harbor found me and animated me. My body hadn't decayed. I'd sort of mummified. Ava ended up with custody of me as a necromancer, and now here I am."

With an uproarious laugh, Grandpa Lynn clapped Alfred on the back. "I am definitely going to want to hear the full version of that story."

"Gramps, we're here because someone has locked Lucifer out of Hell. He was wondering if you'd be willing to see if you can get through the gates as a ghost."

"Ha!" Grandpa clutched his stomach and chortled. "That old cuss is still running around causing trouble?"

"You know Lucifer?" I asked.

"Oh, yes. He's quite the social butterfly. I suppose I might owe him a favor. He helped me out with a tight financial pinch I was in many, many moons ago. I'd be happy to come, but I'm afraid I'm attached to this old castle. I can't leave it."

"Part of my powers when I was alive before was the ability to command ghosts."

"Do you think you can help me leave the castle?" Lynn asked.

Alfred grinned. "I think I can. If you're willing to let me try."

"Hot dog, let's get to it." Lynn straightened up and walked around the desk. "I haven't left this place since before I died." He squinted at Alfred and lowered his voice. “If this works, I'm going to be asking for quite a few trips out and about in the world."

Alfred sighed. "Now you know why I don't tell many people. All the ghosts in the world and probably in the Inbetween would be coming to me for help."

"It's too much for one person. I wonder if this is something you could teach me?" I grinned at him. "Cause I could always use another power."

He snorted. "We can certainly try."

Five minutes later, he'd done something to Grandpa Lynn that made it so Lynn could leave with us. I hadn't been able to see what it was, but Alfred had walked around the middle of the library with his eyes closed. "Basically, I'm looking for the connection," he'd whispered when I'd asked.

Sure. Of all the weird things that had happened in my life over the last year or so, this wasn't a scratch on the surface, so I rolled with it. Why not?

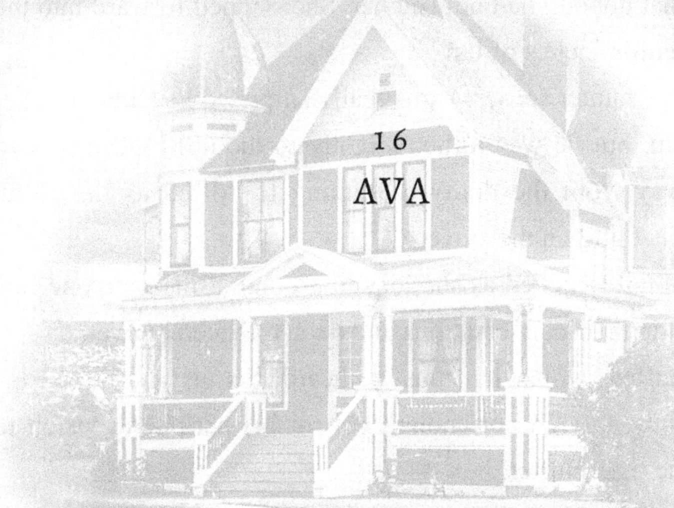

16
AVA

TWO HOURS LATER, everyone had gathered back at my place. The living room was full, and the kitchen was full. Even the conservatory had a couple of people in it. I meandered around, talking with everyone like this was some sort of party rather than a solemn group of people going to attempt to break the devil into Hell.

I say "attempt" because, let's face it, the odds were stacked against us. Most everyone here had tried at least once. Tried and failed, and yet, here we are again. We liked to believe in second chances around here. Sometimes third and fourth.

Ian sat perched in a kitchen chair. He'd pulled it to the wall nearest the large arched doorway from the foyer. From my vantage point in the living room, I could see both Ian and Zoey, who stalked down the stairs in her tiger form.

She loved doing that when we had guests. They either oohed and aahed or completely freaked out.

At the moment, nobody had noticed her. Coincidentally, everyone was turned away from the foyer at this exact moment.

Everybody but me.

I kept my spot and hid a smile as Zoey looked around, clearly irritated that nobody had noticed her. She stepped forward into the kitchen, within inches of Ian.

With his hunter senses, I was really surprised he hadn't felt her behind him, but he was turned slightly to the left, with his head turned away from the doorway, talking to Alfred as the ghoul stirred something on the stove.

Zoey's tail twitched as she looked around. Still, everyone was engrossed in their conversations and hadn't noticed her yet.

She huffed, which Ian must've heard, because he turned his head slightly, though not enough yet for his peripheral vision to pick up the tiger shifter.

I knew what was coming and plugged my ears. Zoey opened her gigantic mouth and roared.

Everyone in the kitchen and living room jumped, but Ian... oh, poor Ian.

Ian's ear was inches away from Zoey's big mouth. He squealed and jumped, falling off of his chair and conjuring a sword at the same time. As he bounced off of the kitchen tiles, the sword sliced his leg, and his squeal turned into a scream of pain.

I rushed forward, completely unable to control my laughter. Ian was hurt, and I shouldn't have been doubled over as I hobbled over to him to heal his leg.

It made everything worse when Zoey fell over in laughter too, except she was still in tiger form. She collapsed on her side between the foyer and kitchen and chuff-roar-huffed as she wiggled her paws and rolled around on her back.

That was all I could take. I collapsed to the side and clutched my ribs with one arm and with the other, reached over to grab Ian's leg in an iron grip.

My laughter didn't prevent me from pushing healing magic into his leg. As soon as the blood stopped pouring, I rolled onto my back and looked up at the ceiling as I tried to catch my breath. Everyone else was laughing, too, and the sheer number of people in the room made the volume loud.

"That was *rude!"* Ian yelled and jumped to his feet. He looked at Zoey in dismay, then around the room at the people in various stages of trying to rein in their laughter. "Can we just go?"

Luci, who had laughed as hard as anyone else, stood. "Yes, let's go." He wiped tears from his eyes and gave Ian an apologetic look. "I'm sorry, Ian, but that was too good." Luci waved his hand, and the blood disappeared. Ian's pant leg fixed itself at the same time.

"Yeah, yeah." Ian crossed his arms and gave the perfect imitation of Sammie pouting.

As soon as everyone had gathered their wits, we stepped out onto the back porch. "Do we have everything?" I asked.

They'd come up with bupkis in North Carolina. The two artifacts they'd found relating to Hell had been a necklace that hid the wearer from hellhounds and a weird, small stone tablet that nullified Luci's power.

That one might come in handy someday. I certainly wasn't going to forget it existed.

"I've got my potions," Melody said. "Maybe they'll work. Who knows?" She'd mixed up some potions that would melt metal, cancel out various spells, and one that worked like a small bomb.

Everyone else was pretty much relying on their powers. Drew,

Ian, and Lily had various weapons at their disposal if we got inside, but otherwise, the plan was to batter the gates with power. Now that I had my full magic, I hoped I could make some kind of impact. I hadn't tried since Alfred woke. What was the point of being the most powerful witch in my family if I couldn't open a measly gate?

Luci opened a portal, and we stepped into... nothingness. It was unnerving. Instead of a floor, white smoke curled around our feet. I had to trust that Luci knew where he was going and hoped our footing wouldn't disappear as soon as we moved too far away from the portal.

I stepped to the side to wait for everyone to enter, but some commotion at the back of the group drew my attention. I returned to my backyard to find Alfred holding Winnie in his arms. She blinked sleepily.

"What happened?" I asked.

"She passed out." Mom put her hand on Winnie's forehead. "Not for long. Alfred caught her before she hit the ground."

"Take her inside." I put my hand on her arm and walked in with them. Luci closed the portal, and the whole group went in with us. As we walked, I tried to use my healing magic to dive in and see what was wrong.

Whatever it was, I couldn't pinpoint it. Something wasn't right in her body, but it wasn't like a break or cut. Nothing so straightforward as when I'd healed Ian's slice on his leg.

"I haven't eaten today," she said as Alfred settled her on the couch. "That's probably all it is. Low blood sugar."

"I'll stay with her," Beth said. "You guys go ahead. Our power isn't significant enough to help, anyway."

"I'll stay, too." Alfred crouched beside Winnie and brushed her hair out of her face.

"No," I said. "Sorry, but you're incredibly powerful, and we might need you. Mom will take care of Winnie."

Alfie looked reluctant.

“Plus,” I continued. “Grandpa Lynn is tethered to you.” I nodded toward the real-looking ghost. “If you stay, he stays.”

With a sigh, Alfred nodded. “That’s true.”

“I could stay,” Wade offered. “I’m not sure why I was going in the first place. It's not like I have magic to open the gates. At best, I could provide some muscle to force them open?”

Hank, the new bartender, stepped forward. “Me, too. Would it help if we stayed with the ladies to be potential muscle if they needed it for something?”

Alfred still looked worried, but after a few seconds, he leaned forward and pressed a firm kiss to Winnie's forehead. "Eat and rest, and let these vampires wait on you hand and foot. If you still feel bad when we get back, we'll contact a healer."

That was no joke. Something wasn't right inside my aunt's new body. It was likely just a cold or something, but she'd be following up on it even if that meant I had to drag her to a human doctor. It wasn't like they'd find anything weird in her bloodwork. If witch abilities showed up in medical records, we'd have been outed a long time ago.

Everyone looked at Sam. He shrugged and pointed at Olivia with his thumb. “Where she goes, I go. Plus, I’m psychic now. That might help with something.”

Fair enough. I hadn’t really expected him to leave Olivia’s side. He wouldn't have even back when he was human. “Wallie,

Michelle, Larry, and Zoey are upstairs," I said. "Any of them could help if you needed them."

Wallie and Michelle had popped in a few minutes after we got back from our errands and wished everyone luck, but Wallie wouldn't let Michelle go, a decision I wholeheartedly approved of. Michelle had, in turn, put her foot down. If she couldn't go, neither could Wallie.

I supported that as well.

It took a few more minutes to get Alfred to leave Winnie, but after several kisses and promises to be back soon, we made it through the portal again and began to walk forward through the weird mist.

This whole thing was a gamble, but one we had to take if we wanted to help our friend and get Hell out of the grips of whoever had enough power to lock the devil out of his home.

The group of us looked more like a bunch of scared kids than the badass magic users we were. Luci walked confidently forward, but the rest of us sort of huddled and shuffled.

As we moved through the foggy smoke, the outline of what had to be the gates formed in the distance. It was definitely a sight to behold. I couldn't tell if it was metal or stone, but either way, the gates had been built by someone with power beyond what I could fathom: Luci. He seemed so... not weak exactly, but the man I knew and, if not loved, was fond of, didn't seem capable of this. Yet here was the pudding proof that he had powers unrevealed.

If nothing else, he was a mystery.

We moved closer, and my heart began to race. All of a sudden, this seemed like a bad idea. Olivia or Luci could teleport us away if things got too hairy. We weren't in any real danger out here. Still, something inside me said this was going to go very wrong.

A few minutes later, we stopped in front of the freaking *massive* gates. Holy crow, they were ginormous. This close, the materials were more obvious, and it was a mix. Stone, metal, and even bits of wood had been melded together. It was amazing and totally terrifying.

It seemed impossible that we'd be able to get through this, but… in for a penny.

"Who wants to go first?" I asked. No one answered. I glanced over at Luci, and he gave me a look. "Are you volunteering? I've already tried six ways from Sunday."

I sighed, steeling myself with a deep breath before walking forward. My hands shook as they touched the gate. I expected alarms to go off or something, but nothing happened. I glanced back at my friends, who watched with wide eyes.

I pressed forward, trying to find some way of getting in. The gate didn't budge, no matter how hard I pushed or pulled or blasted it. I ran my hands and my magic along the seams and grooves of the gate, searching for any kind of opening or latch that would let us in.

After another few seconds of failure, I stepped back and tapped into my necromancer side. Using all of the death magic at my disposal, I held my hands out and said, "Open," in my most commanding tone.

Nada.

Ghost-grandpa Lynn stepped forward. "I don't know what I can do other than try to go through."

Luci shrugged. "If you can get in, maybe you can find a way to open it from the inside or gather intel."

Lynn nodded and walk-floated toward the gates. He stopped short a couple of inches shy of the enormous structure. He tried and tried to push forward, but there was nothing he could do to get past the barrier.

After that, Owen, Dad, and I linked our magic and tried again. Didn't work.

They tried individually, then we *all* linked our magic together, everyone but Luci and Olivia. They'd tried many, many times already. I pulled on the group's power, and for a second, the gates rumbled, but then they stopped, and no matter how I exhausted myself trying, they didn't budge.

Melody came forward with her potions, and the explosion one was particularly fun, but when the smoke cleared, it was as though she'd never even tried.

Drew tried lending his boosting ability to everyone in turn.

What happened? Not a darn thing, that's what.

Sam, Ian, Drew, Lily, and Phira tried to physically move the gates. They were the strongest in the bunch, but it might as well have been Wallie trying.

The weaker witches in the coven came forward and individually attempted it since we had no idea what small thing could trigger a change.

Nothing triggered, nothing moved.

Finally, everyone but Olivia and Luci had given it their all. I looked at the devil and his daughter, exasperated. "You two give it a whirl or let me link up to you and pull on your magic. Maybe between me, you two, and Drew, it'll work."

Olivia stepped up and put one hand on the gate. "Open up, you absolute piece of sh—" She stopped talking because, to my amazement, and by the sounds of the gasps of the people behind me, their amazement as well, the gates opened.

Luci stumbled forward and stared into the darkness behind the gates. "It looks normal," he whispered.

"What can you see?" I stood on my tiptoes and stared over his shoulder. As far as I could tell, it was pitch black beyond the gates.

Luci turned and looked at me. His face slowly morphed from shocked to devilishly pleased.

"Pure Hell."

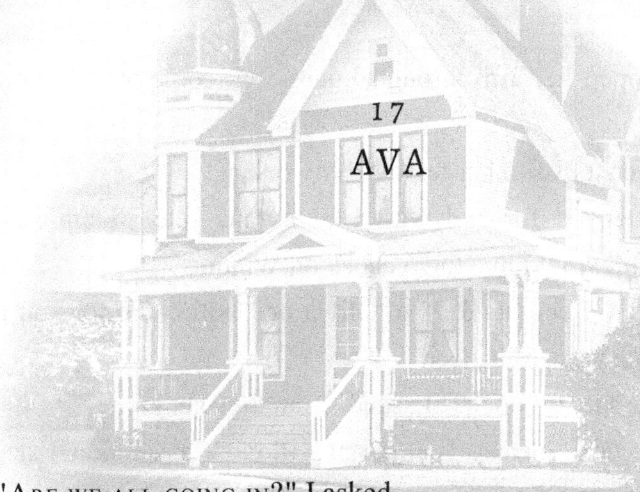

17
AVA

"ARE WE ALL GOING IN?" I asked.

Luci shook his head. "Oh, no. I can't have this big of a group traipsing around in there. I don't know who has been let out of their cells or what sort of chaos they've managed. I don't even know who is responsible for this lock. I'd love some help, but too many would make things worse, not easier."

"Why did it work?" Olivia asked. "Why now? I've tried, how many times?"

Luci stared at her with the wheels turning behind his eyes. "At least a dozen. Probably more."

Olivia sighed, her shoulders slumping. "Then why this time?"

Luci shrugged and then gestured towards the door. "I've got to get in there. We can figure out why later."

With a glare at the gates, Olivia turned toward what still looked like pure inky blackness to me. "I'm going, too."

"And me." I stepped forward. "You might need me."

Drew put his hand on my shoulder, and his brother and sister stepped up and crossed their arms. The hunters would be joining us.

Where Olivia went, Sam went. There would be no arguing that.

Phira looped her arm through Luci's. "I'll come to help you, dear."

He pressed a kiss to her temple. "My queen."

Alfred stepped forward with Dad by his side. "I am very powerful, but I would like to go check on Winnie."

Luci held up one hand. "Go. Olivia or I will come for you if we need another necromancer."

"Is the portal still open?" I asked. "Can they get home?"

"Yes. Go now, please. That portal will close as soon as I step through these gates."

Dad pressed a kiss to the side of my head. "Be safe." He hurried after the crowd, which was already almost out of our view.

Luci waited a few more seconds with his head cocked as though he were listening to them all leave. "Okay," he finally said. "They're gone."

With a determined look, he turned toward the still-open gates of Hell. "Let's do this."

Staying on their heels, Drew, Ian, Lily, and I followed Luci, Phira, Olivia, and Sam through the gates.

Stepping into the darkness felt icky, like walking through cobwebs. "What is this?" I asked, shuddering as the sensation passed.

"The powers of Hell," Luci answered gravely. "Let's be careful."

The group stayed close together. As quickly as the gross sensation had hit me, it was gone, and I could see properly.

We were in a courtyard. It wasn't as big as I might've imagined, but creatures meandered everywhere. "What in the *literal* hell?" I asked.

"I suppose you'd call them zombies," Luci said. "They're souls that have been trapped here." He paused. "Well, it's more than that. They've been here a very long time and are past the point that torture would do them any good. In a way, I've broken them, and they are no longer sentient. Not really."

"Were they evil?" Drew asked.

"Oh, yes. I don't torture those who do not deserve it, nor do I allow anyone else to do so." Luci shook his head. "I said something about all vampires ending up here, which is true, but those who lived a good life and tried to be good people don't have the worst afterlife." He chuckled. "At least, not when I'm in charge. I have no idea what's happening to them now, though it's a good sign that these souls are still roaming about, somewhat free to go where their mindless brains take them."

I shuddered as one came close, then reached out with my necromancer magic. "Stop."

It stopped. "Turn around." Slowly, the creature shuffled in a circle to face the opposite direction.

I blew out a breath. "Wow."

"You can command them, but you cannot animate them the way you could a ghoul." Luci smiled at them a little bit... was that fondness in his expression? Seriously, what a weirdo. "If you're ever here and need protection, they can assist you, but any necromancer could use them. If you encounter one more powerful than yourself, watch out."

I arched an eyebrow at him. "*Are* there necromancers more powerful than me in here?" As far as I knew, I was the most powerful on Earth, save maybe for Alfred now that he had his human body and magic back. We hadn't yet put that to the test.

Luci tapped the side of his nose. "We'll see."

Why was I not comforted by that answer?

Luci strode toward a gigantic castle-like building. How had I not noticed that immediately? I looked around, trying to focus on everything in sight, but the buildings and beings were somehow slippery. If it wasn't within a few feet of me, I had a hard time keeping my gaze on it or really processing what I was looking at.

Before he put his foot on the bottom step, the big door at the front of the castle cracked open. My heart froze as I moved closer to the steps. Everyone stayed close, and we all stared, apprehensive about what we were about to face.

The giant door creaked open before us, revealing a dark path made of black stone. Out from the shadows came a figure cloaked in black robes, leaning on a wooden staff. She threw the hood back, revealing a pale face and bright blue eyes. Her wrinkled skin was somehow both saggy and pulled tight against her skull. It was an odd sight. Luci growled deep in his throat, then said her name. "Helga."

The name sounded familiar, but I'd definitely never seen this old crone before.

"This is who locked you out of Hell?" Olivia asked.

"I wouldn't have thought her powerful enough," Luci said softly.

The woman shuffled forward and pointed her staff at us with an evil smirk on her face. She muttered one word, and as she spoke, the staff glowed a menacing red. "*Mori.*"

I threw up my hands and tried to blast her with power. I didn't have time to put any form to it, but enough raw magic would knock her on her butt.

My magic hit hers with a thunderclap, then, to my utter shock, we froze in place as she unleashed powerful bolts of energy. They shot through the air and threatened to tear apart our very souls if they touched us.

I fought as hard as I could, barely recognizing that Olivia, Phira, and Luci were doing the same beside me. Drew's power filled me, more than I'd ever felt, yet still, it wasn't enough. I couldn't break us free of her immense power.

As we struggled, one of those bolts of magic hit its mark. Electricity—lightning—shot right into Lucifer's chest, and he fell.

The loss of Luci's power meant we couldn't hold against this Helga, yet, she didn't try to harm us further. She let out the most stereotypical witch laugh I'd ever heard as she sprinted past us and out the gates. I would've tried to stop her, but Phira began to scream as Olivia staggered backward into Sam's arms.

"No," Phira howled. She dropped to her knees beside Luci with tears pouring down her cheeks.

When I looked at the devil's face, my stomach dropped to the ground. I echoed Phira's word in a whisper. "No."

Olivia blinked several times with her hand covering her heart. "Power," she said softly. "I'm full of power."

With a wave of her hand, the gates swung shut behind us with a mighty clang.

"Olivia?" I asked.

She clung to Sam and looked down at her biological mother and father. "He's dead," she said in a voice filled with despair, as though she'd lost all hope.

I ran forward and dropped to my knees to heal Luci, but when I touched him and delved to find the problem, I recoiled in horror. There was nothing there. Olivia was right.

The devil was dead, and there wasn't even enough left of him for me to animate.

"He's dead," Olivia repeated, "and I have the power of Hell."

IF YOU ENJOYED SEEING Hailey and Jax again, make sure you check out their series, Fanged After Forty.

IF YOU ENJOYED HEARING about Luci going to Florida to get a key from a hunter there, check out Blair and Lily's series, Hunting After Forty.

See what's next for Ava in A Normal Midlife.

Don't miss two series set in the new academy: Godmother Training Academy and Geography & Ghost Hunts (Middle Grade).

AN INHERITED MIDLIFE

WITCHING AFTER FORTY BOOK 16

L.A. BORUFF

Dedicated to Louisa Rosati. May you find a magical chasm of power to send you on your own adventure.

1
AVA

THE TIME CHANGE from Scotland to the east coast of the United States threw me way off. Drew and I had portaled home, then driven to the location the tentacle monster was last seen, a cave on the beach about an hour north of Shipton Harbor, and I was seriously wishing I could take a nap. How could going through a portal cause so much jet lag? It made no sense.

We stared at the water. Unlike the cave just down from my house, this one flooded at high tide.

"Did she text back yet?" I sat down on a large rock next to the opening of the cave. There was no way I was waiting inside the dark, creepy thing.

"No," Drew replied with an edge of annoyance in his tone. "She doesn't always reply. That's Pearl for you." He slipped his phone into his pocket and scanned the beach. "I'm guessing the creature is ocean-bound. The one we fought at our rehearsal dinner had been heading for the ocean when it saw us coming for it."

I snorted. I couldn't help it. The visual of Lucifer Morningstar being chased by a giant tentacled monster still cracked me up. Nobody could ever take that away from me. It was a cherished memory now. Some would say a core memory, even. Our dear friend Satan still hadn't told us how the monster had gotten out of Hell. Well, monsters, plural. There were apparently more.

"I agree with the monster being in the ocean. If it was somewhere in town, we'd definitely have heard about it already." I dug a hole in the sand with the toe of my sneaker. The water had already come in a little since we arrived, so we had about an hour to wait, give or take.

Pulling out my phone, I texted Olivia. **Are you coming?**

She'd better be coming. The three dots appeared, indicating that she was typing, then disappeared. Seconds later the dots reappeared. Frowning at the screen, I tried not to be annoyed. My intuition was telling me she was ditching the opportunity to fight another monster. I furrowed my brow as if she was in front of me, but then she replied, and I had to relax. Man, I was tired and grumpy.

As soon as trick or treating with Sammie is done, Sam is taking me away for the week. A total surprise. It's been way too long since we had adult time. Sorry I can't make it.

She deserved a week away, and if Drew and I couldn't handle one measly giant sea monster, what good were we? Still, the corners of my mouth dipped into a deep frown. I sighed and tried to reign in my irritation. I needed a nap and a Snickers, STAT. I couldn't be mad at her for reconnecting with her hubby. Since Sam had become a vampire, things had been weird between them. It would be really good for them to get away and work on their relationship.

Have fun. I'll tell you all about the monster battle when you get home.

I scrolled through my texts. Everyone had other more important things to do and couldn't come to help us.

How convenient for them. Ack. Maybe it was going to take an ice cream Snickers.

"Did you get a hold of Lily or Ian?" I asked and Drew shook his head.

"Conveniently busy."

"Looks like it's just you, me, and the monster. Do you have a plan?" I had no clue how to fight a giant monster. It wasn't undead, so my necromancer powers wouldn't work on it. That meant I had to embrace my witchy side and that fancy-yet-deadly lightning magic I'd recently developed.

Lightning magic and of course praying to the universe that my powers wouldn't glitch during the fight and cause my untimely and far too early death. "Hey, promise me if I die, you'll have my dad bring me back."

Drew jerked his gaze to meet mine. The muscles in his jaw worked as he focused on me. "He can't make you like Larry, Zoey, Alfred, and the cats. He doesn't have that kind of power. I'm not sure any other necromancer could."

That was true. I had this special once-in-a-century all-powerful ability to heal the undead and make them look alive. They could even eat food, although they didn't need to. Lucy ate more than most of the rest of the house, much less enough for one little cat. She loved that she wouldn't gain a pound.

"Okay, if I die, and I don't look crazy, *and* Dad can get to me and reanimate me right away, then cool. If my body is messed up, then not a ghoul. In that case, have Wade turn me. Or Sam." I could handle being a vampire. Maybe.

Drew shook his head. "I don't think…" He paused as if having a thought, then a sensual smile formed. "On second thought, Sam says sexy time is more intense."

Yeah, Olivia had told me the same thing. In great detail. Vividly. "Vampire it is."

Drew chuckled and pulled me up. I stumbled—on purpose—into him. Wrapping his arms around my waist, he kissed my nose. "I'll have Wade turn you, but only if Luci isn't able to heal you."

"Deal," I said before pressing my lips to his.

The air swirled with dark magic, vibrating over my skin in the familiar way I'd grown used to. Either Olivia or Luci materialized nearby. Since I knew where Olivia was, I didn't even look at Luci as I said, "Not today, Satan."

The devil chuckled and glided over to us. Drew didn't release me, but I was okay with that. My husband could hold me forever.

Luci looked between us with a pleased smile. He could be so odd at times. "I can't stay." He looked around, and I wondered if he could sense the monster. "High tide will be here soon. Summon me when he shows, and I'll come to help."

Then he vanished without telling us where he was going or why he couldn't stay. Luci wasn't typically super generous with details.

Rolling my eyes, I called out, "Chicken!"

"I heard that." His voice carried on the wind. Or was that in my mind? I didn't have time to analyze any of that because a howl-like sound echoed from the ocean. It sounded somewhat like a dying cow and a hissing snake battling for dominance. The eerie keening made my skin crawl.

"Of course, Luci would leave just as the monster comes." I narrowed my eyes while searching the ocean for the creature. "If you're still listening, the monster is here!" I didn't have time to summon the devil, plus he didn't want to fight the monster. That was clear when he did his little pop-in, checked out the area, and left like his life was on the line and not mine and Drew's. He'd also been running from the one that had chased him at our wedding. The hunters had taken that one out.

How had the devil survived for so long as King of Hell while being such a coward?

"So, what's the plan?" I asked again as Drew and I turned to face the water.

"Don't die?" he offered with a slight grin. Then he conjured two swords and handed one of them to me.

Hunters could conjure their weapons but nothing else. Drew had told me that their weapons were spelled to come to the hunter when called. Kind of like how I could summon Luci, only Drew's weapons actually listened and came.

Another dying-hissing-cow sound rumbled through the air, but it was closer now. My stomach churned with anticipation. I'd never fought an actual monster before. Not unless I counted the vampires in Milan, but they'd been vampires, AKA undead, which was entirely my wheelhouse.

This creature was different. I couldn't control it or command it.

Another roar from the beast sounded and this time the ground shook. I flexed my fingers around the sword and spread my feet, readying myself for an attack. Drew moved to stand a few feet away, wielding his sword like a fantasy warrior. Well, okay. That was pretty hot.

Okay, Ava, focus.

The sound of something large breaking the surface of the water caught my attention. The round head of the beast emerged along with eight tentacles moving around like ginormous wiggling worms.

We were outnumbered—eight massive, long arms against four. This was not going to end well.

The monster slithered closer and when it got out to the shallow part of the water, it lifted its snake-like body into the air.

Not creepy at all.

The monster locked his gaze onto us and roared again, then charged a *hell* of a lot faster than I was prepared for. I squeaked as I ran to my left, attempting to get out of the way of one tentacle only to trip over another, landing across it. Rolling off the surprisingly squishy thing, I had to fight off a gag because the tentacle was slimy and cold.

So gross.

Movement from the corner of my eye made me whirl around to see a large furry tentacle come at me. I ducked, then jumped up and swung the sword, slicing through it. Blue liquid poured out of both sides of the cut tentacle and splashed everywhere. This disgusting monster had blue slime for blood.

"What in the world is this thing?" I yelled as I backed away. My black t-shirt and blue jeans were splattered with blue goop, which did *not* smell good.

"The other one was not like this," Drew said as he sliced through a tentacle that had spikes all over it.

"Lucky me." I swung at another tentacle and the blade of my sword broke. During my hesitation, thanks to my shock, that tentacle, which felt like it was made from solid stinking stone, slammed into me, knocking the wind out of me and tossing me a few yards down the beach. I hit the sandy ground and slid a few more feet on my butt.

Struggling to catch my breath, I glanced up to see how Drew was doing. As I lay there gasping, the monster raised a tentacle and pulled it back like it was going to strike. I couldn't scream because it was so hard to breathe at the moment. No air would fill my lungs to power my vocal cords.

At the last second, Drew saw the looming tentacle and ran with inhuman speed to the water. He dived into a wave just as the raised tentacle began shooting balls of fire at him like a flamethrower.

Seriously, people, you can't make this stuff up. How and when exactly did this become my life?

The monster slithered into the water, heading straight for Drew. I panicked and lifted my hand, finally able to suck a breath in. With everything I had, I blasted the creature with my power. Lightning shot from my palm and hit the monster in the side of the head.

My rotten luck: it only accomplished making him madder than a cat stuck in a plastic bag. I knew how mad a cat stuck in a plastic bag could be. It happened to Snoozer just last week while Lucy and I wheezed with laughter.

Don't judge. We got him loose… eventually.

The furiouser-than-ever—yes, I know furiouser isn't a word, but this big effer was so angry a made-up word was warranted. Besides, I'm an author. It's my right—monster whirled around and flew toward me, crazy fast. Holy crap. I still couldn't breathe normally enough, so I shot him with another lightning bolt. Then another. Thank goodness, my magic allowed them to keep coming.

Pushing myself off the ground, I tried to run, but one of the tentacles—the slimy one, ew—circled my waist and lifted me off the ground like I weighed no more than little Sammie. Just great, I was about to be eaten by the tentacle monster from Hell. Literally.

I tried to conjure a sword or *any* kind of weapon, but my magic wasn't obeying. I was a witch and darn powerful necromancer so conjuring things should be that hard. After begging my magic to let me conjure a rocket launcher, I quickly gave up on summoning deadly objects. I placed both hands on the tentacle and pushed my magic into it. And again, nothing.

Really? Of all the times to fritz out, my magic picks now. Thanks a lot.

I looked down in time to see Drew rush forward and stab the thing in the chest while it was focused on me. My strong, hot hubby must have hit the heart because the tentacle holding me loosened, and I fell to the earth. Despite the fact that he'd been too far away to get to me in time, somehow Drew was there to catch me.

The monster crashed to the ground, shaking it enough that I vibrated in Drew's arms. I tried to take a deep breath, but my chest still hurt as he put me on my feet.

"Are you okay?" Drew asked as he ran his hands over my body, searching for wounds.

"I got the wind knocked out of me. Nothing is broken." At least I didn't think so.

Gods, I hoped not.

"That was fast." Luci's voice was a not-so-welcome interruption of Drew's frantic checkup.

I glared at Luci with my lip curled. "Thanks for the help."

He lifted one shoulder, waved his hand toward the monster, and it disappeared. "It was not my intention to make you two fight it alone."

Right. "Chicken. Why didn't you disappear it back to Hell, to begin with?"

He ignored my question. "I can pop you home."

Drew shook his head and lifted me back into his arms, then began moving toward his SUV. I wiggled so he would put me down. I wasn't a light person. Besides he'd been just as beaten up as I had.

"Ava," Luci called out to me.

We stopped, and I jumped, nearly falling out of Drew's arms when Luci suddenly appeared in front of me. I jerked hard enough that Drew set me on my feet.

Luci frowned then leaned forward to kiss my forehead. Stepping back, he winked at me and vanished.

Drew wrapped an arm around my waist. "What did he do?"

"He healed me." I took a deep breath and sighed in relief when it didn't hurt. Even that knot in my back from sleeping wrong the other night was gone.

I leaned into Drew, healing him as I snuggled his neck. "Let's go home. I need a scalding hot bath to wash off the monster slime."

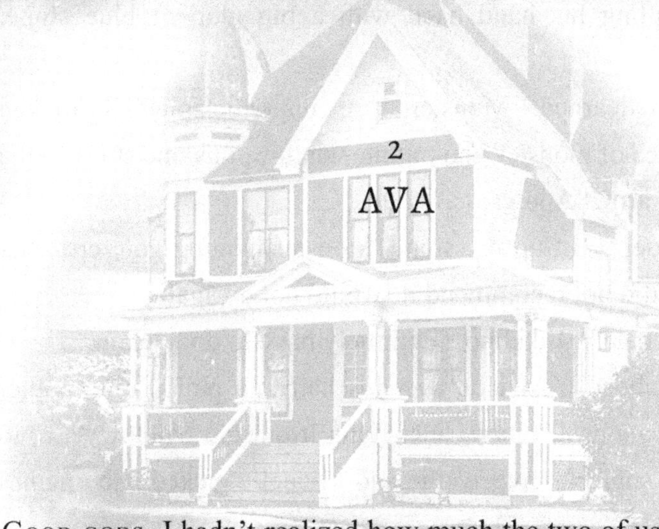

2
AVA

Good gods, I hadn't realized how much the two of us stank until we climbed into Drew's SUV. The windows couldn't be rolled down fast enough or far enough. Maybe I should have asked Luci to do a cleaning spell before he left. I focused on my magic and tried to get it to do that thing where it picked up dust and tornadoed it to a trash can. I could feel a little bit of an attempt on my magic's part to budge the blue blood and sticky tentacle slime, but no dice. It wasn't happening.

"Remind me the next time we fight a monster to put my hair up." I curled my upper lip as I pulled a chunk of monster flesh from my hair and flicked it out the window. At least I thought it was flesh. If it wasn't, I did *not* want to know what it was. It took a minute to work out of my strands of hair without breaking my individual strands. It was hard enough to keep my hair healthy and strong without adding toxic monster slime to the list of things drying it out.

Drew chuckled as he pulled out onto the highway, heading

back home. "I didn't think about it because the last tentacle monster wasn't this messy." He grimaced and scratched behind his ear, pulling his hand back with a big glop of blue slime. "Blech."

"Lesson learned. Monsters are unpredictable." I flicked another piece of monster goo out the window, this one stuck to the back of my arm. "And gross."

A shudder went up my spine. Monster hunting got zero stars from me. I did not recommend it. Would not do again.

Unfortunately, I'd almost definitely have to do it again.

Drew rubbed his hands over his hair and pulled out another big glob of monster blood, then flung it out the window. "So, to change the subject, have Wallie and Michelle picked baby names yet?"

I shook my head. "No. And Wallie has shot down every name I've sent to him." It was difficult not to feel bitter. Some of those names had been fantastic. Who didn't love the name Ruthie? Or if it had been a boy, Seelie?

They were crazy. My son and his girlfriend had recently found out that they were having a baby. A girl, which explained why my powers were wonky sometimes. I was the last female witch on my mother's side, which made me powerful because I'd inherited all the magics from prior generations, all my ancestors' power. Our theory was with a new baby girl coming, my witch magic would split itself and the sweet baby would get potentially half of my witch powers. Plus, she would be a quarter necromancer, as well. I was looking forward to teaching her all about her powers. Wallie had necromancy, but he didn't have my level of power. Michelle, Wallie's girlfriend, was a water witch. The baby girl would get powers from her side, too.

This little bundle of joy had a good chance of being fairly powerful.

The kids were lucky to have their own personal small village to help raise the baby. I, for one, could hardly wait to get my hands on her, whatever her name was going to be.

"I can't wait for the little miss to arrive," I said with a smile.

Drew nodded, which dislodged a gooey chunk of monster from his hair. I watched in disgust as it fell into his jean-covered thigh. Drew just picked it up and tossed it out his window. The shower I was going to take when I got home was going to be so hot it would hopefully melt the top layer of my skin off along with the monster sludge.

"We should've stayed in Scotland," I grumbled. "Got some of your hunter friends to go after the monster." I wasn't bitter about being called away from my honeymoon. Sure, we'd been at the tail end of it, but still. Ugh.

"Pearl got us to come, then has been completely unreachable. She had some reason or another to want *us* specifically to be the ones who took care of the monster."

"That woman has a lot to explain."

Maybe instead of an ice cream Snickers, I would chop up three or four Snickers bars and blend them into a cup full of chocolate ice cream and chocolate milk. Or three or four Snickers bars and a couple of the Snickers ice cream bars into the milkshake. Now that sounded good.

As I daydreamed about incredibly fattening ice-cold desserts, we fell silent. Without complaining constantly, sleep began to intrude on my bright, sunny disposition. I was heading for an adrenaline crash. I rested my head on the SUV's interior door frame, ignoring the fleeting thought of monster goop getting all over it, and breathed in the crisp night air. If I kept my face in the wind, I could just ignore the disgusting smell.

The sun had just begun to set. Where had the day gone? The fight hadn't taken all that long, but the drive was a good hour and a half each way and it'd been nearly three before we'd made it home from Scotland, even with a portal to go through. I hoped we made it back home in time to see some trick-or-treaters, especially Sammie.

Drew got behind a big pickup truck. He liked to find someone going a little bit over the speed limit and sort of stick with them on the interstate. He called it drafting, though I wasn't sure that was the technical definition of drafting someone.

I dozed off at some point, waking when the car suddenly slowed. Sitting up in my seat, I saw the truck he'd been drafting had drastically lowered its speed. "Why is it slowing down?"

"I don't know. I thought he might have a police radar. We were flying for a while."

Just because Drew was a cop, didn't mean he always followed the rules. He wanted to get home as bad as anybody would, police officer or not.

The truck slowed some more, then slammed on its brakes. Drew tensed and did the same as a deer leaped out in front of the truck. The man driving the truck missed the animal by swerving to the left, around the creature, but we weren't so lucky. Drew pushed the brakes to the floor as the deer slid up and onto Drew's hood in agonizing slow motion like we were all in the middle of a movie scene. It slid off and then straightened up, seemingly unhurt, then turned its head to glare at us. In a heavy New York accent it yelled, "Hey! I'm walkin' here!"

Drew just stared at the deer as it walked to the other side of the road as slowly as it pleased. I, on the other hand, burst out laughing. I was gross and tired and a talking deer, who was hopefully a shifter and not a literal talking deer, well, it just made sense because this was my life. It was crazy and zany and sometimes dangerous, but I didn't think I'd ever want it any other way.

Well, maybe just a teeny bit less zany. I could use a nap once in a while.

Needless to say, I was wide awake for the rest of the drive home. We pulled into our driveway just in time to see Sammy trick-or-treating at Winston's front door.

Alfred was giving him some candy as we parked and got out of the car. When Sammie saw us he ran over, his arms out like he was about to give us a hug. I stopped him before he got monster gross all over him. He was the cutest little vampire I'd ever seen. He had white makeup, hair slicked back, fake fangs, and a black tux with a cape. Too cute.

Sammie inspected our clothing and asked, "Why are you dressed in gross costumes?" He shook his head. "I could've helped pick out a better costume."

"It's not a costume, buddy, we had to go kill a monster," I said and patted him on the head. Olivia turned and as soon as she saw us, she burst out laughing. Halfway bent over, she gasped and covered her mouth as she tried and failed to get it together.

"Laugh it up." I rolled my eyes at her. "You got to be here doing fun stuff with Sammie while we were being attacked by giant tentacles."

Olivia managed to get her mirth under control and straightened. "Think of it as bonding time for a newly married couple."

I might've believed her if she hadn't started laughing again.

3

OLIVIA

"When will you be back?"

A tiny ache formed in my chest at my soon-to-be six-year-old's question. Brushing a few strands of his blond hair from his forehead, I said, "We'll be back Friday. That's only five days away. And you're going to be having so much fun with Meme and PopPop that you'll forget we're even gone."

He scrunched up his face. "I guess that will be okay."

A laugh escaped me as I tucked the blanket around him. "Mommy and Daddy need time to ourselves. We're better parents when we sometimes go away together, and *you* deserve time with all of your grandparents too."

Sammie nodded and yawned. "Okay, Mommy, but you guys have to take me next time."

He was too cute. As right as I was about needing time with just Sam, I was going to miss my little guy "I promise we'll do a family vacation when Devan and Jess have a break from school."

Sammie's eyes lit up. "That would be amazing! And we can invite Ava and Zoey and Larry."

After kissing him on the forehead, I stood up. "Go to sleep, we'll talk about it more when we get back."

Sam entered the room. "Night bubby."

"Night, Dad!"

We waved at Sammie as we pulled his bedroom door closed before making our way downstairs. I paused outside his door when I heard his voice again. Sam grinned at me when Sammie said, "And Snoozer, and Lucy, and Papa Lucy, and Mama Phira, and…" His voice trailed off into a yawn. The boy really wanted a vacation with his whole family.

Luci was waiting for us when we reached the living room. Next to him sat our suitcases. Sam hadn't told me where we were going, hence why Luci was creating the portal to our lovey-dovey vacation destination and Phira had packed my suitcases for me.

My bio-dad smiled at us. "You two ready?"

We nodded and Luci waved a hand, creating the portal in a split second. Sam gathered the luggage, and we walked through the portal and onto a beach. The moonlight glinted off of the water, which was calm. Warm air swirled around me as I whirled around to face Sam with a big smile on my face. He looked like the cat who ate the canary. Very satisfied with himself. "Surprise. We're in Jamaica."

It looked like absolute heaven on Earth. Yet… "Why in the world would you bring me to a beach?"

Sam's face fell in disappointment. "You don't like it?"

Oh, that had been the wrong first reaction. "No, I love that we're here." I threw my arms around him. "Sorry, that came out all wrong. I'm just concerned about you."

He set our luggage down and wrapped his arms around my waist, pulling me close. "We can enjoy it at night. Besides, the beach will be near empty after sunset. Humans don't like to swim in the dark."

Oh, he had a point there.

"And I'll protect you in the water." He gave me a sideways grin, making me laugh.

"I can protect myself." I poked at his ribs, and he jerked to the side. "But you're welcome to do it."

Laughing, he grabbed me in a bear hug and lifted me off the ground, nuzzling my neck. When he pulled back to meet my gaze, his dark blue eyes darkened in the way they did when he smelled blood. "Let's get checked into the hotel and enjoy a little *us* time."

Desire stirred in my belly. "Yes, let's."

Sam picked me and the luggage up and rushed to the hotel using his vampire speed. Of course, he slowed down when we got closer to the humans. The lobby and downstairs of the hotel were gorgeous. It was open air, which was so insane to me. What did they do when it rained? There had to be doors that came from somewhere, but as we walked in and toward the desk, I couldn't find them anywhere. It made for a very cool effect. Sam let me down as we got close to the reception area.

Sam smiled at the man behind the counter. "Hello. We have a reservation under Thompson."

The man behind the counter about fell over himself to be overly courteous. I wished I could whisper to Sam and ask him what he'd done to make us seem so VIP.

After Sam got the key card and promised the attendant we didn't need him to walk us, we headed back outside and toward a cluster of small cabins right on the beach. "What was that all about?" I asked.

Sam shrugged. "I have no idea. Your father made the reservations. He insisted."

Hmph. "Probably someone who owes him a favor." I didn't want to know the details.

The cabin was perfection, and I was checking out our bathroom, which had a huge garden tub in it, when Sam came up behind me, brushed my hair from my neck, and placed a soft kiss at the bend where it met my shoulder. A moan escaped my lips, and I leaned back into him.

"That tub is big enough for the both of us."

I smiled. "I was just thinking the same thing." Turning in his arms, I studied him for a few moments. "You need to feed."

The mention of feeding made his fangs drop. With his chiseled cheekbones, strong jaw, and haunting eyes, seeing the tips of his sharp teeth poking out from under his lips was unbelievably sexy. Who knew I'd become a vamp groupie?

Probably I wouldn't feel this way about any other vampire. It was just because it was Sam and I loved him so much.

Probably. I did enjoy a hot vampire novel now and then.

Without a word, he tightened his hold on me and sank his fangs into my throat. I almost had an orgasm right there in the middle of the bathroom floor. My body wanted to crumple, but I managed to stay upright, though Sam had to hold me pretty tight. I let my head relax against the bathroom wall and lost myself in the sensation of feeding my husband.

It was a heady feeling.

When he finished drinking, he released me just long enough to turn on the water to fill the tub, then began to undress me slowly.

The problem was, I didn't want slow. We had so few moments where it was just the two of us, I wanted to be greedy with my husband.

I started to help him with removing clothing, but he grabbed my wrists with one of his hands, holding them over my head. "Let me take my time with you."

"You know patience is not one of my strengths." I nearly whined at him.

"Believe me, I know."

The growl in his voice made it too hard. I couldn't take it. I used my magic to remove his clothes and smiled proudly at him. "I don't need patience when I have magic."

He arched one dark brown eyebrow at me and leaned in close to my ear. "Do you want a spanking?" he whispered.

Heat filled my entire body at that question. "You promise?"

That sped him along. We were undressed and in the tub in record time. I loved that man and all the things he did to me.

THE NEXT MORNING, I woke to the warmth of the sun shining through the doors we'd left wide open, overlooking the ocean. I sat up and sighed at the amazing sight. All I had to do was walk out the door, across the deck, and down two stairs, and I was on the beach. From the looks of it, the high tide would be mere feet from the stairs.

It took me several seconds before I realized the sun was out and streaming all over the both of us. The both of us meaning right on Sam. “No,” I whispered. Freaking out, I rushed to the sliding door and jerked the curtains close. When I whirled around, Sam was still sleeping peacefully.

Or he might’ve been dead because I’d carelessly left the curtains and door wide open!

I rushed to the bed and pulled the blanket off him, which woke him up. “What are you doing?” he asked groggily.

Running my fingers over his skin and lifting his arms to inspect every inch of him, I said, “The curtains were open. Sunshine everywhere. I’m so sorry. Are you hurt?”

He shook his head and sat up, taking my hands, and holding them. “No.” He glanced at the window now blocked by the blackout curtains.

“Are you sure? The sun was streaming on both of us.” I watched his features change to curiosity. Hang on. How was he awake during the day? Usually, he slept like the dead during sunlight hours.

He looked at the curtains again and back at me. “Open the curtains.”

“What? No. Are you suicidal? It was your choice to be a vampire rather than a ghoul, you can’t kill yourself now.” My panic made my voice a few pitches higher than normal.

He kissed me softly. “I’m not suicidal. I have a theory. Trust me, please.”

I took a deep breath and straightened. When I didn’t move, Sam pointed to the curtains. “Go on, open them.”

“I don’t like this experiment,” I grumbled but moved to the sliding glass door. Slowly, I opened the curtains.

The sun touched Sam’s hand, and he just stood there and stared at the spot where the rays met his skin. There was no sizzle, no smoke. He stood, circled the bed, and crossed the small distance to stand beside me. My grip on the plastic rod that opened and closed the curtains tightened. "How do you feel?"

"Fine. Okay. It's warm, but not burning. My skin feels a little itchy. It's only uncomfortable, though. My eyes don't like the bright light, but there's no pain." He smiled wide and turned to me, then he stepped out of the still-open door.

I gripped his hand. "What are you doing?"

"Come on. It's fine."

I studied him for a long moment before releasing his hand. "If I start to smell smoke, I'm portaling you back inside."

We stepped out onto the deck. The smell of the ocean and sand washed over us. Being in the tropics was a little different than our seaside home in Maine. The sun was warmer, and the smells of the salt water and sand smelled like warmth and relaxation. Living on the beach in Maine was nothing like being on the beach in Jamaica.

Sam closed his eyes and sighed happily. "It's not bad. I'll wear glasses and have maybe an umbrella or something, but Olivia…" He looked at me with hope spread all over his features.

"I think I can be out during the day."

"How is this possible?" As much as I would love for it to be true, what if we were out in the sun and whatever this was wore off? Then what?

"I don't know."

I pulled him back inside and closed the curtains again. "I'm going to order room service. We need to figure out why you're awake and can go out in the sun. We can't risk you frying."

Sam didn't eat food, so I ordered my breakfast, then sat on the bed, facing him. "What's our theory?"

He leaned forward and kissed my nose. "Your blood."

"What?"

"Think about it. Usually, I only drink a tiny bit. It never affected me like Jax said it would. I mean, I do get the buzz from your magic, but I don't go into bloodlust because of it or anything. Last night I got a little too carried away and drank more than I ever had from you." He ducked his head, as if ashamed of losing control.

I framed his face in my hands, forcing him to look at me. "I'm perfectly capable of stopping you if you get too crazy with me. Don't feel bad. I love how our sexy time is a little rougher than it was when we were normal humans."

Desire darkened his blue eyes. "Me, too." He kissed me and I melted. "I think your blood has to be what's allowing me to be up and in the sun this morning."

It made sense because I was part fae and my blood had magical properties. "When we get home, we'll talk to Wade and maybe call Jax to get his opinions on it." Wade was barely older than Sam in vampire years, really. He might not know.

"I was just going to suggest the same thing. Until then, I want to enjoy the beach and the sun while I can." Sam pulled me into his arms and kissed my neck.

I was so happy that he was happy. This vacation was exactly what we needed.

Later that evening, Sam and I were relaxing in our room after a day in the sun. We had a blast. My phone rang and I frowned at Ava's dad's number. "Hello?"

"Hello, sorry to bother you, but can you portal me to the North Pole?"

Um… "Sure, I guess. It's cold up there."

John laughed. “Not much colder than Maine. I tried to get ahold of your father instead, but he didn’t answer.”

“So true on most days. It will only take a sec?”

“Yes, five minutes, tops.”

“Okay, then, I’ll be right there.” I hung up and turned to Sam.

He answered before I could ask. I still forgot that his vamp hearing allowed him to hear things no one else does. “Go ahead. I’ll be here waiting when you get back.”

A few minutes later, I portaled to Maine, grabbed John, and opened a portal to the North Pole, not expecting to land in the middle of Santa town. Holy crap, this place was real. I had to take a moment to get my bearings, and from the look on his face, so did John.

The North Pole was unlike anything I'd ever seen before. It was a bustling town, with shops, cafes, and what looked like a never-ending stream of elves. The streets were filled with reindeer tied to posts outside of stores and elves beaming at one another as they carried packages back and forth. Santa's workshop loomed over the city in the distance like some jolly castle. It was like Christmas coming to life.

The castle/workshop was made of the same snow-white stone as the rest of the city. It glowed brightly with the countless Christmas lights that decorated every window and doorway.

"Thanks for coming," Luke cried as soon as he spotted us. "We have a bit of a pickle."

I stared open-mouthed at a man who wore a white undershirt that showed off the luscious muscles in his chest and arms and fuzzy red pants. "My gods, you're gorgeous," I blurted out before I could gain control of my mouth.

He gave me a half-smile. "Thanks."

John cleared his throat. "Now then," he said. "Let's get to work."

I saluted them, then scanned our surroundings. "Are those reindeer? And a sled?"

Cocking my head, I stared at the handsome man again. "Holy sh—"

"Yes," Luke said, interrupting me. "That is Santa Claus, the real one."

"Whoa," I whispered. "So cool."

Santa held out a hand to me. "Welcome aboard, Mrs. Thompson."

"Olivia," I said with a smile as I shook his hand. This was surreal. How was any of this possible? Snapping out of my dazed state, I pointed at John. "I'm gonna want some details later." As much as I wanted to stay, I was on vacation with my gorgeous, just-as-hot-as-Santa husband and didn't want to spend any unnecessary time away from him.

Then I stepped back through the portal, heading back to my little cabin in Jamaica to tell Sam *all* about Santa

4
AVA

STANDING BACK to admire the front of Winston, I cocked my head to try to pinpoint what else it needed. I'd taken down the purely Halloween decorations and put fresh pumpkins out on the porch steps. Drew had brought home a couple more pots of mums to add to the fall décor, as well.

Sammie was visiting and currently chasing Zoey the tiger around the yard. Thank goodness I didn't have close neighbors. At least no human neighbors. We needed to come up with some sort of ward that made people driving by see nothing and nobody. A mirage.

That might freak out the mailman, though.

My phone chimed. I pulled it out of the back pocket of my jeans. It was a group text from Olivia.

I have news for everyone so we're having dinner at Luci's on Friday night.

Friday night? What day was it? I clicked on my calendar app.

Oh, it was only Monday. I replied, **That's a long time to wait for news. Tease!**

Olivia: **LOL sorrynotsorry**

Beth: **Baby news?**

Leave it to my mom to ask that question. She was over the moon happy that Michelle and Wallie were having a baby. I was too. Who wouldn't be excited to have a baby in the house again? But still, it was a bit cheeky to ask Olivia, especially in the group text.

Luci: **Your mother and I would be perfectly happy if it were a baby. In fact, we encourage it.**

Oh, geez, here they went.

Winnie: **Us, too! Alfred says he'll babysit.**

Alfred: **Any time.**

Sam: **Good grief.**

Olivia: **No, no. Everyone calm the heck down. There's no baby. It's good news, though. Not saying anything more until we get back Friday. See you then.**

I put my phone back in my back pocket and placed the last mum in its place as I called, "Sammie, Zoey, come inside and wash up for dinner."

We were eating dinner earlier than normal because Alfred and I had a meeting with the Vikings. I'd wanted all hands on deck, but what could they do? They were just necromancers, after all. Still, I had a pit of worry deep in my stomach that I couldn't shake.

Luci showed up just as we were clearing the table and went into the living room to sit with my parents. Winnie and I helped Alfred clean the kitchen so he wouldn't use it as an excuse to miss the meeting. After all, the whole thing was about him anyway.

I was drying the last plate when Winston groaned, announcing we had visitors. I felt their particular blend of dark magic at about the same time. He also shook the floorboards, indicating he didn't like our guests too much. I was right there with him on those feelings. "It'll be okay, Winston. We need to at least speak with them. Better it be on our home turf." The first time they'd come, he'd opened the door to let them in. He'd obviously since changed his mind.

I put the plate in the strainer and walked to the door. Winston opened it for me, and I greeted the Vikings. As before, there were three. I only knew the elder's name. Arne. They wore nondescript clothing, jeans, and tees that wouldn't stick out in anyone's mind.

"We agreed to wait until after the honeymoon. Now we want Alfred back," the Viking elder said.

I frowned at him and almost slammed the door in his face. What I really wanted to do was scream and tell him that they couldn't have Alfred, under any circumstances. But I'd promised they could come and plead their case, and that we'd at least listen to what they had to say.

"Please come in," I said with a forced smile and stepped aside to let the trio inside. Luckily, Winston didn't react. I just hoped he remained quiet while they were here. They weren't getting Alfred, nor probably anything they wanted, but I would like to avoid an all-out war with them.

After closing the door, I led the Vikings into the living room. Drew joined us a few seconds later and stood behind the armchair I sat in, like a regal guard. My hunter husband watched the Vikings closely, ready to strike if he needed to.

That made me happy in a twisted kind of way.

Arne nodded toward Alfred and Winnie, who glared back at

them. "As we said before, we'd like Alfred to join us again. Start anew as a human. There is a ritual that can be done to make him reborn as a human. He would not have to depend on a necromancer to keep him alive." The elder turned his nose up and looked at me when he said it.

My electricity power *really* wanted to surface but settled down when Drew placed a hand on my shoulder. I didn't bother to correct them about Alfred depending on me to stay animated. The Vikings most definitely didn't need to know about the chasm in the caverns under my house.

"Well, Alfred is happy here," Winnie said as she held Alfred's hand. "You're wasting your time and ours."

Alfred looked so uncomfortable with the whole thing. It made my chest ache for him.

"Alfred, it's ultimately your choice," I offered, hoping that if he spoke up and told them to go away that they would.

I doubted it, but at least I'd have a justifiable reason to zap them with my powers if they refused to take his word. I didn't want a war, but I also wouldn't be bullied. Drew squeezed my shoulder at that thought. We were a magically bonded couple; he felt my emotions as though they were his own. I felt his as well. Right then, I was clinging to his calm.

"Why do you want Alfred to join you again?" Mom asked.

The elder Viking ignored her and met my gaze. "Because he belongs with us. Not here."

Oh, no, he was so wrong there. "Alfred is my family. He belongs here."

That was entirely true because Alfred was my ancestor. My dad's necromancer line had started with Alfred. That was something I was still researching so I didn't know if he was like a grandfather or great-times-infinity uncle or what.

The elder opened his mouth to reply when the house shook, but I didn't think it was Winston protesting. Right after the tremors, the sound of a large animal running upstairs echoed through the living room. Seconds later Lucy-Fur flew down the stairs screaming in horror. Zoey, in tiger form, was fast on her heels.

They ran into the living room, circled us, then headed to the kitchen. There was a crash that sounded like it came from the conservatory, then the back door slammed shut.

I closed my eyes and took calming breaths as I slowly counted to five. When I opened my eyes, everyone was staring at me, waiting for answers. I shook my head. "I'm not getting involved this time. I'm sure it's some female cat thing."

Lucy was always doing something to make Zoey's tiger mad.

Larry appeared in the archway of the living room and pointed toward the back door. "I'll, ahh, go check on them." Then he was gone.

It was a good thing that Lucy was immortal. At least the tiger couldn't kill her. Well, she could've in theory, but Lucy would reanimate as long as her collar was on.

We spent a few more minutes discussing how Alfred was not leaving, mostly us politely putting them off as Alfred looked supremely uncomfortable, before the Vikings left.

Arne gave me one last long look. "We won't stop trying to get him back."

"And we won't stop telling you no." I shut the door softly in his face, waited until I felt his power move well down the driveway and slowly disappear, then turned to Alfred and asked, "Why don't you want to be human again?"

He shrugged. "It's a dark spell. The act of doing dark magic is what bothers me the most. I won't go down that road again. It is a slippery slope."

"How dark are we talking? Because there's gray, light gray, lighter gray, sort of an off-white, then if you go darker there's darker gray, off black, half black, eggshell black, and a couple of others. It's not until you get to near black that things get dicey. And of course, if you do pitch black you spend the rest of Eternity down there with me." Luci grinned at everyone when we all turned to look at him like he lost his mind. I didn't even know when he'd arrived. He hadn't been here when the Vikings were.

Alfred rolls his eyes. "It requires a human sacrifice."

Now that was pretty dark. I held up one hand. "No, nope, we're not doing that. If you want to be human again, Dad and I can do the spell like Winnie and Mom did. Just need to find a new body." I stepped closer to Alfred and took his hands. "It's up to you. I'm happy with you as you are. But I'll be happy as long as you are, no matter what you choose. Except not the sacrifice route. Then I won't be happy."

With a gentle squeeze of his hands, I let go and headed out the backdoor to check on that grumpy white cat and furious tiger.

5
OLIVIA

I STOOD BACK and admired my autumnally decorated living room and dining room. After we got home today, I ran over to the farmer's market and grabbed a bunch of mini pumpkins and gourds, which now adorned the middle of my table.

I was loving Luci's gothic mansion more and more each day. After all, black went with everything, right?

Sam came up behind me and wrapped his arms around my waist while kissing my neck. A happy sigh escaped me, and I leaned into him. His warmth seeped into me, filling me with love and lots of passion for my vampire.

"Doesn't everything look gourd-geous?" I snorted at my joke. Ever since I picked up the gourds, I had the urge to incorporate the word into as many sentences as possible.

"Not as pretty as you," my husband said, kissing my cheek.

Just then the fiddle solo in *Devil Went Down to Georgia* started playing throughout the house. I burst out laughing while Sam asked, "What the heck is that?"

"Luci's new doorbell. I ordered it for him a few days before we left." I walked down the hallway to the foyer. "We can set it to play any song. I thought this one was appropriate."

I pulled the door open and smiled wide at Ava and Drew, noting that Ava's parents, John and Beth, along with her uncle Wade, Alfred, and Aunt Winnie were not far behind them. "Welcome, come in."

Leaving the door open, I made my way back to the dining room. They knew the way.

Luci entered wearing his usual black slacks and white button-down shirt, but tonight he had a black apron on. He carried a large platter of appetizers. "Good evening."

"Don't you mean gourd evening?" I grinned at him as he chuckled.

"Ava, your bestie has a new obsession with the word gourd. Please make her stop." Luci winked at me to let me know he was teasing.

Ava waved him off. "She'll get bored with it. Hopefully soon." She handed me a bottle of red wine and stared at me for a long while before saying, "You're glowing."

"You mean I'll get gourd with it? And it's because I fell in love with my husband all over again. This vacation was just what we needed to reconnect. Nice and peaceful. No drama. No monsters." I smiled at Sam, who was talking with Drew on the other side of the dining room.

"That's great. At least one of us had a drama-free getaway," Ava said as Drew and Sam moved closer to us.

Drew hugged Ava and she cuddled into his side. "Three-fourths of our honeymoon was perfectly pleasant."

"Yeah, if you didn't count the ghosts that liked to hang out with us because they figured out we could see them." Ava rolled her eyes.

Phira entered the room with Sammie, Jess, and Devan in tow. Each one of them had a dish. Phira said, "Dinner is ready. Everyone, please have a seat."

Everyone chose their seats, pretty much in the same places we always sat when we had dinner together, whether here or at Ava and Drew's or somewhere else like with the coven or at the local witchy B&B. As they piled their plates with food, I bit my lip and barely held in my words. Ava asked, "Spill it, Olivia. What is your big news?"

I sat up and held my hand out for Sam to take it. "Sam and I discovered that if he drinks directly from me, not only can he stay awake during the day, but he can go out into the sun."

Wade stared at us, wonder dancing across his face. "How is that possible?"

I shrugged. "I assume it has something to do with my fae blood."

Phira shook her head as she dabbed at the corners of her mouth with her napkin. "Fae blood doesn't do that. Vampires used to hunt us down for our blood because it gave them a high and induced bloodlust. It's never been recorded that it enabled them to walk in the sun. If it had, the vamps would have never created rules forbidding vampires from feeding on fae."

My brows dipped. She had a very good point. One that I hadn't taken into consideration. "Then how in the world can he do it? My blood doesn't affect him like it would other vamps."

Phira shook her fork at me, agreeing. "It couldn't, because if it did, he'd be high every time he drank from you."

"Could be that you aren't full fae," Ava said, then took a drink of her wine.

Luci sat at the head of the table making little humming noises as he ate. I gave him a pointed look before saying, "It has to be something about our bond, then. Us being mates definitely makes him able to walk in the sun and keeps him from being a druggie. We spent all week testing it at the beach."

I looked at Wade and wondered if he'd be willing to test the theory. "Wade…"

Luci reached out and grabbed my wrist. "You still have enough fae blood that will very likely affect Wade, and not in a good way. Besides, as your mother said, it's not your fae blood. It must be mine."

Kablooey. Mind blown. How had I not even once considered that it was my father's side causing the vampire-improving effects? I stared at him with narrowed eyes. "Would you like to test that?"

Ava grinned. "Yeah, Santa, give us a vial of your blood to test."

"I will not. I'm not your lab rat to do your little experiments on." Luci went back to eating, utterly unperturbed.

"You wouldn't be the lab rat, Sam and Wade would. We just need a tiny bit of your blood." Ava took another drink of wine while eyeing Luci. It was all I could do to not laugh at the two of them. She looked like the vampire, ready to suck him dry.

Luci stared back at her, then said, "Why don't you just keep your grabby hands over there, and fill Olivia and Sam in on what happened with the Viking necromancers."

Oh, what a way to deflect. I turned my attention to Ava. "What happened?"

She made a growl-like sound. "They're persistent, but Alfred told them no. I told them no. Winnie said heck no. Even so, I'm sure we haven't seen the last of them."

Winnie snorted. "I'll take them apart piece by piece and feed them to Zoey."

We all had a good laugh at that, although a big part of me completely believed Winnie was capable. Ava told us about the meeting, which hadn't gone very well. When she was done, I looked at Alfred. "You don't have to do anything you don't want to. I, for one, like you the way you are."

He gave me a forced smile. My heart ached for him. He was struggling with what to do. Becoming human again had to be tempting. I just hoped he knew that we were all here for him. We were a family. A little dysfunctional, but a family still.

6
AVA

Oh, man, I really don't like mornings. I descended the stairs into pure chaos. Mom and Dad were finishing their breakfast in the dining room. I stepped off the last step as Wallie helped Michelle put her coat on in the foyer as Winston made some sort of clacking noise in another room. I hadn't even realized the kids were here yet. "You guys leaving already?"

"If they come on." Zoey nodded her head toward my parents. A few seconds later, Winnie came shuffling down the stairs, wearing a silky nightgown with the robe, which theoretically should've made it a modest outfit and appropriate to wear to the table, but was hanging off of her shoulders, dragging behind her on the steps. As a result, her spectacular new breasts were very nearly falling out of the side of the barely-there gown. "Uh, Win?" I raised my eyebrow and stared pointedly at her chest.

"Sorry," she mumbled. "It's early." As she tied her robe, she looked back and glared at Alfred as he descended the stairs. "You sure you won't go with us?"

"Uh, Aunt Winnie?" Wallie tapped her on the shoulder. "We should get going."

She sighed and waved her hand. In a shower of sparks, her gown turned into jeans and an extremely tight tee that showed her midriff. Slippers turned into cute white sneakers and her hair curled itself into soft ringlets framing her face. She snapped her fingers and a set of luggage appeared behind her.

Mom and Dad walked up, their luggage having appeared from somewhere. "Ready?" Mom asked as she gave Winnie a once-over, lingering with almost-but-not-quite disapproval on her exposed stomach. Mom understood why Winnie dressed the way she did. Heck, we all understood *why*. We'd all probably do the same. That didn't mean we loved looking at it.

"Great," Wallie said. "Everyone ready?"

A lump formed in my throat. Sometimes he was the spitting image of his father. Clay had been organized, the one ushering us out the door. He'd been the planner and executor. I'd taken over and I did all right at being organized, but not like he had.

It didn't matter how long Clay had been gone or that I'd remarried. I'd never forget how wonderful he'd been. I missed him every day. After clearing my throat, I pulled the kids in for hugs one at a time. "Be safe. Don't walk alone in the city."

"Yes, yes, we'll brush our teeth and tie our shoes." Wallie pressed a kiss to my cheek. "We'll be back in two days. Enjoy the quiet house."

I snorted. "This house is never quiet."

Alfred pulled Winnie aside and as I hugged Michelle, resisting the urge to rub her still-flat belly, they whispered together. I tried not to listen; I really did.

"I can stay," Winnie said, her tone soft and sympathetic.

"No, you go. I don't want to ruin your fun. If I go, that's what I'll do." Alfred's mousy voice was sad. My chest tightened. I wished there was something I could do for him, but he had a choice to make. No one could make it but him. We all knew what he'd do, but he had to figure it out himself.

When I pulled away from giving Zoey a hug, Winnie was walking out the front door, Alfred headed toward the kitchen, and tension was thick in the air.

"She really wants him to go," Mom murmured as she pressed a kiss to my cheek. "She's worried about him."

"Try to have fun," I called out the door. "I'll keep an eye on Alfred."

Winnie waved over her shoulder and got in the back of the car.

"Why aren't you having Luci or Olivia portal you?" I asked.

Zoey rolled her eyes. "Winnie says we need the road trip experience."

Mom, Dad, and Winnie were taking my car, while Wallie was driving himself and Michelle with Zoey and Larry in the backseat.

Personally, I'd rather have portaled than road-tripped *any* day, but Winnie could be pretty insistent sometimes.

They were driving up to Portland for a weekend of shopping. While the older adults were going to see a show, the younger ones were shopping for baby clothes and furniture and whatever else they could find for the baby. "At least call Olivia or Luci to portal back the shopping." I reached into my pocket for my phone, then pulled my credit card out of the little wallet attached to my phone case. "Take my card. Get anything and everything you need."

Wallie shook his head. "Thanks, Mom, but I've got my trust fund and Michelle has money. We want to do this ourselves."

I pressed the card into his hand. "Then do this. Whatever your most expensive purchase is, put it on my card and it's my shower gift."

Wallie finally relented and took the card. "And if you want, put it all on there," I said as I shut the door behind them.

I thought I had the last word, but Wallie opened the door, said, "No!" and then slammed it shut again.

"You're grounded," I called through the window by the door, but he was already halfway to the car. He couldn't have heard me.

As much as I would have liked to go with them, I had a book deadline. With Drew working a double today, it'd be the first time in what seemed like forever that I'd have the house to myself. Mostly, anyway. Alfred was still here, but he was the quietest of all of us. I was planning to use the calm day to get some writing done.

Slipping into my office, I fired up my computer, then went to the kitchen for some coffee while the old laptop warmed up. I should buy a new one, but there were always other things to do besides figuring out which computer I needed.

There was just enough coffee left for one cup. At least they'd saved me some. Knowing Alfred, he'd start a fresh pot soon.

With my coffee in hand, I made my way back to my office. As I sat at my desk and prepared to focus, Alfred stopped at the door. "I'm going for a walk to clear my head."

"If you need to talk, I'm here."

He nodded and gave me a forced smile. "I know. Thank you."

When he left, I turned on my playlist, opened my document, and got comfy. *Let's do this.*

Then my phone rang.

Of course.

I considered turning off the ringer and flipping it over so I wouldn't see the screen light up with a call, but it was my hubby calling. I always wanted to talk to him.

"Hello, handsome."

Drew chuckled and I could feel his face heat through our bond. It always did when I called him that. He got bashful, which was all the cuter. How could he not know that he was gorgeous? "Grandmother called and wants us to check out a rogue necromancer."

I twisted my mouth and leaned back in my chair. "She knows you're retired, and I am *not* a hunter, right?"

Plus, there was that little problem with my powers.

"She knows and doesn't care. She said Owen is available to help us but has no way to get him to us without flying him, which would take most of the day."

Yeah, flying was faster than driving but not faster than portaling. Before I agreed to leave the comfort of my house and my plans of writing all day, I needed more details. "Did she tell you anything about the necromancer?"

"He lives in a small town outside of New York and has been raising the dead, both people and animals, like it's an Olympic sport."

I snorted. "Were those her words?"

He chuckled. "No, I may have embellished a bit. I've been hanging out with you too much."

"Hanging out with me is fun." And dangerous most days. "I bet the town folks are freaking out."

"Yep."

I sighed loudly for dramatic effect. "I guess. I'll call Olivia to come with. She could help with magic if mine fails."

Although Olivia was fae, she also possessed other, more advanced, magical abilities, thanks to being the devil's daughter.

"Good. I got the second shift covered. Be home in fifteen."

That was great news. "See you soon. Love you."

"Love you more." He hung up before I could argue with him about who loved whom more.

I sent Olivia a text. **Drew and I are going rogue hunting. We need you to come.**

She was free because Phira was in Faery, Luci was doing devil stuff, whatever the H-E-double-hockey-sticks that meant, and Sammie was with Olivia's adoptive parents, who she *still* hadn't told that she knew she was adopted.

Instead of texting me back, she walked into my office seconds later out of nowhere. "Heck, yes I'm in. Wait, what kind of rogue?"

A smile tugged at my lips as I told her what Drew had said about the necromancer. "The only creatures we have to deal with are undead ones. I can control those as long as my powers don't decide to check out. Owen is going too. Can you go get him while I get dressed and wait for Drew?"

She saluted me, then vanished. I turned off my computer, with a forlorn wave at my day of writing, then took my coffee cup to the kitchen. After I rinsed it and put it in the dishwasher, I left Alfred a note about where I was going, then headed upstairs to dress in my comfy stretchy jeans and a black t-shirt, *and* I remembered to put my hair up in a ponytail.

Just in case.

7
AVA

THE FOUR OF us stepped through Olivia's portal right into a graveyard straight out of a horror movie. Dead animals wandered aimlessly around the place in varying stages of decomposition. Skeletons standing frozen in place brought back memories of the time I'd raised an entire cemetery of them to help me fight. I'd been very new to using my powers then and hadn't meant to raise that many, but they'd helped me, so no complaints there. Skeletons themselves didn't bother me. Heck, until recently, I'd lived with one. Now Larry was all fleshed out now as long as he kept his crystal from the chasm on him.

The real gruesome part of the scene was the dead bodies. The corpses that hadn't fully decomposed.

Zombie central. Yuck. Thankfully, zombies weren't real.

"Oh wow. This is disturbing," Olivia said next to me.

"Yep, a little." Okay, a lot.

The sound of people had us turning around. Outside the gates of the graveyard fence, a small crowd had gathered. Crap. That was all we needed.

Owen frowned. "This is going to be tricky."

A bright smile spread across Olivia's face. "I can put up a glamour wall and explain that we're shooting a movie or something."

"I'll go with her and talk to the police that just pulled up," Drew said.

They left to do their thing, and I turned to Owen. He'd cleaned up since he'd left to become a hunter. His hair didn't look nearly as oily as it had, and he'd cut it in a way that accentuated what a sharp jawline and high cheekbones he had. He also looked like he'd buffed out some. All that combat hunter training, no doubt. "How are we going to do this?"

Owen scanned the graveyard. "Let's get the bodies back into their graves. Then we can deal with the animals."

Okay, I could do this. Closing my eyes, I focused on the undead, the ones shuffling around the place while Owen reanimated the bodies. To test my weird, flaky powers I focused on only one of the wandering ghouls. Opening my eyes, I locked onto the closest one to me, a teen boy. Too young to be dead or undead. Poor kid.

Sending out my death magic to him, I caught his attention and smiled. "I'm going to put you back to rest and arrest the man who did this." I spread my arm out indicating the carnage around us.

He followed my hand, looking at the other ghouls and bodies, furrowing his brows. I'd learned from my training with Owen, back when I'd first opened myself up to using my necromancer powers, that I should never give the undead a chance to request to stay animated. They had to be magically bound to a necromancer to stay animated. I did *not* have any more room in my house for another ghoul.

Before he could answer me and possibly ask to stay above ground, I pushed my magic into him and said, "Go back to your grave and rest."

Sometimes speaking to them as if they were alive worked. Sometimes I needed to use force. I got lucky with this one. He seemed to not want to be here. Or he was just confused about being a ghoul?

I glanced over at Owen, and he had managed to get several of the dead bodies reanimated and heading to their graves. Wow, that made me look like a slacker.

Raising my hands, I hoped my magic would work and blasted out my powers to all the ghouls as I said, "Go back to your graves."

They all turned to look at me at once. I froze. Something wasn't right. Then they started moving toward me. Uh-oh. No, that wasn't what I'd wanted. "Stop. Go back to your graves."

I thrust my hands out to them as if that would make my powers work right. They stopped but still looked confused. I did it again, throwing out my hands along with my power. The third time was the charm. The ghouls went back to their resting places, shuffling slowly back to their graves and climbing down to lie in their coffins.

I had to encourage a few of them along, the ones who didn't want to stay dead. My heart broke for them, but death was a part of life. I simply couldn't animate everyone who wanted to be alive. That would be three-fourths of the world's dead.

By the time all of the people were underground again, Olivia and Drew had rejoined us. The crowd at the gates was gone as were the police. "Thanks for taking care of the spectators," I said.

Olivia bounced on her toes. "I used compulsion. And it worked!" She was so proud of herself.

"Ah, your demon side is coming out," I teased, and she swatted at me.

"I should make you reset the gravestones and rebury them." She winked at me. She wouldn't do that because she loved using her magic any chance she got.

Olivia snapped her fingers, reminding me of something Luci would do. Within seconds, the graveyard was clean and looked as though it hadn't just had bodies and ghouls everywhere.

I turned to Owen. "We just need to return the animals to the forest and find out who did this."

He nodded. "We should be able to track him with our powers."

I understood what he meant. If we combined our necro powers, we could do a locator spell that would tell us where any other necromancers were in the area. "Ready?"

He nodded and together, we animated the dead animals and directed them to the forest. Once they disappeared into the trees, I turned and spotted the skeleton of a dog. "Hey, where'd you come from, Rover?"

His skull jerked over in my direction, then he took off. Crap.

"We have a runner!" I yelled and raced after the dog. He was fast, like a greyhound chasing a fake rabbit around a track.

I threw out my hands sending my magic to him and yelled, "Stop!" Nothing happened. Of course. I did it again. Still nothing. Great. Looked like I'd met my quota for my powers working well for the day. Third times a charm? We'd see.

When I threw my hands out again, lightning flew from my fingertips, striking the dog skeleton. I was so glad that it had already died. If it'd been alive I would've fried it.

The four of us spread out to trap the dog. We managed to keep him within our circle. The dog darted toward the space between Owen and Drew. Moving fast, Owen lunged at him, falling on top of the skeleton. Bones went bouncing off in different directions.

Well, that was one way to stop a runaway skeleton dog.

I pushed out my powers to gather up the bones as Drew helped Owen to his feet, but they reformed all on their own before my power even got to them. Once the dog was back together, it took off into the forest. Bah! I wasn't at all in good enough shape to be chasing the undead.

Pushing my legs to move faster and ignoring the burn in my muscles, I ran after the skeleton. A few feet into the thick forest, we skidded to a stop. A tall, thin man stepped into our path. He had a wild look about him. His aura was dark, indicating that he'd been using dark magic for a while.

Owen stepped forward while Drew positioned himself in front of me. My protector. Have I mentioned how much I love that man?

I didn't need protecting, though I loved the gesture. Moving forward to stand beside my overprotective hunter hubby, I glared at the rogue necro. "Why are you raising the dead?"

Olivia stood on my other side and crossed her arms, waiting for the rogue to answer.

He glared at the four of us. "I'm building an army to protect my property against the end of the world."

Olivia and I glanced at one another. Olivia mouthed, "Cray-zee."

I agreed.

"The world is not ending, and you can't just raise the dead and set them loose." I lifted my hand in the air but stopped as dark death magic washed over me.

Owen frowned and scanned the area. Just then a dozen or so ghouls stepped out of the shadows, surrounding us.

Well, crap.

The mix of animated skeletons and fleshed-out ghouls rushed toward us and for a microsecond, I panicked. Then Drew pushed his hunter power into me, giving me a boost. It was a small boost, but enough to knock me out of my what-in-the-world state of mind.

I rushed forward while calling to my powers, deep in my core, and thankfully, they responded. I directed my magic toward the ghouls in front of me. A blast of energy came out and knocked them back several feet. I hurried over to Owen and held out my hand. "We can combine our magics and unanimate them."

He nodded and took my hand, linking our fingers to form a solid connection between the two of us.

Drew and Olivia stood behind us with their backs to ours, fighting off the ghouls and skeletons. From the corner of my eyes, I caught glimpses of vines and tree branches picking up ghouls and tossing them away from us. Olivia was getting so much better at using her magic. That made me smile as I forced another skeleton to crumple, its magic gone.

Drew was fighting his way to the necromancer without much forward progress. That gave me an idea. I nudged Owen's arm and pointed with our linked hands. "Direct the power to the necro. We need to disable his magic."

Owen nodded. "Good idea."

We turned our focus to the necromancer and blasted him with everything we had. The energy ball hit him in the chest, knocking him backward. He hit a tree and slid to the ground, unmoving. He was out.

All of the ghouls and skeletons dropped like lead weights. Olivia used her magic to open up the earth under them. Should we have sent them all back to their original graves? Probably. Did I have the energy? Absolutely not.

I really couldn't muster the magic to send them all home, and Owen had never been powerful enough for a large magical event like that.

While she worked to bury them, Owen and Drew bound the necro's hands to get him ready to take back to the hunter compound in North Carolina. They had the means to deal with rogues.

When all the skeletons and ghouls were buried, Olivia and I walked over to the guys. I gave Owen a quick hug. We might have only known each other for a little over a year, but he was family. After all, he'd lived with me during that time and mentored me. I was so thankful for him.

I pulled out of the hug and lightly punched him in the arm, noting how much firmer it was. "The hunters have you working out?"

Owen chuckled and ducked his head. "It helps with fighting monsters."

"Yeah, I can see that." Especially after fighting the tentacle beast a little over a week ago. If Drew didn't always go to the gym before the roosters woke up, I'd go with him. I just wasn't a morning type of girl.

"Don't be a stranger," I said to Owen.

"I'll try not to." He picked up the unconscious necromancer like he weighed nothing, then moved closer to Olivia.

Olivia curled a hand on his biceps and her eyes widened. "You're right, Ava. He's been working out." She giggled when Owen blushed. "I'll be right back."

They vanished through a portal, and I turned to my husband, who watched me with heat in the depths of his eyes. "What?" I asked.

He wrapped his arms around my waist and pulled me close. I draped my arms over his shoulders. "Just admiring how beautiful you are."

I crinkled my nose. "What do you want?"

He laughed and swatted my rear, drawing a squeak from me. "Nothing. I like hunting with you."

"Why is that?"

"I can always count on things going crazy."

That much had been proven true. "I think I might be cursed to have a lifetime supply of crazy." I grinned, showing my teeth.

"Always an adventure." He kissed my nose. "Keeps it fun."

It was an adventure for sure. A charge of magic filled the air moments before Olivia materialized next to us. "You guys ready to go home?"

"Yep," Drew and I said at the same time.

In a blink, we were standing in Winston's living room. The first thing I noticed was an odd nervous energy in the air. Stretching out my senses, I searched the house for anyone else. No one was here.

The floorboards rippled, then the heat kicked on.

"Winston is in a mood," Olivia whispered.

"Yes, it seems so."

My thoughts turned to Alfred, then I remembered he'd gone for a walk. We'd only been out a couple of hours. Alfred knew the town pretty well. He'd gone into town shopping countless times since he'd been returned to looking like a human. It wasn't like he looked like a zombie anymore. He'd be fine. It'd do him good to clear his head. Then, I'd be here if he needed to talk.

Olivia grinned at me. "You want to come over? Carrie is coming by, and I thought you would like a girls' afternoon."

"Oh, that sounds fun. I'll be over after lunch." I tried to remember the last time I'd seen Carrie. It had to have been the wedding, and we hadn't talked much then with everything that had been going on. It would be great to just sit and chat.

8
OLIVIA

I HAD JUST FINISHED CLEANING the kitchen of my lunch mess when the dulcet tunes of Van Halen filled the air. Now the doorbell was playing Running With the Devil. With a snort, I used my magic to open the front door. Ava and Carrie were on the other side. Having powers was super handy sometimes.

Their footsteps echoed through the large mansion as they made their way to the kitchen. I met them halfway and directed them to the family room that had a spectacular view of the ocean. With a wave of my hand, I created a fire in the fireplace.

Carrie sat on the sofa with a smile. "You're getting good at using your magic."

I beamed at her as I plopped into the armchair beside the couch. "Thanks. I compelled someone this morning."

"That's great. You're embracing your father's powers." Carrie glanced around the room. I realized she hadn't seen more than the foyer of Luci's house before.

"Would you like a tour?" I asked. I'd planned on handing out wine glasses and getting a little bit day drunk with the girls, but Carrie'd never had a tour.

Her eyes lit up, and Ava chuckled. "It's always a trip to explore this house," she said. "Let's go."

I conjured three glasses of perfectly chilled wine. They hovered in midair in front of us. As I grabbed mine, I spread my arm toward the door to the living room. "After you."

The living room was big and impressive, but we didn't linger. "Come on, the upstairs is the most interesting part."

At the top of the stairs, I pointed out Sam's and my room and then Sammie's. Down the hall was Phira and Luci's room, when they were here, which seemed to be less and less lately. Luci was always around, popping in and out, but they stayed in Faerie a lot and often even in Hell.

"Here's where the house gets interesting." I grabbed a key from the top of the door frame and unlocked it, then opened a door at the end of the hall. "This door hasn't always been here. We added the door and lock to keep Sammie out. If he got lost down here it'd take us ages to find him. I'm actually convinced this part of the house is in another dimension."

Another hallway stretched in front of us, impossibly long. "Pick a door and open it." I clasped my hands in front of me, excited by what was about to happen. I'd never opened the same door twice. Each and every time I came down this hallway, usually just for the fun of it, I found a room filled with something new or decorated with a new and specific theme.

Carrie giggled and hurried forward, skipping the first two doors to open the third on the right. "What in the world?" she whispered.

Ava and I exchanged an amused glance and moved behind Carrie to see what was in the room she'd opened. It was entirely full of bean bag chairs. A lion sat on a beanbag in the middle of the room, holding a book in one hand and a mug of something steaming in the other. He turned his majestic head toward us and I belatedly realized he was wearing glasses.

And a tweed suit. Also, he was sitting in a way that big cats weren't supposed to, all upright and proper. "Pardon me," he drolled in a deep, rich British accent. "I'm reading here."

"Sorry." I waved at him as I reached around Carrie and pulled the door closed.

We stood in the hallway for a full five seconds before we burst out laughing.

"Pick another one," Ava said and clapped her hands.

"Okay." Carrie turned in a circle, then went back one door and threw it open.

It was the most ordinary of all the rooms I'd seen so far. One wall had several bookcases, and a sofa and loveseat were positioned in front of a fireplace. It wasn't too different from the family room downstairs. "Weird," I said as I stepped inside. The far wall was lined with windows, but the curtains were nearly shut on all of them. A little light came through the crack in the panels on each one. I stepped deeper into the room and turned around. "See anything odd?"

"I don't trust stairs. They're always up to something."

"Who said that?" I turned in another circle, looking for the source of the voice. "Did either of you do that?" I asked. They both had magic and might've been able to mess with me.

Ava and Carrie looked thrilled but shook their heads as they tiptoed around the room.

The same voice spoke again, and it was the most deadpan I'd ever heard. "I'm so good at sleeping I can do it with my eyes closed."

I snorted. "Are you telling jokes?" I called to the room at large.

"Terrible jokes," Ava said under her breath.

The room replied, "Two men walked into a bar. The third man ducked."

All three of us laughed at that one.

"Still a terrible joke," Ava said. "Despite the fact that I laughed."

"Time flies like an arrow. Fruit flies like a banana."

I started giggling and couldn't stop.

"Every time I take my dog to the park the ducks try to bite him. That's what I get for buying a pure bread dog."

My giggles turned into roaring laughter. Ava and Carrie leaned against each other to keep from falling over. I collapsed onto the couch, which enveloped me in a comforting embrace to continue laughing.

"I used to hate facial hair, but then it grew on me."

My stomach was starting to hurt from laughing so hard. Tears rolled down my cheeks.

The door to the room flew open and the lion walked in. "Out!" he roared. "You must get out."

My laughter died in my throat as the king of the freaking jungle ushered us out of the room. Why had I gotten so tickled? The jokes had been cute, sure, but not funny enough for me to roll around clutching my side in laughter.

The lion repositioned the glasses on his nose and peered down at us. Carrie and Ava looked as consternated as I felt.

"What was that?" Ava asked.

"That couch is cursed. It tells jokes and ensnares its victims in laughter until they go mad. Then it forces them to do its bidding."

"How and why does my father have that thing in his *home*?" I asked.

Ava nodded. "Yeah, why not destroy it?"

"He keeps it here because it's dangerous. He has yet to find a way to destroy it, so until he does, it can't hurt anyone here." He smoothed one strand of his mane back into place. "That is, unless you silly women go exploring and get into trouble."

"Now hold on." I held up one finger, but the lion looked at his wrist, at an expensive-looking watch.

"Please excuse me. I have a meeting with my accountant I really can't miss." He went back into the beanbag room and closed the door.

I wasn't done with him. I opened the door right after he shut it, but the room was empty of everything but beanbags, bookshelves, and books.

"Let's go back to the family room," Ava suggested. "This is officially freaky."

She was not lying.

After carefully locking the door to that mysterious and dangerous hallway back, we got back to the family room, and I conjured enough wine to make our glasses flipping full.

Sammie came into the room with his tablet. He'd been out with my mom and dad, but they'd dropped him off just after I got back from helping Ava with the rogue necromancer. Thankfully, I'd had enough time to get in the door and change. I'd gotten some sort of dirt stain all down the front of my shirt. Yuck.

He crawled up on the couch between Ava and Carrie and grinned at them. "Hi!"

Carrie ruffled his hair. "Hi there, little man." She looked up at Ava and then at me. "I wanted to run something by you guys. You know I've been teaching for well over twenty years. While I love teaching, I feel a change is needed."

I lifted my brows. "What kind of change?"

Ava shook her head but smirked. "I don't think I could handle any more changes."

The three of us laughed and Carrie explained her idea. "We have a growing magical population here in Shipton Harbor. With Ava's granddaughter on the way, I was thinking it would be the perfect time to open a private magical academy."

"We don't have that many magical children here. The shifters either homeschool or send their kids to public schools." Ava leaned over and tabbed on Sammie's tablet screen, making him giggle.

"We could open it nationally. Put in portals. There's *definitely* a need for it worldwide." Carrie looked at me, then Ava, then back to me. "You're not the only mom with a gifted, magical child and no school to send him to. It wouldn't have to be limited to kids, either. We could offer a la carte courses that adults could take too."

Now that piqued my interest. "Oh, I would totally take some classes. There's so much I need to know." I could imagine all the magical courses that I could take that could actually help with my powers. Especially since I was half god, or was it angel? Luci still hadn't confirmed if he was some kind of a god or a fallen archangel.

Ava perked up. "I'd love to take classes too. Sign me up!"

Carrie laughed. "I was hoping that the two of you could teach some classes."

Ava crinkled her nose. "I don't think I'd be good at teaching. But Dad would love it. I could ask him."

"Yeah, I'm not sure I'm teacher material." I'd barely raised my first two. My ex-husband was such a scumbag it was a miracle Devan and Jess had turned out so well. They were great kids, despite the fact that Carter and I had been ill-equipped to be parents. Sammie was my do-over child, my opportunity to prove I could be a good mom. My happy, happy surprise, that I loved to the ends of the earth. I loved my older two just as much. I'd just made a lot of mistakes with them.

Carrie shrugged and said, "I was hoping, actually, that you would run the school. Be headmistress or whatever you'd want to be called."

I stared at her with my mouth hanging open. It wasn't very suave of me, but I was floored that she thought I could run a school. "I couldn't do that."

"I don't know, Liv. You're super organized, fair, and kind. And incredibly bossy. I think you'd be great as the headmistress," Ava said.

Carrie nodded. "I agree with Ava. There isn't anyone I would trust more to take the job. The three of us could be partners."

The headmistress of a magical school?

I'd never had to get a job. When I'd married Carter and moved away, I'd made it clear to my adopted parents that I didn't want the flower shop. They'd also had other companies and investments. None of which I was interested in running or owning.

But the academy gig, that was intriguing. "Okay, count me in.

Obviously, I'd need to run everything by Sam, but as long as he agrees, I'm willing to give it a whirl."

We spent the next few hours planning out classes and making lists. Sammie was also a big help, surprisingly, with ideas about the type of classes we could offer. We couldn't use all of his suggestions. I just couldn't see how conjuring toys would be helpful.

After Ava and Carrie left, I made dinner. By the time Sammie and I finished eating, Sam had woken.

He walked into the kitchen and wrapped his arms around my waist from behind. Then he kissed my neck, which made me want to drag him back upstairs for a bit of fun time. "Good evening," I said, a little breathless and all kinds of turned on.

"Evening," he replied and moved to the refrigerator where we kept the bagged blood. Sam didn't want to feed from me all the time. He was still a newbie vamp and needed to feed more often than an older one. If he drank from me daily it would start to take its toll on me, so he supplemented with blood bags.

While he drank his blood from a large coffee cup, I told him about the academy. He smiled at me. "Ava's right, the job is perfect for you."

"Thanks," I sat in his lap and twirled his dark hair at the back of his neck with my fingers. "I knew you'd agree. I told the girls I had to run it by you, but never once did I think you might not agree."

We spent a couple of hours playing a game with Sammie since his dad slept most of the day now. We usually let him stay up on the weekends to spend more time with his father. Sam missed time with his son. It was great that we had my blood as an option as Sammie got older. Now Sam could go to games or recitals, whatever Sammie got into.

After putting Sammie to bed a couple of hours later than normal, Sam and I settled onto the sofa for a movie. Phira and Luci wandered in a few minutes later and snuggled together in the oversize armchair. I watched them for a few moments, noting how in love they were. A smile tugged at my lips. I was so lucky to have them and my parents. Some people had no parents. I had four. Six if I counted Sam's.

There were about thirty minutes left of the movie when Sammie came sniffling into the room. I'd been so wrapped up in the romantic comedy I hadn't felt him get up. His eyes were filled with tears. I sat straight up and held my arms open for him. "What's wrong, baby?"

He climbed into my lap and snuggled into me. "I had a bad dream. There was a giant marshmallow monster attacking you and Ava."

I hugged him close. "It was just a nightmare. Ava and I are okay. Plus, we can take care of any monster that comes our way, even giant marshmallow monsters."

Luci came over and placed a hand on Sammie's head. My father's eyes flashed red for a moment then returned to their normal dark brown. Then he disappeared.

Alrighty then. That wasn't suspicious.

Actually, it wasn't. He was always doing crap like that. It made sense to him but not at all to the rest of us.

I kissed Sammie on the forehead and stood to take him back to bed. Phira rose from the chair and held out her arms. "Let me. I'll sing him to sleep."

"Thanks," I said as I handed Sammie over to her.

By singing him to sleep, she meant that she'd use her magic to chase away bad dreams. Maybe I needed to look into dream catchers. Sammie had been exposed to some pretty crazy stuff in his young life. We had to protect him in any way we could.

9
AVA

"So, he just jumps off the building?" I pointed at the screen and narrowly refrained from throwing popcorn at it.

Olivia and Sam were having a movie night with Luci and Phira, so Drew and I had decided to follow suit. The problem was I wasn't the biggest fan of action movies and Winston was being a supreme brat tonight.

Drew and I had settled on the couch with a bowl of popcorn between us, ready to watch the movie. But as soon as we'd hit play, our cats LucyFur and Mr. Snoozerton had started chasing each other around the living room, knocking over a vase and creating general chaos. We'd paused the movie to try to contain them, but they weren't willing to be contained. I'd managed to convince Lucy to chase Snoozer outside and we were about fifteen minutes into the movie.

"Yes, but he's trained to—" Drew snapped his mouth shut when Winston's kitchen cabinets began slamming open and shut. I paused the movie and waited patiently for my house to stop having its snit. "Are you done?" Drew asked a few seconds later. "I wish you could just tell us why you're so upset."

"I know. Do you have a leak?" Winston was a magical house. Our running theory was that all the magic users who had lived in him over the hundreds of years since he'd been built had imbibed him with magic.

It had to help that there was a massive source of magical power running underneath the basement.

"He's always repaired himself before hasn't he?" Drew asked.

"Yeah, except when he was empty. He needed a lot of work when I moved back to Shipton, but once I agreed to stay, he fixed himself." I sighed and looked up at the ceiling. "Maybe he's just feeling neglected."

"Maybe," Drew conceded. He got up and headed to the kitchen. I followed, then went over to the kitchen, inspecting the cabinets as I walked around. Everything seemed to be in order, but Winston had focused his irritation on this room. I opened the cabinets one by one, checking for anything that might seem out of place.

Nothing.

"Come on, let's try to finish the movie before Snoozer does something to make Lucy mad and our night descends into chaos."

"So much for our quiet night in the house," Drew said and threw his arm over my shoulder to press a kiss to my temple.

"Any night we're together is better than a night apart," I said in my most sickly-sweet voice.

Drew laughed and said, "You're right. Let's get back to the movie before Snoozer and Lucy come back in and ruin the whole thing."

We both laughed and headed back to the living room, eager to watch the rest of the movie, even if I didn't love it.

The moment we got settled in, something crashed in the kitchen. I cocked my head and listened. Lucy and Snoozer were chasing each other around upstairs. Their little footfalls sounded like the world's tiniest elephants.

"Enough is enough. Winston, stop!" It wasn't like I was correctly deciphering what had him so upset.

"What could he want?" Drew asked.

I shook my head. "I'm not sure." I stood and went to the stairs. "Alfred?" There was no answer. He hadn't been down since we got home and settled in for our movie.

Winston went crazy. The floors shook and the windows rattled.

Lucy-Fur appeared at the top of the stairs with a grumpy look on her face. "What in the cat yak is going on?"

Snoozer appeared behind her, yawned, then said as plain as the long fluffy tail on his butt, "Alfred." It was kind of more like Meolfred. He couldn't talk like Lucy could, but when he wanted to get the point across, his meows sounded incredibly close to words.

Drew and I froze and stared at the dark gray Maine coon. Then it hit me. "Oh, my gosh. Alfred never came back from his walk."

Lucy twitched her tail. "What kind of friend are you that you hadn't noticed he was missing?"

I glared at the white cat. "If you knew he wasn't back yet, why didn't you say anything?"

"I'm not his keeper," she said and walked off. "Come Snoozer, I'm not done playing."

Snoozer let out a few low meows like he was muttering under his breath and followed behind Lucy, down the hall and out of sight.

Shaking my head, I raced up the stairs and to Alfred's room. One, I wanted to make sure he wasn't in there after all, and two I needed something personal of his so I could do a locator spell. In most cases, I didn't *need* one, but the spell would be stronger if I had something with his energy on it.

I picked up his tablet. He used the thing all the time for lists, recipes, and social media. His cell phone sat beside the tablet. He hadn't taken it with him on his walk. Holding the tablet, I closed my eyes and spoke the chant for my locator spell.

Nothing happened.

Panic tightened my chest, and I tried again.

Nothing.

"What is it?" Drew asked.

"The spell isn't working." I couldn't stop the slightly panicky tone in my voice.

Drew grabbed my hand and threaded his fingers with mine. "Try now."

After a few deep breaths and an attempt to center myself, I did, aided by the flow of Drew's power mingling with mine. It gave me a boost, but I still couldn't locate Alfred.

I pushed out my senses to see if I could feel him. He was still a ghoul, after all. My necromancer powers would pick up on any ghoul in the area.

The only ones I sensed were Lucy and Snoozer in the house. No other ghouls were anywhere nearby.

Fear settled her icy fingers in my spine. I locked gazes with Drew. "He's gone. I can't feel him."

I left Alfred's room and made my way back downstairs and to my office. My phone was on my desk. I usually left it there when I was at home and didn't have plans to go anywhere. Picking it up, I texted Olivia.

Alfred is missing. Ask Luci if he can sense him.

A moment later Olivia materialized beside me. "When was the last time you saw him?"

"This morning right before we went to New York to deal with that necromancer. Alfred said he was going for a walk. I hadn't even noticed that he never returned." I was an awful niece and friend.

While I stood there, wracking my brain for where he could be and why I couldn't sense him, Luci appeared beside Olivia. "I can't sense him either. Did you try a locator spell?"

I pursed my lips at him. "Yes, Sir Satan, of course. That was the first thing I did."

He closed the distance between us and grabbed my hands, holding them gently. "Let's try together."

I sighed. Luci was the King of Hell, so in a way, he also had death magic, didn't he? He dealt with evil creatures and demons. Closing my eyes, I opened up to Luci.

Warmth blossomed in my chest, and a deep, ancient power filled me. Holy crow. I could do a lot with this magic. It was wild though, unpredictable. No wonder there were these big, amazing, awe-inspiring things he could do, and then sometimes he couldn't have tied his shoes with his power.

His magic wasn't as evil as I'd imagined it to be. It was definitely dark gray, but not black. That was interesting. Luci was a complex fellow, to say the least.

Together we focused on Alfred, searching through the town and beyond until we covered the whole island.

There was no sign of Alfred.

When Luci let go of my hands and stepped back, I wrapped my arms around my waist. "He's gone," I whispered.

Drew pulled me into a hug. "We should call Winnie."

I nodded even though I hated to spoil her weekend. But she'd be *so* mad at me if I didn't call her as soon as I realized he was gone.

After texting my dad, Olivia opened a portal for them to come home right away.

Within minutes, my house was full again, which was the way I liked it if push came to shove. A quiet evening with Drew would be nice, but I loved having my family here.

Winnie paced the living room, wringing her hands. "You can't sense him at all?"

"No, I'm so sorry. I tried a few different types of locator spells. Drew boosted my power then Luci and I tried together. He's—"

Winnie whirled around to glare at me. "Don't say it!" Then her eyes filled with tears. "I knew I should have stayed. He *insisted* I go and have fun. He was so worried about those damn Viking necromancers."

The Vikings! Of course. I felt like doing the movie-trope hand-on-forehead slap for my stupidity in not remembering the Vikings. They had to be behind this. It was time to show those Vikings what it meant to be a warrior.

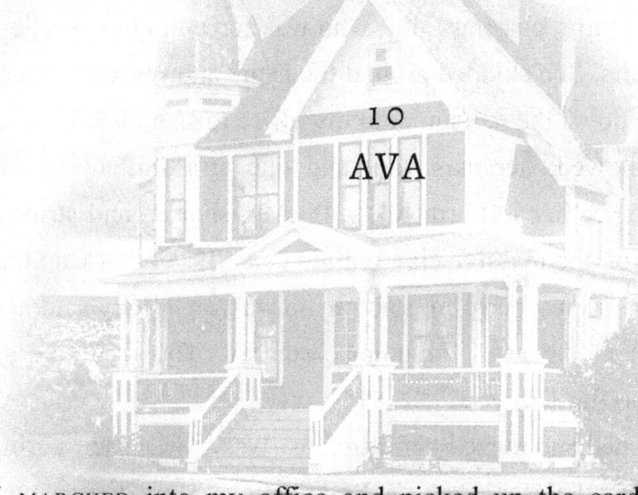

10
AVA

I MARCHED into my office and picked up the card the Viking leader had given me, then I dialed his number with hands shaking.

It was rage, not fear. Alfred was okay, we just had to get him back.

He was fine.

Really.

While I waited for him to pick up the phone, I tapped my foot against the floor.

"Hello, Mrs. Walker." Arne's voice sounded way too smug. Far too pleased with himself. I couldn't tell by his tone if he'd done it, but I wanted to think I could hear his voice.

"I need you three to come to my house. Tonight. Now." I didn't give them time to argue. I just hung up and squared my shoulders, ready to go to battle.

Stomping coming from upstairs drew my attention to the ceiling of my office. Now someone was running. Then Zoey yelled, "Lucy! Stay out of my room!"

Good grief, what now? Were they incapable of giving it a rest for a minute when we were in the middle of a crisis?

I walked out of my office to see Zoey, only halfway shifted into her tiger form, chasing Lucy, who was screaming as she flew down the stairs. She skidded around the stairs and reversed direction to come down the hall and into my office to stand behind me.

Zoey followed, her ears, tail, and one arm shifted. It was unnerving to see her left arm fuzzy, thicker, shorter, and striped. Not to mention the massive claws at the end. "If you hock up one more hairball on my bed I'm going to shave you," Zoey said and glared down at the cat. "Including your tail. You won't be so pretty with no fur, will you?"

Lucy gasped and pursed her little lips. Was… was she wearing lipstick? I peered closer. She was. Red lipstick. "How do you even know it's me and not Snoozer?"

Zoey's face reddened as she replied, "Duh, you idiot, I'm a *shifter*. I can smell you all over your *hork*!"

Lucy shrugged and licked her paw as if to say *sorry not sorry*. Oh, she was a horrid little thing sometimes.

Zoey lunged for Lucy, trying to go around me and catch the little white rat. I caught Zoey by wrapping my arms around her waist and using her momentum to haul her around in a circle. Zoey was thinner and a bit shorter than me, but geez she was strong. We nearly completed two rotations as Lucy squawked and scrambled to the back of the room, under my desk.

"Don't make me use my power over you," I said through clenched teeth as I fought valiantly to stop Zoey from going after Lucy. Drew raised his eyebrows. He would step in if needed, but he didn't have quite the same parental relationship with Zoey that I did. More like a step-parental thing. Maybe a beloved uncle.

She stopped fighting me. “It’s gross to come home to a giant hairball on my bed.”

Yeah, I got it. I’d be livid too. Turning to Lucy, I said, “No more hairballs in Zoey’s room.” I leaned in close and lowered my voice to be more menacing. “Or else I’ll make you hairless for a week. No. A month.”

Lucy gasped. “You wouldn’t.”

I glared at her. “Try me.” I tapped the stone on her collar. “I can take this back and control your beauty and health myself.” It was a mean threat, but she needed to understand she couldn’t do *any*thing she wanted to.

Just most things.

Lucy walked off, grumbling under her breath.

I ignored her because I simply didn’t have time for cat drama right now.

We moved into the kitchen to wait for the Viking necromancers to arrive. Mom and Dad were already sitting there with Winnie sobbing in Mom’s arms.

The familiar wave of necromancer power touched my awareness seconds before a knock sounded on my door. How had they arrived so quickly? It hadn’t been twenty minutes.

Winston opened it as the rest of us turned and glared toward the front door. The Vikings stood there. Arne still had his hand raised from knocking. He looked unsure for a split second before composing himself into his normal superiority.

“Come in. Have a seat.” I clipped the words out, my temper reaching its boiling point. I’d had all I was going to take out of these creepy ancient necromancers.

They glided in, somehow giving the illusion of wearing robes despite their attire of jeans and tees.

Once the three of them were settled on the sofa, and I was in one of the high-back chairs with my entire entourage behind me—except for Winnie beside me in the other chair. "Where is Alfred?" I asked with a tight jaw.

The two cronies on the right looked at one another but their fearless leader spoke. "We left him here with you."

I held out my hand and conjured the truth stone from out of my desk drawer. "I ask you again. Where is Alfred?"

This time Arne glanced at his fellows before looking back at me. "I do not know where Alfred is." The tone of his voice along with the slight sense of confusion that rolled off of him made me feel he was likely telling the truth. However, I didn't trust them one tiny little bit. There was a reason they wanted Alfred to be human again with his powers fully restored and it certainly wasn't for wholesome purposes. I wanted to know why.

Closing my hand around the stone, I activated it, then asked again, "Where is Alfred?"

"We do not know." He was starting to sound irritated, but they didn't know where my ghoul-butler-future-uncle-in-law was.

If they didn't take him, then where in the world was my beloved, great-times-infinity-uncle ghoul? It wasn't creepy. He was my relative on my father's side, and Winnie was my mother's sister.

It was creepy because of how public they made it, but not because of the levels of relation.

"When did you see him last?"

Without hesitation, Arne said, "When we were here yesterday."

Okay, so they didn't know that Alfred was missing or why. I

changed the direction of the questions. “Why do you want Alfred to be fully alive again?”

The leader paused, opened his mouth, closed it, then said in a stiff, cold voice, “We want to be a powerful coven again. Like we were hundreds of years ago. Together we make each other more powerful.”

That made sense and wasn’t all that different from why witches formed covens. There were powers in numbers. Although, a group of necromancers banding together wasn’t necessarily a good thing. Dark powers carry dark intentions. They were the ones who had told me too many necromancers in one place drew trouble.

I didn’t need that in my town.

Plus, there was the issue of their age. The Vikings were hundreds of years old. Normal necromancers didn’t live that long. How were they still living? What kind of dark magic had they done to extend their lives?

Enough was enough. I stood. “I’m stepping in as Alfred’s necromancer guardian and making his decision. No. Under no circumstances can you have Alfred back, alive or undead.” I took a breath and calmed down. Electrifying magic swirled inside me. My lightning powers. They seemed to be the only ones working but I couldn’t control them. At the moment, they really wanted to make crispy Vikings.

I needed to calm myself before I fried the Vikings on my couch. If I did that, I’d have to buy a new couch. I liked the one I had, not to mention I had no time for the task of picking out a new one.

“Alfred is a ghoul by choice. In his mind, this is his punishment for all the things he did wrong when he was alive. You need to leave town and leave Alfred alone." I put magic in my words to make them more of a threat. I couldn't compel people, but I wanted these goons to know I meant business. After all, I was considerably more powerful than they were. I could sense it. They should've been able to as well.

At least, I would be more powerful again once my magic leveled out after Michelle had the baby.

They stood and the leader bowed his head a little. "We will leave Shipton." Walking in unison, super creepy, they went out the front door, which opened for them and then closed behind them.

Winnie opened her mouth and said loudly, "If they didn't—"

I held up my hand. "Wait. They're too close."

As their power lessened and they got farther away, I put my arms around Winnie. "Okay, they can't even hear us with magic now."

"If they didn't take him then where could he be?" Winnie cried out.

I pulled her into a full hug. "I don't know, but we will find him."

She pulled back. "We have to go search for him. Right now. He could be hurt or worse." She started crying again and headed for the door.

I raced ahead of her to stop her.

Drew hurried over and put his hands on her shoulders, looking her deep in the eyes. "I called in a missing person's report. My officers are out searching as much as they can right now. Also, Sam and Wade can go out there and look all night. They've got the skills required to search in the dark."

Sam nodded eagerly. "That's right."

"I can go, too," Zoey said. "I can shift and hit the woods."

Winnie nodded and swiped tears away as Mom pulled her back into her arms. "Come on. It's late and there isn't much we can do tonight. Let's try to get some sleep while those who can search do, and in the morning, we form a plan."

That seemed to calm Winnie a little. My dad came out of the kitchen and pushed a cup of tea into her hands. I smelled the chamomile and a few other herbs that would help induce sleep. Winnie took the cup and sipped it while Mom directed her upstairs, to her room.

Wade exited the hallway, having just come up from the basement. I had no doubt that he heard everything that was said. He confirmed that thought when he said, "I'm in."

Wade nodded at Sam, then Sam kissed Olivia on the cheek, and they headed out the back door. Zoey shifted and followed.

"Thanks," I called after them.

I hoped they found him or at least some clues to where Alfred had gone. We couldn't lose our Alfred. That wasn't an option.

11
AVA

I WOKE up to a note from Wade lying on my bedside table.

We caught Alfred's scent in town but lost it because it started raining. Zoey found nothing in the woods. We're happy to help again tonight. —Wade

I handed the note to Drew. "If they were in town when they lost the scent, that's where us day walkers will start looking."

"Agreed." Drew yawned and got out of bed. "I'll start the coffee."

My heart sad because it was almost always Alfred who started the coffee, I showered and made my way downstairs. It hit me hard that Alfred wasn't waiting for me with breakfast and coffee as soon as I stepped into the kitchen.

I hardened my emotions and steeled my spine. This was not the reality of our future. Alfred would be back and soon.

Drew gave me a sympathetic look and pressed a kiss to my cheek as he passed by me. "I'm going to check in at the station."

As much as I didn't like to be away from him, I wanted him

out there looking for Alfred. "Okay, call me if you find out anything."

He gave me another quick kiss and left.

I sat at the kitchen table just as Olivia appeared with a big cardboard box of coffee with the logo of some fancy coffee shop in Paris, France she loved. To her credit, it was truly amazing coffee. It was just insane that my BFF could just portal over to Paris for coffee. If I'd known she was coming, I would've told Drew not to make a whole pot. That would definitely be going down the drain later.

Mom and Winnie walked into the kitchen dressed and ready to interview the townspeople about Alfred. We finished our coffees and then headed out as a somber but determined group. I drove Dad's new Suburban. It was a mammoth of a vehicle but at least we all fit inside.

Once in town, I parked the SUV in front of the one-hour photo store. Zoey had made up a flier with Alfred's pictures and our contact information. We were going to make copies of them and hand them out as we asked around.

"Hello," I said brightly to the clerk behind the counter. "Could you make about a hundred copies?" I highly doubted we'd need that many, but I handed her the flier Zoey had put together. It had several snapshots of Alfred taped to a piece of paper with our phone numbers handwritten at the bottom.

Five minutes later, flyers in hand, we split up in pairs. Mom and Winnie, Zoey and Larry, Olivia and me, and headed out in different directions. Liv and I went toward the bookstore where I used to work.

Clint was sitting at the counter reading a book when we

entered. He looked up at us and smiled. "It's good to see you." He seemed genuinely pleased.

"Hi, Clint," I said, returning his smile. "How's it going?"

"Can I persuade you to come back to work? Since Owen left town, I seriously miss my days off."

Poor Clint. Not that many people in Shipton liked working in a dusty bookstore. I'd loved my time here, but it just wasn't in the cards now. Who had time? Not me. "No, sorry. I'm happy being the local author and the sheriff's wife." I grinned. I did miss the bookstore, but I just didn't feel right working there with everything going on in my life. No need to drag Clint into my crazy life. He was fully human and didn't need to have anything to do with necromancers, vampires, and witches. And all the other random insaneness in my life.

"I've come in to see if you have seen Alfred. He's missing," I said with a sad note in my tone. I was also hopeful that it would only take a few questions here and there to find him.

Olivia showed Clint the flier, but Clint shook his head. "No, I know who Alfred is, but I haven't seen him in the last couple of days. Is he missing as in *missing?* How long has he been gone?"

"Yes, as in we cannot find him whatsoever. He left yesterday later morning for a walk and hasn't returned, which is completely unlike him"

Clint took the flier. "I'll hang this up on the front door. Man, I hope you find him before Friday. We're expecting a big crowd."

Olivia and I shared a look and I asked, "A crowd for what?"

Clint chuckled. "Sorry, I didn't mean it like that. I hope you find him, safe and sound, and soon, just so that Alfred is safe. As for Friday, he comes in weekly to read to kids and while he's here he always puts in a big book order." He smiled sadly. "The kids love him."

Why had I not known this? "Wow, that's awesome, but no sad smiles. We're going to find him."

Olivia nodded. "Absolutely. Can we leave a few flyers here for the counter as well as the one on the door?"

"Yes, please," Clint answered. "Is there anything else I can do to help?"

"No, but thank you. Just call us if you or anyone spots Alfred." We said goodbye and left the store, then headed next door to Peachy Sweets Bakery. The owner, Kelly Elmore, was busy checking out a customer, so we waited until she was done. My gaze kept drifting to a case full of gigantic cinnamon rolls. Oh, man. Cinnamon and sugar really were a weak point for me.

Kelly and Owen had dated for a short period. I really wasn't sure how or why they'd ended it, though Olivia and I had wondered and discussed it more than once. We just weren't close enough to Kelly to ask her outright and Owen hadn't volunteered any information.

When the customer left with her sweets, Kelly greeted us with a smile. "Hello ladies. How are you both doing?"

"We're good," I said as Olivia handed her the flier. "We're looking for Alfred." She definitely knew who he was. As much as he loved baking, he'd been in quite a few times to discuss recipes with Kelly. "He went missing yesterday. Have you seen him?"

Kelly frowned. "No, not since last week." She stared at the flier. "If you're making flyers, that's not good, is it? Did something happen?"

I glanced down into the case and saw a scone with the name tag, Alfred Scone. Pointing at it, I asked, "What is an Alfred

Scone? And we don't know if anything actually happened, but we can't find him for almost twenty-four hours now."

Kelly looked horrified. "That's not like Alfred at all, is it?"

I shook my head and tried not to let my eyes fill up with tears. Pulling out one of the scones, she cut it in half and handed a piece to me and one to Olivia. "This scone has become my bestseller. It's Alfred's recipe. He shared it with me months ago. I can't keep them on the shelf. I offered to pay him some kind of royalty, but he wouldn't take the money," Kelly said. "I never let him pay when he comes to get pastries, though." She chuckled. "Which he doesn't do often enough. He likes baking them himself too much."

Moaning, I ate my half of the scone. "I recognize this. Alfred makes them at home. Why does it taste better?" I asked.

"Probably my ovens. I have convection ovens and they bake things so much better."

I glanced at Olivia. "Alfred's been talking about wanting one for ages. When we find him, I'll buy him three."

We left a stack of flyers with Kelly, and as we were walking out, she taped one to the window, front and center where nobody walking by would possibly miss it.

Our next stop was Guac On! The owners were there, luckily. "Yes, of course," Hector said. "He came in for lunch yesterday. He had his usual, a chicken burrito with extra queso dip."

"What time was he here?" I couldn't help but be excited. This was the best lead we'd had all day. Nobody else had seen him at all.

Hector's wife, Rosa, checked the computer behind the hostess counter. "I think it was…" She squinted at the screen. "Yes, we sold a chicken burrito with extra queso at eleven, then not another until later afternoon. It wasn't late afternoon because our son would've been excited to tell him about his report."

"Report?" Olivia asked.

"Alfred came in last week and tutored our son. He helped him write a paper on the Vikings that got him an A. He needed a small boost to graduate with honors, and thanks to Alfred, he will. Junior is excited to thank Alfred for his help."

We left a few flyers with them and stepped out onto the sidewalk. "Alfred is so much more involved with people around town than I ever realized." I sighed and looked around. We'd reached the end of the street and hadn't heard from the others yet. "We could drive over to Ben and Brandon's B&B."

Ben and Brandon were twins and witches who belonged to the local coven. They owned one of two of the biggest bed and breakfasts in Shipton.

"Sure, but we don't need to drive." Olivia tugged me into a breezeway between the Mexican restaurant and the bakery. When she was sure no one was looking, she created a portal.

We came out on the backside of the twins' property. It only took seconds for the twins to come out the back door of their large home and advance toward us in a rush, through the gardens where we'd once found the body of a little girl who had been murdered many decades ago. I waved. "Hi, guys."

They slowed and released a big breath at the same time. Ben said, "We didn't know what was materializing on our lawn."

"It's just me," Olivia said with a smile. "Well, us, but the magic was mine."

I took a flier from Olivia and handed it to Brandon. Or Ben. I never could tell them apart. "We came to talk to you about Alfred. He's missing. Have you seen him?"

The twins looked at each other, then shook their heads. "Not for a week or so," Brandon said.

Ben added, "He usually comes by with baked goodies for the guests once a week or so. We have a few long-term guests who are addicted."

Well, okay then. Alfred was just going around town doing good deeds for everyone it seemed. That made my heart happy but also more scared. Where in the world was he?

"How long has he been gone?" Ben asked as he looked over the flier.

"He left for a walk yesterday morning but never came home." The longer he was gone the less likely it was I'd ever see him again. My chest tightened at that thought. I tried to push those negative thoughts out of my mind, but it wasn't easy.

Brandon took my hand and squeezed. "You should call a coven meeting. Even though you're not the High Witch anymore that doesn't mean you can't call an emergency meeting. This more than qualifies as an emergency. We could figure out how to find him together."

"That's a great suggestion. Can you help me out and pass on the word and have everyone meet at my place in about an hour?" With the coven's help, we'd find Alfred. At least I hoped so. I had to hope so.

Ben pulled out his phone and started texting. "Got you covered."

I thanked them again and Olivia opened a portal to take us back to the SUV parked downtown. Rather, the alley beside the bookstore, but that was close enough.

Mom, Winnie, Zoey, and Larry were already waiting when we got there. I frowned at them. "How long have you been waiting?"

Mom said, "Not long."

"We just walked up like two seconds ago," Zoey said.

Winnie sniffed and dabbed her eyes with a tissue. "Everyone we talked to had such nice things to say about Alfred. He's such a wonderful person."

Olivia said, "Us too. Alfred helped so many people."

He really did. "Helps," I said firmly. "Not helped." Olivia looked stricken and Winnie dissolved in tears. "Let's get home. I called a coven meeting."

12
OLIVIA

I SHOT off a text to Phira to let her know that she could bring Sammie over to Ava's if she wanted. My fae mother loved spending time with Sammie as well as Jess and Devan. She was making up for all the years she'd missed with me because she'd been imprisoned in a sort of limbo plane by her father for falling in love with mine.

She texted back a few seconds later. **We just settled in to watch that new superhero movie. Plus, he looks sleepy.**

The bubble popped up telling me she was typing, but then it went away. Then she called. Smiling, I walked through the kitchen and into the conservatory. The coven members were starting to arrive, and the house was becoming noisy. Especially with Winston making one sound or another to greet each person who arrived. The dang house was friendly with everyone but me, it seemed.

"Hi, Fee," I said, using my father's pet name for her. It felt more natural than mother.

"Hello, Breena. This is a much easier way to talk."

I laughed. She still called me Breena. That was the name she'd given me before she'd been forced into the Inbetween, and I'd been given to my human parents a mere hours after my birth. It had been weird being called a different name at first, but it was growing on me. I would forever be Fee's Breena.

She didn't like technology that much, though to give her credit, she had been trying to adapt.

"So, Sammie will be asleep soon?" He was almost six now, but he had always loved his naps. I did *not* complain about that. Ever.

"Yes, even though he denies it." Fee laughed softly, then I heard my youngest son giggle. "He's so tired that he is being silly."

His father was the same way. When Sam got overly tired, he got punchy and silly. "He'll settle down when the movie starts. Tell him Mommy loves him and please tell Sam where I am when he wakes. Ava called a coven meeting so it might be a good idea for him to come over and give everyone an update about the nightclub if they're all still here when he wakes." It was only the afternoon, but he'd had some of my blood yesterday. He might wake early enough to come over.

"I will. Have fun."

"I'll try. Goodbye, Mom." I hadn't called her that often, sticking more to Fee.

There was a pause before she replied with a hint of tears in her voice. "I love you, daughter. Goodbye."

She hung up, and I tucked my phone back into my pocket. The conservatory door opened, and Ava stuck her head in. "There you are. Everything okay?"

Nodding, I smiled and wiped a tear from my eye. How had that gotten there? "Yeah. It just dawned on me that I'm blessed with a large extended family. We have to find Alfred." Having a member of our crew missing had me all in my feels.

"Yes," Ava agreed while grabbing my hand and pulling me into the house. "The sooner the better."

Definitely. This was an all-hands type of situation.

We entered the living room where it looked like everyone had arrived except for Sam, Wade, and Drew, who was still working with the police. Larry and Zoey carried up a couple of extra chairs Ava kept in the basement. Ben and Brandon helped them place the chairs around the living room.

Someone else knocked on the door, and Winston opened it. Sam walked in wearing a wide-brimmed SPF hat usually worn for swimming, long sleeves, and jeans. He came straight over and kissed me. "I'd just gotten up when Phira hung up with you, so I came straight over. Our son was too fixated on the movie to acknowledge me." Geez, I'd just hung up with her about a minute ago. He must've used his vampire speed to run over.

I patted him on the chest. "Get used to it. The older he gets the less he'll need us."

Sam frowned. "He's only six, don't rush it."

I hugged Sam as Ava got the meeting started. "Almost six," I whispered. "You don't rush it."

Ava clasped her hands together and looked around the room. "Thank you all for coming on such short notice. Yesterday morning, Alfred went for a walk and never returned. When I realized that he'd never come home, I did several different locating spells. Drew and I tried as a bonded magical couple. Then Luci and I tried. Nothing worked. It's like he's just gone."

Winnie sobbed from the sofa. Beth pulled her into a hug. "He wouldn't just leave."

Ava nodded. "My mom is right. If anyone has seen him, let me know, please."

Melody stood and faced the room. She was the High Witch now. Ava had been so relieved when Melody accepted the job as coven leader. It'd just been one too many things for her to juggle. "I know for a fact that in the short time, we've all known Alfred, he has touched each of us in one way or another. I propose we combine our magics and see if we can do one massive locating spell."

Winnie looked at Melody with hope in her gaze. Ava nodded, although I could tell she wasn't very hopeful. She also didn't believe Alfred was dead, I could tell that much.

Melody directed everyone outside, through the kitchen and to the backyard, which was relatively private and overlooked the ocean. "The open air and the power of the sea will guide us. Everyone, please get in a circle and hold hands."

I stood directly across from Ava in the big circle and marveled at everyone's powers as they flowed through our connected hands. I let my own magic join the stream and aid in the strength of the spell.

Melody began to chant the spell to find Alfred. Something in Latin, I was pretty sure. Their brand of magic and mine was definitely different, but hopefully, my power would assist. Streams of magic stirred around us before shooting off in different directions. I had hope that one of those streams would lead us straight to Alfred. But as we stood there and continued pushing our powers into the spell, one by one, the streams died out.

Sadness settled over everyone. It hadn't worked.

Winnie started crying again and ran inside. Ava went to follow, but Beth touched Ava's arm. "I'll go."

Once we got back inside, everyone returned to their seats. Ava sat forlornly in one of the high-back chairs. "I don't know what else to try."

"We will all be on the lookout for him," Melody said. "If anyone learns anything at all that might help find Alfred, please call me or Ava." Everyone in the room nodded and looked at us with sympathetic looks on their faces.

Winnie and Beth still hadn't returned, but John walked in and sat down with a sigh.

"While we're here and all together, I wanted to tell everyone about something unrelated. Carrie Treehill contacted me this morning to discuss building an academy for magical beings."

It wasn't totally appropriate to go over this subject right at this moment, but it was done. I raised one hand. "I think Carrie had such a great idea, especially for kids like mine who didn't know they were magical until they came into their powers," I said and added, "Plus I'm excited to take a few of the adult classes."

"Me too. I love learning new things," Melody said. "If any of you would like to teach or work at the academy, get in touch with Carrie or Olivia because she will be the headmistress of the school."

My cheeks heated. "Even though I'll be the boss lady, I'll have an executive team to help me keep it running." No way I was giving up *all* of my free time.

"I'm excited," Melody said before moving to the next big project. "Sam, do you have any updates on the vampire nightclub?"

Sam stood and waved at the room, looking kind of nervous.

"We've narrowed it down to two properties. We placed bids at both and are still waiting on a decision." Sam's eyes lit up when he talked about the nightclub. I was so happy that he was enjoying this project. "Luci is working with Jax on the architecture of the building and keeping it a secret. He said he wants everyone to be surprised at the same time."

I nodded. "He won't even tell me, and I'm his daughter."

Ava chuckled, though she sounded sad. "Because he knows you'll tell all of us."

I shrugged. Maybe. Maybe not.

13
AVA

I FELT like I'd talked to everyone in town, and I still had no clue where Alfred had gone. The Vikings hadn't taken him. I was sure of it because there was no way they could've lied under the influence of the truth stone.

No one else in Shipton would have any reason to kidnap him, so I'd ruled that out. If he'd had enemies, we would've known.

Everyone had cleared out of the house about an hour ago. Olivia had suggested using the truth stone on the coven, but I'd immediately said no. There was nobody in that coven who would hurt Alfred.

One by one, everyone in the coven had stood. They'd volunteered to let me use the stone on them. "Every person who you rule out narrows your list," Ben—or maybe Brandon—had said. I'd nearly cried at their willingness to help and eventually gave in. I went down the line, holding the truth stone, and let them all clear themselves of anything nefarious regarding Alfred.

They were all gone now, including Drew. He'd come home

and within an hour had gotten called into work. He still hadn't replaced Sam as his deputy sheriff. Sam and Olivia had gone home, Zoey and Larry were out looking in the woods again, and Mom had taken Winnie to drive around and search the outer parts of the county.

With the house quiet, I retreated to my office, but I couldn't think about being creative at the moment.

A light knock sounded on the door frame of my office, drawing my attention. My dad entered and sat in the chair to the left of my desk. "I've tried sensing him, and I can't."

"The energy in the house is off balance without him here." That was why Winston had been acting out until we'd figured out Alfred was missing. He'd been trying to tell us something was wrong. The house still wasn't settled. There was a constant vibration in every room. "Winston wants him back as much as the rest of us."

I studied my father for a long while. "You and Alfred have been working on some family tree project and spending a lot of time together. Do you have any idea at all where he would have wandered off to?"

Dad shook his head. "I can't think of anywhere. He loves it here. Loves you and especially Winnie. While you all were in town today, I did a little more digging into Alfred and who he was before he died. I didn't find much. I'm thinking about taking a trip to our family home to take a look at the old grimoires and see if there's anything in our family history."

I sat up straight in my office chair. "Oh, I'd love to go with you. Can I?" He'd mentioned our family home before, but the time hadn't been right to go for a visit.

He chuckled. "Of course, you can go. It'll be a nice father-daughter trip."

"Great. When did you want to leave?"

He looked at his phone to check the time. "Early morning might be best."

"Ugh. I don't do early mornings. What if I call Olivia to create a portal for us and we leave late morning instead?" I grinned at him, knowing he wouldn't mind. He wasn't a morning person either.

"Deal," he said as he stood and came over to kiss my forehead. "I'll see you in the morning."

THE NEXT MORNING, I was up earlier than I planned to be, but I was anxious to see if any news had come in during the night. Plus, it was exciting to go to a family home I'd never been to and possibly meet family members I'd never met.

Being the first one in the kitchen was strange. It also broke my heart because Alfred wasn't there. I made coffee and heated up a cheese Danish. By the time the coffee was finished, Mom entered the kitchen.

"How is she?" I asked, already knowing the answer. Winnie was a mess. Understandably so. If Drew went missing I'd be bat crap crazy. I just couldn't think of anything else we could do to find him except wait to see if he returned. It wasn't like he had a tracking device sewn into his clothes that we could track.

"She didn't sleep much last night. She was up making a list of places that Alfred could've gone. We're going to go through the list this morning and maybe go back out to talk to more people." Mom poured me and herself a cup of coffee.

We sat at the table. "That's good. It'll keep her busy and focused. I'm hoping this trip with Dad will help us find him or at least give us new clues. If we learn about his past, maybe it could help us now."

Olivia walked in the back door with her *good* coffee, a smile, and dressed like she was ready for Faery Court. "Morning."

I eyed Olivia, noting every royal thread of her floor-length, sea-green dress that showed just enough cleavage. The gown was almost too naughty while being elegant at the same time. Her golden hair was pinned up in a beautiful bun that was circled by a braid. Spiral curls framed her face.

Looking closer, I noticed a tiara with diamonds and emeralds in it.

Phira entered the kitchen behind her in a light blue gown in a similar style as Olivia's. Phira also wore her hair up and her tiara was bigger, with diamonds and sapphires.

When they stood side by side like they were at the moment, it was obvious they were mother and daughter.

Olivia handed me a blue crystal. "I'll create the portal to get you to your destination, but I'll be in Faery when you guys want to come home, so Mom helped me enchant that crystal to bring you back. Just think of Winston and a portal will open, bring you back home."

"Oh cool, thanks." I examined the gemstone.

Phira said, "It only works one time."

I nodded. "You two look great."

Olivia patted her hair and grinned. "I am a princess, after all."

She waved her hands up and down her body as if showcasing her new look. "Part-time, but it counts." She was considered royalty in Faerie. Good thing she had us here on Earth to keep her grounded.

My dad entered the kitchen and did a double take at Olivia. "I almost didn't recognize you, Olivia."

"Today, I'm Princess Olivia." She laughed, then asked, "Are you ready?"

Sipping as much of my hot coffee as I could stand within a few seconds, I got up and stood next to my dad as Olivia opened the portal. I'd sent her the address last night before bed, so she'd be prepared to portal us someplace new.

The portal opened in a dusty living room that was seriously outdated. The floors were ceramic titles that looked like stone. The walls were dark gray, also like stone. It was very castle-like, dark, and old. And very dusty.

"Where are we?" I asked.

Dad walked forward to a bookshelf that took up the opposite wall from the massive fireplace. "Tucked away in the hills of West Virginia. The house and property are hidden from public view."

He scanned the shelves, a little lost in his memories, then snapped out of it a bit and waved for me to follow him. We left the living-room-library and entered a long hallway that reminded me of the caverns under my house. As we passed a large window, I stopped and gaped at the gorgeous view of the mountains. The November weather had turned the leaves on the trees every shade of red, orange, gold, and yellow. It was like being in the middle of a fire. Absolutely gorgeous. Maine was spectacular in the autumn, but the Appalachian mountains were something else entirely.

"It's a beautiful view," Dad said, stopping beside me.

"That's an understatement."

"Come on." He touched my arm and I hesitated for just another moment. Before following him further down the hallway, I snapped a picture of the view with my phone. Drew would love this, having grown up in North Carolina.

Tucking my phone back in my pocket, I rushed down the hall. I found Dad in a huge library. The room we'd started in was definitely the living room. Now, this was a library. Row after row of shelves filled the room, and each wall was lined floor to very high ceiling with them. The windows had ancient velvet curtains partially shut over them, and there was a fireplace to the right, but every other square inch of wall was devoted to books.

Dad had pulled out a few old, thick books and set them on one of the long tables at the front of the room. I came over and sat in a chair and opened one of the books. It was a grimoire. And ancient. "Dad, how can we just be here?"

"It's our birthright. This home has been in our family for hundreds of years. Probably built right after Alfred, really. I'd need to research a bit more for details. When I was young and stupid, I didn't care. Now I do."

I traced the runes in the margins of the title page, feeling a spark of magic left behind by the witch or necromancer who'd owned it.

"So, is this place a house or a castle?"

Dad laughed. "Eh, that's always been a bit of an argument in the family. Potayto-Potahto."

I smiled and carefully turned the pages of the grimoire. "I'm calling it a castle."

A sound echoed down the hall behind us that made us freeze and lock gazes. "Does someone live here?"

Dad shook his head. "No. Not for years. It's been magically sealed, which is why it's not crumbling around us. It's probably the heat kicking on."

I frowned. "Why would the heat be on if no one lives here?"

Dad looked at me and stared for a few moments, then blinked rapidly. "Good question."

Another noise sounded. This one was closer. "Is this a magical house? Like Winston?"

"No..." He drifted off and straightened to his full height just as an elderly man entered the library.

The man looked familiar like I'd seen him in family photos or something.

Dad stared at him with his mouth open before saying, "You're dead."

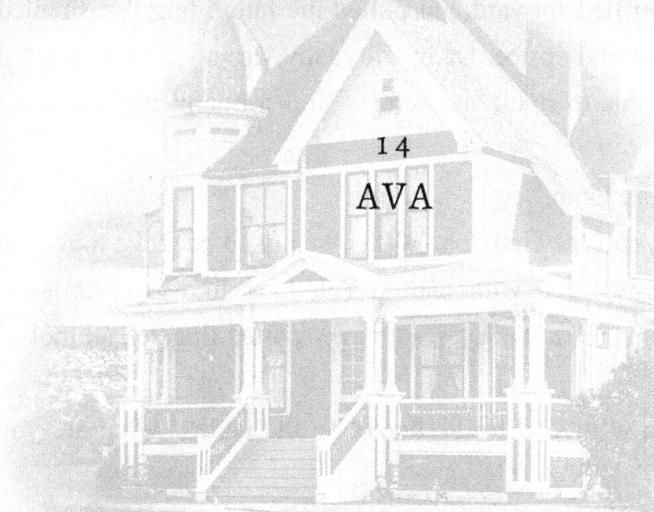

14

AVA

Amusement flirted with the man's expression, "Last I checked, I'm very much dead." He was a ghost. I hadn't even realized it. He was very strong.

Dad shook his head and raced over to the elderly man. They embraced one another for a few long seconds before Dad pulled back. "I never knew you hadn't moved on. He laughed, then hugged the man again.

"I couldn't leave this old house. And your grandmother is here. She's not as strong as I am and can't cross over as often." He looked sad. "She'll be upset she missed you. Also, when I passed, your father was still here. I wanted to keep an eye on him." The man turned to me. "Who do we have here?"

Dad moved to stand next to me. He placed a hand on my back. "This is Ava, my daughter. Ava, this is your great-grandfather, Lynn Howe."

Oh. Oh, wow. I'd never imagined I'd get to meet a member of

Dad's family, ghost or not. He hated talking about his family, so I didn't know much about them.

Lynn shuffled forward and pulled me into a hug. He smelled like ointment and coffee. Dang. He really was a strong ghost. I'd never been able to smell one before. "It is a true pleasure to meet you, Ava."

"And you, Lynn."

"Please, call me Grandpa." When he pulled back, he looked at me with eyes filled with tears. "You look like my late wife, Mary." He swiped at his eyes with age-spotted fingers and looked past me.

Grandpa motioned to the books on the table. "What are you looking for?"

Moving out of the way, I explained. "I lost one of my ghouls. Alfred is related to us, from way back. He was a Viking shaman and powerful necromancer." I glanced at Dad, then back to Grandpa, noting the similarities. The same dark hair, green eyes—like mine—and the same facial bone structure.

"Alfred…Oh yes." Grandpa pointed to a book on a low shelf nearby. I walked over to grab it. As soon as I opened it, I gasped. The first page had a picture, well, a painting, of Alfred when he was alive. It was definitely him. "Can I take this home with me?"

I wanted to read every page and share it with Alfred when we got him back.

Grandpa nodded. "Of course. This home is yours as much as it is mine."

That was a nice feeling. I'd always felt a sense of passing time and ancestry in Winston, but this castle was something else. I wanted to dive in and not come up for months. My life would never allow that. "Thank you."

"No need to thank me. Come. There should be tea in the kitchen you can still use. The spell on the property would have kept it fresh." He left and Dad and I followed him through a winding hallway. "Dad." I tugged on his shirt and let Grandpa get ahead of us. "Why did I know nothing of this place? I mean, I know you were imprisoned, but Mom should've told me."

"I never told her," he said sadly, then held open a giant and heavy wooden door. We went down several stairs, coming out in a gigantic kitchen. I could just imagine it bustling with women in dresses and aprons, cooking over the fire and on the old stove that took up half of one wall.

I wasn't done asking him questions. "Why didn't you tell her?" Grandpa could hear us now.

He looked at us sharply. "Because his father, my son, was pure evil, dear Ava. He was the worst of us."

Dad nodded grimly. "I left when I was sixteen or so. Right after Grandpa died." He swallowed. "Grandpa died protecting me from my father."

"What happened to him?" I asked. "My evil grandfather?"

"The hunters finally got him. He'd gone to a coven meeting and the hunters took them all out. They weren't a good coven." Grandpa pulled out a metal teapot and put it on the ancient stove. I waved my hand and a merry fire flared up. I was just thankful my powers had consented to do it for me without giving me crap.

"The hunters?" I gave Dad a significant look. "Drew couldn't have known, or he would've said. When did this happen?"

"I didn't even know they'd gotten him," Dad said. "I checked on the house as sneakily as I could once I was freed and discovered his grave in our family graveyard. The house had been spelled against the sands of time, so I left it until there was a good time for us to all come together. I told your mother everything once I knew he was dead and you two were safe from him. I want to bring your mother here as well, and show her where I grew up, however difficult that childhood was."

We sat around a kitchen nook that overlooked a courtyard that was a little overgrown. "Ava, how is Alfred alive?" Grandpa asked.

"He's a ghoul, not technically alive. Another necromancer originally animated him." I turned to my dad. "Did you know Bill Combs?"

Dad nodded so I continued. "Bill was a family friend. Anyway, he found and raised Alfred. When Bill was killed by another necromancer who hunted our own kind, Bill's wife gave Alfred to me since I was the only necromancer she knew."

I'd been so freaked out by the idea of taking care of a ghoul. I hadn't known how to care for one.

"Ava had six ghouls tied to her at one point," Dad said, bringing me out of my thoughts.

Grandpa eyed me like he wanted to bow to me. He'd better not. "Yes, we thought they were draining me, so Dad helped me transfer them to their own power source to keep them animated."

"The impressive thing was none of them were draining her. I've never seen a necromancer with so much power." Dad's words, so full of pride, made me blush. I'd never been the center of attention type of girl. That was Olivia. At least it had been when we were in school.

She still liked the attention. It was less annoying now that we were friends. "Well, I am a half-witch. The last witch of the bloodline on my mom's side." I paused, then smiled. "Not for long. My son and his girlfriend are having a girl."

"Congratulations," Grandpa said. "My great-great-grandchild."

"Thank you."

Dad said, "Ava can heal others. It seems to be tied to her necromancer powers because she can fully flesh out a skeleton."

"That is impressive and a rare gift. It only manifests once in a very long while." Grandpa looked at me, maybe a bit awestruck, then rose. "I have something to show you in the library."

Fifteen minutes later we sat around one of the tables with a large piece of thick paper. On it was an extensive family tree, going back to the age of the Vikings.

I took a video of the complete family tree with my phone, then pictures with flash, trying to get every inch in great detail so it would be clear and crisp. I'd have Wallie help me take the images and piece them together to print a copy. The paper was far too long for a single image.

Grandpa tapped one of the names on the tree, toward the bottom. "My grandmother was also a healer. Like you, she was very powerful. Every few generations one of our family is born with more powers than the others. Miraculous powers like healing and controlling the elements." Grandpa looked at me with such praise and pride for me.

"Elements? Like lightning?"

"Is that your gift?" he asked.

"I wouldn't call it a gift. It has a mind of its own." It had saved my butt more than once, though. I couldn't exactly dislike having it. Nor did I love it, though.

He gave me a sympathetic look. "My wife's grandmother had the ability to control fire. It took her a while to learn to control it because she tried to ignore it."

Got it. Don't ignore the electricity powers. I hadn't planned on it. I want to learn how to use them without hurting my friends and family. "Lucifer and I are going to work on controlling the power."

I've just been busy getting married, on my honeymoon in Scotland, and fighting a giant tentacle monster that almost killed me. Now Alfred was missing.

Just then my phone chimed. I glanced to see a text from Wallie.

Mom, Winston is freaking out. It's bad.

Shoot. I showed the message to Dad and stood. "I'm so sorry to run out, my magical house is having a fit and everyone thinks I can calm him."

Grandpa drew me into a hug. "You are always welcome to come back anytime, especially if you're willing to explain the magical house and a person named Lucifer."

"I will definitely be back. I'll bring my husband to meet you. Drew would love you." I pulled out the crystal Olivia had given me and held out my hand to Dad. When he took it, I thought of home and that was all it took. We materialized in the living room.

The whole house was shaking. The cabinet doors were opening and shutting with gigantic slams. The lights flickered, and it sounded like the tiles were falling off of the roof.

"Winston, stop!" I yelled at the top of my voice.

He settled down, but only a little.

Just then Olivia entered the backdoor with Sammie in tow. "I heard your house freaking out all the way over at Luci's."

"Yeah, I don't know what's wrong with him." I looked up. "Winston, please find a way to talk to us." Maybe if we put up a chalkboard or something.

Sammie walked over to Winnie and asked, "Why are you crying?"

"I'm upset because I miss Alfred and wish we could find him." Winnie sniffed, then she blew her nose.

"I know where Alfred is," Sammie said.

Everyone stopped talking and Winston went silent. The complete absence of noise was almost as shocking as what Sammie had just said.

Olivia glanced at me, then asked, "You do? Why didn't you tell us?"

"Sure." He shrugged. "Nobody asked me."

15
AVA

Sammie scrunched his nose. "Yeah, he's in that cave that you guys took me to that time. The one that has all the power inside it."

Everyone looked at Olivia, and she shrugged. "We went out for a walk one day, and we were near the cave, so I showed it to him. That was weeks ago."

Wallie and Michelle came down the stairs. Wallie asked, "What happened that got Winston to stop freaking out?"

"Sammie says Alfred is in the chasm cave," I said, nodding toward the little boy.

Luci opened a portal to the beach, right at the cave's entrance. "Then let's go bring him home."

He didn't have to tell me twice. I ran through the portal, and my whole family, except for Sam and Wade, who were asleep, followed behind me.

We went inside the cave and gathered around the chasm that held the large crystal, a power source in itself. Dad and I had a theory that the crystal was being powered by the ley lines that ran directly under it.

Sammie pointed at the chasm. “He’s in there.”

In the chasm? How was that possible?

Olivia and I inched forward with Winnie clinging to me. I had to put my arm in front of her so she wouldn’t jump in looking for Alfred. I leaned over and whispered, “Alfred?”

The chasm made a deep rumbling sound, then the cave began to shake and bounce. Small rocks rained down as the chasm grew and grew until it was more than big enough for any of us to fall in. Out of the corner of my eye, I spotted my parents grabbing Sammie as he attempted to run forward.

With another giant shake, an unconscious Alfred floated up and out of the enlarged chasm, making Olivia and me jump back a few feet out of the way.

Alfred floated to the ground slowly as if the magic from the chasm was gently laying him down. We stared down at him, each of us shocked beyond belief, then I knelt and pushed healing power into him. As hard as I tried, nothing happened. There was nothing to be healed.

Luci crouched and hovered a hand down the length of Alfred’s body, made a face, then stood. “There is nothing wrong with him. He’s not injured. In fact, he’s human.”

“What?” I stared at Alfred, shock radiating through my body. “Human? How could he be human?”

Winnie threw herself on top of her love. “Why isn’t he awake? What’s wrong with him?”

“He seems to simply be asleep. I’m guessing, though, because this is new to me,” Luci said. “I’ve never seen anything like it. Presumably, the chasm changed him.”

I didn't know what to say about that. This was insane, strange even for me, and I lived in a world of the impossible.

The chasm released a burst of power. It reverberated throughout the cavern with a sound like tiny bells ringing at once. Magic blew out in all directions, hitting all of us. We never had a chance to get out of the way. It happened too fast. When the magic settled, I felt renewed, refreshed, and recharged. I looked around to find everyone looking shocked. Mom was looking at her hands and arms like she was afraid they'd look different or something.

"Is everyone okay?" I asked.

Everyone nodded and Drew muttered, "I feel great. Like a new man."

Okay. That was enough. I was *done* with the weird for tonight. Finished. Finito. "Let's go back to the house."

Olivia used magic to carry Alfred back to the house through the portal outside the cave entrance. Winnie rushed along with him, clasping his hand. "Take him to our room."

I was about to go upstairs with them when Luci caught my attention. He stood very still in the middle of the kitchen with his head cocked, listening to devil things only he could hear. He disappeared, then before I could open my mouth to ask if anyone had any idea where he'd gone, he rematerialized a second later. "I have a lead on Penny," he said, then added in a small voice, "Also I'm locked out of Hell."

See what's next for Ava in A Fiendish Midlife or read the series in one swoop in Witching After Forty Volume One and Witching After Forty Volume Two.

A NORMAL MIDLIFE

WITCHING AFTER FORTY BOOK 17

L.A. BORUFF

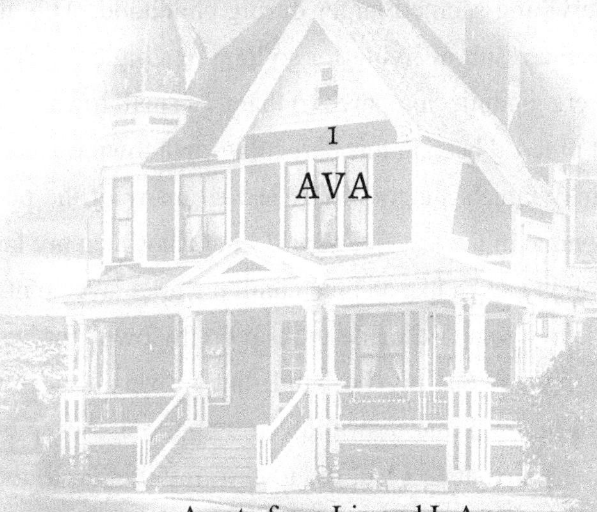

1
AVA

A note from Lia and L.A.:
The beginning will feel very familiar. Stick with it because not everything is as it seems. Welcome to Ava's *Normal* Midlife.
Much love, Lia and LA.

After nine hours on the road with only one short bathroom break, I'd seen enough of the inside of my car to last me a long time. Not to mention driving alone was making me talk to myself, and I wasn't that funny.

Getting out of my Hyundai, I flung the door shut and frowned. Disappointment rolled over me at the sound of the car door clicking shut. Not at all like the sound older cars made when their doors slammed.

With my hands on my lower back, I stretched and scanned the grocery store parking lot. There were exactly three cars, and the building was much, much smaller than I remembered. That was how things were when remembered from the perspective of youth, though. Everything seemed larger during childhood. Although, it could've been a result of living for so long in a big city where the buildings were gigantic compared to that of a small town.

The last time I'd been in this particular small town was last year for my Aunt Winnie's funeral. Why had so many of the people I loved died on me in the last five years? First Clay, then my favorite Aunt—two didn't seem like so much until the grief layered in.

With a heavy soul, I'd made the trip on my own then, too. I'd hated traveling without my husband, but he was gone now. A lump formed in my throat. I swallowed it and took a deep breath. It'd been five years since I lost the love of my life. Well, the first love of my life. The second had left me several weeks ago for a dorm, parties, and medical books.

Thinking of the little devil, I pulled out my phone and sent my college-age son a text. Wallie had insisted I message him the moment I arrived in Shipton Harbor. Nothing like having an over-protective son watching over me. Even if he was watching from Harvard University.

Me: I made it alive. I think. Unless I died and my ghost drove the rest of the way.

Wallie: Your ghost can text? That's impressive. Will you haunt Aunt Winnie's house for the rest of eternity?

Me: That's the plan.

Wallie: Cool. I'll make sure to visit on holidays. If med school kills me, I'll be moving in.

I laughed and replied: Oh, no way. You find your own house to haunt.

Wallie: LOL. Love you.

Me: Love you too. I'll call you later.

After locking the screen on my cell, I slipped it into my pocket and took another cleansing breath. The fresh scent of the ocean filled me. That was when I noticed the crisp, cool air that had wrapped around me like an old friend. I never used to like the cold, but for the last couple of years, I'd craved it. Hello, early hot flashes.

With a sigh, I headed inside the store, wishing Clay were walking beside me. I grabbed the cart while I organized my grocery list in my mind, just as we'd done once a week, every week, during our twenty years of marriage. Another ache formed in my chest, tightening it. I closed my eyes briefly and pushed the loneliness away. Clay would've killed me if he knew I was still grieving him this strongly. We'd promised each other long ago that if one survived the other, we wouldn't mourn. We'd find the strength to move on and learn to live again.

I'd only agreed to the crazy pact because I'd genuinely believed we'd die within months of each other at the ripe old age of one hundred and two. It'd never occurred to me we'd part ways at thirty-eight.

Still, a promise was a promise, and I'd try to keep it. That was why I'd returned to Shipton Harbor, to fix up the old house and put it on the market—hopefully, a quick sale. Then, I could go back home and decide what to do from there.

Here I was in Shipton, but before I went to my family home, I needed a few things. The house was devoid of all foodstuffs, so I had to get enough to tide me over until I figured out how long I'd be in town, which depended on how much work the old Victorian needed. There was no telling what sort of condition it would be in. After all, it'd been empty for a year.

As I grabbed a buggy and headed around the produce department, picking up enough of my favorites for a couple of days, for the hundredth time I wished Aunt Winnie had left me enough money with the house to have a caretaker oversee the property. Instead, it had been boarded up for a year.

Looking at the apples, I fought my sadness. It could've been a lot worse. At least I still had my baby, Wallie. I focused on the mission—sell the house and make enough money to get back to what was left of my life. To the home my son grew up in. To Philadelphia.

That didn't mean it would be easy to sell the home that had been in my family for a couple of hundred years. If I was correct, the house had been built before the town even officially became a town. I'd never paid too much attention to the history of it or anything. Maybe I should've.

"Ava?"

The sound of the familiar voice of one of my best friends made me smile as I turned. "Snooze."

I laughed at the face he made right before pulling me into a tight hug. Being wrapped in his arms felt weird because he'd never been a hugger, not really. At least he hadn't been in high school.

He also pretended to dislike the nickname our best friend Sam and I had blessed him with, way back in the day. We'd started calling him Snooze because he'd slept through most of our classes, and his real name was Winston Snoozerton.

His name echoed in my mind. "Snoozerton. Why does that sound so familiar?" I muttered more to myself than him. It was like there was something that had happened very recently to make that name important, but what?

By the raised brow Snooze gave me, he heard me. "Um, because it's my name. Are you feeling okay?"

"I'm fine." As soon as those words left my mouth, I wasn't so sure I believed them. "I meant that I heard it recently, but it wasn't you." I waved a hand and pretended that I wasn't losing my mind. "It was probably on the radio on the drive over. Road fatigue."

He gave me a tight-lipped smile while watching me like I was about to crack at any moment. "Probably, but you know you can call me if you need to talk."

"I will." I pulled him into another hug before turning to my buggy. "I have a long night of cleaning ahead of me." I finger-waved as I walked away. "Talk to you later." Something about seeing Snooze made me uncomfortable. Meh. I didn't want to talk about Clay or selling the house. Snooze would very likely give me a lot of crap about letting go of the home I grew up in. Heck, he, Sam, and I had been in the attic and backyard more than anywhere else growing up.

I sped around the store after that, snatching anything I could think of that I'd need for the next twenty-four hours or so. If I didn't remember it now, I'd figure out how to live without it. Five minutes later, I lugged four bags to the car, leaving the buggy at the corral. I'd rather rip my arms off than make two trips.

"Ian, Drew! I got him." A woman with long black hair pulled into a ponytail yelled from across the parking lot. She was athletic and gorgeous in tight pants and a leather jacket. I could only assume she wore a shirt underneath the jacket because I couldn't see it from where I stood, blocking the front door of the grocery store.

She was chasing a guy that looked like he could be the stunt double for Alan Rickman.

All-righty then. I stepped forward, shaking off the weird chase scene I'd just watched, as two guys careened around the corner of the store, coming in fast.

Uh-oh. Too fast. Their facial features were similar, so brothers? Perhaps this was the aforementioned Ian and Drew. The younger-looking with a smaller build darted to his left to go around me. The older, beefier one, had dark hair streaked with silver. He darted left, but then corrected right.

He was about to plow right into me but noticed just in time. He slowed and reached out with his left hand, grabbed my hip, and time slowed. We locked gazes, and I hitched a breath as I stared into his eyes. A bone-deep knowing filled me before an image of the silver fox and me locked at the lips formed in my mind.

Drew. He was Drew. He flat didn't look like an Ian.

What made a man *not* look like an Ian?

Not a clue.

The vision disappeared, taking Drew with it. Well, Drew didn't disappear, but he was already across the parking lot with Ian and the woman who looked like she stepped out of an urban fantasy novel.

Shaking my head, I walked to my car. What in the devil rides at midnight had just happened? Hmph. It'd been a driving-fatigue delusion. Had to be. That crazy stuff didn't happen to me. That was the sort of thing the kids videoed and put on social media.

The drive to the house only took about fifteen minutes, and I did my best to put the strangeness out of my mind as I drove. Shipton Harbor was a small town, but the house wasn't *in* the town. It was on a cliff overlooking the ocean on the outer edges of the city limits.

At the moment, the ocean was calm with medium-ish waves breaking. The scent of saltwater, sand, and sunshine swirled around me, welcoming me home. This was the only thing I'd missed about Shipton Harbor. Well, that and Winnie.

Maybe Sam and Snooze, a bit.

The beautiful, old, gothic Victorian stood tall against the blue sky with puffy white clouds. With the lights off—not because the electricity was cut off, but because no one was there—it looked sad and, well, dark. I stood beside my car and stared at the home I grew up in. So many emotions churned inside me. A voice from deep inside my mind said to keep the old place and start a new life.

I wasn't sure I wanted to start over. I was forty-three, for crying out loud. Where would I even begin? Things were done now. I could live simply, retire, and enjoy eventual grandchildren. That would be plenty.

Bracing myself, I grabbed my grocery bags and fished the house key out of my pocket. This was the big moment. Time to find out how bad the house was inside. It'd been empty for the last year, since right after Aunt Winnie's funeral. I'd only had the power and water turned on a few days ago, so at least I'd have that. Probably.

My phone jingled my son's text tone in my pocket. My baby was keeping tabs on me. I couldn't help but smile. He'd come to Shipton Harbor with me and cleaned out the house last year. The perishables, anyway. It'd been hard on both of us, him helping me in place of his father. He'd risen to the occasion. Wallie was a great kid. Now that he was settled in at college, I had no reason not to take care of this and get the house sold.

I'd been putting it off for too long, dreading the flood of emotions I was sure would overwhelm me at any moment.

On the other hand, those emotions could've been waiting to catch me off guard. Hit me when I wasn't expecting them. I needed to keep an eye on them. Keep them locked down tight.

The door creaked as if it was making the only sound the house had heard since the last time I closed it, or was it a sad kind of greeting? A cry for help? I couldn't tell.

I suppressed a shiver as I entered the open first floor. Everything was exactly as I'd left it. Furniture covered in sheets, boards on the windows, the whole shebang. The air was stale and smelled of dust.

Hurrying to the kitchen, I put the grocery bags on the dusty white tablecloth-covered kitchen table and flicked on the light. To my relief, it came on. It'd be dark in a few short hours, and the last thing I wanted was no power. That saved me a phone call to the electric company. They were lucky.

I opened the fridge and sniffed, then groaned while covering my nose. I'd scrubbed it before leaving it, but it had still developed a smell. At least it was still clean, but I had to get rid of the smell.

Smart grocery store me had thought of this. I'd picked up some baking soda.

Unpacking my bags, I opened one of the boxes of baking soda and put it in the corner to start absorbing the smells. The freezer was next. I slid the second box in and remembered I'd forgotten to buy a bag of ice. This old fridge didn't have an ice maker, so I was SOL for my Diet Cola for a while.

On that thought, I studied the fridge straight out of the seventies. Perhaps older? Shoot, I didn't remember when my grandmother had bought this thing. Long before she died, and that was when I was nineteen.

I might have to replace this dinosaur to put the house on the market. I'd know for sure when the realtor came by. For now, I'd get the place ready for visitors.

Grabbing a towel out of the cabinet where they'd been all my life, I smelled it. It still had a faint scent of the homemade detergent Auntie used. She'd scented it with dried roses. Smiling, I dampened it and wiped out the cabinet my Yaya and Aunt Winnie had always used for dry goods, then put away the rest of the food.

The women in my family were a little New Age.

With the kitchen settled, for the time being, I went out to the car to unload my suitcases. When I came inside, I dropped the suitcases next to the stairs, then scanned the living room. The boards needed to come down, but I wouldn't be able to do that myself. I'd deal with that later. Maybe call Snooze and Sam to come over to help.

That sounded like a great plan. It'd been too long since the three of us had been together, anyway.

Picking up my computer bag, I took it to the downstairs master bedroom that had long ago been converted into an office. About halfway there, a white blur leaped at me from the stairs like some humongous furry bat. I screamed but managed to catch the beast in both hands.

"Excuse me Miss Lucy-Fur, you can't jump out at me like that. I'm old and could have a heart attack." I adjusted the beautiful, long-haired white cat in my arms to keep from dropping her.

She meowed at me in rapid bursts like she'd missed me or was blessing me out for staying gone for so long.

"Lucy, you can retract the claws." I bent over and lowered the monster diva to the ground. She looked at me and let out several more meows. "I hear ya', Lucy."

Well, crap on a cracker. I didn't buy cat food. Turning to the kitchen, I wondered where the grumpy feline had been. Wallie and I had searched all over for Lucy last year with nothing to show for it. That crazy cat hadn't wanted to be found. It was a good thing she was resourceful. She'd probably hit up a few neighbors for food when and if she couldn't hunt.

I opened the cabinet with the canned food and pulled out the tuna while pulling out my phone to make a grocery list. She was a special kitty and would only eat the most expensive food on the market, no thanks to Winnie for spoiling her.

Lucy purred loudly and rubbed against my legs. After draining the water from the tuna can, I emptied the contents onto a plate and lowered it to the ground. "Eat up, Miss Lucy."

My thanks were the growl-like sounds she made when she ate something she loved. It was a good thing I'd picked up tuna for myself. I laughed at the cat and left her to her meal. "I'm heading to the office."

As I walked past the front door, someone pounded on it loud enough to wake the dead in the next town over. Geesh. I cursed after I collected my heart off the floor and put it back in my chest. I might've screamed a little.

Marching over to the door, I jerked it open, about to bless out whoever was trying to break down the door but stopped short when I found my best friend standing on the other side. His brown hair was its usual unruly mess, which looked amazing on him. Dark blue eyes sparkled as he smiled at me.

As I took in his sheriff's uniform, I burst out laughing. "You didn't need to knock like you had a warrant for my arrest."

Sam Thompson, my best friend since the first grade, chuckled. "How do you know I don't?"

"I know. I've been too depressed to get into trouble." I meant it to be funny, but it came out pathetic.

Shaking his head, Sam's smile fell, and he stepped closer like he was going to hug me. I stepped back. I couldn't. I'd finally got my emotions under wraps. If I hugged him, the floodgates would open up. Instead, I held out my hand. "It's great seeing you again."

He took another step, forcing me backward.

"Sam, don't you dare."

He leaped forward, grabbed my arm, and pulled me into him, hugging me tight. The feel of his arms around me brought on the waterworks.

Sam was a great hugger. So had Clay been. I gripped his shirt and buried my face into the center of his chest. "Jerk."

"It's good to have you home." The door clicked shut.

Home. Was I home? There was a nagging feeling that I was missing something. Then there was the guy in the grocery store parking lot, Drew. There was definitely a connection there, and I'd never even *seen* him before.

Whatever that had been, and despite the tears, it was so good to see Sam. He really did feel like home.

Lucy-Fur

This situation was maddening on a whole new level. At first, I'd been confused about where I was because this house wasn't the same Winston I normally lived in. It'd been boarded up. I wasn't even sure how I would have gotten out if I was actually here for the year it was empty. How did I know that it had been empty for a year?

I don't know.

That witch cursed us all and now we're stuck in this normal world. Ava doesn't even have a clue.

"*Ava. Snap out of*—meow, meow, meow." Damn it all, I wasn't a talking cat in this messed-up dream. I was just a cat! "*Ava, you have to*—meow, meow, meow." Someone knocked on the door, and that guy Ava knew walked in.

"Oh, good, Sam—meow, meow, meow." Even he couldn't understand meow. Meow, meow, meowmeowmeow.

Meow.

Meow.

2
OLIVIA

THE GIANT DOOR CREAKED OPEN, and a shiver ran down my spine as I stared at the dark path made of black stone. We were walking into Hell, actual Hell, to face an unknown evil. My nerves jangled, and I tried to swallow the lump in my throat.

"Are we ready for this?" Phira asked, her voice trembling slightly.

I looked at her, then at Sam, and finally at my friends. Each one had a determined expression on their face. We were in this together.

"Stay close," Luci warned, his eyes scanning the darkness ahead. "We don't know what's waiting for us."

"Is it always this dark here?" Lily whispered, crowding behind me as we ventured deeper into Hell.

"Sometimes," Luci answered quietly. "There's a strange heaviness in the air that wasn't here before."

As we continued along the dark path, I couldn't shake the feeling that something was watching us, waiting to strike. The anticipation gnawed at me, making me more determined to uncover whatever secrets lay ahead.

Around a bend, a figure cloaked in black robes stood off to the side of the path. They almost blended in with the shadows, but their pale faces and bright blue eyes caught my attention like a beacon in the darkness. My heart raced as I tried to decipher if they were friend or foe.

"Luci," I whispered, trying not to draw attention to the mysterious figure. "Do you see that person over there?"

His gaze followed mine, and I could sense the tension building within him. "I do," he said cautiously. "Stay close."

"Who are they?" Phira's voice trembled, betraying her fear.

"Unknown," Luci replied. "But we need to be prepared for anything."

As we approached the figure, I braced myself for a confrontation. Instead, the robed figure stared at us, an eerie calmness in their bright blue eyes.

We stepped forward, and the figure moved onto the path and pulled her hood back. A woman, an old woman who looked like evil incarnate. Geez. The look in her eyes was chilling. Fear gripped my heart, but I had to be strong for my friends.

"Leave now," she hissed, her voice barely above a whisper. "This isn't your fight."

"Who are you?" I demanded, my voice shaking with anger and fear.

"Leave," the witch repeated, her word dripping with menace.

Luci stepped forward, his power radiating from him like a force field. "We're not going anywhere until we find our friends," he declared, defiance in his voice. "And if you stand in our way, you'll regret it."

"Very well," she said coldly. "You've sealed your fate."

"Olivia, watch out!" Phira shouted in time for me to turn my head as Luci's hands glowed with a blinding light, and before I could react, he blasted power toward us. The impact of the blast was jarring, sending us hurtling through the air as our surroundings changed rapidly. I screamed, desperate to help my friends and Luci.

As we flew back, unable to stop the torrent of magic sending us wherever Luci had wanted us to go, the witch struck Luci with a bolt of magic like a thousand daggers. His anguished cry echoed in my ears. I watched in horror through the rapidly closing portal as the life drained from his eyes, his body convulsed, and then fell limp. The pain and terror were palpable, a cold shiver running down my spine. Behind him, everyone else fell to the floor. It was like they were put under a sleep spell, but not Luci. The magic that hit him was different.

"Luci!" I screamed, reaching out for him but finding only emptiness as the portal closed behind us. My heart ached with grief and determination. The last image I saw was his lifeless body crumpling to the ground before everything went black. His eyes had been absolutely devoid of any life. He was dead.

I woke up on a soft bed in an unfamiliar room. The walls of the unfamiliar room seemed to close in on me, their rough texture a stark contrast to the smooth black stone of Hell. Soft shafts of sunlight filtered through the windows, casting eerie shadows across the floor. The décor wasn't anything I'd pick out for myself, although it was beautiful. Soft shades of blue and gold accented midnight blue walls. I shivered from the magic coursing through me, and tears fell unchecked as the memory of Luci's death flooded back. I blinked them away, determined not to let grief consume me. There wasn't time. I needed to save my friends. Thank goodness I'd sent Sammie to my adoptive parents before we'd gone to Hell. However, my beloved Sam was under a spell in hell. At least, I hoped that was all that b—witch had done to them.

Movement next to me startled me. Looking down, I smiled sadly at my sleeping bio-mom. I considered leaving her to sleep because she was going to be devastated when she woke. Luci was the love of her life.

Placing a hand on Phira's shoulder, I gently shook her. "Fee. Wake up." She didn't respond so I said, "Mom." It was the first time I'd said it out loud, but she was asleep, so it didn't count.

Her eyes fluttered open, her tear-streaked cheeks glistening in the dim light. "Olivia," she choked out, her voicc barely audible. "Is he...?" She sat up on the bed beside me, then gasped and covered her face. "My Luci." When I touched her arm, she threw herself toward me and sobbed into my shoulder. I held her tight, trying to offer solace even as my heart shattered.

"I know." I swallowed the lump in my throat and fought off the sobs threatening to take over. "Luci would want us to avenge his death and save our friends." I didn't know what else to say other than I hoped this whole nightmare wasn't real. That I hadn't just lost my father right when we'd started to become a family.

My aunts, Scorpia, Evie, and Octavia walked into the room, their faces etched with concern. That explained where we were. Each one radiated a unique aura—Scorpia's strong presence, Evie's gentle grace, and Octavia's fierce determination.

Phira cried harder with her sisters here. Even though they'd always included me, I still felt like an outsider. I might be a little envious of their love for one another. I never had sisters.

"Olivia, what happened?" Evie asked softly, her eyes full of worry.

I recounted the events leading up to Luci's death and how he'd expelled us from Hell to Faerie. My voice shook with emotion, but I forced myself to continue, knowing that we needed their help. “Luci died saving us. I think all of my friends are under some kind of spell. I need to get to Hell and find them.”

I paced the length of the room at the foot of the bed. My mother and aunts got quiet. I glanced at them. “What?”

“Your power,” Evie said.

“It’s different,” Octavia said.

Scorpia nodded. “A lot.”

I looked at myself while searching within to measure my magic. Sure enough, I was packing a lot of power. Hell power.

I locked gazes with Phira as she said, “Luci gave you his magic.”

"I have to go," I whispered after moving Phira into Evie's arms. "You'll take care of her?"

"Of course," Evie said with a sad smile. "Leave her to us."

I had Hell magic, which meant I could get into Hell. Closing my eyes, I called on the magic and focused on getting into Hell. I’d been there a few times without Luci’s power, so it shouldn't be hard to do.

Nothing happened. Determined to avenge Luci's death, I tried again to get to Hell, but no matter how hard I focused, I couldn't open a portal. My frustration grew with each failed attempt, making me feel more and more helpless.

It didn't help that this magic coursed through me, a power so raw and fierce I didn't dare try to harness it. If I did... I couldn't be sure it wouldn't burn me up instead.

“I can’t get in." I looked at my aunts and mother on the bed. "The witch must still be blocking it somehow.”

"Maybe you should try getting to Earth instead," Scorpia suggested. "You're used to making portals back and forth from there."

Good idea. I focused on home and tried teleporting. Nothing. Dang it. I tried creating a portal. My heart leaped when one started to form, then all hope died when it fizzed out. Double dang it.

I tried again and again, but still, the portal wouldn't form. Desperation clawed at me. I was losing control.

As panic threatened to overwhelm me, Octavia handed me a cup of calming tea.

I took deep breaths, and sipped the warm liquid, letting it soothe my body and mind. “I need to get home to my kids and figure out how to save my husband and friends. I'll save them," I vowed, my voice steady and strong despite the turmoil inside me. "And I'll make the witch pay."

With determination burning in my heart, I wouldn't rest until my friends were safe and Luci's death was avenged.

3
AVA

The renovations on the house were going so smoothly that I kept waiting for the other shoe to drop. I'd expected there to be at least one thing to go wrong. The contractor said the old house was in better shape than he'd initially thought. When did that ever happen?

I stood in the middle of my living room, surveying the progress of the renovations. The air smelled of sawdust and paint, and I couldn't help but smile. It'd only been three days and already so much had been done. At this rate, I could get it on the market as early as next week.

A knock on the door interrupted my musings of quick sales. It was a miracle I heard it over the construction noise. I opened it to find my other childhood best friend looking tense.

He had a sheen of sweat on his brow despite the cool fall weather. "Sam," I exclaimed, surprised but pleased to see him. "What brings you here?"

He didn't answer right away, fidgeting with the zipper of his leather jacket.

I raised my eyebrows. "Sam?"

He sighed and shrugged. "Can we talk? It's important."

The urgency in his voice made me step to the side. "Of course. Come in." After closing the door, I led him to the kitchen.

He eyed the man in the living room, banging on the mantle with a hammer. "Er, privately?"

"Sure, sure. Come on, the office is untouched and has a perfectly thick door."

Inside the office, we sat on the sofa against the wall across the room from the desk. He opened his mouth and then shut it. I waited for him to gather his thoughts. After another few seconds, he said, "This is going to sound crazy. For some reason, I feel I can tell you."

"Sure, Sam, you can tell me anything. I'm not promising that I won't make fun of you, but you can tell."

I waited for him to speak. What the heck was going on with him? His hands were shaking slightly. Sam wasn't the nervous type, not even slightly. "Are you okay?" I asked softly, concern lacing my words.

He took a deep breath before responding. "I've been having these dreams...they feel like memories of a past life. They're so weird but *so* vivid."

Oookay. He was this upset over a few dreams? "What kind of dreams?" I asked, trying to keep my tone even. Maybe they weren't dreams. Maybe they were like that weird vision I'd had when that guy at the grocery store touched me. Drew.

I'd had a couple of other daydreams, or whatever the heck they'd been. Only the other two had made even less sense. One had been about a skeleton named Larry. Another that Lucifer freakin' Morningstar lived next door. As if that were even possible.

"In one dream," he continued, "I'm a vampire and you're this powerful witch."

I laughed but he held his hand up. "That's not the weirdest part."

I lifted both brows. How much weirder could it be?

"Olivia and I were married."

Okay, that *was* freaky. "Olivia?" I asked, aghast. Well, crap. No wonder he was sweating bullets. "Olivia from high school, the hag of the harbor? The serpent of Shipton?" We had quite a few fun names for her like that.

He nodded gravely. "We were married, and she had this power over me that no one else had.

I stared at Sam for a long second, then burst out laughing. "Olivia Johnson? Mean girl Olivia who thinks she's better than us?"

"No, you laugh, but it was so freaking real."

"Didn't you date her a few years ago?" That couldn't have gone well.

He scrunched his face up. "Yeah. That was the worst date I'd ever had. She's still a bitch."

Duh. I could've told him that. In fact, I'd tried to before he went on the date. I hadn't seen Olivia since high school. She'd been horrible back then. I couldn't *imagine* her being married to Sam.

"What did you do in the dream?" I asked curiously.

"We fought a lot of demons and monsters together," he answered, his expression turning serious. "In one of the dreams,

I'm a vampire. It was like we were saving the world or something. It was crazy."

Sounded like it. I mean, *Olivia*?

"Oh, and you were married to Drew Walker, and there were these people after us, bounty hunters."

A shiver ran down my spine at the mention of Drew. That was who I saw at the grocery store yesterday, and something about them had seemed off. Now, hearing his name again in connection to Sam's dreams, I couldn't shake the feeling that something unbelievable was happening. "How do you know Drew?"

Sam gave me a side-eye kind of look. "Yeah, how do *you* know Drew? He's in town with his sister Lily and brother, Ian. They're bounty hunters."

Bounty hunters made sense given how I'd watched them take down that greasy-looking guy. "Do you know where they're staying?" I got up and walked a circle around the room, completely freaking out. "I need to speak with Drew."

"Um, Ava are you okay?" Sam got up and followed me out of the office.

Shaking my head, I flapped my hands a little, trying to get the skin-crawly feeling to go away. "No, nothing has been okay since I got here. I don't know why but everything seems a little too... I don't know. Like it's too normal, too perfect."

"What about Drew?" he asked.

"Your dreams, are they nighttime dreams or daydreams?"

I walked into the kitchen and a flash of... something... ran through my mind. It was fast, but it was kind of like a zombie standing at the stove, cooking.

Insane. Impossible. Why did it make me feel sad?

"Drew, yeah, him I ran into yesterday. Literally. He was

chasing some guy and he touched me, grabbed me to keep from running me over. As soon as he touched me, I knew his name and it was like we had this insane connection."

Pulling out his keys, he said, "I'll drive. They're staying at the Shipton Bed and Breakfast."

"You know where they are?" I exclaimed.

He opened the door. "Yes, come on."

"Yeah, okay." I yelled at the construction crew to let them know I was heading out. "Maybe it'll help us make sense of all this."

Sam nodded, still looking tense as we headed to his cruiser.

"Thanks for coming," I said as we drove towards the Shipton Bed and Breakfast where Drew and his siblings were staying. "I'm really glad you're here with me."

"Of course," Sam replied, a hint of a smile on his face. "We're in this together as usual. All we need now is to grab Snoozer."

I snorted but then cocked my head at him. "Could we?"

"Nah, he's probably at work."

He pulled up a long driveway and parked. "Are you sure this is the right place?" I asked, eyeing the charming Shipton Bed and Breakfast. The building had a welcoming, homey feel to it, with its warm yellow paint and white trim. However, the thought of finding Drew there made my stomach churn.

"Positive," Sam replied, his grip on the steering wheel tightening slightly. "I did a little digging after dreaming about them, and he and his siblings are staying here." We got out of the car and walked towards the entrance, the gravel crunching beneath our shoes. My heart hammered in my chest, nerves making me jittery. I took a few deep breaths, trying to calm myself, but what if I couldn't keep my cool around Drew? What if he thought we were crazy?

Please. He'd definitely think we were crazy.

"Ready?" Sam asked, pausing at the door. He glanced over at me, his eyes searching my face for any sign of hesitation.

"Let's do this." I gave him a small smile.

With one last nod, Sam pushed open the door, and we stepped inside. The interior of the bed and breakfast was just as cozy as the outside. A fire crackled in the hearth, casting flickering shadows on the walls. We approached the reception desk, where a friendly-looking woman greeted us with a warm smile. "May I help you?" she asked, her eyes traveling between Sam and me.

"Hi, we're looking for Drew Walker," Sam said, trying to sound casual. "Is he around?"

"Ah, yes. Mr. Walker is in the parlor with his siblings," she replied, pointing down a hallway. "Just follow that corridor and take a left at the end. You can't miss it."

"Thank you," I murmured, my voice barely audible.

As we made our way down the hallway, my heart raced even faster. In just a few moments, we'd be face to face with the man from Sam's dreams—and apparently my past life husband. "Here goes nothing," Sam muttered as we entered the parlor. The room was dimly lit and filled with plush armchairs, and the occupants engaged in quiet conversations.

There, in the far corner, sat Drew. My breath hitched when our eyes met. He started and held my gaze, his teal eyes widening slightly in what looked like recognition. "Ava," he breathed.

The sound of his breathy, surprised voice ran all through me in the most delicious, shivery way. He stood and walked over to us, getting what *should* have been uncomfortably close, yet I loved it. If anything, I wanted him to get closer.

His tall, muscular frame towered over me. "Y-yes," I stammered, my cheeks flushing. "This is my friend, Sam."

"Nice to meet you both," Drew said, shaking our hands, but somehow his gaze never left me. "Sorry for almost running into you the other day." He shook his head as though he wasn't believing his eyes. "Have we met before? What brings you here?"

"Um, uh, we, uh," I began, glancing at Sam for support. Which question to answer and how to make the words come?

He gave me a reassuring nod, then continued for me. "It's kind of a long story, but I had a strange dream that involved you, Ava, and a past life. It was so vivid and detailed that we couldn't help but wonder if there might be some truth to it."

I wasn't so sure I thought it was *true,* but it was something.

"Really?" Drew raised an eyebrow, his expression a mix of curiosity and disbelief. Oh, yeah. He thought we were nutso. He surprised me by saying, "Well, I've always been open to the idea of past lives, so I'm intrigued. Tell me more."

Sam hesitated for a moment before launching into the details of his dream, recounting how he'd been a vampire and I was a powerful witch and necromancer hybrid. As he spoke, Drew's eyes never left mine, as if he were searching for something. "According to the dream," Sam continued, "Ava was married to you, Drew. Now that we've met in this life, we thought it might be worth exploring the possibility of a connection between us all."

There was a brief silence after Sam finished speaking, during which Drew's gaze bored into my very soul. I squirmed uncomfortably under his scrutiny.

"Interesting," Drew finally said, breaking the silence. "I won't lie, the moment I laid eyes on you, Ava, I felt drawn to you. It was like déjà vu or something as if I'd known you before. I didn't want to say anything because it sounds crazy, right?"

"Right," I whispered, my heart pounding in my ears. "Maybe there is some truth to Sam's dream. Maybe we did know each other in a past life." My voice was unusually frail for me, but it was the best I could muster.

"Maybe," Drew echoed, his teal eyes still locked on mine, creating a sense of tension and unease.

I shifted in my seat, trying to shake off the chilling sensation that crawled up my spine. I couldn't put my finger on it, but something strange was happening in this room. Was it the heavy air or the lingering unease between us? Or the *insane* attraction I had for Drew.

"Maybe we should go," Sam said, sensing my discomfort.

"Sure," Drew agreed. "But can we talk again soon? I'd like to explore this connection further."

"Yeah, I suppose," I replied, my voice barely a whisper. I didn't want to talk again. What I wanted was to not leave him, but I couldn't say that. "Let's do that."

"Great," Drew said, smiling warmly at me as we walked out of the room.

As soon as Drew was out of sight, I picked up the pace, suddenly desperate to make space. "Let's go," I whispered as we walked out the front door. "Come on, come on."

Once safely in the car, Sam and I exchanged glances, each of us obviously unsettled by the encounter. We drove to the house in silence, both lost in our thoughts. Maybe Drew and I *had* met before, but neither of us remembered. That was the only explanation that made sense. There was no way we'd been married in a past life. That was ludicrous. Still, I couldn't shake the feeling that there was something else going on here—something I wasn't seeing. As we reached my street, an uneasy feeling settled in the pit of my stomach. Whatever was happening, it wasn't going to be simple. Sam dropped me off and I waved as I stood in front of my front door as though it was going to open for me.

It didn't. Now that would've *really* been weird.

A sense of relief washed over me when I stepped inside. This day had been so freaky.

I called out for my kitty, needing the comfort of my furry companion after such an intense day. "Lucy-Fur, Mommy's home," I cooed in my best baby voice, spotting her curled up on her favorite armchair.

"Meow," she grumbled, clearly unimpressed with my attempt at cutesy conversation.

"Did you miss me, sweetie pie?" I scooped her into my arms and nuzzled my face into her soft fur.

"Meow," she repeated flatly, squirming in my embrace, obviously annoyed by my display of affection.

"Fine, be that way," I said, setting her down with a huff. "You're a pretty girl, yes you are, but just so you know, things around here might get weirder before they get better."

She gave me another meow, almost like she was trying to tell me something.

"Lucy-Fur, I wish you could talk to me," I whispered, tears pricking my eyes. "I don't know what to do."

LUCY-FUR

IF SHE TRIES to kiss me, I'm gonna bite her freakin' nose off. Why on earth do humans talk to their pets like infants?

Once again, I tried to talk to her, and again it all came out in meows. That didn't stop me from trying, though.

"*We have a spell*—meow, meow, meow." I growled in frustration and tried again. "*I'm trying to* meow *you.*"

Ava continued with the sickly sweet voice. "Sweet baby, are you hungry? My precious girl, want to go for a walk?"

"*For a walk? Who walks a cat? I can walk myself, thank you very mu*eow, meowmeowmeowmeow." This is meowing ridiculous. I'm going to lose my meowing mind. "Meow, meow, meow…"

4
OLIVIA

"A ROYAL BALL? I don't have time for a ball. I need to get to Earth to find my friends and avenge my father." Royal ball my left butt cheek.

"Olivia," Octavia said, her light brown hair cascading down her shoulders as she approached me. "You don't have to do this. We can cancel the ball if it's too much for you right now."

Scorpia shook her head. "It's tonight, so we can't." She gave me an apologetic look. "Sorry."

"Thank you for understanding," I replied, my voice wavering a bit. "But I can't come. I get it if you can't cancel, that's fine. It's important to our people, and I want to honor that. I can't attend is all."

Octavia and Scorpia exchanged glances, their expressions softening. "All right, yes. Of course." Octavia conceded, placing a gentle hand on my shoulder. "We're here for you, Olivia. Whatever you need, let us know."

"Thanks," I whispered, offering them a small smile. As much as I appreciated their support, the weight of terror for my husband and children and the grief for my father wore on me.

Amid my inner turmoil, a messenger burst into the room, his face flushed and breathless. "Your Highness," he said in a pant, addressing Scorpia. "King Mitah requests your presence, as well as Lady Olivia and Lady Phira, in the throne room."

"Very well," Scorpia replied, before turning to us with a reassuring smile. "Come, let's see what my brother has to say." She led the way, her golden gown shimmering as she glided through the palace.

Phira and I exchanged worried glances as we followed, our footsteps echoing around the marble halls. The last time I'd been in the castle, it had been made primarily of polished woods. The time before that it was like it'd been weaved out of nature herself.

The air felt heavy and still, leaving me with a sense of unease that settled in my stomach like an unwelcome guest. I couldn't shake the feeling that something was amiss. I had to get home.

Upon entering the throne room, I marveled at the intricate detail of the carved wooden doors and the stunning stained glass windows, depicting scenes of Fae history. Was this the same castle transformed, or had I visited a different castle every time?

There was no time to admire the beauty around me, as King Mitah spoke with a fae holding a clipboard. I'd dealt with him several times. He was kind, but I also had zero desire to piss him off. "There you are," he called out, smiling at our arrival. His voice held a note of affection, but the tightness around his eyes betrayed the gravity of the situation. "Please, come closer." He beckoned us forward, and we approached with measured steps, apprehension gnawing at the edges of my thoughts. He held out his hands. Phira took one, and I took the other.

“I’m so pleased to see you two up and about. Are you well?”

Phira sniffed. “My Luci is gone.”

Mitah frowned and drew both of us into an awkward group hug, then walked us over to a large round table. “Do have a seat.”

"Thank you, Your Majesty," I managed, trying to ignore the gnawing feeling that his words were merely a prelude to something far more dire.

"Your Majesty," Phira hesitated, her voice cracking with emotion. "Luci--" she choked on the name of her loved one, tears welling in her blue eyes.

"Phira?" I asked, my heart pounding hard against my chest, fearing the worst.

"Luci is gone," she whispered, the words barely audible as they tumbled from her quivering lips. A heavy silence filled the room as if the weight of a hundred stones pressed down upon us.

She seemed unable to say anything else.

"Forgive me for asking this of you now," the king said gently, releasing us from the hug, "but I need to understand what has happened. Olivia, can you tell me everything that has occurred since you woke up?"

Taking a deep breath, I recounted the events, starting with entering Hell. “I don’t know what she's planned or why she locked down Hell, to begin with, but I have to get to Earth to see if Ava has learned anything new.” I hoped to Hell that Ava was alive and on Earth. "More importantly, I must find my husband and children."

Mitah sighed heavily. “I'm so sorry, dear niece, but we can’t cancel the ball. Guests are already starting to arrive." He cupped my chin and said, “You must show your people that you're observing our customs. You are a Faery princess, after all.”

And the new ruler of Hell. That thought made my chest tighten and tears fill my eyes. I shook my head. "I have to get home."

"Olivia, I understand the urgency of your situation," King Mitah began, his voice firm yet gentle. "This is also important."

I stared at him in disbelief. "You want me to attend a ball? Now?"

"Your presence will reassure them and give them hope in these troubled times," he explained. "As half Fae, half goddess, you're a symbol of unity between both worlds. It's crucial we put on a united front."

"I'm sorry, Uncle, but I cannot. I must go continue to break through to Earth or Hell."

"Perhaps if we asked our people for help," Scorpia suggested. "Many faeries have ancient magic we've yet to tap. Together we could punch through that barrier."

The King frowned, skepticism etched into his features. "It may be a valid option. The full moon approaches—an auspicious time for such powerful magic."

A spark of hope lit within me. Maybe with help from my uncle's subjects, I could finally break through and return to the human world or Hell.

"Let's do it," I said, steely determination in my voice. "It's time to call upon the magic of Faery."

The King and Scorpia exchanged glances, then nodded.

"Very well," Mitah proclaimed. "We shall ask for volunteers

tonight, then plan to perform the spell under the light of the full moon."

“The full moon? When is that?” I could never determine the time while in Faery.

“It’s in two days,” Evie said.

"The volunteers must understand the risks," Mitah warned. "Magic of this caliber often comes with a price."

"We shall endeavor to impart the magnitude of our request," Octavia said. "For now, we must get Olivia ready."

We stood, but Phira stayed in her seat. She hadn't even noticed we'd gotten up. "Fee?" I whispered.

"I've got her." Scorpia pulled Phira to her feet with gentle hands. "She'll not be in attendance tonight." She directed her words toward her brother, the king, and her voice left no room for argument.

He pursed his lips, but his eyes were full of sympathy. "Very well. Have someone sit with her."

Scorpia nodded once, and my other two aunts shepherded me out of the room. "Come dear, we'll get you ready."

Oh, boy.

Later that evening, after I'd been washed, plucked, lotioned, and painted, I entered the grand ballroom, taking in the enchanting sight before me. The entire time a team of fae helped get me ready, I'd focused on my magic and Luci's, trying to tap into it. Desperate times meant I had to at least attempt to harness it.

A soft golden glow from countless sparkling chandeliers bathed the room in a soft glow, casting their light on the polished marble floor. A large fireplace provided warmth to the room, while ornate tapestries adorned the walls, depicting scenes from Fae history and mythology.

My gaze turned to the crowd of elegantly dressed Fae, dancing gracefully to a lilting melody played by a group of musicians stationed on a stage. Their attire was nothing short of mesmerizing—gowns, robes, and suits made of the finest silks and satins shimmered in the light, embellished with precious stones and intricate embroidery. I couldn't help but feel awestruck by the beauty of it all.

I danced my fingers over the smooth, silk fabric of my gown. It embodied the very essence of this magical evening. The deep blue fabric hugged my modest curves before flowing out gracefully at my hips, creating an elegant silhouette that was both regal and enchanting. Delicate silver embroidery adorned the neckline, drawing attention to the pale skin of my shoulders and the simple pendant resting just above my collarbone. It was a dress truly befitting a half-goddess, half-Fae princess. I shivered at the thought of Scorpia attempting to force me into an extravagant dress with layers upon layers of petticoats—thank goodness she'd relented.

"Are you enjoying the view?" Octavia asked, appearing beside me with a knowing smile.

"Hard not to," I replied, still trying to take in the breathtaking scene before me. I sighed heavily. Usually, I loved the Fae balls. Sam and I had been to a few. The last ball had been all nature themed. It had been breathtaking in its own way. Today, all I wanted to do was get to Earth and find out what was going on.

Scorpia fluttered over, her dark purple wings glowing. She didn't have actual wings. They were part of her custom. "Smile, Liv. We have to put on a good show."

I smiled slightly, not feeling very happy. My heart ached from the loss of my father and not knowing what happened to all my friends. If I was honest with myself, I was barely hanging on to my sanity. I'd squashed the strong emotions to be dealt with once I got out of Faery. I couldn't let them out or I'd be as much of a basket case as Phira.

King Mitah glided through the crowd, robes sweeping behind him. He took my hands. "You look radiant as always, my dear."

"And you look positively ancient," I teased, though my heart wasn't in it. He chuckled, his eyes sparkling with mischief.

"Tease all you like, but we have serious matters to discuss." Boy, was he right about that.

His expression turned serious. "The barrier between realms remains strong. We've tried every spell we know, and still, we cannot break through."

That was news to me. He must've had his sages working while I was getting ready.

I was starting to see why Luci had gotten so frustrated when he got locked out.

"Come," he said. "It's time to talk to our subjects." He walked over and quieted the band. "All right, everyone," King Mitah announced from the small stage. "Please gather around. We have important matters to discuss."

The room fell silent as the Fae turned their attention to their king.

"First, I'd like to introduce you to Princess Olivia," he began, gesturing for me to join him on the stage. "As many of you know, she's the daughter of our beloved Princess Phira who has recently returned to us after a long absence. Princess Olivia is half Fae, half goddess, but was raised human. She's a fitting symbol of our desire to coexist with other creatures."

I took a deep breath and stepped forward, trying to ignore the butterflies in my stomach as I faced the curious gazes of my people. This was my chance to prove myself to them, to show them that I was worthy of their trust and loyalty.

"Tonight," I began, my voice steady despite my nerves. "We come together not only to celebrate our culture and traditions but also to face the challenges that lie ahead. The realm of Hell has been seized, and Lucifer is dead." It nearly ripped me out of my numb cocoon to say that. "We don't yet know the witch, but I implore you now to lend me your magic on the night of the full moon so that I may force my way to Earth and Hell and rescue my family and friends. Hopefully, I'll also be able to take our revenge for the death of Lucifer, a friend of the Fae." Scorpia had coached me about how to phrase it. I'd memorized her words.

A stunned silence fell over the glittering ballroom. Then one by one, the fae began stepping forward as a murmur of assent rippled through the crowd. "For Olivia and Luci, I volunteer my magic," they pledged. More and more fae came forth until over a hundred had gathered before the dais. A surge of determination filled me. My heart swelled until it was in danger of bursting from my chest. These fae had offered a tremendous gift—to lend their magic and help me get home.

I gazed out at the sea of volunteers, tears flowing freely down my cheeks. "Thank you, all of you, for this tremendous sacrifice. Together, we will break through."

The applause that followed my speech made my cheeks warm, and I couldn't help but smile as I looked around the grand ballroom. It was a breathtaking sight - the crystal chandeliers glinted above us, casting warm light on the Fae as they twirled across the polished marble floor. Their laughter and chatter filled the air with a lively energy that was contagious, but impatience and worry still gnawed at me. What if, even with all their magic combined, it wasn't enough? No, I couldn’t think that way. I'd find a way if this didn’t work. I just wasn’t sure what that was yet.

5
AVA

I WAS *SO* LOOKING FORWARD to spending a nice quiet day reading. It was Sunday, and the construction workers had taken the day off, leaving me alone in the house. Perfect day for some me time.

I was on my way to the kitchen when someone knocked on my front door, their knuckles rapping out a fast, nervous beat. When I opened the door, I found Snooze looking down, gazing at his shuffling feet as he moved around.

His slumped shoulders and hesitant demeanor were so unlike his normal, carefree personality. Something was eating at him.

"Hey, Snooze. What's up?"

He glanced up at me and forced a smile. Sadness and uneasiness radiated off of him. I'd been extra sensitive to others' emotions for as long as I could remember. Clay had called it empathic, but he'd been prone to being fanciful.

Lucy brushed against my leg, purring in greeting. She trotted over to Snooze and wound herself around his ankles, gazing up at him with an expression so adoring it was almost comical.

I didn’t think I’d ever seen her so affectionate with anyone before, not even me or Aunt Winnie when she'd been alive.

He scooped her up and buried his face in her fur, seemingly drawing strength from her affection. When he raised his head again, his gaze held mine. "Ava, there's something I need to tell you. About Crystal, and why we're really here." His voice was low and urgent. Crystal was his girlfriend. I'd met her a few times over the years, but never really liked her.

The sharp click of heels on the pavement behind Snooze made him tense up and flinch a bit. We both turned to see his girlfriend striding up my front walk, an unpleasant smile twisting her lips.

Snooze placed Lucy gently on the ground and took a step back from me. What was with that?

Crystal stopped in front of us, arms crossed. "Well, isn't this cozy? What are you two up to?" Her tone was light, but her gaze sharpened.

Snooze shook his head. "Nothing. Just, you know, saying hi." He wouldn't meet my gaze, which made me glare at him in suspicion.

Crystal's smile widened, but it didn't reach her eyes. "Lovely. Why don't we all go inside and *say hi*, then?"

Trapped, Snooze could only nod. My heart sank as I realized that whatever he'd been about to tell me would have to wait. Crystal had ensured it.

Before we could enter the house, Lucy let out a fearsome yowl and launched herself at Crystal, claws unsheathed. Crystal shrieked and stumbled back, batting at Lucy.

Snooze rushed forward and grabbed Lucy, pulling her away from Crystal, but Lucy twisted in his grip and broke free, charging at Crystal again with an ear-splitting shriek.

"Lucy, no." I lunged for my cat, but she evaded me easily. Snooze made another grab for her as he said, "Crystal, I'm so sorry."

I couldn't help but think he wasn't trying all *that* hard to catch Lucy. In fact, he seemed torn between stopping the attack and allowing it to continue.

Crystal's eyes narrowed. "What's wrong with that cat?" she yelled. She took another step back, poised to flee if Lucy attacked again.

"I'm so sorry," I said, though I wasn't. Lucy had never behaved aggressively before, but I couldn't blame her for disliking Crystal. I liked her less and less every second. "Let me put her inside."

I scooped Lucy into my arms and carried her into the house, depositing her in my office. "Stay," I ordered, then shut the door.

Lucy let out a growl-like meow, scratching at the door. I ignored it, hoping she'd settle down.

When I returned to the front porch, Crystal had a hold of Snooze's arm. "You need to keep that beast under control," she snapped.

Snooze looked apologetic, but he didn't touch or comfort Crystal. That was interesting.

"I'm *so* sorry about that. Lucy's usually so well-behaved." As I said the words, I didn't believe them.

A loud crash came from inside the house. When I turned to look inside the foyer, I could just see the office door banging open. Then a white blur as Lucy streaked out, heading straight for Crystal again, yowling like a maniac.

Crystal shrieked and stumbled backward. "That cat is possessed!" She turned and ran for her car, scrambling inside and locking the doors.

Lucy scratched at the car door, creating a horrible sound as she tried to get in.

Finally, Snooze looked over at me. "Guess I'll go get the cat." He shrugged, then walked over and gathered her into his arms. "Easy, girl," he murmured. Lucy purred and nuzzled against him, her aggression disappearing as quickly as it had appeared.

Snooze met my gaze, a wry smile tugging at his lips. "I guess she doesn't like Crystal."

"No kidding," I said. "But why?"

I had a feeling *he* knew why. I crossed my arms over my chest and gave him the look that said he better fess up.

Snooze's expression turned serious. "That's what I was trying to tell you."

I frowned. "What is it?"

"Crystal isn't what she seems," Snooze said as he looked over at the car. "She's not human. She's a—"

Before he could finish, a searing pain shot through my skull. I clutched my head, gritting my teeth against a flood of images in my mind's eye.

A woman with dull brown hair and eyes to match, smiling triumphantly. The same woman tried to ruin my wedding. She was supposed to be locked up in Hell.

The pain vanished as fast as it came on, leaving me stunned. I stared at Snooze. "What's going on?"

Snooze set Lucy down, his expression grave. "You're starting to remember things that have been hidden from you." He paused. "Crystal has somehow put us in a dream world of her creation."

I swayed on my feet, dizzy with confusion and disbelief. "Magic? Memories? What are you talking about?"

"You're not an ordinary human, Ava," Snooze said softly.

"You're a necromancer-witch. And Crystal has been manipulating you for reasons only she knows."

I blinked at him. His words were completely insane.

"You have to remember Ava. Remember who you are—a powerful necromancer who once had six ghouls bound to her. The Ava who summoned Lucifer at Christmas two years ago. You're married to Drew Walker and best friends with Olivia."

Okay. Hold up. Now I *knew* he was freaking insane. Friends with Olivia? Might as well go watch pigs fly through the blue skies.

Snooze stepped closer and reached out to me, Lucy still in his arms purring like a little motorboat.

"What?"

He spoke again, but I didn't hear him. My mind whirled with his claims. Memories surfaced, bringing on another headache. Staggering to the side, I sank into the rocking chair that had been there as long as I could remember.

Holy freaking crap. Memories flooded my brain. Magic, necromancy. Aunt Winnie, Yaya... Mom and Dad. Oh, my heavens. Drew.

Then I remembered walking into Hell. A dark witch blasted Luci, killing him. That was the last thing I remembered before ending up in this weird, abnormally normal world. A world without magic.

As if the thought called to my power, a tingling warmth spread through me. Sparks of light danced across my fingertips.

I gasped. At that moment, I remembered it all. I knew the truth.

I had powers.

And Crystal was my enemy.

That must have been why Lucy had such a strong reaction to her.

I stared at Snooze in shock. I wasn't even remotely able to process the fact that my twenty-something-year-old Maine coon cat was a real live man in this world. Was this a parallel universe? A total illusion? It didn't *feel* fake.

Rage flooded me, and my power built with it. I flung out my hands, directing a blast of energy at the car where Crystal cowered. The windows shattered outward with a terrible crash and the engine made a grinding noise before emitting a cloud of black smoke. Crystal shrieked in terror.

I smiled at her.

I was back.

Crystal scrambled out of the smoking car, fleeing down the street in a panic. I watched her go with grim satisfaction.

Then I turned to Snooze. "*How* are you human right now?"

He averted his gaze to focus on stroking Lucy's long white fur. I put my hand on his arm. "Tell me."

He nodded and took a deep breath. "I used to be human. The year I came to live with your family, I was cursed to live as a cat by the god who gave me my power. I didn't die when I jumped from the stairs when you were sixteen. The magic wouldn't let me get off that easily."

I had totally freaked out when Snoozer jumped from the top of the stairs, landed weirdly, and didn't get up. I'd instinctively pushed my magic into him, not knowing then that I had the rare ability to heal people. I'd thought he was dead at the time and that I'd animated him. "Are you saying that I didn't animate you?"

"No, you healed me, with the help of my curse." He sat in the rocking chair to my left.

I shook my head in disbelief, but why was I so shocked? It was par for the course with my life. A laugh bubbled up inside me. "This is crazy. Completely nuts." I grinned at Snooze. "Then, magic always is."

I reached over and squeezed his hand. "Okay. Okay, so, where do we go from here? How do we break this curse?"

Snooze frowned and looked at the now-sleeping Lucy in his arms. Oh, man, no wonder she'd gotten so mad at Crystal. Lucy was head-over-heels in love with Snoozer. "That, I don't know. The god who cursed me didn't provide an instruction manual, but as nice as it's been to be human for the last few days, I don't want to break my curse. I mean, I used to want to, but then you came back to Shipton and stayed. Then I found Lucy. If I turned human again, I wouldn't have any of you."

"Makes sense," I said, pulling him and Lucy into a hug. The pretty sleepy kitty grumbled about humans being touchy. She could talk again. Snoozer and I laughed. "We need to figure out how to wake up from this spell or get back to our world or whatever is going on, but you should know, when your curse is over, you'll still have me. No doubt the rest of the people in my crazy life will agree."

Snooze looked at me with watery eyes and nodded. "Thank you." He cleared his throat, then said, "I'm pretty sure this is a sleeping spell and dream world. I just don't know where to begin with breaking this curse. We don't have any spells in this reality."

He might've been right about spells, but I had my magic and my determination. That had to be good for something.

6
OLIVIA

THE PALE LIGHT of the full moon washed over the clearing not far from the royal gardens, casting a silvery upon the gathered Fae, their wings shimmering like a thousand rainbow-hued stars inside the ancient stones that formed a perfect circle. I stood in the center of that circle in a simple white gown and no shoes, my heart pounding in anticipation about the spell we were about to perform. The risks loomed large in my mind, but I couldn't let fear stop me from trying to break through the barrier that had ensnared Hell and kept me from my friends.

Phira and Scorpia had said that being barefoot helped us to connect to the earth beneath us, and to draw on the natural magic that flowed throughout Faery.

"Your father once told me that he's the reason there are gateways to different worlds," Phira said as she joined me. "He said when he created his first portal, it opened up the possibility for other worlds to do the same."

That was interesting. “Do you think when he pushed his power into me, he closed the gates to all worlds?”

Phira nodded. “I do. To reopen them, you'll have to create your first portal using his magic, at least, I'm guessing.”

"If that's correct, it's also the reason I couldn’t open a portal.” That made sense. Luci created a portal differently from the way I did them. He'd never said why. I'd assumed that he never thought I’d need to learn his special technique.

"Are you ready, Olivia?" Scorpia asked, her eyes filled with concern as she placed a hand on my shoulder.

The sounds of soft voices drew my attention to the forest around me. More fae volunteers entered the clearing. Geez, there were a lot of them. Hope that we’d succeed filled me, along with a sense of determination. I nodded, swallowing hard. "Let's do this." I leaned into Phira and whispered, “You don’t have to do this. There're more than enough people here.”

A tear slid down Phira’s cheek, glimmering in the moonlight. “I have to,” she whispered. “For Luci. You must avenge him, Olivia. You must destroy that witch for what she’s done.”

“I will,” I vowed. “I give you my word.”

Phira squeezed my hands, her gaze burning into mine. “I *am* staying behind in Faery. My heart is too broken to return to the human world, but I'll be here for you if you need me.”

I pulled her into a fierce hug, blinking back tears. “I love you, Mom,” I whispered. Hearing me call her mom made her sniff louder and hug me tighter. I'd said it before, but this was the first she'd heard it.

Phira pulled out of our embrace and smiled sadly. “I love you, always. Tonight, we have work to do.”

Yes, we did. I was ready. The last two days waiting on the full moon had been torture. It'd been at least three days since I'd seen any of my friends or family besides Phira and the fae.

Mitah approached me as the fae formed a circle around us. "If things on Earth get critical, I want you to know that you can call on me. I'll send my best warriors to assist you."

Oh, wow. That was a huge deal. "Thank you. Hopefully, I won't need them, but it's generous of you to offer."

Mitah placed a smooth, obsidian stone in my palm, which pulsed with energy. "Hold this in your hand and make your request. I'll hear it and send the warriors to you."

I slipped it into my pocket, hoping I'd never need to use it. I was about to thank him again, but he turned to the crowd, which had begun to form a circle around us. "Thank you for coming to help my niece get to Earth. Tonight, we come together as one, united by our love for Faery and our desire to help our princess. We'll channel our magic under the light of this full moon, attempting to break the barrier between realms. Remember, there are dangers involved, so only join if you're willing to face them."

A chorus of determined voices rang out, affirming their commitment. My heart swelled with gratitude and admiration for these brave Fae who'd chosen to stand beside me.

"Very well," Mitah said, his voice filled with pride. "Form a circle around Olivia and join hands. Concentrate your energy on the fae next to you, allowing your magic to flow through one another until it reaches Olivia."

Hands clasped mine, and I closed my eyes, focusing on the task at hand. Heat surged through my veins as if every fiber of my being were alight with magical fire. The energy of the Fae enveloped me, an unstoppable force shattering my previous limitations. A chorus of chanting in an ancient Faery language filled the air in a rhythmic beat. The energy built as Phira hummed a low melody, and King Mitah called up the fae magics within each of us, gathering it in the center of the circle.

"Feel the power coursing through you, Olivia," Phira whispered in my ear. "You can do this."

"Breaking barriers is what you were born for," Scorpia added, her faith in me unwavering.

Electricity crackled around us as our intertwined magics grew stronger. My chest tightened with emotion, and I opened my heart to the magic, letting it guide me toward the barrier. With each second that passed, the power grew stronger, until it felt as if the very air around us vibrated with energy.

The ground beneath us was cool, but the air charged with electricity. Tiny sparks of light danced around our hands as we clasped them together, creating a glowing web over the center of our large circle. We lowered the web over the combined magic. The web and the ball of power snapped together with a force that almost put me on my backside. Thank goodness Phira and Mitah had a good hold of my hands.

The full moon's energy fueled our power, amplifying the energy in the center of the circle.

"Release it, Olivia," Mitah commanded, his voice resonating with authority. "Break the barrier."

I raised my hands to the sky, releasing the pent-up energy in a torrent of light that shot toward the heavens. The world around me blurred, consumed by an eruption of color and sound, as our combined magic collided with the barrier.

For a moment, it felt as if time itself had stopped. And then, a resounding crack echoed throughout the night, accompanied by the shattering of the invisible wall between our worlds.

I stepped forward, peering through the portal. On the other side was Ava's cozy kitchen, dimly lit by an overhead light. Beth and John sat slumped at an oval wooden table, clutching steaming mugs of tea.

"We did it." I turned to all the Fae. "Thank you so much for helping me."

The Fae cheered, their voices triumphant, and I found myself swept up in a sea of grateful, joyful embraces. We'd done it; we'd broken through the barrier.

I hugged Phira, then Mitah. He seemed a little shocked at my boldness, but I didn't care. He was family, even if he was the King of Faery. "Thank you again," I whispered in his ear before pulling away from him.

Mitah gave my hand a gentle squeeze. "Any time, Princess. Now, go find your friends and avenge your father."

With a deep breath, I stepped through the portal into Ava's kitchen. Beth turned to look at me, then gasped, while John leaped to his feet, knocking over his chair in the process.

"Olivia?" Beth whispered, her eyes widening. "Is that you?"

Nodding, I stepped forward and into the embrace of my best friend's mom. Beth held me tight. "Where's Ava?"

"Hell. At least I hope she and the others are there." Stepping out of her hug, I moved to the table and sat down. I told them everything I remembered, starting from the moment we entered Hell.

"We didn't know what happened. Just that no one returned, and we tried to locate them, but we kept hitting a wall. Then we tried to get into Hell with no luck." Beth said, her voice trembling.

John covered her hand. "We'll get them back."

"You bet we will," I said.

John didn't look very convinced. "We tried everything. Locator spell. Alfred and I combined our powers and tried to get into the Inbetween and Hell. Nothing we tried worked."

I frowned as I scanned the dining room and kitchen. "Where's everyone?"

"Wallie and Michelle are in school, but they've been helping with spells and research. Larry and Zoe don't have magic but helped as much as they could. Wade's asleep in the basement. Winnie…" Beth stopped, and her eyes filled with tears.

My chest tightened at the thought that something terrible had happened to Winnie. "What happened?"

"You know how Winnie hadn't been feeling well?" John asked.

I nodded, and Beth said, "She found out that she has a form of witch cancer. There's no cure for it." Beth wiped her eyes and sniffed. "We checked out the cause of death for both of our bodies before we inhabited them. None of the medical records said anything about the cancer in Winnie's body. She and Alfred are searching for a new body that's cancer free."

Holy freaking crap. What? Poor Winnie and Alfred. "What can I do to help?"

"Not much until they get back. We've been focusing on getting Ava and everyone back when we're not at the school." Beth took a sip of her tea.

I watched the two of them for a while, thinking of what they said. Then it hit me. They'd done a lot in a few days, and why did they need to be at the school? "How long have I been gone?"

"It's been a month," John said.

My heart clenched. A month? For me, it had only been a few days since Ava vanished. How long was I asleep? Why hadn't my fae family told me how long it had been? I gasped again as I thought about my son. "Sammie."

Beth placed her hand on my arm as I jumped from the table. "Wade went to your adoptive parents' house and compelled them to believe that you and Sam went on an extended vacation. It's okay. Your parents were more than happy to have Sammie for the summer, and Sammie has been having a fun time. We've checked in on him and sent him your love. He's asked for you a lot, though."

Relief shuddered through me. My adoptive parents were the best people anyone could ever ask for. So were Ava's and Wade. "Thank you for thinking about that."

"Carrie said she could take him if your parents started asking too many questions, but it hasn't been necessary." Beth patted my hand and stood. "Would you like some tea?"

I used to not be a tea drinker, but Phira loved it, and I found that I liked it too. Especially the herbal ones. "Yes, please. Then we can get to brainstorming how to break Sam and our friends out of Hell so I can go get my son."

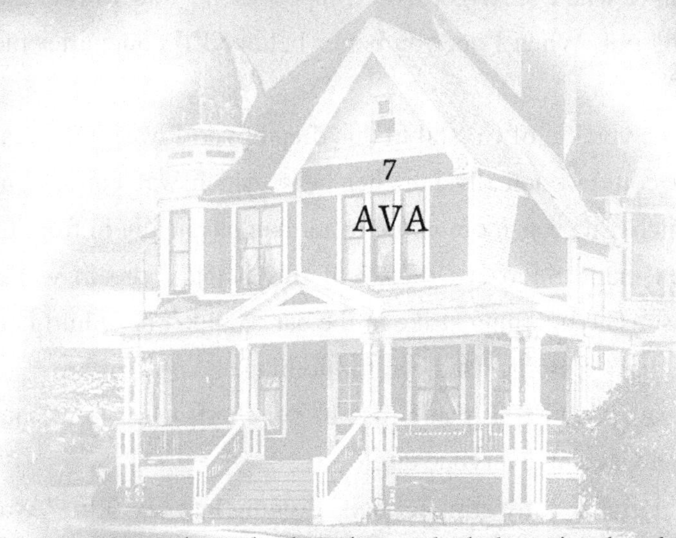

7
AVA

I RUMMAGED through the cluttered shelves in the dusty attic, tossing aside cobwebs and old boxes in my frantic search. Where were my grimoires? My spell books? I needed to find a way home, and magic was the only way I knew how. This world was possibly a sleep thingy but that didn't mean my power was gone. I had access to my raw magic but without any finesse.

If Drew were here, this might not be so bad. Sam and Snooze had been brought up to speed. It'd pissed Sam *way* off when he remembered. We'd tried to go find Drew, but he'd already checked out of the BnB.

"Ava, stop." Crystal's voice echoed behind me. "You need to accept that there's no way back."

I whirled around, glaring at her as my lightning magic stirred under the surface. "I'll not accept that. There has to be a spell, a portal, something."

Crystal stepped forward. "You'll only hurt yourself. I removed all magic from this world. Let it go."

"Let it go?" I stood and faced her, electricity arcing off my fingertips. "I won't let it go. You trapped me in this world, and I'm getting out. When I do, you better believe I'll come after the real you."

That the version of Crystal in this dream world wasn't the real Crystal. I couldn't actually hurt her here, which was convenient for the witch. She was more in my head than physically in front of me, which made Snoozer's theory of this being a dream world make sense. The lightning strike in the car wouldn't have hurt her. Her dramatic screaming had been for nothing.

My heart pounded as panic rose in my chest. I had to get out of here and wake up everyone else.

Crystal grabbed my arm, her nails digging into my skin. "Ava, stop this madness." She couldn't hurt me, yet somehow her grip was painful.

This world was weird.

I wrenched my arm from her grip, stumbling back. "Don't touch me. I have to find a way back, I have to—" My foot caught on a floorboard, and I tumbled to the ground, books and dust raining around me. I curled up, hugging my knees to my chest as tears pricked at my eyes.

Crystal crouched beside me, resting a hand on my back. "I'm sorry," she whispered. "But you can't go back. You have to accept this is your home now."

I shook my head, squeezing my eyes shut. No. I refused to believe that. There had to be a way back, there just had to be. I wasn't stuck here. I wasn't.

Crystal sighed, giving my back a final pat before leaving me alone in the attic, surrounded by the remnants of my desperate search. I wouldn't give up. Not yet. There was still hope. There had to be. I just needed to find it.

I stayed in the attic for hours, searching through a set of paranormal women's fiction books that I'd written years ago. It was the only thing close to a magic book I could find. Unfortunately, I hadn't put in real spells in that series.

After a while, exhaustion overtook me, and I lay on the floor in defeat, staring at the ceiling. At some point, I drifted into a restless sleep.

In my dream, I was in my old attic, but this attic was different —it was tidy and organized, not a mess of scattered books and dust. There, on a shelf, was a single leather-bound book I didn't recognize.

I pulled the book off the shelf and opened it. The pages were blank at first, then words and symbols began to appear. I turned the pages until they didn't want to be turned anymore.

It was a spell. A spell to counteract a sleeping spell. Holy crow. My heart leaped. That was it. The way home I'd been searching for. I read through the spell repeatedly, committing each word and gesture to memory. When I finished, a surge of power flowed through me, waking me.

I sat up and scanned the attic around me. It was still a mess and not at all like the one in my dream. I wasn't sure it had even been a dream since I was currently living in a made-up world. Thanks to Crystal.

Folding my legs into a pretzel in the middle of the dusty, messy attic floor, I closed my eyes and focused on the spell from my dream. I chanted while visualizing myself waking up in the real world. Magic swirled around me, causing the papers to blow in a circular motion.

Then a snap of power burst from me like a rubber band snapping.

I woke up with a start, my heart pounding. For a moment I was disoriented, unsure of where I was. The walls of the room I was in were stone and there was no window. This wasn't the attic.

Oh, thank goodness. I was awake and in Hell. Drew slept beside me, his chest rising and falling with deep, even breaths. Sam, Lily, Ian, Snoozer, who was a cat again, and Lucy were curled up in various spots around the room, all asleep.

I did it.

I shook Drew's shoulder. "Drew. Wake up."

He grunted but didn't open his eyes. I shook him harder. "Drew. It's important. Wake up, please."

After a few more shakes, his eyes blinked open, still heavy with sleep. "Wha—Ava? What's going on?"

I took a deep breath, trying to figure out how to explain it because I wasn't sure I fully understood what was going on. "We've been under a spell that sent us to a dream world," I said, meeting his gaze. "Everything was normal and boring, but it wasn't right. You and I never met. Sam didn't marry Olivia. It was awful."

"Whoa, slow down," Drew interrupted, now fully awake. He studied my face in the dim light as if trying to determine if I had lost my mind. Yeah, that was possible.

After a long moment, he let out a breath. "You're serious, aren't you?"

Something told me he didn't remember his dream world experience. "What was the last thing you remember?"

He bunched his brows together as he thought about it. "We got into Hell. Luci was shot with dark magic and died. Then I saw you in the parking lot of the grocery store. What in the world? Ian, Lily, and I were bounty hunters."

"Yeah, dream world. Crystal is behind it. I *think* the dark witch was a distraction." A distraction for what, I hadn't a clue. "Anyway, help me wake everyone up. We need to get home and figure out our next move."

He nodded and moved to wake up his sister and brother while I woke up Sam and the cats. I wasn't sure how the furballs had made it to hell with us, but with those two, it also didn't surprise me much. Lucy always had to be where we were like she craved magic and action.

Sam yawned and stretched, blinking at us in confusion. "What's going on?" Then he met my stare and widened his eyes. "Holy crap."

I hugged him. "Your psychic mind wouldn't let you fall under completely, thank the gods. You and Snoozer helped me realize it."

"Yeah. That was weird, and I never want to do it again." Sam looked around. "Where's Olivia?"

"I don't know. I'm hoping she's in the real world, trying to get us out." I glanced over to Drew. Lily was awake, rubbing her eyes, and it seemed Drew was having a hard time waking Ian. Turning to Sam, I pointed at the cats. "Wake them up."

Sam reached over and placed a hand on Snoozer and shook him. I slapped at Sam. "Stop."

While Sam got the cats up and going, I moved over to Drew. By the time I got across the room, Ian woke up. "We need to figure out how to get home." I glanced at Drew, and he squeezed my hand.

"What's the plan?" Ian asked. "How do we get out of this place and back to the real world?"

“I don’t know. We could search for a portal out of here. There should be gates or something.” I was about to summon Luci but then remembered he was dead. Sadness squeezed my heart. I’d grown to like the devil since he came into my life.

“We could look for Luci’s throne room or something,” Sam suggested.

“That could work. Maybe he’ll have something in there that will help break us out of here,” I said, heading to the door out of this room. "Let's go home."

8
OLIVIA

"THERE HAS TO BE A WAY." I threw my hands up. "I have all this power now but can't do *any*thing to help." I paced around Ava's living room like a caged animal. My nerves were shot, and my new powers buzzed under my skin, itching to be unleashed. We'd been brainstorming for hours, trying to find some way to break into Hell and rescue Ava and everyone else stuck there. The whole situation was frustrating, to say the least.

"Oh, Liv," Beth said, her voice soft and sympathetic. "I know you're desperate to help and save them all, but your powers are still new and unpredictable. We need to be cautious when trying to break into Hell."

"Sam, Ava and the others are trapped in *literal* Hell." Even with all of Luci's magic, I still couldn't get into Hell. I was starting to understand what my father had felt when he'd been locked out for so long. He'd kept it together remarkably well. It helped that none of us had been trapped there. "I hate not knowing what to do." Feeling helpless was the worst.

I stopped pacing and turned to look at Ava's mom. Her golden-brown hair fell just past her shoulders, but she had it pulled up. Her light green eyes sparkled with determination. She was right, but it didn't make me feel any less useless. How could I have these extraordinary abilities and still not be able to do anything?

"I know, Beth," I sighed, running a hand through my blonde hair. "It's just, I can't stand feeling so useless, you know? I want to get in there and get something done. Rescue them."

"Of course you do," she replied, giving me a small smile. "But we have to be smart about this, Olivia. If you go charging into Hell with no control over your powers, who knows what might happen?"

I clenched my fists in frustration, my eyes welling up with tears, and glanced around the room filled with books on witchcraft, maps, and scribbled notes. This was freaking overwhelming, all of this crap on me and me alone. John and Beth were helping, but they weren't equipped for magic of this caliber.

As much as I wanted to disagree with Beth, she really was right. I couldn't risk losing control of my powers in Hell and endangering everyone even more.

"Fine," I relented, wiping away a tear. "We'll keep thinking of other solutions, but we've got to hurry. They need us."

"Of course," Beth agreed, placing a hand on my shoulder. "We'll find a way to rescue them, Olivia. I promise."

Determined, I paced around the living room, my eyes darting from one book to another, searching for anything that could help us. The scent of old leather and musty pages filled my nostrils, but it did little to calm my nerves.

"I don't care how risky it is," I insisted, slamming my fist onto a pile of maps, causing them to scatter across the floor. "We have to do something. We can't just sit here and let them suffer."

John, who'd been quietly observing from a corner, finally spoke up. "Olivia, we know you want to help, but remember what happened with the ocean? Your powers are still new, and if you lose control in Hell—"

A shiver ran down my spine as the memory of the blood-red waves crashing against the shore flashed through my mind. The horror in the eyes of those who'd witnessed my failed attempt to teleport to Hell still haunted me. I cringed. I'd accidentally turned the entire ocean into blood earlier when I'd tried to teleport to Hell. That had been a nightmare to fix. At least, I *think* I fixed it. "I've got a better handle on my powers now. I can do this."

"If you make it, but then you lose control in Hell?" John asked. "How would we get you out then?"

"All right, I get it," I said, swallowing hard. "There has to be some way we can use my powers without putting everyone at risk."

"Maybe there is," John suggested, his gray-blue eyes filled with hope. "Let's keep trying to find a spell or talisman that could help focus your powers. It might not be a perfect solution, but it's worth a shot."

His words were like a lifeline, and I clung to them, desperate for anything that could give us an edge. Together, we began combing through the books, our fingers trailing along dusty spines as we searched for anything that might help. They had a ton here. They'd gone everywhere they could think of in the month I'd been gone, collecting tomes from the school, the hunters' headquarters, and Luci's house. Ava's living room was chock full of books now.

My heart raced as I paced the living room, my mind reeling

from the terrifying memory of the ocean turning red. The salty taste of iron still lingered on my tongue, a constant reminder of my uncontrollable powers.

I took a deep breath and tried to calm my racing thoughts. We needed a plan, not reckless action. As I paced, trying to come up with a plan, a strange tingling started in my fingertips. I frowned, glancing at my hands. Before I could wonder what was happening, a burst of searing heat shot through my body. I cried out in alarm.

Beth and John rushed to my side. "Liv, what's wrong?"

I gritted my teeth against the burning sensation flooding my veins. "I don't know...my powers..."

The heat intensified until my clothes erupted into flames. I shrieked, batting at the fire and tumbling to the floor. In my panic, I lost control of my powers completely.

"Earthquake!" Beth cried.

John grabbed us and pulled us under the dining room table as I managed to get my clothes to stop flaming. The tremors intensified, objects crashing to the floor all around us. From what I could see, the entirety of the kitchen cabinets had fallen onto the floor.

"Liv, you have to stop this!" John shouted over the chaos.

"I'm trying," I said through gritted teeth, but the more I tried to restrain my powers, the more they slipped through my grasp like sand.

The earthquake finally eased, leaving destruction in its wake. I sagged against the floor, exhausted and demoralized.

“We'll figure something out," John said gently. "For now, just try to stay calm."

I stood up on shaky legs, brushing dust off my clothes. "There has to be a way to get into Hell," I said.

"Okay, what about this? What if we try summoning a god? Rhiannon, for example. She's a goddess of magic. She's known to be helpful, right?"

Beth furrowed her brow, clearly not thrilled with my suggestion. "Olivia, you know that summoning gods is dangerous. They're powerful beings, and we can't predict how they'll react. After what happened with Lucifer, you want to summon another supernatural being?"

I bristled at her tone. "Lucifer turned out to be a good thing. Rhiannon isn't evil as far as I know. She could help me. We need help," I snapped, frustration seeping into my voice. "We can't just twiddle our thumbs."

"I understand your desperation, believe me. Rhiannon might help, yes but she could also make things even worse," Beth argued. "We have to find another way. Summoning is too dangerous, especially now that your powers are unstable." She crossed her arms, her green eyes filled with empathy. "There has to be another way."

"What do you suggest?" I threw my hands up again as John cleaned up the mess in the kitchen. Winston groaned and shuddered, but a crack that had formed in the middle of the kitchen wall disappeared. "I should just sit here and destroy everything around me through sheer accident?"

I sighed, biting my lip. "I'm sorry." As much as I didn't want to admit it, Beth was right. Summoning a god could lead to unforeseen consequences, especially considering my unpredictable powers.

"No, of course not," Beth said. "We'll keep researching, find spells or talismans to help focus your power. There has to be a way to harness magic that doesn't involve consorting with demons or deities."

But *I* was part demon, wasn't I? "Fine," I conceded, sitting on the sofa next to her. The thought of struggling with these powers alone, not knowing if I'd ever gain control, made me feel sick with dread. I didn't know if I was strong enough. I didn't know if any of us were. I slumped into an armchair in the living room, staring into the empty fireplace. "I just wish Luci was here," I said softly. "He always knew what to do in situations like this." He was random but usually very helpful.

A heavy silence fell over the room. I didn't need to see their faces to know they were exchanging worried looks, unsure of how to respond.

"Let's keep searching the books," John chimed in from the corner, his gray-blue eyes scanning the pages of a dusty tome. "There must be something in here that can help us. There're dozens of books we haven't searched."

"All right," I agreed, reluctantly picking up a book from the coffee table. "We also haven't made a dent at Luci's, but the problem with doing that is it could take days or weeks to get through all the rooms in that darn house."

I flipped through the pages of book after book, each one filled with ancient spells and cryptic symbols, praying that one of them would hold the key to Hell.

An hour later, I tugged at my hair in exasperation, nails scraping against my scalp. How were we supposed to do this if every option seemed to lead to disaster?

Jumping up, I paced back and forth in the living room, my mind racing with possibilities. John's search for a solution would take time, but I couldn't just sit idly by. I needed to practice my abilities, to prepare for the inevitable confrontation with the witch. With a deep breath, I focused on channeling my powers, attempting to summon a small gust of wind.

"Uh, Olivia?" Beth called out hesitantly. "Maybe you should start with something smaller, like—"

"Like this?" I interrupted, holding up my hand, expecting to see a tiny whirlwind dancing on my palm. Instead, I stared at a glass of water on the coffee table that had turned into wine. "Well, that's not what I intended."

"Ooh, party trick," John joked as he inspected the glass. "You'll be a hit at social gatherings."

"Very funny," I muttered, trying again to focus my energy.

"Hey, at least it's not blood this time, right?" Beth chimed in, flashing me a supportive smile. I appreciated her optimism, but I couldn't help feeling disheartened by my lack of control. Each attempt to harness my power resulted in more chaos, from books flying off shelves to lightbulbs exploding overhead.

"Olivia, maybe we should take a break," John suggested, shielding his eyes from the shower of sparks. "We don't want to cause any more damage."

"Or run out of lightbulbs," Beth added, sweeping up the shards of glass scattered across the floor.

"Fine," I grumbled, gritting my teeth as I willed my powers to subside. "But we can't give up. I have to get better at this."

"Nobody's giving up," John assured me, placing a comforting hand on my shoulder. "Rome wasn't built in a day. You'll get the hang of it."

"Exactly," Beth agreed, nodding enthusiastically. "Besides, how many people can say they've turned water into wine? You're practically a miracle worker."

Despite the setbacks, my friends' encouragement lifted my spirits. They were right; I couldn't expect to master my abilities overnight.

"Look," John exclaimed half an hour later, his eyes sparkling with excitement as he held up an ancient-looking tome. "I found a spell for a talisman that could help balance your powers. It might be just what we need to open a portal to Hell."

"Really?" I asked, my heart pounding with hope. "That's amazing."

"There's no guarantee it'll work," Beth cautioned, peering over John's shoulder at the faded script.

"Right," I sighed, my relief giving way to the familiar weight of uncertainty. "At least it's a start."

"Exactly," John agreed, his optimism undiminished. "We can't expect everything to fall into place overnight, but we're making progress."

"All right, then," I said, determination surging through me. "Let's get to work on this talisman. What do we need?"

"According to the spell, we need several rare herbs," Beth explained, scanning the list of ingredients. "I think we have most of these either in the conservatory or at the school."

"Great," I replied, grateful for their resourcefulness. "Once we've gathered everything, how do we put it all together?"

"Apparently, it's a pretty involved process," John admitted, tracing a finger along the intricate diagrams in the book. "But don't worry. We'll figure it out."

As we set about gathering the necessary ingredients and deciphering the spell, I couldn't help but feel a glimmer of hope. With every step forward, we were inching closer to rescuing my husband and best friends.

9
AVA

I CREPT through the dark caverns of Hell with my friends at my side, determined to find Crystal before she could unleash any more chaos.

As we turned a corner, a familiar-looking figure came into view behind thick iron bars. I peered at the nameplate beside his cell.

What in the ever-loving literal Hell? It was Julius Caesar. Now that wasn’t something I saw every day, and yet... Why was I not surprised? Luci loved to collect things. Collecting souls kind of fit in there with his whole aesthetic, given he was the king of Hell.

Or used to be.

I still couldn’t believe he was gone.

"Ave, citizens of Rome," Julius purred in a smooth voice.

I snorted. "Sorry to disappoint, there, Julie, but we're not *actually* in Ancient Rome."

He blinked at me, clearly confused. Talk about being stuck in the past. "Dear lady, where are we?"

"Hell," I replied flatly.

He paused, then said, "Ah. That explains a great deal. Mayhaps you could help me find my way out?"

I shook my head. "Afraid not, Julie-boy," I said as we moved on. "You're stuck here for the long haul."

He sighed in frustration, but we'd already moved on. A few empty cells down, we spotted a portly man gorging himself on a turkey leg. I read the nametag, but I knew exactly who it was. He looked just like his paintings.

Henry the freaking eighth.

"Come now, darling, won't you give me a son?" He leered at me through the bars, grease dripping down his double chin.

"You seem like a fertile enough lass."

I rolled my eyes. "In your dreams, buddy," I said as we walked past him. Welp, good to know all the rumors about him being a lech had been true. I should write a letter to his descendants on the throne in England.

I quickened my pace, wanting nothing more than to escape his vile gaze.

"Well, isn't this quite the rogues' gallery," Drew muttered beside me, making sure he was between me and the cells. I couldn't help but agree.

In the next cell, Cleopatra lounged on a chaise while gazing at her reflection in a hand mirror. "You will rule Egypt again, never fear. It is your destiny," she promised her reflection.

I looked at her skeptically as Lily said, "Unless you can find a way out of this cell, your dreams are pretty much toast."

She turned to us sharply, her gaze filled with defiance. "Never doubt my power. I'll escape and reclaim my throne." She stood as if to argue, but we'd already turned to see Marie Antoinette a few cells down. She sat on the floor, blonde curls tumbling over her shoulders as she played with a doll. She looked up and smiled sweetly at us. "Would you like some cake?"

Ian burst out laughing, as did Lily, but they ducked out of sight as I did my best not to react, not wanting to encourage her delusions. The poor former queen really had lost her mind.

The man in the last cell was the most chilling—a familiar figure with cold, calculating eyes—Ted Bundy, the infamous serial killer. He regarded us with a predatory stare. A shiver ran down my spine. I faced monsters regularly, yet that man scared me more than any of them ever had.

Ted leaned forward, and I stepped back, edging closer to my friends.

"I see you," he whispered.

Holy frick that man was unnerving.

Drew squeezed my hand reassuringly. "Don't worry," he said softly. "He can't hurt you."

I swallowed hard and quickened my pace, eager to move away from this hallway of horrors. We had a mission, after all—to find Crystal and put a stop to her chaos and get home. Not particularly in that order. These historical figures, villainous as some may be, were merely a distraction. The real danger still lay ahead.

As we hurried down another dimly lit stone corridor, a shriek rang out behind us. "Off with her head."

Lily snorted. "How original. As if we haven't heard that one before."

I smiled, glad for her humor in this place of gloom.

My heart pounded in my chest as we ventured further into the depths of Hell. Drew, Sam, Snoozer, Lucy-fur, Ian, and Lily walked cautiously alongside me, each one as determined as me.

The air was thick with the heat and stench of sulfur, but I couldn't let it distract me from our mission. "Keep your eyes peeled, everyone," I whispered. "We don't know what we might run into down here."

"Or who," Drew chimed in, his eyes scanning the shadows.

Sam nodded in agreement. Snoozer stayed close to my side, while Lucy padded beside him. Ian and Lily brought up the rear of our group.

As we continued our search, we stumbled upon a doorway down a long, narrow hallway. The entrance was a massive iron door, it's surface covered in intricate carvings of tormented souls and demonic figures. With a heave, I pushed the door open, revealing a dark dungeon.

"Look at this place," Sam muttered, his voice barely audible over the distant wails of anguish echoing through the halls.

"Seems cheery," Lucy quipped, flicking her tail disdainfully.

The dungeon was a labyrinth of narrow stone passages, each lined with rows of cells on either side. Flickering torches mounted on the walls provided an eerie illumination, casting dancing shadows across the damp floor. The smell of decay and despair hung heavy in the air, only amplifying the unease that had settled over our group.

"Ugh, can you believe people used to live like this?" Lily remarked, peering into one of the cells.

"Or die like this," Ian added. "I don't think anyone in here was living the high life." He grimaced as he eyed a pair of shackles.

"Let's find a way out of here," I said, my voice wavering. "The sooner we can put this place behind us, the better."

We pressed on, navigating the winding passages and checking each cell as we went. The walls wanted to close in on us, and the air grew colder with each step. I couldn't help but feel weighed down by the oppressive atmosphere.

"Is it me, or are these cells starting to look a bit like fancy hotel rooms?" Sam asked as we passed a cell with a four-poster bed draped in moth-eaten velvet.

"Maybe Hell's trying to give them a taste of their own medicine," Lucy-fur suggested, eyeing the bed skeptically. "You know, make them live in luxury they can't actually enjoy."

"Seems fitting," Drew murmured, rubbing his arms against the chill.

Suddenly, Snoozer let out a low meow. We followed his gaze to a dimly lit corner of the dungeon where a figure was chained to the wall. As we cautiously approached, my heart leaped into my throat, and hope coursed through me.

"Lucifer," I gasped, rushing to his side. He looked pale and weak, but there was no mistaking that familiar face. "You're alive."

"Never thought I'd be so happy to see the Devil himself," Ian muttered, his eyes wide in disbelief.

"Oh my god, could you lot solve a mystery any slower? I thought you were never going to get me out of here," Lucifer rasped, wincing as he shifted against the chains. "I'm alive but not exactly thriving. I gave my powers to Olivia before blasting her and Phira to Faery. That left me vulnerable."

"Let's get you out of here," I said, working to free him from his restraints. Tears coursed down my cheeks as I thought about how happy Phira and Olivia would be. The others joined in, each taking a chain and pulling with all their might. Drew used his newfound power of enhancing others' magic to give mine a little boost to break the chains, and Sam's strength helped a lot.

"Thank you," Lucifer whispered as the last chain fell away. He straightened and sniffed, straightening his soiled clothing. I waved my hand and changed him with magic into a neat but simple suit. He sighed in relief and gave me a big smile. "Oh, thank you." His expression hardened. "Now, let's find Crystal."

"Right," I agreed, my mind racing as we resumed our search. If Lucifer was powerless, how were we supposed to defeat Crystal? There was no telling what kind of power she'd amassed down here. There was no time to dwell on that now.

"Listen," Drew said suddenly, stopping in his tracks. "Do you hear that?"

We all strained to listen, and sure enough, an unmistakable chorus of demonic voices echoed through the hall. They seemed to be chanting something, growing louder and more fervent with each passing moment.

"Sounds like we're getting closer," Sam said, his voice tight with apprehension.

"Stay sharp," I warned, gripping my weapon. "We don't know what we're walking into."

As we rounded a corner, Lucy-Fur muttered, "I have a feeling we're about to find out."

"Lucifer, we need to tell you about Crystal," I said, my voice urgent. "She's the one behind all of this. She's taken control of Hell and is planning something terrible."

"Yes, I know," Lucifer said, his expression heavy with annoyance. "That little witch was the one who chained me up. How did she gain so much power?"

"I don't know," I admitted.

"All right," Sam said, clapping his hands together. "What's our plan? We can't wander around Hell, hoping to stumble upon her. How do we get out of here?"

"Actually," Lily piped up, a mischievous grin on her face, "I might have an idea. When we were passing through those cells with the historical figures, I noticed a map etched into the wall in the hall. It seemed to show the layout of this place, including what appeared to be some sort of throne room."

“I don’t need the map. But you do have a point about her taking over the throne room,” Lucifer said, taking the lead as we continued through the corridors. “While I’ve been chained up, I listened and observed. Crystal has gained a fan club since she’s been down here.”

“She has a demon army?” I asked.

Luci nodded and I cursed.

As we moved through the dungeon, my thoughts raced with possibilities, worry consuming me about walking into the unknown.

"Watch out!" Drew shouted, pushing me aside as a fireball hurtled towards us from a dark corner. We managed to dodge it, but the searing heat left a singed patch on the wall where we'd stood moments before.

"Damn it," Ian cursed, struggling to regain his balance. "Crystal must've set traps for us."

"Looks like it," I muttered, my heart pounding in my chest. "We need to be more careful."

"Agreed," said Luci, his eyes scanning the shadows for any signs of danger. "Let's proceed with caution."

We continued our search for Crystal, navigating the labyrinth passages which became increasingly treacherous. We faced a series of obstacles, from hidden pits filled with writhing serpents to enchanted doors that required answering riddles to pass through. Thankfully, Luci knew all those answers. Each challenge left us more exhausted than the last, but I refused to give up. We'd come too far to turn back now.

"This is ridiculous," Luci muttered. "I miss portaling."

After what felt like an eternity, we stumbled upon a massive chamber at the heart of the dungeon. Its walls were lined with grotesque statues of demons locked in eternal torment, their anguished expressions hauntingly lifelike.

"Is this...?" began Sam.

"Crystal's throne room," I finished for him, my gaze drawn irresistibly to the small figure seated on the dais at the far end of the room. She was just as blah-looking as she'd always been. Mousy brown hair, weak features.

"Look," whispered Lily, pointing at the army of demons kneeling before Crystal's throne. "She's somehow gained control over them."

"Crystal!" I called out, my voice echoing through the chamber as I stepped forward, anger and determination fueling me. "Release these demons and surrender yourself."

"Ah, Ava," Crystal's voice rang out, cold and mocking. "I've been expecting you." She rose from her throne, the assembled demons parting before her like a dark tide. "But you're too late, I'm afraid. My reign has only begun."

"Your reign?" I spat. "You're nothing but a power-hungry witch who's playing with forces she doesn't understand."

"Maybe so," Crystal replied, her eyes glittering. "But I understand enough to know that I'm now unstoppable. Once I unleash my demonic army upon the world above, there will be no one left to defy me."

"Over our dead bodies," Drew growled, brandishing his weapon. Apparently, hunters could conjure their weapons even in Hell.

"Exactly," Crystal said with an evil grin, raising her hand. The demons sprang into action, rushing toward us at a terrifying speed. They looked like they were ready to tear us apart.

"Fight them off!" I shouted, my heart pounding in my ears as we braced ourselves for the onslaught.

The battle erupted into a chaotic whirlwind of snarling demons of all shapes and sizes, some with razor-sharp claws, others with rows of serrated teeth. Weapons flew around us as each of us did our best to hold our ground. Drew conjured another sword using his hunter power and slashed through the air, felling one demon after another, while Ian and Lily worked together with their weapons. Sam darted through the shadows using his vampire speed and strength, striking at vulnerable points with precision.

"Watch your back!" I yelled, sending a blast of energy from my palms that incinerated an advancing demon. My heart raced as adrenaline coursed through my veins, my magic responding to each moment with newfound urgency.

"Thanks," Drew called out, grinning despite the dire situation.

Lucy-Fur hissed, her fur standing on end as she clawed at a demon, her sharp nails leaving deep gouges in its flesh. Lucifer, still weak but determined, fought a two-headed demon with deadly accuracy, using a sword Drew had produced.

"Crystal's getting away!" Sam shouted, pointing toward the far end of the chamber where Crystal was making a hasty retreat, using the battle as cover for her escape.

"Go, we'll handle these demons," Ian urged as he battled demons alongside Lily.

"Be careful," I warned as Sam, Drew, and I broke off from the group, sprinting after the retreating Crystal.

We chased her through a labyrinth of twisting corridors, the sounds of battle growing fainter behind us. Our breaths came in ragged gasps as we pushed ourselves to the limit, determined not to let Crystal slip away.

As we turned one final corner, we found Crystal standing before the massive, iron gates of Hell, her hands raised as she chanted. The air crackled with dark energy. We were running out of time.

"Stop," I yelled, but Crystal only laughed, the sound echoing through the chamber like a sinister melody.

"Too late, Ava," she taunted. "The gates are opening, and there's nothing you can do to stop it."

"Think again!" Lucifer shouted, appearing beside me. Lily, Ian, and the cats fell in line behind us. "Ava, Drew, listen carefully. We can escape this place with the demons and go find Olivia. Once I have my powers back, I'll be able to put the demons back where they belong and deal with Crystal once and for all."

"Can you do it?" I asked, hope flickering in my chest like a tiny flame.

"Trust me," Lucifer said, his eyes filled with his signature devilishness. "I've faced far worse than Crystal and her control over *my* demonic horde."

"All right." I nodded. I trusted that he'd get things done when he needed to. This was one of those times when he *needed* to. Right after we get home and found Olivia. "Let's do this."

The eerie glow of the gates bathed Crystal's face in a ghastly light, casting sinister shadows across her features. Her laughter rang through the chamber like nails on a chalkboard, and I clenched my fists, ready for battle.

We charged toward her, weapons at the ready. Crystal snarled and summoned a horde of demons to intercept us. I threw out my hand, shooting electricity at them. They scattered in all directions. Cowards.

"The gate is opening!" Luci yelled, pushing me forward. "We have to go now."

I didn't need to be told twice. We raced toward the portal. With a burst of speed, we leaped through the portal as it closed behind Crystal. Darkness enveloped me, and for a heart-stopping moment, I thought I'd be lost in the void between worlds.

Then I tumbled out the other side, landing in a heap of limbs on cold, hard concrete. The slap of my hands and knees against the ground was the only sound in the empty alleyway.

I stood up, brushing grit and grime from my clothes. "Drew? Sam? You okay? Luci?"

No response. I was alone.

10
AVA

PANIC ROSE, making it harder to breathe. Where the crap was I?

I yanked my phone out of my back pocket. Wherever I was would be easily figured out as soon as I got on the internet and the map app.

It was dead. Oh, come on.

I ran out of the alley into a busy sidewalk, startling a young couple walking by. "Sorry, excuse me," I said. "Do you know where I might find a phone?"

The woman eyed me warily and pointed across the street. Then she looped her arm around her husband's and tugged him down the sidewalk.

I muttered a quick thanks and glanced where she pointed.

Well, I'll be damned. A pay phone. I hadn't seen one of these since…I didn't know when. It'd been a while.

As I crossed the street, I patted my pockets. Son of a... I didn't have any change on me. I didn't have a purse or any form of ID. Nothing. Did collect calls still work?

Picking up the receiver, I stared at the keypad. Holy freaking crap. My mind went blank. I couldn't remember my own phone number. When was the last time I called the house? Not since before I moved out, right after Clay and I married. What was the number?

Well, poop on a cracker. I glanced around and considered asking someone if I could use their cell phone. Nah, I didn't need anyone hearing my conversation when I finally reached someone at home.

Mirror. I could conjure Yaya's antique handheld mirror. Mom and I had fixed it so we could charge it whenever we wanted to visit with Yaya. It was her way of communicating with us from the other side.

I scanned the sidewalk, noticing that it wasn't as busy as it was a few moments ago. Good. Closing my eyes, I focused on the mirror. It appeared instantly. Smiling, I touched the top of the glass and pushed a tiny bit of magic into it. "Yaya, are you there?"

"Where have you been, child?" She appeared, her aged face filled with worry. "It's been too long since you visited me."

"I thought you didn't recognize any time passing in there?" I asked, ducking into the alley before someone saw me talking to an antique hand mirror. If I angled myself right in this alley, they might think I was just on the phone.

She chuckled. "That's true. I was just pulling your chain. What can I do for you, my beautiful girl?"

Geez, this made me miss my grandmother so much. This wasn't quite the same, though it was so good to see her face. "I called you to see if you still remembered the house phone number?"

She blinked at me twice. “You don’t know your own number?”

“It’s in my phone. I just push a button. But I haven’t called the landline in years.” Decades, maybe.

She rattled off the number.

"Thanks, Yaya. Love you, but I gotta go."

"Love you, too, Sweetie." She disappeared, and I shoved the mirror handle in my back pocket before I hurried over to the pay phone and pushed zero for the operator. When someone answered the line, I almost laughed. It was living in the nineties. “I’d like to make a collect call.” I rattled off the phone number that I now remembered as if I'd never forgotten it.

The phone started ringing, a tinny electronic sound. "Pick up," I whispered. "Please, just pick up."

After four rings, a familiar voice answered. "Hello?"

I nearly collapsed in relief. "Mom. Thank goodness I reached you. We have a problem..."

She gasped. "Ava."

"Ava?" Olivia's voice echoed in the background, followed seconds later by my father's.

"Is that Ava?"

"Yes, now you two hush so I can find out where she is and why she's calling from a Boston area code."

I didn't take the time to ask her how she knew what a Boston area code was. At least I knew where I was now. I gave her the highlights of the story that turned into me rambling on about demons, portals, and escaping through the said portal only to end up scattered across who knows how many miles.

"Ava, slow down," Mom said at last. "Are you hurt? Where are you now?"

"I'm in Boston. I don't know where the others ended up." I ran a hand through my hair, clenching the phone with the other. "Mom, it's bad. Really bad. We have to seal that portal before it gets worse."

"The cats materialized in the living room a few minutes ago. Lucy-Fur said she didn't know where anyone was. That you were in Hell, then walked through a portal, and she and Snoozer appeared in the living room." Mom let out a breath.

I was so relieved that the cats had made it home. I wasn't sure what I'd do if I lost them.

"Sam called right before you. Olivia is leaving now to get him. I'll send her to you when she gets back. What's the address?"

I rattled off the one on the payphone. I couldn't believe it was there. "Thanks, Mom."

"I'm so happy you're alive. We didn't know what happened." Mom's voice cracked. I wished I could hug her.

"See you in a little bit."

"Bye, Dear."

I disconnected and leaned against the brick wall of the building. A cafe of some kind. Just then, someone walked out of the cafe, bringing the sweet and savory scent of food with them. My stomach growled like it was possessed.

Hopefully, Olivia wouldn't be long.

Two minutes later, a portal formed in front of me, and Olivia rushed out and ran into my arms, pulling me into a hug.

"I missed you," I whispered. I hated the thought of how much I'd hated her in the dream world.

"I missed you." Olivia pulled back and looked me over. "Ugh, you need a shower."

I snorted out a laugh. "Yeah, among other things." With a

wave of my hand, I cleaned myself up. "Do you know where everyone is?”

“Sam is at your house. I gave him some of my blood so he could stay awake.” Olivia grabbed my hand and closed her eyes. Her magic–Lucifer’s magic–wrapped around me like it was searching for something. “We're off to pick up Drew.”

She closed the portal she'd stepped out of and created a new one. We walked out into an empty field to find Drew on his back on the ground. Rushing over, I dropped to my knees. "What's wrong?" I gasped. That was when I saw the phone at his ear. Oh, thank heavens.

“Yes, Grandmother. We're fine. No one is hurt. I’ll find Lily and Ian and make them call you. Ava and Olivia are here. I’ll talk to you later.” He listened a little while longer. “Love you too, Pearl.”

Then he hung up and met my gaze. Snaking his hand around the back of my neck, he pulled me down for a lingering kiss.

I broke it when Olivia cleared her throat.

“Where are Ian and Lily?” I asked. "And how is your phone charged? Mine was dead."

"You know I keep a jump charger in my pocket. It's a hunter habit. Ian ended up in Washington State. Lily went to France, of all places.” Drew shook his head. Then looked at Olivia. “She says you're more than welcome to save picking her up for last.”

He texted Olivia the addresses so she could bring up a map. I stood and looked over her shoulder. “How do you know where to portal to if you've never been there?”

“I used to wonder the same thing about Luci when he did it. Now that I have his power, I also have his knowledge. It’s weird, but I understand why he does what he does and why he won’t do some things." She flashed me a grin then opened a portal and said, "That one will take you guys home. I'm taking door number two to grab Ian."

Then she was gone before I could tell her that her father was alive. Well, she'd know very soon. It'd be a more than pleasant surprise.

Drew and I happily took our portal home.

Mom swept me into a fierce hug as soon as I stepped through, and Dad's arms circled us both a moment later. I closed my eyes and leaned into their warmth, along with the scents of cinnamon and coffee that meant safety.

"You should get some rest," Mom said after a long moment, smoothing a hand over my hair. Her fingers trembled. They must've been so worried. "Maybe a shower first."

My cleaning spell must not have worked so well.

After a quick shower, Drew and I headed downstairs for some food and coffee. When we reached the first floor, we found Luci cross-legged on the floor of my living room, eyes closed, hands resting on his knees. His breathing was slow and steady, almost trance-like.

"What's he doing?" I whispered to Sam as he handed Drew and me a cup of coffee.

"Meditating," Sam replied. "He said something about trying to connect with the spirit realm to get information on Crystal."

"Is it working?"

Sam shrugged. "Hard to say."

Just then, Luci opened his eyes. "You two looked refreshed."

"How did you get here?" I was certain that Olivia hadn't come back yet.

Luci stood and dusted off the sleeves of his suit jacket, the same one I'd conjured for him. “I walked right out of Hell into my house. I came over a few minutes ago. He looked around. "I assume Olivia is still picking people up.”

“Yeah, I think,” I said, turning to the delightful smells coming out of the kitchen.

Beth walked by. “Olivia should be back any minute. Come eat.”

Didn’t have to tell me twice. I was starving.

11
OLIVIA

I STEPPED out of the portal into Ava's living room with Lily following behind me. I took a moment to take it all in, the smells of home-cooked meals, the warmth radiating from the fireplace, and the faint sound of laughter coming from the kitchen.

We made our way into the kitchen to find Beth stirring something on the stove.

My heart leaped as I spotted Luci sitting at the dining table, waiting for us. The moment our eyes locked, I gasped and staggered backward.

"How?" I whispered. "How are you alive?"

He stood and I flew into his arms, sobbing my heart out. I couldn't have stopped the tears if my life depended on it. He was *alive.* Alive! Holy freaking crap.

"I'm sorry for that," he said into my hair as he squeezed me tight. "Where's Phira?"

Stepping out of our embrace, I held his gaze. "She's in Faery. I can't get back there."

I'd figured out about an hour before Sam called me, with the help of the talisman that John created, that I could portal from place to place on Earth, but I couldn't portal to Hell or Faery.

Luci sat at the table. "You won't be able to until we recreate the spells I've done over centuries."

I stared at him as I lowered myself into the chair in front of him. "What spells?"

Ava came in and sat beside me and asked, "Yeah, go back, why aren't you dead? I never did get that answer."

I leaned over and hugged my best friend as her phone rang again. She held up one finger. "One sec, that's Jax and Hailey."

As she stepped into the living room to talk to them, Beth said, "They've been using their powers and connections to try to look for you or break into Hell."

"Have they found Ransom yet?" I asked.

Beth shook her head sadly. "No, not yet."

When Ava returned, I gasped. "Wait, do you know how long you've been gone?"

She shuddered. "I've already had that freak-out, yeah."

I glanced over at Drew. "What about your job?"

Wade raised one finger. "I went over and made them think he'd taken a leave of absence and that they knew all along." He glanced at Sam. "The bar's fine, too."

Luci glanced at Ava and then at me. "As we entered Hell, I wasn't put into a dream like the rest of you. From the moment we walked through the gates everything felt wrong, like it was under a spell. I sensed Crystal's presence coming at me with a massive amount of power. There was no way I could resist it, so I had to decide to try and save all of you."

He paused for a moment. "I took my power and pushed it into Olivia, right as I shoved her and Phira into Faery. This reset a lot of the spells I'd put into place, one of them being the ability to travel between realms. I was hoping that Olivia would find a way to get back to Earth. And she did." He reached over the table and patted my hand. "My girl figured out a way and now we're all safely in our own realms."

I shook my head. "I didn't do it alone. Just about all the fae turned up to help boost my power and direct it to create the portal to get back here."

"It was you who created the portal. That allowed Crystal to reopen the gates to Hell, which we still need to close," Luci said. He sighed. "Powerless, I was vulnerable to Crystal. She didn't want me, though. She wanted my power," Luci said. "That was when she blasted me with her magic and locked me in the dungeon."

"We saw you die," Ava said.

I nodded. I had the same confusion.

Luci nodded. "The moment you crossed through the gates, I'm fairly sure you were under Crystal's spell. You saw what she wanted you to see. I believe that she wanted you guys out of the way so she could get out of Hell and find Olivia. She's power hungry."

"I'm glad she didn't get a hold of your power," Ava said with a shudder. "I couldn't imagine what she'd do with all that power."

I agreed. "Most likely try to take over the human realm too."

Luci stood and walked around the table to stand in front of me. He held out his hand. "We need to close that hole in Hell."

"We?" I placed my hand in his, and he pulled me to a stand,

then he touched the talisman around my neck. “Clever but you won’t need that anymore.”

“Thanks, it was John and Beth who found the spell for it.” I took off the talisman and handed it to Ava. Facing Luci again, I asked, “What do I do?”

He waved for me to follow him. As we entered the living room, I used Luci’s magic within me to move the furniture so there was a space in the center of the room.

When I faced my father, he took my hands in his. "You'll need to focus your energy on the gates. Remember, it's not about brute force. It's about finesse. You have to feel the connection between you and the magic."

I took a deep breath and closed my eyes, focusing on the sensation of power stirring within me. It pulsated like a heartbeat, eager to obey my commands. I hoped I didn’t create any more earthquakes.

"You’re doing great," Luci encouraged. "Now, channel it toward the gates. Feel the connection between your magic and the broken pieces."

As I directed my energy toward the gates, the shattered fragments of the gates reached out to me, longing to be whole again. It was as if they clung to my magic like a magnet. Well, Luci’s magic, because there was no way I was keeping this much power. I concentrated, attempting to weave the pieces together.

"Easy," my father warned, sensing the strain in my efforts. "You don't want to create another disaster."

I slowed down, focusing more on control than power. As I did so, the gates began to mend, each piece finding its place and locking into position. The sensation was exhilarating, like solving a complex puzzle with my mind alone.

"Keep going," Lucifer urged, pride evident in his voice. "Almost there."

As I continued to work, I sensed that Luci still had a tiny bit of magic in his life essence. Like a true god would have.

Our combined magics formed a unique bond—one I'd never forget. Together, we mended the once-broken gates, sealing the hole that threatened to unleash Hell upon the world.

A sense of balance washed over me as the gates clicked shut and locked into place. “It’s done," I breathed. "Now, I think it's time I give you back your magic."

"Are you sure?" Luci asked with a hint of teasing. "It's not too much for you to handle?"

I chuckled with a mixture of relief and exhaustion. "Yeah, it’s a lot, and I've had it long enough now. Besides, you kind of need it to rule Hell and all that."

Because I sure as *hell* didn’t want the job.

"Fair enough," he replied with a smile.

Closing my eyes, I focused on the energy that pulsed within me, visualizing it as a bright, swirling ball of light. I imagined handing it to my father, like passing a baton in a relay race. As our hands met, the power transferred from me to him, a sensation both electrifying and comforting.

"Wow," I muttered as the last remnants of his magic left me. "That was intense."

"Thank you, Olivia," Luci said. "I'm grateful for you holding onto my power for me. You held onto it well—even if it was only for a short while."

"Hey, what are daughters for, right?" I joked, trying to lighten the mood. My heart swelled with pride, knowing I'd helped my father regain control over Hell.

He drew me into a tight hug, then pulled back, closed "I'm now going to go deal with the demons. He stepped back and created a portal, then waved and disappeared.

How did he make it look so easy?

12
AVA

THE LAVENDER-SCENTED CANDLES FLICKERED, casting a soft glow over the pentagram I'd drawn in chalk on the dining room table. There were several different ways to do a locator spell, and I'd already tried two of them while Luci and Olivia closed the gates to Hell.

Neither spell had worked, which told me that Crystal was hiding herself with magic.

Now I was hunched over the map of our small town, determined to find Crystal. My hands trembled with a mixture of anxiety and unyielding resolve. I was trying to find her by, I don't know, *feel* or something. Needless to say, that wasn't working either.

"Crud," I muttered under my breath as my latest attempt at a locator spell flickered out like a dying firefly. That was the fourth or fifth time it had failed me, and I couldn't help the frustration. This wasn't supposed to be so difficult. I was supposed to be super powerful and all that crap. Fate was conspiring against me.

"Okay, Ava," I whispered to myself, "time to bring out the big guns." It was always a risk to dip into my necromancer powers for non-dead-body magic, but desperate times called for desperate measures. Besides, what could be more important than finding Crystal right now?

With a deep breath, I gathered my focus and let the ancient energy of my necromancer lineage surge through my veins. Power like a bolt of lightning coursed from my fingertips all the way down to my toes, electrifying every nerve in my body. I shuddered at the sheer power of it all. Man, when I'd gotten my powers back, it had really taught me how freaking much I *had* to begin with. I must've gotten used to them.

"Here goes nothing," I said as I concentrated on the item that belonged to Crystal—a delicate silver locket she'd left behind. I gripped it between my fingers, feeling its cool metal press against my skin, and began the incantation once more.

"Guided by the spirits, past and present,
Lead me to the one whose heart is absent,
Through land and air, across the sea,
Reveal the path for me to see."

The words flowed from my lips like a sacred hymn, and the spell gained strength with each syllable. The locket vibrated in my hand as the combined power of my earth witch and necromancer abilities mingled together, creating a potent force that refused to be ignored.

"Come on," I murmured, willing the spell to work this time. "Find Crystal."

"Here it is!" Olivia announced, bounding into the room with a picture clutched in her hand. She handed it to me, and I grimaced at the image of Crystal and Penny, their arms around each other as they laughed at some long-forgotten joke. Gross. Probably them laughing about torturing kids or something.

"Perfect," I said, placing the picture in the center of the pentagram. With a deep breath, I closed my eyes and began chanting the incantation that would activate the spell.

"By the power of earth and air,

By fire's warmth and water's care,

Guide me through the darkness clear,

To where the missing one appears."

As the last word left my lips, a pulse of energy radiated from the picture, causing the pentagram to glow with a soft, ethereal light. I opened my eyes and studied the map closely, praying that we were on the right track this time.

"Looks like it's working." Olivia beamed, her blue eyes sparkling with excitement. "Nice job, Ava."

"Thanks," I replied, unfortunately not bolstered by her enthusiasm. "I hope you're right." I set up a little tripod and set the locket over the map. The spell would charge itself and keep looking for Crystal. It was an older spell but tended to be more effective than the quick ones.

"Sam and I are going to go pick up Sammie while you work on that." She rubbed her hands together nervously. "To us, we haven't seen him in a day or three, but to him, it's been more than a month. I hope he doesn't think we abandoned him."

"Sounds like a plan," I agreed, giving her a nod of approval. "Mom said she checked on him several times and he was having a good time with your parents. He'll be fine."

"Of course," Olivia said, but she didn't sound too convinced. She gave me a quick hug before hurrying out of the room with

Sam in tow. Their footsteps echoed in the foyer, leaving me alone with my thoughts and the map.

As the hours passed, I poured over the map, trying anything I could think of to make it pinpoint Crystal's location. The sun dipped below the horizon, casting long shadows across the room, and I had to take a break. This wasn't working. I headed into the living room to join my family. They'd checked on me several times, force-feeding me and putting drinks to my lips, but I'd mostly ignored them. "This could take several days," I said with a sigh as I sat in the big high-back chair and stared at Michelle and Lucy. "Lucy-Fur, you're going to give Michelle a heart attack," I teased as the cat vigorously kneaded her paws into Michelle's belly. She glanced up at me with a look of pure contentment on her furry face before returning her attention to her feline task. What the heck? Where'd my evil cat go while we were in dreamland?

"Oof, she's getting in there," Michelle remarked, wincing but not making any move to stop Lucy's biscuit-making session.

Zoey and Larry wandered over to join us, settling themselves into the cozy couch across from Wallie and Michelle.

Mom and Dad had gone to the Rune Academy to prepare for the godmother classes that were starting in a few weeks. It had taken us several brainstorming sessions to name the place. Who knew naming it would be harder than actually opening the school?

Lily was chatting with her hunter friend Blair and some guy named Reed. I didn't ask, mostly because her brothers were within earshot. They were way too overprotective of her, even though she was as kickass as they came.

"Hey, everyone," Drew called out, entering the room with his phone in hand. His expression was grim, casting a shadow over the warm ambiance of our gathering. "I got several messages about demon sightings. We might need to go out. I'm getting texts from Pearl, they're all over."

Ian, Lily, and Blair all pulled out their phones. As if on cue, their cells began to ding and ping and ring various tones. Lily rolled her eyes. "Yep. Demons."

"Demons?" Wallie's eyes widened, and he exchanged worried glances with Michelle and Ian.

"Great," I muttered under my breath, my chest tightening with a mixture of fear and frustration. "As if we didn't have enough on our plates already. I thought Luci was supposed to be taking care of it."

Drew shrugged and typed on his phone. "It's being handled. Do what you can in the meantime." He tapped one more time. "Sent." He met my gaze. "Luci better hurry."

A few minutes later, the phones stopped beeping. Then Drew's rang. We all glanced at each other before Drew answered. "Hi, Dad, you're on speaker."

"They all just disappeared," his dad said in a rush. "The streets are clear, and everyone seems to be safe."

When I'd first met Marcus Walker at the wedding, I'd gotten the impression that nothing could rattle him. If it did, he sure wasn't going to show it to anyone. "Lucifer must have put them in Hell where they belong," I said.

"Good." Marcus was quiet for a while before asking, "Is everyone okay?"

Drew smiled a little. "Yeah, Dad, we're good. Ava has a powerful location spell brewing. We should know where Crystal is in a day or so."

"Good. Call us if you need us."

Drew hung up and a relieved smile spread across his face. "Thank goodness," he murmured, crossing the room to pull me into a tight embrace. "It's been too long since we've had some peace around here."

"Tell me about it," I mumbled into his chest, savoring the warmth and security of his arms around me.

"Speaking of which," Drew said, pulling back to meet my gaze. "Now that things seem to be settling down, how about some alone time with my wife? We haven't had a moment to ourselves in ages."

Alone time was a luxury for us, and I couldn't deny that it sounded more appealing than ever after the recent chaos. "Okay," I agreed, allowing him to lead me away from the map and our worries, if only for a short while.

13
AVA

THE NEXT MORNING, I lay in bed, watching Drew sleep. He wasn't really sleeping, but I pretended that I didn't sense his wakefulness through our bond. Being away from him for a month made me want to cling to his side, not letting him out of my sight. He felt the same way–another feeling I got from our bond.

A month. Time in the dream world or whatever it was hadn't felt like a month. A few weeks, at most but not any longer than that. Of course, Crystal had counted on that as a distraction.

"Are you going to watch me sleep all day?" Drew's low tone was thick from sleep.

"I just might," I said as I draped across his chest with my ear to his heart. The thump, thump soothed me. "I remember not having magic and not knowing about magic. At the same time, something was wrong. Everything felt so off."

He wrapped his arms around me and kissed the top of my head. "Yeah, same with me. At least Lily, Ian, and I were bounty hunters. The weird part was, we actually got along while hunting. Normally we argue non-stop."

I snorted. Drew and Ian often butted heads. Both of them were headstrong with alpha personalities. Even though they argued, they loved each other. When it came to Lily, they were in sync about protecting their baby sister.

Releasing a dramatic sigh, I said, "I guess we should get up. I need to check on the tracking spell and figure out what we're doing today."

He nodded as he traced circles on my bare back. It felt amazing and I didn't want to move.

We cuddled for another thirty minutes before I had to get up and go pee. When I exited the bathroom, Drew pulled me back to the bed with a devious grin.

One satisfied hour later, Drew and I made our way downstairs. After grabbing a cup of coffee, I headed to the living room where Michelle, Wallie, Zoey, and Larry sat talking.

The first thing I noticed was Lucy-Fur nestled up against Michelle's belly, purring. I sat on the loveseat and motioned to Michelle. "What did you do to my cat?"

Michelle laughed. "Nothing. I think she likes the baby."

Drew sat beside me, watching Lucy. "I'm not sure that's a good thing."

"I can hear you," Lucy said without opening her eyes.

"We know." I arched an eyebrow at her, but she still wasn't looking.

Lily walked into the room and did a double take at Lucy whispering to the baby. Then Lily shook her head and looked at Drew and me. "Ian and I were talking about the necromancers, and I was wondering if y'all had a chance to go through the RV? I mean, there could be anything in there—clues, spells, creepy dolls."

"Actually," Sam interjected, emerging from the kitchen with his mini-me–Sammie–behind him. "The RV isn't there anymore."

"Where is it?" I asked as Olivia walked in behind Sammie.

"Luci moved it."

As if talking about the RV summoned him, Luci materialized beside Olivia. His sudden appearance startled everyone, but we should've been used to it by now. He stood there, impeccably dressed in a tailored suit, with a smirk that could only be described as matter-of-fact. "Ah, yes, about that," he said and adjusted his cufflinks. "I took the RV to my house. You're welcome, by the way."

"Your house?" I struggled to process this new piece of information. Why did the Prince of Darkness have an interest in a necromancer's RV? Then again, he did like to collect things.

Odd things.

“It's not outside and you don't have a big garage,” I added.

“Oh, I put it in one of my rooms. Hang on, let me look.” Lucy reached into his pocket and pulled out a scroll, the kind that was made of parchment and looked like some sort of declaration of independence should've been written on it. It looked far too large to have fit in his pocket in the first place. With a flick of his wrist, he unrolled it.

And unrolled it.

And unrolled it.

It kept rolling until it crossed the living room and headed out into the hall.

"What in the world?" I asked, getting to my feet to see what was on the paper. I had to snort.

“Is that...?" Michelle asked, her eyes wide with surprise.

"Indeed," Lucy replied, smirking as he traced a line on the map with one manicured fingernail. "This, my friends, is the path to the RV's current location." It was a map of his house. All his collection rooms, everything.

We leaned in for a closer look. The map was intricate and beautifully illustrated, depicting corridors, wings, staircases, and doorways. There were even tiny, ornate symbols scattered throughout, their meanings unclear.

“Your house isn't that big,” I said.

Olivia snorted. “You need to come over and go exploring with me again. I swear every time I go looking for something the house seems bigger.”

"Great, so we're supposed to follow this map?" I doubted our ability to navigate such a complex layout.

"Correct." Luci grinned, unfazed by my skepticism. "You'll find the RV tucked away in the eastern wing, down a corridor marked with a crescent moon, up two flights of stairs, and behind a green door adorned with golden ivy."

"Sounds simple enough," Drew muttered.

"Come now, where's your sense of adventure?" Luci chided, his eyes sparkling with mischief. "Besides, you've got me to guide you."

"Okie, then, let's do this," I said, trying to instill some confidence in the group. We all shared a collective deep breath and then set off, following Luci to his house, which was on my property across the expansive lawn from my house.

The mansion itself was an enigma, each room more opulent and bizarre than the last. The eastern wing was shrouded in shadows, the air growing cooler as we ventured further down the crescent moon-marked corridor. At one point, I could've sworn a painting's eyes follow us as we passed by.

"Two flights of stairs," Luci reminded us, gesturing toward an ornately carved staircase that spiraled upwards into darkness.

"Of course, it's up there," Michelle grumbled, rubbing her pregnant belly. "Uphill both ways."

"Stay close, everyone," I whispered. When we finally reached the top, we stood before a door that matched Luci's description perfectly: green with golden ivy snaking across its surface.

"Here we are," Lucy announced, placing a hand on the doorknob. "Behind this door lies the elusive RV."

I looked across the hall to a door that had a gold star on the door. "What's in there?" I asked moving to the door.

"You don't want to go in there," Luci said and motioned to the room with the RV in it.

I chuckled. "Okay, I *so* want to go in there now." I opened the door with the gold star and froze. "Holy..."

Olivia stepped up next to me. "Wow." She walked into the room ahead of me.

It was a veritable shrine to the entertainment industry, with shelves upon shelves of memorabilia. Gold and platinum records adorned the walls, and glass cases displayed everything from signed guitars to bedazzled costumes.

"Welcome to my little slice of musical heaven," Lucy beamed, gesturing for us to step inside.

"Wow," Michelle breathed, her fingers hovering over a rhinestone-studded glove. "This is incredible."

We spread out in the room, looking at all the stuff. I was super tempted to take home a microphone that said *Nashville, TS, rained out concert, May 2023*. "Uh, Luci? This date hasn't happened yet."

He raised his eyebrows and joined me. "Oh, yes, well." Carefully taking the microphone away, he put it on its stand. "I'm sure it's a typo."

Not believing him *at all*, I moved on and came across a box full of papers. "Are these contracts?" I asked, reading the fine print with growing disbelief.

"Indeed," Luci purred with twinkling eyes. "I've been offering my, er, *services* to certain individuals in exchange for a small favor here and there."

"Services?" Zoey asked. "What kind of services?"

"Let's just say I have the ability to give one's career a little, ah, *boost*," Luci replied cryptically. "In return, they provide me with some unique items for my collection. Or other favors as I see fit."

"Wait, so you're saying that these pop stars owe their success to you?" I asked incredulously, scanning the list of names on the contracts.

"Only a select few," Luci admitted. "But it's a mutually beneficial arrangement, I assure you. No soul collecting. I stopped doing that *years* ago."

"Still," Michelle said, shaking her head in disbelief. "This is wrong. You can't manipulate people's lives like that."

Drew scoffed, his face flushed with anger. "It doesn't matter if you gave them a boost or not. It's the fact that you're using their success for your personal gain."

"Besides, it's deceitful. People should earn their success through hard work and talent, not because of some supernatural intervention."

Luci rolled his eyes and strutted to the center of the memorabilia room. "Oh, please. As if any of you are innocent of cutting corners or making less-than-ethical choices." His dark eyes sparkled with mischief.

"Not even close," I said.

"Allow me to provide an example," Luci said and pointed to Michelle. "Remember the time you lied about being sick so you could get out of helping your sister move?"

"Hey, I—" Michelle started, but Luci cut her off.

"Or Sam," Luci continued, his tone dripping with sarcasm, "how about the time you hacked into your professor's computer to change your grade on that exam?"

"Uh, well, see—" Sam stammered, his cheeks turning a deep shade of crimson. He turned and stammered, "Well, Ava *borrowed* that library book and then spilled coffee on it. You never returned it, did you?"

I snorted. "A library book is nothing. Olivia flashed the whole track team during our senior year of high school," I said.

Olivia's mouth fell open, but she laughed and said, "Drew drank so much at our wedding that he started dancing on the tables."

"I've yet to see video evidence of that," Drew said, then added, "Ian was stalked by a bunny shifter once."

Drew and Lily burst out laughing at that one.

Ian wasn't amused. "You wanna tell secrets? Lily has a boyfriend. He's a wolf shifter."

Drew stopped laughing and jerked his gaze to his sister. Lily rolled her eyes. "He's not my boyfriend."

"He's your mate," Ian added.

Lily opened her mouth and then closed it.

Ohhh, it was true. I stepped closer to her and whispered, “Congrats.”

Lily grumbled, “Thanks, but it’s complicated.”

"Okay, that's enough," I said and looked at Luci. "The point is what you're doing is wrong."

"Perhaps," Lucy admitted with a shrug. “It's my wrong to commit. Let’s go search through the RV.”

He walked out of the room, and we all followed.

"He's got like six guitars signed by Elvis over there," Olivia hissed behind my back. "I gotta find my way back to this room."

No joke. I wanted to hunt for anything Black Sabbath as soon as possible.

We’d spent the rest of the afternoon searching through the RV and didn’t find anything remotely interesting. Definitely not as interesting as the music room, but at least it got our minds off Crystal for a little while. That was something.

14
AVA

IT'D BEEN two days since I started the tracking spell to find Crystal. The sun peeked through the curtains of my bedroom as my locator spell tingled against my consciousness, waking me from my sleep.

A surge of magic flowed through my veins.

Holy freaking crap. The locator spell found Crystal. I jumped out of bed and ran downstairs after throwing on a bra and some leggings. As I ran down the stairs, I pulled my hair in a bun. Not gorgeous, but I'd do.

Everyone else was already up. Drew, Ian, Lily, Sam, and Olivia sat at the large kitchen table enjoying coffee. That wasn't an unusual occurrence since I normally didn't get out of bed until tenish.

"The locator spell found her." I moved to the map at the end of the table. "There she is." I could hardly believe it. We had her.

Olivia gulped the rest of her coffee, then created a portal to the location on the map. "Let's do this."

My heart raced as we rushed through the portal, coming out in front of an old abandoned house on the outskirts of town.

Olivia, Lily, and I crept through a back door into a musty kitchen. The guys went in through the front.

We found Crystal perched on the sofa, examining her nails as if she hadn’t a care in the world. This had been a trap, and we'd run right into it. Our only hope was to outpower her.

“You're out of your league, little witches,” she said.

Before I could blink, she flung out her hands, sending a blast of

magic hurtling toward us.

I threw up a hasty shield, her magic sizzling against it. Out of the corner of my eye, I watched Olivia cast a spell. Vines grew out of the floor, wrapping around Crystal's arms and legs.

With an angry shriek, Crystal tore free of the bindings. She snapped her fingers, and half a dozen demons materialized from the shadows, eyes glowing red.

What the actual Hell? I looked at Olivia. “I thought Luci sent them all home.”

“So did I,” Olivia said, hardening her stare on Crystal. “I sent a message to Luci. He should be here any moment.”

“Good.” We were going to need his help.

“Get them!” Crystal screeched.

The demons leaped at us, all claws and gnashing teeth. Olivia and I fought side by side, magic crackling through the air as we dueled the creatures. I hurled a lightning bolt at one demon, banishing it in a burst of light.

Lily charged forward with a large dagger in one hand, fighting off her own demon. Drew, Ian and Sam fought off a group of demons together, Sam blending in with the brothers as though he'd battled with them for years.

As we defeated the last of the demons, I turned to see Crystal attempting to sneak away, edging along the wall toward a side entrance.

"Not so fast," I said, flinging a binding spell at her. This time, the magic held.

Crystal struggled against the magical ropes, curses spewing from her lips. I strode over to her, electricity arcing off my finger-tips. "How did you get so powerful?"

She bared her teeth in a vicious grin. "Wouldn't you like to know."

"Tell me," I said, "or I'll make you wish the demons got you instead."

Crystal laughed. "You think your petty threats scare me?" Her grin widened. "Now that you have me," she purred, "what are you going to do with me?"

Before I could answer, Luci appeared in a burst of flames, scowling at Crystal. "Well, well. Look who's all tied up."

Crystal paled. Luci had his magic back. The whole room could feel it. He wore it like a cape, thundering around him as the room darkened.

Crystal didn't respond to him, but she was nearly shaking.

Lucifer snapped his fingers and the bindings fell away. "You've caused me no end of trouble, little witch. It's time you paid your dues." He grabbed Crystal's arm in an iron grip and created a portal with the other one.

He took Crystal through the portal and Olivia and I stepped closer to watch what he was going to do to her.

"Wait, the Devil has a Department of Motor Vehicles?" Olivia asked, her blue eyes wide with disbelief.

"Apparently so." I couldn't help but chuckle at the absurdity of it all.

In the middle of what looked like a Hellish version of the DMV stood Crystal, her eyes wide with horror as she took in her surroundings.

"Please tell me they have to wait in line for hours like the rest of us." Olivia snorted as Crystal whirled on Luci, fists clenched.

“You can't do this!” she shrieked.

The smell wafted out of the portal. Something like burning rubber mixed with stale body odor.

"Yikes." Olivia cringed. "Luci really does have a sense of humor."

Lucifer gave her a cold smile. “My dear, I’m the king of Hell. I can do as I please.” He leaned close, lowering his voice to a menacing purr. “Welcome to the eternal DMV.”

Crystal’s face registered shock and horror as her gaze landed on the endless rows of people standing in lines that seemed to go on forever. She glanced around, her mouth agape, as she listened to the cacophony of impatient murmurs and groans from the eternally waiting damned souls. She let out a bone-chilling scream of rage and despair. “No. No, this isn't happening!” She grabbed at Lucifer, her nails raking across his arm. “Get me out of here.”

Luci didn't even flinch. “I'd watch your tone, witch. Remember," he said, his voice low and menacing as he towered over her. "You're here because of *your* actions. You'll leave when I say you can leave." With that, he strode towards a door marked 'Eternal Suffering,' leaving Crystal standing in the middle of the Hellish DMV, looking utterly lost and terrified.

Behind him, Crystal collapsed to her knees, her scream of "No!" echoing through the room.

The last thing I saw before the portal closed was Crystal's anguished face. After everything she'd done, it was almost satisfying—but still, a fate I wouldn't wish on anyone.

Later that night, Olivia, Sam, Drew and I gathered in my living room, discussing the day's events over glasses of wine. It was nice to breathe for a moment. We still needed to find Penny and Bevan but at least this threat was handled.

Sam sat in an armchair with Olivia in his lap. Little Sammie was upstairs with Zoey and Larry. Ian had gone to bed. Lily had gone back to Florida via a portal Olivia created for her.

"Do you remember how I smelled berries at Penny's house?" Sam asked.

I nodded and he said, "I smelled berries again when we found Crystal."

"So, Crystal had been in Penny's house before we got there. I'm betting she took that journal that was missing off the desk," I said.

"I'll have to ask Luci if he could hunt for the journal to see why Crystal wanted it. Maybe it could lead us to Penny and Bevan," Olivia said.

Penny and Bevan had escaped Hell several months back and we hadn't been able to find them. We did have the shifters spread the word about them just in case they decided to start up another shifter fighting ring.

Olivia sighed, rubbing her temple. "Must there always be another crisis?"

I gave her a sympathetic look. Our lives had been nonstop drama.

“Comes with the territory, I'm afraid,” I said. “When you're dealing with magic and monsters, there's never a dull moment.”

Olivia groaned. “Remind me again why I married into this family?”

Sam laughed and pulled her close, kissing the top of her head. “Because you love me, of course.”

“Lucky for you,” Olivia said dryly, but she was smiling.

“Hate to tell you, bestie, but you're the one who dragged Sam into this, technically. You're the half-goddess, half-fae, remember?"

Olivia beamed. "Oh, yeah."

"I’m happy you're both in our lives,” I said, snuggling into Drew a little more. “And I’m *so* happy that our lives aren't normal.”

15
AVA

THE MORNING SUN cast a warm glow on the cobblestone path leading up to the Rune Academy. Excitement buzzed in the air as Olivia and I stepped through the iron gates, our heels clicking in unison. The first day of godmother school had finally arrived, and we were more than ready to take on our roles of helping Mom and Dad run the school. This was so cool. We weren't just going to be helping. There were several classes we planned to take ourselves.

"Can you believe the day is finally here?" Olivia whispered, her blue eyes twinkling with anticipation. "We're doing this."

All the hard work was coming to fruition. I smiled at her with a surge of pride and confidence in our joint venture. "It's going to be amazing," I assured her. "We've worked so hard for this moment, and now it's here."

As we approached the grand entrance, I spotted my parents waiting for us.

"Morning, ladies." Dad pulled me into a hug. "You both look radiant today."

“So do you and Mom,” I said with a laugh. He was so excited.

"Thank you," Olivia replied with a silly bow. She shifted gears, going into organizer mode. "How are the preparations going? Is everything on schedule?"

"Everything's running smoothly," Beth answered, tucking a strand of her brown hair behind her ear. She held a clipboard in her hands, her gaze scanning the list of tasks she'd meticulously organized. "The classrooms are set up, the refreshments are being prepared, and our new students should be arriving any minute."

Olivia nodded, satisfied with their progress, but still wanting to ensure every detail was perfect. "And the teachers? Are they all set?"

"The godmothers have their own teachers." Mom shrugged. "I didn't want to grill them about it or anything."

"They’re good to go and eager to start the school year," Dad assured her. "I spoke to their head sugar daddy."

We froze and stared at my father. "What?" Mom asked. "Their who?"

He grinned and said, "They call the male godmothers *sugar daddies*."

"How long have you known that?" Mom stared at him with her mouth open. I’d known about their name but hadn’t thought to tell Mom and Dad.

I chimed in before Dad could answer, "You were just holding that and waiting for the right time, weren't you?"

He burst out laughing. "I've been *dying*."

"Great," I said after we had a good laugh on the front lawn of the school. "Now, let's get ready to welcome our new students and give them the best first day we possibly can."

As we dispersed to our designated positions, I couldn't help but feel a sense of accomplishment wash over me. This school was going to help so many magical and supernatural beings.

As our new students filed in, a mixture of nerves and excitement radiating from them, I noticed Zoey standing off to the side. She seemed lost in thought, her gaze fixated on a group of women chatting about their new adventure at Rune Academy.

"Hey," I said, pressing my shoulder into hers. It was something the ferret shifter, Dana, had told me cat shifters did. Touch was important to them to settle their inner animal. Zoey's tiger was a huge cuddle bug. "What's going on in that head of yours?"

Zoey startled before offering me a small smile. "It's nothing. Just watching the new students, you know? They're all so excited."

"Of course they are," Olivia chimed in, joining us. "This is a big step for them. The first day of the rest of their magical lives." She shook her head. "It's still weird that the godmothers don't come into their powers until their forties."

"Yes, but for them, this is like high school, or maybe college." Zoey sounded wistful. "I never got to have that, you know? A real education, I mean. It's just, sometimes I wonder what it would be like to attend high school, even though I'm too old now."

"Hey, it's never too late to learn," Dad said as he and Mom approached us. "You can always pursue your education in other ways."

"True, I guess." Zoey nodded, taking a deep breath. "Sometimes I think about how great it would be to experience walking down those hallways, making friends, learning from teachers who care..."

"If this is something you want, then we should explore your options," I suggested, trying to offer my support. "Get you tested to see where you're at and look at what you want to do after you graduate."

"Here at Rune Academy, you wouldn't have to worry about your ears or your tail popping out," Olivia added. "You could be yourself."

"That *is* a plus." Zoey's eyes lit up with hope. "Okay, I want to do this."

Before she could get too excited, Zoey's phone dinged with an incoming message. She glanced at the phone and frowned as she read the message. I glanced at it without reading anything. I didn't want to invade her privacy, but my curiosity was piqued. It was pretty long.

"What is it?" I asked.

Zoey looked at me, her face pale. "I don't understand." She handed her phone to me.

I scanned the message. Shock and sadness bubbled inside me while my chest tightened. After calming myself, I read the message out loud.

"Hi, Zoey. I can't believe it's you. I wasn't sure at first but, then I went to your social media accounts and saw your videos and knew it was you. Sorry, rambling. My name is Rowan, I'm your cousin on your mom's side. I've recently come across some information that, well, it's going to sound crazy, but everyone in the pride thinks you and your parents were murdered years ago."

The air felt suffocating, each word feeling heavier and more restrictive than the last. A torrent of emotions swirled through my mind—confusion, fear, anger. But most of all, I was consumed by an overwhelming need to protect Zoey and help her uncover the truth.

This was the first real clue we'd got about her parents and

pride. I handed her phone back and held her hand. “You can message her back and even arrange to meet with her, but I’m going to be there. I’m not letting you do this alone. Take it from someone who's investigated her mother’s death, it’s not an easy thing to do.”

“Plus, you'll be learning about your life before you were abducted. That will trigger memories that you don’t want to remember,” Olivia said, pulling Zoey into a hug. “We’ll all help with research and emotional support and anything you need.”

Dad and Mom nodded. “You’re family,” Dad said.

Zoey teared up and her ear popped out. “Thank you. I’m not sure I know what to say to her or how to reply.”

I pulled her out of Olivia’s arms and held her close. “Be honest and tell her what happened. You don’t have to go into details right away, just the highlights.”

She nodded. "Yeah, okay."

All I could hope for was that her pride wouldn't try to take her from me. She deserved a place with them, but Zoey was like a daughter to me, and I wasn’t to let her go without a fight.

READ a FREE Witching After Forty story here: A Witching Babymoon.

See what’s next for Ava in A Grand Midlife.

Don’t miss two series set in the new academy: Godmother Training Academy and Geography & Ghost Hunts (Middle Grade).

Catch up with Hailey and Jax: Fanged After Forty

Catch up with Blair and Lily: Hunting After Forty

A GRAND MIDLIFE

WITCHING AFTER FORTY BOOK 18

L.A. BORUFF

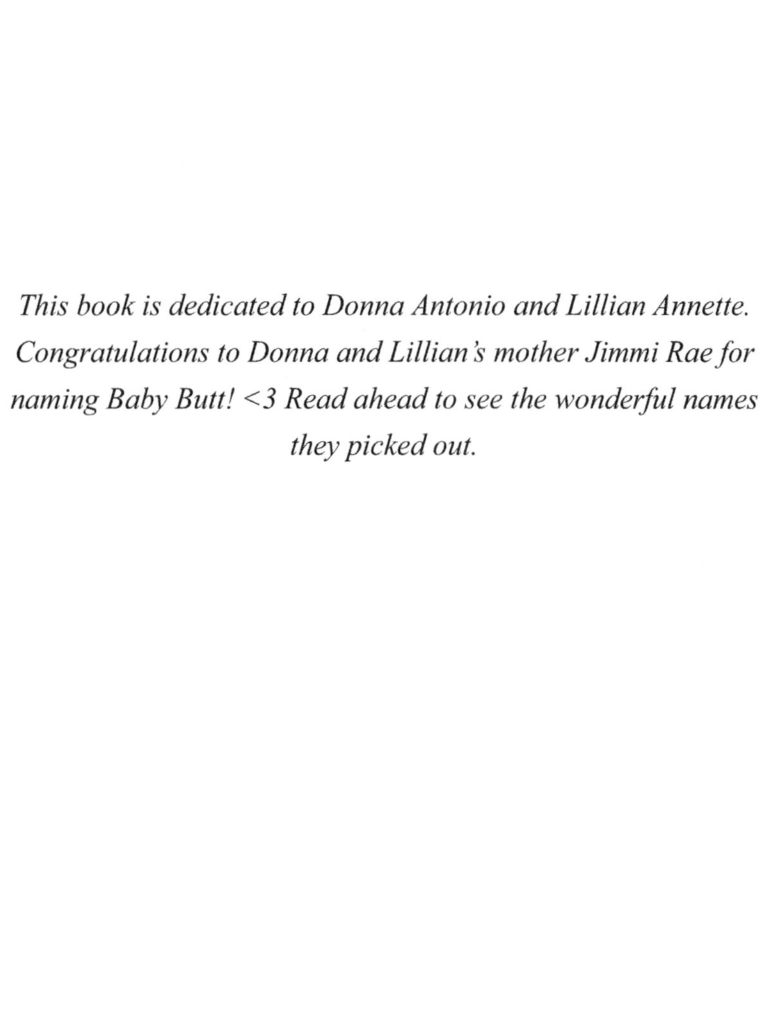

This book is dedicated to Donna Antonio and Lillian Annette. Congratulations to Donna and Lillian's mother Jimmi Rae for naming Baby Butt! <3 Read ahead to see the wonderful names they picked out.

1
AVA

SHOCKED BEYOND ALL REASON, I stopped mid-step, causing Olivia to slam into my back.

My bestie yelped, walking around me to stand at my side. "What in the ever-loving, fire-burning, *what*-has-my-father-done-now heck?"

We'd just gotten back from Rune Academy, tying up last-minute things and checking on how the summer program was going. The godmothers had just started up their classes. Zoey had gone with us, but she'd left about an hour ago after getting a message. Someone from her biological family, a cousin, had found her on social media and reached out. That was something Zoey and I hadn't thought of. We'd have to deal with it soon.

I pointed to a new building in the once-empty yard between Luci's house and Winston, my magical Victorian.

"There's an extra freaking house in my backyard." It was smaller than Winston and much smaller than Luci's gothic mansion, but it was still a house that hadn't been there this morning when we left for the academy.

Despite not being all that big, the house was lavish, with stone siding and big bay windows and a chimney puffing out wispy trails of smoke.

Completely and utterly over Luci's crap, I stormed over to the monstrosity of a house just as Lucifer himself sauntered out of my backdoor, munching on a sandwich stacked with all the fixings. Was that from *my* fridge?

"Dude," I called. "Your house is right there." I jabbed my finger at his pristine gothic mansion, the one, for the record, he'd never asked permission to put in my expansive side yard.

He blinked innocently, then ignored my comment and gestured toward the new house. "Don't you love it? It's a pool house."

I pursed my lips and glared at the devil, trying not to let my nostrils flare too much as Olivia snickered at my side. "We. Don't. Have. A. Pool,"

Luci paused mid-chew and glanced around. "Oh, shoot. Yeah, I guess we don't."

The infuriating devil snapped his fingers and whoosh. There was a huge in-ground pool, rimmed with slate tile and tropical plants. Steam rose from the heated water into the air.

I pinched the bridge of my nose. Times like this I wondered how was this my life. Not that I was complaining, exactly, because my life was pretty freaking wonderful, but this man-god-mischief maker was pretty dang annoying sometimes. "Luci, it's cold most of the year here. A pool is useless."

"Hmm." Luci tapped a long finger against his chin in thought. With another snap, a retractable pool cover emerged, sleek and state-of-the-art. "There, now it'll stay a balmy eighty-five degrees. You're welcome."

My eye twitched. Beside me, Olivia gave a low whistle before she giggled and said, "Dang, Dad. Those are crazy expensive. Like twenty grand at least."

Lucifer waved her off. "Oh, I confiscated it from a drug lord in South America. He won't miss it. It's always hot there."

Good grief. Before I could comment further, the pool house door creaked open, and a man shuffled out. He had kind of wild hair, mostly brown. It was wavy more than curly and desperately needed a cut. Not a trim. A big cut. He also had a wild beard, long and untamed. Wild Mountain Man was all that came to mind.

"We'll talk about this later," I grumbled to Lucifer. Then I smiled as sweetly as I could at the stranger and held out my hand. "Hi. I'm Ava. I own this property. Who are you?"

The man studied me for a moment, then glanced at Olivia before settling his attention on Luci, who then introduced our new neighbor. "This is the werewolf that the kids and I saved in Australia last month. Now he has a place to stay, or any of your guests." He beamed. "I figure you'll want a place for in-laws and whatnot."

The *kids* Luci was referring to were Michelle, Wallie, Zoey, and Larry. They'd found the werewolf in the woods close to a cabin made of candy while they were on Wallie and Michelle's babymoon—their last vacation before the baby arrives.

"He can't remember his name," Luci added.

Olivia nudged me as the werewolf approached. "Hey, maybe Sam can get a read on him, find out something about his past."

I raised an eyebrow. "I thought Sam didn't have control over his psychic powers yet."

"Worth a shot, though, right? Plus, it'll be good practice for him." Olivia pulled her phone out and called Sam.

With his vampire speed, Olivia's husband and my lifelong best friend, Sam, arrived within seconds.

Olivia asked, "Think you could do a reading on our new friend here? See if you get any hits on his identity?"

Sam frowned, shoving his hands in his pockets. "I dunno Liv. It's not like I can just turn it on and off. This psychic stuff is still new to me."

"Please?" Olivia clasped her hands together pleadingly and batted her lashes at him. "Just try."

"Yeah, c'mon Dad, you got this," Little Sammie popped up beside us eagerly.

I jumped and clutched my heart. Geez. I did not know where the kid came from. My guess was from my house, since he enjoyed hanging out with Zoey and Larry.

Sam sighed. "All right, all right, I'll try."

He turned to the werewolf, who'd watched the exchange curiously. Sam stepped forward, and the werewolf widened his eyes, looking like he was ready to run. Sam held up his hands. "Easy. I have to touch you to get a good reading. This is still new to me, but I won't hurt you."

After another second, the werewolf nodded and stood still while Sam placed his palms on either side of the wolf's head, closing his eyes in concentration.

We waited with bated breath. A little part of me was proud of Sam for embracing his new powers as easily as he had, although it didn't surprise me all that much. We'd grown up together, and he'd always known about my witchy side.

After a long moment, Sam dropped his hands. "Sorry, nothing. It was just static."

Little Sammie tilted his head. "That's sad how you can't remember your name." Before we could stop him, Sammie grabbed the werewolf's hand.

"Your name is Ross," he stated confidently.

The werewolf blinked in surprise. Heck, we all blinked in surprise.

"Ross." He breathed in and out a few times and blinked. "Actually, I think you might be right. That sounds familiar. It feels right."

Olivia tousled Sammie's hair. "Very good."

I grinned at my little buddy. It made sense that Sammie's powers were more potent than his father's, given that Sammie was part psychic, part fae, and part whatever Lucifer was. God? Not *the* God, but a god.

Pointing to Winston, my old magical Victorian house, I said, "C'mon, let's go talk with Zoey about her cousin and figure out what to do with that bombshell."

Luci followed Ross into the pool house as Olivia and I entered my house through the conservatory. When we entered the kitchen, the wonderful savory aroma of spaghetti surrounded us. Michelle stood at the stove, stirring an enormous pot of sauce. Wallie hovered close by. "Come on, honey. Please sit down and let me finish dinner."

Deciding to let my son learn on his own to not bother a pregnant woman who was clearly nesting, I focused on my two adopted kids, Zoey and Larry.

They sat at the kitchen table, waiting for us. Zoey's tiger ears and tail were out, and she'd taken off the contacts she wore in public that masked her yellow cat eyes. Her tail twitched from side to side. She was stressing over what to do about her extended family who, until earlier today, thought she was dead.

Zoey *was* dead, technically. I'd animated her as well as all the kids who'd died in the shifter fight ring that Olivia, Drew, Sam, and I had taken down a little over a year ago. I'd animated the kids to find out who their families were so I could give them some kind of closure. Many of their relatives hadn't known where their kids had gone.

Zoey had told us she didn't have any family, and that she'd wanted to stay with me. So here we were, over a year later. Gods, it was surreal that it'd been that long already.

"Hey, guys," Zoey said.

I poured four mugs of hot water and set them on the table after putting a chamomile tea bag in each.

Sliding into the seat across from Zoey, I met her gaze. "So, about your cousin reaching out," I began gently. "How are you feeling?"

Zoey bit her lip, looking down. "I don't know. Part of me wants to talk to her, find out what happened after I ran away. But another part..."

I reached across to squeeze her hand. "You're scared," I finished for her. "Scared they'll reject you, or that you'll find out something you don't want to know."

Zoey nodded, eyes shimmering with unshed tears. "What if they're the ones who killed my parents? Or they didn't even look for me?"

The pain in her voice broke my heart. I wished I could erase the trauma of her past. As powerful as I was, time travel wasn't something in my bag of tricks.

"I can't promise it won't hurt," I whispered. "But don't you think it's better to know the truth?"

Zoey stared into her tea silently.

"You mentioned your parents were shot," Olivia prompted gently. "Did you see who did it?"

Zoey shook her head, her tiger ears drooping. "No. It happened so fast. One minute we were having dinner, the next there were gunshots. I hid, but my parents didn't get up. I shifted, and as a tiger somehow I knew, beyond a shadow of a doubt that they were dead. I ran out the back door and kept running. For days, weeks maybe. I was so scared."

She took a shaky breath. "Eventually, some humans found me. I guess they thought I was just a regular tiger. They took me to this big cat rescue place. Honestly, it wasn't so bad at first. I got to be around other tigers. But then..."

She trailed off again, fresh tears spilling down her cheeks. What horrors had this poor girl endured?

Larry wrapped an arm around her, drawing her closer to him. The poor guy looked as helpless as I felt.

I moved to kneel beside her, enveloping Zoey in a fierce hug. Larry came with her until we were tangled in a three-person hug. "It's okay. You're safe now. Whatever happened, we'll get through it together."

Zoey clung to me, body shaking with sobs. I held her until the tears slowed, stroking her hair.

"Sweetie, I know this is hard," I whispered. "But don't you want to find out what really happened that night? Why your family thought you died too?"

Zoey lifted her head, yellow cat-eyes glistening. "I do, but it's scary. What if whoever killed my parents is still out there?"

I took her hands in mine. "Then we'll face them together. Me, Drew, Olivia, Sam, Michelle, Wallie, Larry—we're all here for you. I even think Luci would do anything to keep you safe as well."

Zoey managed a small smile. "You're right. I should at least talk to my cousin, see what she knows."

I squeezed her hands encouragingly. We both looked up as Michelle waddled to the table, one hand supporting her pregnant belly. "Ava's right. And I'm sure Baby Butt will help to protect her Aunt Zoey."

Zoey laughed softly. "I'm not sure I want my family to explode like that evil witch did."

Yeah, that had been unexpected. Wallie and Michelle had gotten into a lot of trouble in Australia on their babymoon. Olivia and I got there just in time, but we ended up being unnecessary. Baby Butt had exploded the dark witch from the womb. My granddaughter was going to be a powerful witch one day. And more than likely a handful to raise. It was a good thing that Michelle and Wallie had an enormous family to help.

"I wanted to make dinner for everyone, but this one insisted on doing it," Wallie said, kissing Michelle's cheek. She swatted him playfully.

"I gotta keep busy, or I'll go crazy waiting for this little one." Michelle grinned, then added, "Dinner is ready. We're doing buffet style tonight."

After everyone had full plates, we sat down to eat. Someone was missing. "Hey, where's Ian?"

"Oh, he said he wasn't hungry," Michelle replied through a mouthful of pasta. "More for us."

I frowned. That was odd. Ian was usually the first one at the table.

The ringing of my phone interrupted my thoughts. "Oh, it's Drew." I answered it, putting it on speaker. "Hi, Honey. How's the investigation going? You're on speaker, by the way."

Drew's voice echoed through the kitchen, along with Lily's enthusiastic hellos. "We must have just missed you at the Rune Academy," Drew said. "We just left."

"We did too, recently. We must've been there at the same time and didn't realize it." He and Lily had been called in to investigate a murder at the godmother training center in one wing of Rune Academy. My parents had told Olivia and me about it moments before we left. Of course, at the same time, Drew had texted me to let me know he wouldn't be home for a few days. I didn't know how I was going to survive without him.

On the flip side, I got my bed again.

After we chatted for a few minutes, Drew hung up. I looked at Olivia. "Where's Phira? I haven't seen her in a few days."

"She's having a blast in Faerie with Jess and Devan." Olivia twirled pasta onto her fork. "Might even stay the whole summer."

After dinner, I found Ian sitting alone on the back porch steps, staring up at the night sky. Slivers of moonlight illuminated his brooding face.

"Hey." I leaned against the railing. "You okay? You've seemed a little off lately."

He stood and looked at me. "Nothing." Then he went inside without another word.

Nothing, my big toe. There was definitely something going on with him, but I wasn't really close enough to force the issue. I'd have to remember to mention it to Drew the next time I talked to him.

2
OLIVIA

As I loaded the dishwasher the next night with Sammie's and my plates from dinner, Sam let out a heavy sigh. He'd been researching his family history with little luck.

"Still nothing?" I kept my tone light as I started the dishwasher.

Sam ran a hand through his hair. "Nope. I just wish I understood my powers better. It's like I have this unwieldy thing inside me that could burst out at any moment." He met my gaze.

I dried my hands and went over to rub his shoulders reassuringly. "I know. We'll figure this out." An idea struck me. "Why don't we go see Jeanne Maclay at the academy? She's the expert on psychic abilities. And classes are surely done for the day by now, so if we hurry, we can catch her before she goes home for the weekend."

Sam's eyes lit up with hope. "That's brilliant. Maybe she can give me some guidance on how to manage all this." He gestured wildly at his head.

I smiled. "Exactly. I'll call Zoey to watch Sammie while we're gone."

I picked up my phone. After two rings, the sweet dead tiger picked up. "Hey Zoey, sorry for the late notice, but could you come over and watch Sammie for a little bit? Sam and I need to make a quick trip to the academy."

"Sure, no problem," Zoey chirped, her voice bright and cheerful through the phone. "I'd love to spend some time with my favorite little man. I'll head on over."

I smiled as I hung up, thankful for such a willing and eager babysitter on short notice. Zoey doted on Sammie as if he was her own little brother.

Soon after, the doorbell rang, announcing Zoey's arrival. Sam and I gave Sammie big hugs and kisses goodbye.

I ran through a quick list of instructions—bedtime, snacks, emergency numbers—which Zoey waved off. "We'll be fine. Now go," she said with a playful shooing motion.

With our son in excellent hands, Sam and I headed out into the deepening dusk, off to the academy to hopefully gain some clarity around his emerging psychic abilities. I slid my hand into Sam's, giving it a supportive squeeze as we set off.

As we stepped through the shimmering portal into the academy, I gave Sam's hand another reassuring squeeze. "We'll figure this out," I said gently.

We navigated the halls of the Rune Academy until we found Jeanne's classroom. She was busy setting up for next week's classes, arranging crystals on desks and scribbling notes on the chalkboard. Her short black hair framed her face, and she hummed cheerfully as she worked, occasionally moving items around the room with her mind.

"Hey, Jeanne," I called out, catching her attention. "We need your help."

"Olivia, Sam." She jumped slightly and chuckled. "What brings you here?" Jeanne asked, her eyes twinkling with curiosity.

Sam explained his predicament, detailing his newfound psychic abilities that seemed to have unlocked when he turned into a vampire. I chimed in with examples of what Sam and Sammie had done so far, hoping it would shed some light on the situation. "Sammie has dream visions. He knew where our friend was when he went missing and no one else could find him. Ava even did several different locating spells, but Sammie had a dream and knew right where he was."

"Interesting," Jeanne mused. "I think I have a few ideas on how to help. Let's start by running some tests, and then I'll teach you some basic exercises to gain better control."

I glanced over at Sam, who nodded in agreement. "That's not all," he chimed in. "When we were placed into a dream world without magic by a witch, and I didn't go fully under her spell. Somehow, my psychic powers seemed to protect me from the worst of it."

"Very curious indeed," Jeanne said, tapping her chin. "Are there other psychics in your family?"

"Yes," Sam said. "While going through my mom's ancestry research, I found out that my seven-times great grandmother, Cassandra Thompson, was a psychic."

"Ah, Cassandra Thompson," Jeanne exclaimed and leaned forward. "Her name is quite famous in psychic circles. She was a powerful woman who made significant contributions to our understanding of psychic abilities. How fascinating that you're related to her. It is odd, though, that the power should surface in you, a male descendant. It's only been known to pass down to the females."

"Could it have anything to do with him being turned into a vampire?" I tried to make sense of the situation.

"Perhaps," Jeanne replied thoughtfully. "The combination of supernatural forces at play could have caused an unexpected awakening of his latent psychic powers."

"Can you help us?" Sam asked, his voice tinged with hope.

"Of course," Jeanne said with a reassuring smile. "I'll do everything in my power to help you both understand and control your abilities."

"Thank you, Jeanne." Relief washed over me.

"Could my transformation into a vampire and Olivia's Fae heritage have something to do with our son's psychic abilities?" Sam asked, looking at Jeanne for answers.

"Very likely," she replied, her gaze flicking between the two of us. "Fae power could have unlocked the psychic power from your side of the family, allowing it to manifest in Sammie. It could explain why his abilities are so powerful."

"Is there a way I can learn to control and better understand these powers?" Sam inquired earnestly.

"Of course," Jeanne smiled warmly. "I actually run a psychic powers for beginners' class here at the academy—granted, it's mostly children who attend, but I believe you'd still find it beneficial. The summer session is starting soon, which tends to have far fewer students than the fall semester. It would be an excellent opportunity for you to learn more about your abilities."

"Thank you, Jeanne," Sam said gratefully, his eyes shining with hope. "I'll take you up on that offer."

We chatted a bit more before it was time to leave. As we

walked toward the portaling room, I glimpsed a fuzzy white tail disappearing around a corner. "What is that cat doing here?"

Sam chuckled. "Who knows what she is up to?"

Curiosity piqued, we followed her, but when we turned the corner, she was gone.

"Should we search for her?" Sam asked.

I shook my head. "No, let's leave her be. If she gets stuck at the academy, that's on her. She's resourceful enough to find her way back."

Sam agreed reluctantly. He hated leaving any loose ends, but sometimes, it was best to let things be. Lucy could handle herself just fine in the academy. If not, then she'd be sure to let us all know about it when she returned home.

With one last look down the empty hallway, we continued our way to the portaling room, hearts lighter with the newfound knowledge and hope Jeanne had given us.

"Since we're on this side of the castle, let's go check on the renovations," I suggested to Sam. He nodded in agreement, and we made our way up a few floors to find where Beth, John, and a couple of teachers were magically renovating a part of the castle.

As we approached, a wall crashed down right in front of us with no warning. The noise startled me, and out of shock, I froze the wall with my Fae powers. Pieces of the stone wall floated in midair, suspended by my magic.

"Whoa, Olivia, nice save," John called, grinning as he surveyed my handiwork. He carefully stepped through the floating pieces and stopped. "Can you hold them there a few more seconds?" he asked. "There's something embedded in one of the larger pieces of stone." He plucked it from the rock—an amulet.

I let the stones float to the ground, but the moment John

touched the amulet, Sam groaned and clutched his head. "Ugh, I just got this horrible feeling washing over me." He pressed his hand against the wall as if to steady himself.

"Are you okay?" I asked, worried as I clutched his arm.

Sam blinked a few times, then straightened up. "Yeah, it's gone now. Went as fast as it came. Must've been a psychic fluke," he said dismissively.

Leaving John and Beth to the renovations, I opened a portal, and we walked through into our kitchen. I looked out the window and saw Luci and Ross stepping out of the pool house.

Leaning my head out the kitchen door, I waved to them.

"Hi, Olivia. Sam," Luci said smoothly, a knowing glint in his eyes.

Sam and I crossed the yard to see what was going on. Ross looked twitchy, like his skin was too tight or he was just uncomfortable.

What the heck?

Oh, yeah. The full moon was coming tonight. "Feeling all right, Ross?" I tried not to sound too concerned.

"Yeah, I'm fine," he stammered a bit, trying to regain his composure. "Just, you know, the full moon."

"Ah, right." I nodded sympathetically. "How's that going to go?" I glanced at my father with an eyebrow up.

Luci patted Ross on the shoulder. "Don't worry, I'll be taking him to Hell for the next few days. That way, he can avoid the worst of the transformation."

"Thanks." Ross looked relieved for a second, but then he started getting even more twitchy. Lucifer placed a hand on his shoulder and they vanished.

Sam glanced at me. "We thought vampires were bad."

I chuckled in agreement. Werewolves were a whole new ballgame. Nobody knew much about them yet.

"Finally home." I sighed, stretching my arms above my head as we walked through the door and into the living room.

"Mommy," Sammie rushed toward us, his little face lit up with excitement. "Guess what happened while you were gone?"

"Let me guess." I scooped him up into my arms. "You and Zoey had a dance party in the living room, complete with disco lights and cat backup singers?"

"Close," he giggled. "Zoey let me bake cookies with magic,"

"Delicious and educational." Sam raised an eyebrow. "I'm almost jealous we missed it."

"Can we go see the cookies?" I set Sammie down and ruffled his hair. "I could use a sugar fix after today."

"Race you there," Sammie shouted, dashing toward the kitchen before I could even take a step.

"Slow down, kiddo," Sam called teasingly. Sam was faster than any of us, but he always let Sammie win the race, of course.

"Never," Sammie's laughter echoed down the hall as Zoey and I followed at a decidedly more leisurely pace. When we stepped into the kitchen, Sam and Sammie were sitting at the table, munching on chocolate chip cookies that were shaped into cats and bats.

A few weeks ago, Phira had shown Sammie how to bake with magic and the little guy practiced every chance he got. It surprised me that the kitchen wasn’t a floury, sugary mess.

"Save one for me," I warned them, grabbing a cookie for myself and taking a seat next to Sam. "So, what's the verdict? Are our baking skills in danger of being outshone by magic?"

"Absolutely," Sam declared, grinning at Sammie. "These are amazing, buddy."

Zoey laughed. "Watching him bake with magic was fun. I'm almost jealous that I'm not magical."

Sammie grinned at her. "You have magic. You shift into a tiger. That takes magic."

"I think you're right, little man." Zoey patted his head, then waved before heading to the back door. "See you guys tomorrow."

"Bye, and thanks for looking after Sammie." I walked her to the door. I wanted to ask her about her family and if she'd decided if or when she was meeting them. At the last second, I didn't ask. I'd get an update from Ava tomorrow. Zoey needed some time.

"Maybe you can teach your old mom some tricks someday," I suggested, giving Sammie a wink as I leaned over and kissed the top of his head. "For now, though, it's time for bed."

"Aw, but it's still early," Sammie protested, his enthusiasm tempered by the mention of bedtime.

"Nice try." I checked the clock on the wall. "It's way past your bedtime, mister. Time for teeth brushing and pajamas."

"Fine." He slid off of his chair and trudged toward the bathroom. "Night, Mommy. Night, Daddy."

"Goodnight, kiddo."

"Sometimes I wonder if living in this magical world is robbing him of a normal childhood," I mused, taking another bite of my cookie.

"Normal is overrated," Sam replied, reaching over to squeeze my hand. "Besides, just look at us—we're anything but ordinary, and we turned out all right."

"Speak for yourself," I teased, rolling my eyes. "I'm still not convinced you're not an alien in disguise."

"Touché," he laughed, leaning in to give me a kiss. "Now, how about we enjoy the rest of our evening before it's our turn for bedtime?"

"Sounds perfect." I snuggled close to him as we continued eating our cookies, enjoying the quiet moments of our extraordinary life together.

3
AVA

"Really? Is Ian not eating again?" I muttered under my breath as I glanced at the empty seat where my suspicious hunter brother-in-law should've been. I hadn't had a chance to talk to Drew about his brother yet. I didn't want to worry him while he was working on a case, but Ian had been super weird since Drew had been gone.

"Maybe he's just not a morning person," Beth suggested, buttering her toast. My mother always had a soft spot for giving people the benefit of the doubt.

"Or maybe he's up to something nefarious," John countered, sipping his coffee. He eyed the door, expecting Ian to burst in any minute now. "Anyway, the new wing of the academy is coming along nicely. We might be finished early."

"Great news." I tried to shift the focus away from Ian's absence. I felt a twinge of worry about what he was up to, but I couldn't let it consume me. I had enough to worry about at the moment.

As if on cue, my phone rang, displaying Alfred's name on the screen. I answered, hoping for good news. "Hey, Alfred. What's up?"

"Hello, Ava. I'm calling with an update on Winnie." His voice held a mix of urgency and concern. "She's not doing well. We've tried everything, but we're still searching for a suitable body for her."

While I'd been in the dream world, my aunt Winnie had found out she had an incurable form of witch cancer. When we'd returned from Hell and the crazy dream, Alfred had taken her to find another new body to magick into. It had worked once. Why not again? We couldn't lose our Winnie. Worse came to worst, if she died, I'd animate her, but then we'd have Alfred alive, and Winnie animated. We'd only *just* gotten Alfred back to life. What a mess.

I frowned, stirring my coffee absentmindedly. "What are the requirements again?"

"We need a witch's body, young enough but not too young, healthy, and no family," Alfred recited. "It's proving to be rather difficult to find someone who fits the bill. We're heading to a new city today, so hopefully we'll have better luck there."

"Keep me posted." A wave of sympathy and grief for Winnie. Witch cancer was a cruel and unforgiving disease. "We're all rooting for her." Then a thought came to me. "If anything, you could tether her ghost to you until we find one. Or animation."

"Yeah, that's an option. Winnie says we'd do that as a last resort." He sighed, then said, "Talk to you soon." With that, he hung up.

After breakfast, my parents headed to the Academy to start

their day. I used magic to clean the kitchen, then settled into my office for a few hours of writing.

About thirty minutes later, Zoey entered the office and sat on the love seat against the wall across from my desk. Her nervousness wafted off of her and hung in the air between us. "I think I'm ready to call my family now," she said softly, wringing her hands together.

"Okay, sure." I offered her a warm smile, trying to ease her nerves as I joined her on the love seat. "Just remember, it's important not to tell them what happened to you—that you're a ghoul now. We don't want to cause any unnecessary panic or confusion."

"Right," Zoey nodded, her gaze fixed on the floor. "I just...I don't know what to say to them, you know? It's been so long, and I've changed so much. I was just a little kid."

"Take a deep breath and speak from your heart." I placed a reassuring hand on her shoulder. "For now, we'll play it by ear. Just be honest about how you feel, and they'll understand."

"Okay." She took a shaky breath, her eyes meeting mine with newfound resolve. "Let's do this."

Together, we settled onto the living room couch and started a video call with Rowan. As her face appeared on the screen, I watched the surprise in the girl's eyes, quickly replaced by joy.

"Zoey," she whispered, her voice cracking slightly. "I can't believe you're alive. We all thought...well, it doesn't matter now. You're here."

"Hi, Rowan," Zoey replied, her voice barely more than a whisper. "Yeah, I'm here."

"Where have you been?" Rowan asked. "Why didn't you contact us sooner? The pride mourned you."

Zoey hesitated, glancing at me for guidance. I gave her an

encouraging nod, and she took another deep breath before answering. "I've been through a lot." Her voice grew stronger with each word. "I didn't know how to contact anyone or even where I was from."

"How did you not know where you were from?" Rowan looked like she was about to cry. "I'm not trying to sound harsh, but I just don't understand."

"I didn't know what state I was in," Zoey said. "I just ran. And ran. And then I had no idea where to go."

"Zoey," Rowan said gently, reaching out as if trying to touch her through the screen. "You've always belonged with us. With your family, with the pride. We just want you to be safe and happy."

"Thank you," she whispered, wiping away a tear. "I'm not sure where I want to go from here."

"Hey, it's okay," Rowan assured her. "What matters is that you're alive, and we can start making up for lost time."

As they continued to talk, I was so proud of Zoey for facing her fears and reconnecting with her family. Despite the secrets and consequences that still loomed over our heads, we'd figure this crap out.

"Speaking of family," Rowan said, her gaze shifting between Zoey and me. "We moved further south a few years ago. The pride is living near New Orleans now. In the bayou."

I raised an eyebrow. "The bayou? Really?" I'd vacationed down there before. It was a gorgeous place.

"Yep," she confirmed. "Mom and Dad wanted to be closer to nature, so we moved out here a few years ago. It's amazing—the air is fresh, the wildlife is abundant, and the shifts feel like nothing I can describe. There's magic in this place."

"Wow," Zoey breathed, her eyes wide with wonder. "That sounds incredible."

"Trust me, it is," Rowan replied, grinning. "You'll have to come down for a visit sometime. I think you'd love it."

"Maybe," Zoey murmured, glancing at me uncertainly.

"Absolutely," I chimed in, trying to keep the mood light. "Zoey definitely deserves a vacation."

Another face appeared on the screen, and my heart skipped a beat. A man stared back at us, a mixture of disbelief and raw emotion etched across his rugged features.

"Zoey?" he choked out, his voice thick with tears. "Is that really you?"

"Hi," she whispered, her own eyes filling with tears once more. "I think I know you, but my memory isn't great."

"It's okay. I'm Gerard, your uncle and Rowan's dad. Where are you, sweetheart?" he demanded, his tone desperate. "We thought you were dead. Please, tell us where you are. We need to see you, to hold you..."

"I'm in Maine," Zoey stammered, struggling to maintain her composure. "Ava found me, and she's been taking care of me."

I took her hand and gave it a reassuring squeeze.

"Maine," Gerard repeated, as if tasting the word for the first time. "That's so far away." He shook his head. "It doesn't matter. We'll come to you, Zoey. Just tell us when and where."

"Actually," I cut in gently, "I can make that part easy. I can have a portal created for you. Just call ahead, and we'll have it set up."

Gerard looked surprised. "A portal?"

"Ava is a witch," Zoey said. "My family, er, my Maine family is made up of a bit of a mix of supernatural people."

"That's amazing. I'm so glad you found a family to care for you. Thank you," Gerard breathed, his eyes shining with gratitude as his gaze shifted to my face. "We'll make plans as soon as possible. I can't wait to see my girl again."

"Me too," Zoey whispered, her voice thick with emotion.

As we disconnected the video call, the weight of it all pressed down on me. The secrets we would be keeping from Zoey's family, the potential consequences of our actions... It was all a lot. But it was better than telling them the truth, at least for now. My inner voice told me there was more to the story about her parents' death and Zoey's disappearance from the pride land.

"Are you sure about this?" Zoey asked, her voice barely more than a whisper.

"Of course," I replied, placing a comforting hand on her shoulder. "Family is important, Zoey. And if there's one thing I've learned over the years, it's that love—and a little bit of magic—can heal even the deepest wounds. Plus, they may be able to help fill in the gaps of your memory of your parents and their deaths."

As she leaned into my embrace, lordy. I hoped that I was right. For all our sakes.

That evening, the conservatory was a haven of flickering candlelight and the sweet scent of herbs as I worked on my latest magical project. The air hummed with energy, and I felt alive—a powerful force of witchery and necromancy combined.

"Hey, Ava." Olivia waved as she and Sam entered the room. Sammie ran in behind them and darted inside the house, yelling, "Hi Ava," as he went to search for Zoey and Larry. Or maybe one of the cats.

Olivia hopped onto a stool beside mine and asked, "What are you working on?"

"Infusing some amethyst stones with magic for the ghouls' Halloween costumes," I replied, grinning. "I know. It's months away, but I want time to make it right. Zoey, Larry, and the cats are going to look fabulous."

Sam raised an eyebrow but said nothing. He had seen enough in his life to know better than to question my magical endeavors.

"Actually, I need your help, Sam," I added, shifting my attention to him. "I want to do some research on Zoey's family. You still have contacts at the police station, right?" I could easily have had Drew do it, but I didn't want to wait until he got back from his hunt.

"Sure," he answered, his voice betraying a hint of curiosity. "You think there's something fishy about them?"

"Maybe, maybe not," I mused. "But with all the secrets we're keeping, I'd rather be safe than sorry."

"Sure, makes sense." Sam pulled out his phone. "I'll call the station."

As he stepped away to make the call, Olivia watched him with concern and pride. Her husband had come a long way since discovering his psychic abilities, but she worried about him constantly.

"Are you okay?" I asked her, my voice gentle.

"Oh, yeah, I'm fine," she murmured, her eyes never leaving Sam. "Sometimes I just can't believe how different my life has become in the last year or so."

"Yeah." She was *not* wrong. "But would you trade it?"

She puckered up her lips and squinted her eyes. "Not for all the designer shoes in the world." After cocking her head, she added, "Maybe I'd change Carter's attitude."

Sam returned then, his expression serious. "Okay, so I talked to one of the officers on duty. Gerard and Rowan don't have a record in the human world."

"Hmm," I chewed on my bottom lip, mulling over this new piece of information. "No news is good news, I suppose."

"Agreed," Sam said thoughtfully. "But it's something. We can keep looking into it if you want."

"Thank you, Sam." I nodded. "Please do. It's just a feeling I have. Something isn't right." I sighed. "Olivia, could you pass me my phone?" I asked, as I continued to infuse my magic into the amethyst stones. The Halloween costumes were coming along nicely. I'd test them out on the cats later to see if I needed to adjust the spells.

"Here you go," Olivia replied, handing me my phone. "Who are you calling?"

"Blair." I tapped her number on the screen. "She's the new shifter-hunter liaison. Maybe she can help us with Zoey's family."

"Good idea." Olivia turned her attention back to the stones. "May I?" She held her hand over them.

"Hey, Ava, nice to hear from you." Blair's cheerful voice rang through the speaker, and I grinned as I nodded at Olivia.

"Hi, Blair. How's it going?"

"As good as expected, I guess." She sounded genuinely pleased to hear from me.

"I was wondering if you could help me with something," I asked.

"Of course. What do you need?"

"So, a long story short, I need you to do some checking on a shifter. My best friend, Sam, had his police friend run a check run for my adopted daughter Zoey's family, but they don't have any records in the human world." A crash came from inside the house.

Sam rolled his eyes and headed in. "I thought maybe you could ask around the shifter world for us."

"Sure thing, Ava." Her voice was firm and full of resolve. "I'll start asking around right away. Text me their info, give me a day or two, and I'll get back to you."

"Thanks so much, Blair."

"Happy to help, Oh, hold on a sec." There was a brief pause, and then another familiar voice came through the speaker.

"Hey there, beautiful." My husband's voice sparked a longing I've been feeling since he left a few days ago.

I grinned in surprise. "Hey, I miss you. What are you doing in Florida?"

"Miss you too," he replied, his voice tinged with warmth. "We hit a dead end on the investigation and portaled back here to do some research. Just wanted to say hi to everyone and let you know I'm thinking of you all."

I glanced at Olivia, who waved her hand in a hello gesture. "Olivia says hi as well."

"Tell her I said hi back. And please keep me posted on the Zoey situation."

"Will do," I promised.

"Back to work." I refocused on the amethyst stones. It was comforting to know we had friends willing to help us, even far away. Now, all we needed were some answers.

4
AVA

"CAN you believe Snoozer was once human?" I shook my head as I stared out the kitchen window. Olivia had come over early this morning and made coffee for me. For once, I was already up when she walked in.

I know. It shocked me too, but I just can’t sleep that well without Drew here.

"Seriously." Olivia chuckled. "I can't even imagine."

"Neither can I," Sam said, then yawned. It was past his bedtime. "I mean, who would've guessed?"

"Apparently, only Yaya knew all along." I sighed. "Poor Snoozer. I wonder what he did to get cursed like that."

"Must've been something big." Olivia sipped her coffee. "It does make me look at him a little differently now."

"Same here," Sam agreed. "I keep trying to picture him as a person, but all I see is a very hairy man with pointy ears and a bushy tail."

"Thanks for that mental image, Sam." I wrinkled my nose. "I'll never be able to unsee it now." I had no idea if the way Snoozer looked at the dream world was the way he had looked when human, but that was how I pictured him now.

"Anytime," he replied with a grin. "That's what friends are for."

"Speaking of friends." Olivia nodded toward the door. "Look who decided to grace us with his presence."

We turned to see Snoozer sauntering into the room, dragging a small hand mirror behind him. It looked heavy for a cat to carry, but he managed to drag it along with an air of perseverance. The mirror had Yaya's spirit imprinted on it, allowing her to communicate with us from beyond the grave. She'd done something before she died to make sure she'd be able to talk to us again. It wasn't *her*. Yaya was at peace and far away from our reach. It had her memories and knowledge up to the point she imbued the mirror, however, so when needed, we could put a bit of magic into the mirror and speak to Yaya.

"Hey there, Snoozer." I scratched him behind the ear. It was so weird, knowing that I was actually scratching a human man behind the ear.

I did *not* want to think about the times he'd been nearby while I changed or showered.

A few seconds later, Lucy came in and sat in the doorway of the kitchen. "He wants you to talk to Yaya," she said with an air of boredom. "You know, since he's apparently the hot topic of conversation."

"Is there anything else he'd like to share before we contact Yaya?" Olivia asked, her tone teasing but gentle.

"Like what, his favorite brand of catnip?" Lucy shot back,

rolling her little kitty eyes. "I think he's shared enough for one lifetime, thank you very much."

"Fair enough," I conceded, chuckling at Lucy's typical snarky response.

Snoozer set the mirror on the floor by my chair before stalking off to find a private spot in the conservatory to take a nap.

"Seems like he's not too keen on discussing his past," Sam said.

"Can't say I blame him," I agreed. "It must be hard, knowing you were once human and now you're… well, a cat."

"True," Olivia nodded. "But he's still Snoozer, your cat."

"Absolutely," I smiled with a renewed sense of appreciation for my feline-witch friend. "Now, let's see if Yaya can shed some light on this mystery."

I picked up the mirror, taking a deep breath before letting my magic flow into it and calling out Yaya's name. The surface of the mirror shimmered like water, and my grandmother's familiar face appeared. She looked as though she'd been interrupted from some important task, but her expression softened when she saw me. A surge of grief went through me, but the actual Yaya was at peace, so I couldn't let that get to me.

"Hello, Ava, my dear." She smiled at me in the loving way only my Yaya could. There was something about a grandmother's love. "What can I do for you?"

"Yaya, we have a bit of a mystery on our hands," I began, glancing over at Sam and Olivia for support. "It's about Snoozer."

"Ah, that old cat," she said with a knowing smile. "What has he gotten himself into now?"

"Well, it turns out that he used to be human." I watched her reaction closely.

She didn't react so much as chuckle. "Ah, yes. I thought you might find out, eventually. I wasn't sure if his curse would ever be revealed to you."

"It has, and I was hoping you could fill us in on his background," I said.

Yaya nodded and met my gaze. "You see, many years ago, I was approached by the goddess Ceridwen. She is the Welsh goddess of wisdom and mother of the famous bard Taliesin. She was surrounded by white cats who carried out her orders on Earth." Yaya paused for a moment.

"Go on," I urged.

"Snoozer, or rather the man he once was, is one of Ceridwen's descendants—a witch," Yaya continued. "He had committed some grave offense, and Ceridwen deemed it necessary for him to be punished."

"What did he do?" Sam asked.

Yaya shrugged. "Ceridwen never told me. She sentenced him to a hundred years as a cat to learn humility. So, I'm guessing he wasn't a very nice witch."

The room fell silent as we processed this new information. A pang of sympathy for Snoozer and the life he'd left behind. Then again, he should have known that he'd be punished, eventually. What goes around, comes around and all that jazz.

"Yaya, why didn't you ever tell us?" I asked quietly, slightly betrayed by her omission.

"I was forbidden by the goddess to tell anyone. It was a secret that I had to carry alone."

"I understand," I said softly, trying to push aside my hurt feelings. After all, Yaya had been bound by a divine command—who was I to question that?

"Thank you for telling us now," Olivia chimed in, offering Yaya a reassuring smile.

"Of course," Yaya replied, her eyes glistening with unshed tears. "Since I didn't reveal it to you, it seems I can speak of it. My promise to Ceridwen even held in this echo because I tried to tell you the last time we spoke, but I couldn't. I only wish I could have done more for him."

"Well, he always has a home with us. He did say that he didn't want the curse broken." That I could understand. He had a family and a girlfriend. Plus, human servants to feed and clean up after him. "He's contrite."

We said our goodbyes, and I ended the call by cutting off my magic from the mirror.

Later that afternoon, I was in the middle of folding laundry when my phone rang. "Hello?"

"Hey Ava, it's Rick."

Rick was the ferret shifter whose sons had been taken by Penny and Bevan in their shifter fighting ring. The same one where I found Zoey. I've kept in touch with Rick and his wife, Dana.

"Hi, How's the family?" I asked. When I called earlier, I'd talked with Dana about Zoey's uncle and pride.

"Good, thanks. Dana and I just found out that she's pregnant with twins. We are over the moon excited and so is Zane." Rick's voice was filled with excitement.

Zane had also been taken to the fight ring, but I was able to find him and several other shifter kids alive. Their younger son had not made it, unfortunately. It was a sight that still haunted me to this day and probably always would. "Congrats,"

"Thanks," he said. "Listen, I've been looking into Gerard and Rowan, but I can't find anything on them. Nothing good or bad."

"Really?" I furrowed my brow, glancing over to see Ian hovering suspiciously near the doorway. He seemed to think he was being stealthy, but he stood out like a sore thumb. I ignored him, letting him think that he was being sneaky. "Thanks for trying, though."

"No problem. If I find anything else, I'll let you know," he said before hanging up.

As soon as I ended the call with Rick, my phone rang again. This time, it was Blair. All the news was coming in.

"Hey Ava, I managed to dig up some info on tigers," she started without preamble. "It's all a bit vague, but from what I can gather, it seems they're clean."

"Clean?" I repeated, still worried.

"Yep. No laws broken. Gerald is the alpha of the pride and seems to be a good leader. Tigers don't live in packs like wolves do. They have a pride, but it's more like an extended family who lives kinda nearby but also kinda spread out. They get together now and then for a meal, but it's not the commune kind of situation that many other shifters live in. They still answer to their alpha, and if there are any issues, the alpha steps in to help. But overall, it doesn't seem like there's anything to worry about."

"Interesting. So, is it safe for Rowan and Gerard to visit?" I asked.

"Best I can tell, it should be fairly safe. "

"Thanks, Blair. I really appreciate your help."

"Of course. Let me know if you need anything else." She hung up.

It wasn't much, but it was better than nothing. Maybe, just

maybe, it would be safe for Zoey to get to know her uncle and cousin. Now, all I had to do was find her and share the news.

Leaving Ian to his weirdness, I found Zoey in the herb garden, her hands dusted with soil as she lovingly tended to the plants. The sun cast a soft glow on her face, emphasizing the peaceful expression she wore while working with the earth.

"Hey, kiddo," I called out to her, my voice full of warmth. "I have some news."

Zoey looked up from her gardening, curiosity lighting up her yellow cat's eyes. "What's up?"

"Blair managed to find some information about how tiger shifters live. Apparently, they don't form tight-knit communes like other shifters. They're more like an extended family, living separately but getting together occasionally." I watched her closely, gauging her reaction.

"Really?" She paused, deep in thought. "You know, that does sound familiar. It's been so long since my parents were alive, but that feels right in my mind somehow."

"Blair thinks it should be safe for Rowan and Gerard to visit us," I added, hoping this would give her some peace of mind.

"Good," she replied, wiping her hands on her jeans. She paused for a second, then nodded. "I'll call them and invite them here."

We went inside, and Zoey wasted no time calling her newfound relatives. As she spoke to Rowan and Gerard, the conversation seemed to flow easily—a good sign.

"Are there any hotels nearby?" Gerard asked through the phone.

My protective instincts kicked in, but before I could stop myself, I blurted out, "You can stay with us."

As soon as the words left my mouth, I regretted them. Sure, it might've been perfectly safe for them to visit, but actually having them in our home was another matter entirely. I wasn't sure how they'd take the news of me being a necromancer. I tried to hide my unease as Zoey continued the conversation, finalizing their visit.

"Looks like we'll have company soon," Zoey said with a smile once she hung up the phone. She seemed more hopeful and happier than she'd been since Rowan first emailed her.

"Yep." I forced a smile of my own. "It'll be... interesting."

"Indeed," chimed in Lucy from her perch on the back of the sofa, watching us with her usual feline indifference. "Never a dull moment around here, eh?"

"Tell me about it," I muttered, wondering just how many surprises our new guests would bring with them. "Ugh, what was I thinking?" I groaned, rubbing my temples. "I mean, it's great that they're coming to visit, but why on earth did I invite them to stay with us?"

Zoey grinned at me, clearly amused by my frustration. "Well, at least all the ghouls look like actual people now. No worries about trying to hide Larry in skeleton form."

I snickered at the mental image. "True, that would have been a disaster. It's hard enough keeping track of Lucifer and his antics without having to worry about our guests discovering our supernatural secrets."

As if on cue, Luci strolled out of the kitchen, munching on something that looked suspiciously like one of my freshly baked cookies. We hadn't even known he was there, which just went to show how stealthy the ruler of Hell could be when he wanted to.

"Ah, Ava, Zoey," he drawled, pausing mid-chew. "I heard you talking about your upcoming visitors. Rowan and Gerard, right?"

"Yep," I confirmed, suddenly very self-conscious. Had he been eavesdropping on our conversation?

"Interesting," Lucifer mused before his eyes narrowed, and he squinted at something in the distance. "Oh, hang on. Look outside."

Zoey and I exchanged puzzled glances before we moved to the window. What could possibly be so interesting that it warranted Lucifer's attention?

As we looked out into the backyard, I sighed in annoyance, and maybe a little teensy bit of relief. There, nestled among the few trees between the houses, stood a small home that matched our new pool house perfectly—a perfect little twinsy cottage. "For your soon-to-arrive guests," Luci said and popped another bite of cookie into his mouth.

"Well, at least we can still get a little privacy and have them close by."

"Consider it a favor," he replied with a cheesy grin, crumbs tumbling from his lips. "I thought you might appreciate a little extra space."

It would be nice not to have Rowan and Gerard underfoot the entire time they were here. "Thank you, Luci." I said it mostly sincerely.

Mostly.

"Anytime, Ava," he said with a wink before disappearing back into the kitchen, presumably to devour more of my cookies.

"Looks like we'll have a bit of breathing room after all." Zoey stared at the new addition to our backyard.

"Thank goodness for small miracles."

5
AVA

I STOOD IN THE CONSERVATORY, my fingertips barely grazing the surface of the amulet we'd discovered in the RV where our Viking necromancer *friends* had been crashing. The dark magic emanating from it prickled against my skin, raising goosebumps on my arms despite the warmth of the sun streaming through the glass walls. Something powerful and sinister lay hidden within its depths, but for the life of me, I couldn't figure out why the Vikings had it or what they'd used it for.

As I continued to ponder the mysteries of the amulet, Lucy crept silently into the room through the cat door, her eyes wide with mischief. Unbeknownst to her, I'd caught sight of her reflection in the antique mirror hanging on the wall in front of my workstation.

That darn cat carried a small, fluffy, white kitten by the scruff of its neck, trying her hardest to be as inconspicuous as possible. But with a cat like Lucy, inconspicuous was a relative term.

"Lucy-Fur," I called out, trying to keep a straight face as she jumped at the sound of my voice.

The kitten mewled softly, its tiny paws flailing in the air as Lucy looked around, feigning innocence.

I put one hand on my hip. "And what do we have here?"

"Absolutely nothing that concerns you," Lucy replied, her words somewhat muffled by the white fluff dangling from her lips.

"Go put that kitten back wherever you found it," I ordered, trying to sound stern.

"I don't see what the big deal is." She lowered the kitten to the ground with a surprising delicacy. "It's not like it was doing anything important. You know, other than being abandoned by its mother and crying its tiny little heart out."

"Is that supposed to make me feel bad?" I asked skeptically, unable to resist the urge to reach down and stroke the kitten's soft fur. It purred contentedly at my touch, clearly none the wiser about Lucy's intentions.

Okay, so her guilt trip worked a little. But I wasn't going to let Lucy know that.

"Maybe just a little," Lucy admitted. "I mean, come on. Look at that face. How could you send it back outside?"

"Okay, fine." I sighed, knowing that arguing with Lucy was an exercise in futility. "But how are you going to feed it? You're not exactly lactating, are you?"

"Rude." She snorted, then looked down at the small kitten and licked the top of its head. "I hadn't really thought that far ahead," she admitted sheepishly.

"Obviously," I snorted before grabbing my phone to call Olivia for backup.

"Hey," Olivia answered on the first ring cheerfully. "What's up?"

"Lucy found a kitten," I explained. "It's really young and needs bottle-feeding. Want to go to the store to pick up some supplies?"

"Of course," Olivia replied without hesitation. "I'll be there in a few minutes."

"Thanks, Liv." I ended the call. "She's on her way."

"Excellent," Lucy purred, clearly satisfied with her victory. "Now we just need to come up with a name for our tiny new family member."

"Let's focus on getting it fed first." Once Lucy started brainstorming names, there would be no stopping her.

Olivia arrived, and we drove to the local pet store. Once there, I couldn't help but buy all the things a kitten would need. Like a new litter box. They say have as many litter boxes as you do cats. Snoozer and Lucy were outside during the summer more than inside, but I bought one more just in case.

I also picked up a bunch of new toys for the kitty. And maybe a heated bed.

And some treats.

And a cat tree.

That was all, though!

"Wait," Olivia whispered as we stepped out of the store, gripping my arm tightly. "Isn't that Ian?"

"Where?" I squinted, my gaze following hers to find Ian loitering near the corner of the street, looking lost and disoriented.

"Hey, Ian," I called out, hoping to catch his attention. He didn't respond, just continued to stare blankly in the opposite direction.

"Something's not right," Olivia murmured, and I agreed.

We put our purchases in the back of Olivia's SUV. When I looked up again, Ian had started walking down the sidewalk away from us.

"Should we follow him?" Olivia asked.

"Yeah." I closed the back door to the SUV, then started down the sidewalk, following Ian at a discreet distance.

We crossed the road and tried to catch up with him. "Hey," I tried again, louder this time. "Ian."

He turned down a side street that led toward the ocean. When Olivia and I rounded the corner, he was waiting for us. "Why are you following me?" He looked genuinely puzzled.

"We called your name, but you didn't answer," Olivia cxplained, her brow furrowed. "Are you okay?"

That was the question of the decade. Ian had been acting weird for the last few days. Maybe a week or so.

"Sorry," he said, rubbing his temples as if trying to clear his thoughts. "I'm not myself today."

"Clearly," I muttered under my breath, still uneasy about his strange behavior. For now, we had a hungry kitten waiting for us back at home, and our hands were already full dealing with magical amulets and getting the house ready for Zoey's uncle and cousin. One problem at a time.

Back at home, I fixed a bottle for the baby kitty, then I searched for Lucy. I found her in my office, curled up on the sofa with the kitten tucked into her side, sound asleep. Lucy wouldn't let me wake the tiny fluff ball to feed her, so I grabbed my laptop and headed to the living room.

I plopped down on the sofa, my laptop perched on my knees and the amulet from the Vikings sitting on the coffee table. The screen's soft glow filled the dimly lit room as I furiously typed away, scouring the internet for anything that might help me understand the mysterious object.

"Find anything interesting?" a familiar voice drawled, oozing sarcasm. I stifled a yelp of surprise as Lucifer materialized beside me, smiling mischievously, like he'd just won some sort of celestial bet.

"Jesus," I muttered under my breath, clutching at my chest in an attempt to calm my racing heart.

"Wrong deity," he quipped, giving me a pointed look before his gaze landed on the amulet. "Still trying to decipher this little trinket, I see."

"Little trinket?" I raised an eyebrow, letting out a humorless chuckle. "This little trinket was connected to Viking necromancers, in case you forgot."

"Ah, yes, how could I forget?" he mused theatrically, rolling his eyes. "You mortals, and your penchant for dabbling in things you don't understand."

"Speaking of which," I said, irritation bubbling up inside of me. "Any chance you could enlighten me, or are you just here to make snarky comments?"

"Both," he replied with a devilish grin, turning on the charm. "Since you asked so nicely, I suppose I could take a look."

Lucifer reached for the amulet, turning it over in his hands with a thoughtful expression. The surrounding air crackled with energy as he studied it, and I held my breath, waiting for him to reveal its secrets.

"Interesting," he murmured, looking up at me with a newfound seriousness. "This amulet holds the same dark magic that the witch in Australia was using."

The witch he meant was the one in the candy cottage who had kidnapped Michelle and Wallie for the purpose of draining their powers. She especially wanted Baby Butt's power, which was already pretty powerful even then.

"Wait," I interjected. "You mean they were drawing from my powers?"

"Exactly." He narrowed his eyes. "Unlike the witch, who merely wanted a boost of your kids' abilities, those necromancers would have drained you dry, killing you in the process. In doing so, they would have prolonged their lives."

"Fantastic." I groaned, rubbing my temples as if I could somehow massage away the horrible implications of what he'd just told me.

"Cheer up." He gave me a playful nudge. "At least you've got a cute new kitten to keep you company."

How did he already know about that? "Just another complication I don't need."

"I'll leave you to it, then," Lucifer said with another signature grin as he handed the amulet back to me, then vanished.

I set the amulet on the coffee table because holding it for long periods of time weirded me out. Since I now knew that the thing had been used to siphon my powers, there was only one thing to do with it. Destroy it.

Lucy walked into the living room, carrying the kitten with Snoozer trailing behind. They jumped up on the sofa and lay down with the kitten nuzzled between them. It was the cutest thing I'd ever seen.

Having a baby kitty in the house sure was adorable, at least.

6

OLIVIA

THE LATE AFTERNOON sun cast a warm, golden glow on Ava's house as Sammie and I walked over from next door. Sam was busy preparing Red Lipped Mary for its grand opening, the *official* grand opening. Sam and Wade had a few kinks to work out from our soft opening a few weeks ago.

"Hey, Ava," I called out as Sammie and I entered through the conservatory.

"Hi Olivia, hi Sammie," Ava greeted us with a smile.

Zoey rushed down the stairs. "Is it time?" Her voice came out in a squeaky growl.

"Yep. Are you ready?" I gave my adopted niece a side-hug.

"Yes. I'm ready."

"Relax, kiddo. They're family," I reminded her, giving her a reassuring hug. I pulled back, and she smiled at both of us, then reached up to pat the top of her head, feeling for her tiger ears. They weren't there. "Ears are gone." Zoey gave a nervous laugh, and she felt her backside. "Tail is gone. How are my eyes? The contacts feel weird."

Ava framed Zoey's face with her hands. "You look perfectly human. Eyes are clear. But if you do have a slip up, just tell your uncle and cousin that you were in an accident that makes it hard to control some of your tiger parts."

Zoey relaxed. "That's a great idea."

With a wave of my hand, I opened a portal to a spot we'd agreed on in the woods near Gerard's house.

"Gerard, Rowan, welcome, I'm Ava, and this is Olivia and Zoey," she said, gesturing to each of us, in turn.

"Nice to meet you all," Gerard said, shaking our hands as they stepped through the portal. "Rowan and I have been looking forward to getting to know you all better."

"Same here." Zoey offered a small smile.

"Come on in," Ava said, stepping aside. "Let's head out to the patio. Larry and Wallie have been manning the grill, and it smells amazing out there."

"Sounds perfect." Gerard glanced at Rowan, who nodded in agreement.

Gerard was a salt and pepper gentleman with a definite reddish tint to his beard, which made sense, given he was a tiger. He had a bit of a dad bod, fit, but a small belly. It wasn't unattractive. Rowan looked remarkably like Zoey, though older, with long black hair.

"How close in age are you two?" I asked.

"I was a teenager when Zoey was born," Rowan said. "Thirteen years apart, I think?" That would make Rowan close to her mid-thirties.

As Ava led the way, Zoey seemed so much more relaxed now

that the initial introductions were out of the way. Maybe this family reunion wouldn't be so bad after all.

Ava swung open the door to the back porch, and a blur of dark fur darted out from under the deck and into the house. A sleek gray cat ran past our legs, making a beeline for Lucy and the baby kitten snuggled up together in their makeshift bed in the living room.

"Hey," Lucy yowled as the mama cat launched at Lucy, claws bared. "What the f—"

In a sudden flurry of movement, before any of us could react, the protective mama swiftly delivered a series of resounding whacks around Lucy's ears while shrieking in that way only cats could. She then gently scooped up her tiny, mewling baby in her mouth and dashed out the door, disappearing into the backyard. The scene unfolded in an instant, leaving us all standing in shock.

"Ouch." I winced, looking down at a very disgruntled Lucy. "That looked like it hurt."

"Tell me about it." She licked one paw disdainfully.

Ava stared at Lucy, shaking her head in disbelief. "I *knew* you stole that baby."

"Stole? She abandoned that baby." Lucy hissed indignantly, her fur still bristling from the attack.

"How long did you wait?" Ava asked, crossing her arms.

Lucy didn't answer, instead looking away with a sulky expression.

"Come on, let's leave Lucy to wallow in her kitten-less misery," I suggested, trying to lighten the mood. We made our way back out onto the porch where Larry and Wallie were introducing themselves to Gerard and Rowan. Michelle waved from the corner of the deck where it was shadiest. Wallie had set her up with a footstool and a fan.

"Sorry about that," Ava apologized, brushing off her hands. "Our resident cat burglar had a bit of a run-in with an angry mama."

"Family drama, huh?" Rowan giggled. "Sounds like we'll fit right in."

"Speaking of family," Gerard sat at the big table after Ava gestured for him to. "I'm so sorry my wife couldn't make it. She owns a business back in New Orleans, and she just couldn't take the time off."

"Must be tough to manage a business and family life. What kind of business is it?" I asked, genuinely curious.

"An art gallery," Rowan said proudly. "Mom's really passionate about it. She's always been into supporting local artists and showcasing their work."

"That sounds amazing." Ava's eyes sparkled with excitement. "I've always loved art, but I can barely draw a stick figure. We have a friend in Philadelphia who used to own a gallery. We'll have to introduce them."

"Maybe when things settle down, we can all go visit and have a proper family reunion," I suggested, imagining a fun-filled road trip with everyone.

"Sounds like a plan," Gerard nodded.

"Come on." Ava waved for Gerard and Rowan to follow her. "Let's show you guys where you'll be staying during your visit."

We led them through the beautifully landscaped backyard toward the new guest house situated next to the also new pool house. The warm afternoon sun cast a golden hue over everything, making the scene look like something out of a fairytale. Of course, I'd used a little fae magic to help Ava upgrade the landscaping and decor in the guesthouse. It looked so amazing, if I didn't say so myself.

"Your accommodations," Ava announced with a flourish as we reached the charming little cottage. She pointed next door. "That's the pool house where our friend Ross is staying. He's away for a few days, but he's a really great guy. You'll meet him soon."

I caught myself biting my lip, worrying about how tiger shifters might react to having a werewolf neighbor. But hey, they didn't need to know that...yet.

"Oh, this place is amazing." Rowan looked at the front of the cottage, her eyes wide with admiration. "You guys really went all out."

"Only the best for our family," Ava said, beaming with pride.

Sam strolled into the backyard from our place, wiping his hands on a towel. His face lit up when he saw us. Yes, it's Luci's house, but we've been staying there so long it's beginning to feel like home.

"Hey, everyone," he called, walking over to join our little gathering. "Sorry I'm late."

"Sam, meet Gerard and Rowan," I introduced, gesturing toward our guests. "This is my husband, Sam."

"Nice to meet you both," Sam said warmly, shaking their hands.

"Thanks, it's great to be here," Gerard said with a smile, but his body language said he was guarded. He eyed Sam carefully, like he was trying to figure out what Sam was. I wasn't sure it was a good idea to volunteer the info, so I didn't.

We showed Rowan and Gerard the interior of the cottage,

which was simple but tasteful. Again, I helped. Then after they stowed their bags, we headed back toward the porch.

Sam hung back and walked behind us. A few seconds later, my phone pinged.

Something's off with them. I can't put my finger on it, but one of them is different.

My mind instantly jumped to Gerard, considering he'd been tense since he arrived. However, I didn't want to jump to conclusions just yet. Sam's whole psychic thing was patchy at best.

We'll just have to keep an eye on them.

I tried not to let my suspicions show on my face.

Secrets have a way of revealing themselves sooner or later.

That went also for the secrets we were keeping about Zoey being a ghoul. I agreed with Ava that we should wait to feel out Zoey's family before spilling the details, but the truth would likely come out soon enough.

Sam caught up and gave my hand a reassuring squeeze.

Back on the porch, we settled into the comfortable chairs and sipped our drinks, enjoying the late afternoon sun as it dipped toward the horizon.

"Tell us more about your lives back home." Ava filled up our drinks.

As they chatted, my thoughts drifted to what Sam had texted. My gut told me something was definitely amiss, but for now, all I could do was observe and hope that everything would become clearer in time.

I swirled my iced tea, trying not to focus on the nagging feeling that something was off when Gerard cleared his throat.

"Hey, Zoey," he began, his eyes darting around nervously. "I just wanted to let you know that my wife, while busy at the shop, the main reason she didn't come with us because she and your mom, well, they didn't exactly get along."

Zoey raised an eyebrow, clearly surprised by this revelation. "What do you mean?" she asked, her voice barely more than a whisper.

Gerard scratched at his beard and shifted in his seat. "It's just, uh, they had their differences, you know? We thought you'd remember, and I wanted to let you know off the bat that she held back to avoid any awkwardness with you. She wanted you to feel totally at ease."

A mixture of emotions flickered across Zoey's face as she tried to recall any memories of her mother and aunt. "I don't really remember much, to be honest," she admitted.

Larry put his hand on her back and that helped relax her a bit.

"Well, Heather wanted me to make sure and tell you she loves you, and no drama that she and your mother had will ever cause her to stop loving you."

Zoey smiled, and the tension in the air seemed to ease a bit. Before anyone could say anything else, Ian burst onto the porch wearing a full-on luxury tuxedo. His entrance caught everyone off guard, and we all stared at him in stunned silence.

"Uh, Ian," Ava said, trying not to laugh. "Looking sharp, but why are you all dressed up?"

Ian looked at his outfit, then at all of us. "I thought this was a special occasion," he said ever-so-slightly defensively.

"Special, yes, but not black-tie formal." Sam grinned from ear to ear. "Nice tux, man."

"Come on, guys, cut him some slack." I tried to defuse the situation. Despite my best efforts, everyone continued to tease him.

Wallie snorted, and that sent pretty much everyone on the deck, including me, into giggles.

Ian's face turned a deep shade of red, and he mumbled something about changing before disappearing back into the house.

Ava and I exchanged a glance. What in the world was going on with Ian?

Later that evening, after Gerard, Rowan, Zoey, and Larry went to the guest house and Sam took Sammie home to get him ready for bed, Ava and I sat alone in her living room.

The Viking amulet sat on the coffee table, its eerie glow casting an ominous shadow across the room. We had to destroy it, but how?

"All right," Ava said, rubbing her hands together. "Let's brainstorm some ideas. What's the best way to destroy an ancient, cursed artifact?"

"Throw it into Mount Doom?" I smirked.

"Har-har, very funny." She rolled her eyes. "Come on, let's get serious."

"Fine, what about fire?" It seemed like a logical choice. Fire was known for its purifying properties.

"Okay, let's give it a try." Ava grabbed the amulet and went to the fireplace. After lighting a fire, she threw the amulet into the flames. Several minutes ticked by before the metal began to heat up, turning red before releasing a plume of thick, black smoke that filled the room.

The windows and doors opened, and Winston groaned unhappily.

"Sorry, Winston," Ava apologized, sheepishly. "We'll go outside."

I grabbed the still-smoking amulet with a pair of oven mitts, then followed Ava out the back door. We heard the front door slam shut. It was another sign from Winston that he wasn't happy about all the smoke. "So, fire didn't work."

"Nope," Ava mumbled, coming to a stop a few yards from the cliff. "At least not this fire. Maybe it wasn't hot enough. Any ideas?"

"How about we try to blow it up?".

"Couldn't hurt." She conjured some gunpowder, fuses, and matches.

We dug a shallow hole and poured some gunpowder in, then smashed the amulet into the powder. After setting the fuse, we stood back.

"Here goes nothing." I warned, lighting the fuse and retreating to a safe distance with Ava. The fuse burned down, and with a deafening BOOM, the gunpowder exploded, sending bits of dirt and grass flying into the air.

"Did it work?" Ava asked as the dust settled.

We walked over to the charred hole in the ground, and my heart sank. "Nope. Still there, just a bit dirtier." It was like it didn't even try to die.

"Urgh." Ava groaned in frustration. "What does it take to destroy this thing?"

"We'll need to get creative," I mused. "Acid? It works in the movies."

"Let's give it a shot." Ava locked gazes with me. "I don't have any acid."

"We could search through Luci's garage." I smiled. "There is *no* telling what all is in there."

We raced across the yard to my house and searched the garage. Luci's garage was a technicolor wonderland of auto-related oddities. I loved coming in here. The moment we stepped inside, it was as if we had entered a magical, mechanical circus. Detached car doors of various colors and makes lined one wall, some sporting vibrant decals of flaming dragons or ethereal fairies. A collection of fuzzy dice hung from the ceiling, swaying slightly in a breeze created by a creaky old fan.

"This one's got a mind of its own." Ava tapped a pair of purple dice with a long feather. The dice spun around wildly before abruptly stopping, almost as if offended by Ava's action.

Then there was the shelf dedicated to novelty horns, ranging from a model that made a meowing sound to another one which, when pressed, blared out Christmas music.

"Try that one." I pointed at a horn shaped like a rubber chicken. Ava gave it a squeeze, and we both doubled over in laughter as it let out a comically high-pitched squawk.

Rows upon rows of hubcaps filled another corner, each more ridiculous than the last. One featured a neon pink unicorn, another that looked like a spinning disco ball, and one that had a holographic image of Luci's face.

"Imagine driving around with these." Ava held up the last one. "It's like Luci's watching you drive, judging every turn you make."

In one corner, we found a cabinet full of what seemed to be magical car waxes, one of which promised to turn the car invisible, while another claimed it could transform a rusty old bucket into a shiny new hot rod.

"Think we should try this?" I pointed at a jar labeled, 'Acidic Car Wax: Guaranteed to Strip Even the Toughest Paint!'

Ava considered for a moment, then shrugged. "At this point, I'm willing to try anything."

We went back to the hole in the yard and carefully wiped the acid over the amulet.

"Come on, come on…" I watched as the cream bubbled and hissed.

Instead of dissolving the amulet, the acid just rolled off it, leaving the stupid freaking amulet unscathed.

"Are you kidding me?" Ava threw her hands up in frustration.

"Let's call it a night." I sighed, defeated. "We'll regroup tomorrow and figure something else out."

"Fine." She grumbled and conjured a pair of tongs to pick up the amulet. "But we're not giving up. We're going to destroy this freaking thing, no matter what it takes."

"Agreed." I clapped her on the back. "Now let's clean up this mess before Winston sees it and has an aneurysm."

If a house could have an aneurysm, Winston would.

7
AVA

I WOKE up with the warmth of Drew's arms wrapped around me, his steady breathing a comforting lullaby. It seemed like it'd been forever since I slept next to my husband instead of a few days. Drew had portaled over last night to stay with me, taking a break from the murder case he'd been working on at Rune Academy with his sister.

"Morning, handsome." I snuggled deeper into his embrace.

"Morning, beautiful." He pressed a gentle kiss to my forehead. The sounds of everyone getting up and milling around the house drifted through the walls, but we stayed cocooned in our little love bubble for just a bit longer.

"Gerard and Rowan are here." A smile tugged at my lips as I thought about the two new houses Luci had created. "Did you see our new pool house and guest house?"

Drew chuckled, his chest vibrating against my back. "Well, you know how Luci is. He never does anything halfway. Plus, I think he secretly enjoys showing off."

"Secretly?" I scoffed. "He's about as subtle as a sledgehammer."

"Can't argue with that." Drew laughed softly. "But hey, at least Gerard and Rowan have a nice place to stay now."

"Yeah, they do."

With a deep breath, I reluctantly rolled out of bed, the hardwood floor cool against my bare feet. Drew stretched and yawned before doing the same, ruffling his messy hair as he stood up. I admired his sculpted torso, soaking in his masculine beauty.

He caught me staring and gave me a smug smile.

We dressed with the familiar sounds of the house coming alive in the morning, providing a comforting background noise.

"Ready to face the day?" Drew asked, a teasing smile on his lips as he opened the bedroom door for me.

"Never," I said with mock seriousness, "but let's do it anyway." Hand in hand, we made our way downstairs, the scent of freshly brewed coffee drawing us toward the kitchen like moths to a flame.

As we entered the kitchen, Gerard was leaning against the counter, talking animatedly on his phone. At the sight of us, he hung up abruptly, a guarded look in his eyes. "Morning, Ava," he greeted me, trying to sound casual but failing miserably.

"Good morning, Gerard." I raised an eyebrow at his sudden change in demeanor. "This is my husband, Drew."

Gerard eyed him warily. "Ah, so you're the famous Drew." He hesitated for a moment before reaching out to shake Drew's hand, clearly sensing that he was a hunter. "Heard a lot about you."

I bet he had. The Walker family was like royalty among the hunters. There were all kinds of rumors and stories about each

Walker family member, both from the hunters and the paranormal communities.

"Hopefully all good things," Drew said with a warm smile, gripping Gerard's hand firmly.

"Of course." Gerard's voice lacked any real warmth. "Ava mentioned that your family is trying to change how hunters operate?"

"Indeed," I interjected, hoping to ease the tension between the two men. "Drew's family has been working hard to create a more collaborative environment between hunters and supernatural beings."

"Really?" Gerard looked skeptical, his gaze flickering between Drew and me. "How exactly are they planning to do that?"

Drew kept his tone calm and steady. "By focusing on understanding and communication. We're trying to break down the barriers between hunters and supernaturals, working together when necessary."

"Sounds like a noble cause," Gerard said noncommittally, though with the faintest hint of respect in his eyes.

"Change is never easy." I hoped to reassure him that our intentions were genuine. "But we believe it's worth fighting for."

The sound of laughter and footsteps echoed through the hallway, drawing my attention away from Gerard and Drew's conversation. Zoey and Rowan appeared at the top of the stairs, followed by a grinning Larry. They were all dressed for a swim and made their way down to join us.

"Morning, Drew." Zoey grinned as she approached us. "Didn't realize you were home."

"Hey, kiddo," Drew responded, his eyes crinkling in the

corners as he smiled. He pulled her into a hug, kissing her temple. "Just here for a sleepover."

"Ah, TMI!" Zoey shook her head playfully before leaning up to peck a quick kiss on his cheek, then stepped out of the hug. She then turned to me and said, "We're going swimming. Wanna come?"

"Maybe later, sweetheart," I said, a little envious of their carefree plans. "I've got some things to take care of first."

"'Kay." Zoey grabbed Rowan's and Larry's hands. "Catch you guys later, then." With that, the trio strolled out the back door, their laughter carrying on the breeze as they headed toward the water.

As the door closed behind them, I glanced over at Gerard, acutely aware of how his posture had relaxed slightly. The father-daughter affection between Zoey and Drew seemed to have put him more at ease, and I was grateful for the small moment of levity.

"Your family seems close. I appreciate how you've taken Zoey in and treated her like she's yours," Gerard commented, his voice softer than it had been earlier.

Because she's mine. Instead of saying that out loud, I said, "Zoey and Larry mean the world to me. I've become protective of them."

"Must be nice," he said quietly, almost wistfully. What kind of family life must he have had growing up? Was it filled with love and laughter, or had it been overshadowed by the darkness that he now carried with him?

"Everyone deserves to have people who care about them." I hoped to offer some comfort. "Family doesn't have to be blood."

Gerard looked at me for a long moment, his eyes searching

mine as if trying to gauge the sincerity of my words. Finally, he nodded and offered me a small, tentative smile. "Maybe you're right."

I thanked the gods when Olivia walked in, Sammie in tow. He was dressed head to toe in swim gear, complete with neon green shorts and a matching pair of goggles perched atop his head. His arms were filled with towels, toys, and what looked suspiciously like an inflatable duck.

"Zoey and the others just left for the beach," I told him, and Sammie's face lit up like a Christmas tree.

"Yay!" He squealed and raced out the door, yelling Zoey's name at the top of his lungs.

"Kids," Olivia chuckled, shaking her head fondly as she watched her son disappear into the backyard. "You'd think he'd never seen water before."

Drew handed me a cup of coffee, made just like I liked it. I'd been so focused on Gerard that I hadn't noticed Drew move to the coffeepot. "Thank you."

Drew kissed me. "I'm meeting Lily for breakfast, but I'll talk to you later."

"Wait. I will create you a portal." Olivia raised her hands, fingers dancing in intricate patterns as she wove the magic necessary to open a shimmering portal before us.

"Thanks," Drew said, leaning down to press a lingering kiss to my lips. "I'll be back as soon as I can."

"Be careful," I whispered against his mouth, hating the thought of being separated from him again but knowing it couldn't be helped. There was work to be done.

"Always." He offered me one last smile before disappearing through the portal. It snapped shut behind him.

I took a deep breath and conjured the Viking amulet into my hand. Its cold, metallic surface was heavy, as if it carried the weight of all its dark history. "Let's go see if we can destroy this thing."

"Sounds like a plan." Olivia's gaze fixed on the amulet with a steely glare.

"Gerard." I turned to face him. "Would you like to join us? We're going to check out the chasm on the beach."

"Chasm?" He raised an eyebrow in curiosity.

"You'll have to see it to believe it," I said with a smile. "We hope it might be able to help us with our little amulet problem."

"Sure, why not?" He shrugged, clearly intrigued. "I could use some fresh air."

"Great." I led the way as we made our way down to the beach together.

As we approached the shore, a sense of peace washed over me. The sun was shining brightly, casting a warm glow on the sand and water. The gentle sound of waves crashing against the shore filled the air, accompanied by the distant laughter of Sammie, Zoey, Larry, and Rowan playing.

"Beautiful day." Olivia smiled as she removed her sandals and dug her toes into the soft sand.

"Definitely," I said with a surge of gratitude for this little slice of paradise that I was lucky enough to call home.

"Hey, look." Gerard pointed at the water. Rowan and Zoey were splashing around in their tiger forms, their powerful bodies gliding through the water with ease. Larry stayed close to Sammie, keeping a watchful eye on him as they played in the shallows.

"Seems like everyone is having a good time." I waved at the

kids as we passed by. Sammie waved back excitedly, his face lit up with joy.

We continued further down the beach until we reached a small cave hidden behind a cluster of rocks, with a hum of energy coming from within. We were close to the chasm.

"Here we are," I announced, gesturing toward the entrance. "This is where the magical chasm is."

"Wow." Gerard's eyes went wide with wonder as he gazed into the cave. "It's beautiful in here."

"Isn't it?" I led them inside. As we ventured deeper, the walls shimmered and sparkled, illuminated by the glow of a large quartz crystal—the chasm. The crystal pulsed gently, like the steady beat of a heart, its power radiating outwards.

"Is this what powers Winston?" Gerard looked completely flummoxed.

"Yep," Olivia said. "Winston, the house, draws its energy from this very chasm. It's a pretty remarkable system if you think about it."

Gerard nodded thoughtfully, clearly impressed by the ingenuity of it all.

I steeled myself for the task at hand. "Let's see if this thing can help us get rid of the amulet once and for all." I took a deep breath, clutching the cursed object tightly in my hand before hurling it into the chasm.

"Come on, come on," I muttered under my breath, crossing my fingers, and hoping for the best.

For a moment, it looked like the amulet had disappeared, swallowed up by the powerful energies swirling around the crystal. But then, to our collective shock, the chasm spat the amulet back out, sending it flying through the air and landing at our feet with a soft thud.

"Seriously?" I sighed. "Well, that was anticlimactic."

"Looks like it's not going to be that easy," Olivia said, her brow furrowed in thought as she stared down at the amulet. "We'll have to figure out another way to destroy it."

8
AVA

A FEW DAYS had passed since that mama cat showed up to reclaim her baby, and the house had a somber feel to it. Lucy, my rude, sarcastic talking cat, was depressed.

Lucy hadn't cussed or yelled at anyone in *days*. She hadn't even told me how much she hated the scent of my new flavored coffee. Instead, she'd spent her days curled up on Zoey's bed, sleeping away the hours. Her sadness hung heavy in the air like a fog. The reason for her melancholy? She wanted babies, an impossible feat for a ghoul cat.

I'd tried everything to cheer her up: bringing her favorite snacks, letting her sleep on my pillow, even giving her full control over the TV remote. Nothing worked. It was time to have a heart-to-heart with my feline friend.

"Hey, Lucy." I stood in the doorway of Zoey's room.

Lucy lay curled up on the center of the bed, her eyes half-opened, staring blankly at the wall.

"Go away," she muttered without looking at me.

"Lucy, we need to talk about... well, you know." I walked into the room and sat down next to her on the bed. "We're all worried about you."

"TALK ABOUT WHAT? There's nothing to say. I want babies, but I can't have them because I'm a freak. End of story." She turned fully away so I couldn't see her face.

"Lucy, you're not a freak. You're just unique," I tried to reassure her, gently stroking her fur.

"Unique?" she echoed bitterly. "That's just a fancy word for weird, Ava."

"Fine, you're weird, but we love you because of it, not in spite of it. And I think there might bc a way to help you feel better."

"I doubt it." She stood, stretched, then curled back into a ball, this time with her fluffy white tail covering her face.

I trudged downstairs, the weight of Lucy's sadness still clinging to me like a heavy cloak. As I entered the kitchen, I found Olivia and Michelle sipping tea and chatting about something in hushed tones. The house was filled with the sounds of life going on around us. Wallie attended classes online, Larry and Zoey laughing with Rowan and Gerard in the living room.

"Hey." My voice sounded a bit hollow, even to my own ears. "Have you noticed anything off with Lucy lately?"

OLIVIA RAISED AN EYEBROW, her concern evident in her eyes. "Yeah, she's been awfully quiet these past few days. It's not like her to be so subdued."

"Subdued? Try comatose." I ran a hand through my tangled

hair. "She wants babies. She can't have them because she's a ghoul, but that doesn't stop her from wanting them."

"Aw, poor thing." Michelle's face softened. "It must be hard for her."

"Tell me about it." I sighed. "Any ideas on what we can do to help her?"

Michelle chewed her lip thoughtfully before a slow smile spread across her face. "What about a kitten? We could get her one from the pound or something. What's one more cat in the house, right?"

"Sure," Olivia said, nodding her agreement. "I mean, it's not exactly having a baby, but maybe having something small and helpless to care for will make her feel better. Plus, Snoozer could use a playmate to keep him company."

"True." I loved the idea. "And it's not like we don't have enough space for another fur ball. But what if Lucy doesn't bond with it? What if it just makes her feel worse?"

"We'll cross that bridge when we come to it," Michelle said firmly, her eyes shining with determination. "Besides, Lucy was desperate enough to steal another cat's baby."

"True." A small smile tugged at my lips. "Let's do it. Let's get Lucy a kitten."

Operation Kitty Rescue was officially underway as Michelle, Olivia, and I piled into Drew's SUV.

The local animal shelter was buzzing when we arrived. Families milled about, peering into cages, and cooing over their potential new pets. As we approached the front desk, a pang of sympathy filled me for all the animals waiting for their forever homes.

"Can I help you?" asked the woman behind the counter, her

eyes flicking between the three of us.

"Actually, yes." I put on my most charming smile. "We heard that you just got some kittens in and we're hoping one of them might be the perfect fit for our...uh, friend."

"Your friend?" the woman raised an eyebrow, clearly skeptical.

"Lucy," Olivia clarified, giving me a nudge. "She's been really down lately, and we think a kitten might be just the thing to cheer her up."

"Ah, I see." the woman nodded, her eyes softening. "Well, we have some orphaned four-week-old kittens, but they aren't available for adoption for a few more weeks."

Olivia smiled sugar sweet and touched the woman's hand, forcing her to make eye contact. "Can you let us in to see the babies? How many are there?"

The woman stilled and focused on Olivia. "There are six. Two girls. Four boys."

Olivia looped her arm with the woman's in a way I'd seen Luci do when he wanted something. The two of them moved down the hall to a room where the kittens were being held.

Michelle and I exchanged a glance and followed quickly behind.

Olivia then turned to the woman, not letting her go. She looked deep into her eyes and said, "You only have five kittens. One girl and four boys. There is a typo in the files that you should fix right away."

When Olivia released her hold on the woman, she left us alone.

"What was that new superpower?" I asked Olivia.

She grinned. "I've been practicing my demonic charm, AKA compulsion."

As we entered the kitten room, my heart swelled at the sight of the tiny fur balls tumbling around and batting at each other. It was impossible not to smile, even as I worried about how Lucy would react. One kitten in particular caught my eye: a little tortie with a tremendous amount of sass, who seemed to be instigating the surrounding chaos. She was mostly black, but her face had a line down the center. Half of her face was black and the other half blotchy brown. Oh, my goodness, how sweet.

"Olivia," I whispered, leaning in close. "That one. She's perfect. Look at her bossing everyone else around, just like our Lucy."

"Agreed." Olivia looked like she was ready to gush.

I went over to the kitten and scooped her up. "Let's get this little lady home to her new mom."

"Welcome to the family," I whispered to the kitten. I could hardly wait to show her to Lucy.

The moment we stepped through the front door, the anticipation was palpable. The tiny fur ball in my arms seemed to sense it too, her eyes wide and curious as she took in her new surroundings. I called out, "Lucy, Snoozer. We've got a surprise for you."

There was no response at first, just the quiet creaking of the old house settling around us. Then, the kitten let out a meow that echoed through the hallway, and suddenly it sounded like a herd of tiny elephants above our heads. Lucy came thundering down the stairs with Snoozer right behind her.

"Dear Satan's whiskers, what was that glorious sound?" She skidded to a halt on the living room rug.

"Meet your new baby." I introduced the kitten to Lucy and Snoozer. "You two are now parents."

Lucy and Snoozer sniffed their new family member. It was heartwarming, really, seeing how quickly they took to her. And as Lucy began to boss everyone around again, a familiar sense of normalcy returned. "Her name is Lenore," Lucy declared.

Okay, then. Lenore it was.

Later that night, I walked into the kitchen and found Ian standing by the counter, speaking in a strange language I'd never heard before. He appeared deep in conversation, despite the fact that there was no one else in the room. I checked both of his ears and saw no earbuds or any sign of a phone nearby.

"Um, Ian?" I asked cautiously. "Who are you talking to?"

He jumped, clearly startled, and quickly switched to English. "Oh, uh, just practicing my, um, language skills. You never know when they might come in handy, right?"

"Sure." I tried not to sound as suspicious as I felt. "Well, don't let me interrupt your...language practice."

Backing out of the kitchen, I headed back upstairs. If Ian didn't get his crap together, I was going to have to call Drew.

9
OLIVIA

I WAS JUST ABOUT to sit down with a cup of tea when my phone rang. Ava's name and number flashed on the screen. "Hey, Ava. What's up?"

"I have the most fantastic idea," she said. "You know how Wallie's room has been sitting empty since he and Michelle moved into their apartment a while ago? Well, what if we turned it into a portal room?"

I widened my eyes. That woman really was clever. "Ava, you're a genius. Let me grab Sam and Luci, and we'll head over."

"Great, see you soon." She hung up, leaving me grinning at my phone.

"Sam, Luci," I called, standing up from my cozy armchair. "We're going to Ava's. She's got a brilliant idea for Wallie's room." Sam emerged from the kitchen, wiping his hands on a dish towel, while Luci strolled down the stairs.

As we made our way to Ava's house, I considered the possibilities a portal room would bring. It was perfect. We could have dedicated places to go wherever we needed to go.

Entering Ava's house through the back door, we found her in the living room with Michelle and Wallie. They were sitting on the couch, their heads bent together as they discussed something animatedly.

"Hey, guys," Ava said when she saw us. "I was just telling Michelle and Wallie about my idea for the portal room."

"Okay, so how many portals are we talking about?" I got down to business. "And where do you want them to go?"

Ava thought about it for a moment. "One to the school, another to Michelle's parents' house, one more to Wallie and Michelle's apartment, and maybe even one to Wade's house in Philly."

"Sounds doable." Lucifer nodded his approval.

"Before we jump into creating the portal to Wade's house in Philly, I should probably call Jax," Ava said, pulling out her phone as we made our way upstairs. "You know, just to make sure the house is empty and all."

"Good idea," I said.

Ava dialed Jax's number and put the phone on speaker so we could all hear. Jax answered on the first ring. "Hello, Ava."

"Hey, Jax. You're on speaker," Ava said. "We're working on a bit of a project here, and we were hoping to create a portal to Wade's house. We just wanted to check if it's empty right now."

"Yes, it's currently vacant. Did you need one of my vampires to head over there to test the new portal out?" Soft whispers filtered through the phone. Then Jax added, "Hailey said she could run over there." Hailey was Jax's mate, Ava's friend, and the owner of Ava's old house in Philly.

"That would be nice. Thanks," Ava said, and then hung up.

When we reached Wallie's old room, Winston opened the door for us.

"Winston, we'll need your help with this. First, let's clear out the room and set it up for some powerful magic." I stepped forward but hit an invisible barrier.

I glanced at Ava for a little help because Winston still liked to mess with me. Not as much as he had a year or so ago. Now it was more like a game. He liked to tease me.

Before Ava could intervene, the house shook and the floor to Wallie's bedroom lifted, ceiling and all, dust flying everywhere, and slammed into the upper floor. Banging and creaking sounds came from the attic. Then everything fell silent again. A second later, it lowered, clicking back into place to reveal an empty room as though nothing had happened. Even the freaking dust disappeared. Tentatively, I reached out with my hand to see if the magical wall was still there. It wasn't, so I walked into the room.

"Thanks, Winston," I said.

Winston's reply was a warm, humming feeling under my feet. It was the closest thing to a hug that a house could give someone. I almost asked him if that meant he liked me, but I wouldn't push my luck with the magical house.

Next, Winston started changing the room. The window morphed into a doorway. Then several other doorways appeared around the room. It was more than we needed, but that meant we had room to add more portals later on. They looked as though if we walked through them, we'd step right out to the front lawn. We were a story too high for that to be safe.

Luci stepped up next to me. "Which portal is first?"

"The school since I know exactly where to go." Rune Academy had its own portal room that I'd helped create.

I stepped up and focused my magic into the doorway where the window used to be. My energy was a cool, silvery blue, and I watched the portal to the school take shape before my eyes.

"One down," Luci said as he turned to Michelle. "Since I haven't been to your parents' house, can I pull the image from your mind?"

Michelle eyed him for a moment, then nodded. "What do I need to do?"

"Just visualize where they want the portal in their house. Then we hold hands, and I see where to place the portal." Luci held out his hand.

"Okay." Michelle closed her eyes. "Mom said the hall closet would be the best place."

Michelle placed her hand in Luci's, making him shiver. "Baby Butt is growing so strong. Her power is unlike anything I've felt in a very long time."

I glanced at Ava, who winked at me. We all knew the Baby Butt was going to be a force. It was a good thing that the baby had a village to help raise her and teach her about her powers.

Luci faced the door to the left of the Academy portal. His magic was a vibrant red that crackled like electricity, and he made quick work of creating the portal to Michelle's parents.

Her mom poked her head in when it was complete and waved at everyone. Her little corgi, Roxie, came through the portal and danced around Michelle's feet.

"Come on through," Michelle said. Her parents stepped cautiously through the portal. Kathy and Mark looked around in amazement, their eyes widening as they took in their new surroundings.

"Wow." Mark shook his head. "You guys weren't kidding. This is incredible."

"Amazing." Kathy stepped forward to envelop Ava in a hug. "Thank you so much, dear. This will make visiting so much easier, and we can have the birth here now."

"Anything for family," Ava said, grinning.

Ava bent down and picked up the cutie so Michelle could give her smooches. Michelle was in her last month of pregnancy, so bending down was not as easy for her as it was a few months ago.

Michelle took Roxie from Ava and followed her parents back through the portal.

Wallie and Michelle's apartment was next. That one was easier since there was already a portal in the closet. "Winston, could you just move that portal out?"

He groaned and the closet door disappeared. The portal inside scooted forward to match the others, though on the left wall.

Once it was settled, Ava walked through and back again. "It checks out perfectly."

I moved on to the final portal. Wade's house in Philly. "Where are we putting this one?"

Ava thought about it. "Let's put it in the mudroom off the garage."

"Perfect." When I finished with the portal, Hailey stepped through.

"Hi guys!" Behind her, a tiny dragon flew into the room and did a few circles around us all before landing on Hailey's shoulder. "Meet Flint, my uh, new friend. Kendra calls him my familiar, but I'm not a witch, so I'm not sure that's correct."

Hailey laughed, and Ava stepped closer to her, holding out her hand to the little guy. "Hello, Flint."

"We found him in Australia when we rescued Ransom," Hailey explained.

When Hailey and her tiny dragon left, the sound of the front door opened. We heard it upstairs because Winston made the sound echo so that Ava always knew when someone was there.

"Hello?" a familiar voice called out.

"That's Alfred," Ava said and darted out of the room.

The rest of us followed. We reached the living room just as Ava pulled Alfred into a hug.

My breath caught in my throat at the sight of Winnie, who looked pale and exhausted. She'd lost a good fifteen pounds since the last time I'd seen her, just a few weeks ago.

"Is everything okay?" I asked softly, my gaze flicking between the couple.

"Aw, don't worry about me," she said with a feeble wave of her hand. "Just a little under the weather, that's all."

"No, you're not." Ava wrapped an arm around Winnie's shoulders. Concern was etched on Ava's face. "You look really sick, Winnie. Let's get you upstairs. Wallie, can you make her some soup and bring a couple bottles of water up?"

"Really, it's nothing," Winnie insisted, but her eyes betrayed her.

Luci took that moment to excuse himself. "I'll see what I can find out about this cancer," he murmured for me only to hear. Then he dematerialized.

When we reached Winnie's bedroom, Ava pulled out her phone. "Mom, Dad, Winnie's home, and she doesn't look well at all. I thought you should know."

I watched as Ava listened to her parents on the other end. Her brow furrowed with worry, and she promised to keep them updated.

"Thanks. I'll call you later." She hung up and looked over at Winnie, who was tucked in bed, shivering despite the warmth of the room.

"Let me try something," Ava said, approaching Winnie with resolve. She sat beside her and hovered her hands above Winnie's body. A soft glow emanated from her fingertips, but it seemed to have no effect on Winnie.

"Dang it," Ava said under her breath, clearly frustrated. "Why isn't it working?"

"Maybe you need more power?" I suggested hesitantly.

"Or maybe this isn't something my healing powers can fix," Ava said. There was a crack in her voice that made my chest tighten.

"I could go to Faery and ask my uncle if they have any healers?" I watched helplessly, not coming up with any other ideas.

"That would be great. Thank you." She squeezed my hand and gave me an appreciative look.

With a deep breath, I wasted no time creating a portal to Faery, the Fae realm. The swirling vortex shimmered with ethereal light, and my heart thudded wildly as I stepped through, feeling the familiar tug of magic on my body.

The moment I stepped into Faery, my senses were immediately overwhelmed with the sheer vibrancy of the realm. It was like stepping into a painting come to life, every color more vivid than anything I'd ever seen in the human world. The air hummed with the unmistakable thrum of magic, and it tingled on my skin.

Jess's voice rang out, pulling me from my reverie. "Mom!"

She and Devan appeared at the edge of the clearing, their smiles wide as they ran toward me. They looked absolutely ethereal in fae clothing. Jess wore a flowing gown that shimmered like the morning sun, while Devan's tunic and breeches were the deep green of the forest. The fabric seemed to be crafted from some magical material that made them both look as if they were part of this enchanted land.

They actually were, since they were part fae. Their powers had woken up at the same time mine did.

"Jess, Devan." I hugged them tightly. "You both look amazing."

"Thanks, Mom." Jess glowed with happiness. "We love it here."

"Breena," Phira called out, joining us. Her smile was warm and welcoming, though her eyes held a trace of concern.

My bio-mom called me Breena a lot because that was the name she and Luci had picked out for me, before Phira had been banished to the Inbetween and I was taken from her and placed in the care of my human parents.

"You needed our help?" Phira asked with her brows knitted together.

"Yes," I said, my voice cracking slightly as the weight of the situation settled on me once more. "Winnie is really sick, and we're running out of options."

"Let's go speak to King Mitah." Phira placed a reassuring hand on my shoulder. "He might be able to help."

As we made our way through the lush gardens toward the palace, I marveled at the beauty of Faery. Delicate winged creatures flitted among the flowers, and the air smelled like warm honey and fresh rain. The magic was in every breath I took, and for a moment, I allowed myself to believe that everything would be all right.

"Olivia," King Mitah greeted me with a warm smile as we entered his throne room a while later. "It is good to see you. What troubles you?"

"Ava's aunt Winnie is very sick with witch cancer. Do you think the fae healers could help?" I asked hopefully.

My uncle-king's somber expression told me what kind of answer he had for me. "Unfortunately, there is no known cure for her illness." He tapped a finger on his chin and looked thoughtful. "However, there might still be something we can do."

"Anything," I whispered, desperation edging my voice.

King Mitah squeezed my hand gently. "I already knew of this plight, and I knew of the witch Winnie's search for a body. If you had not come to me now, I would have sent for you tomorrow. There is a fae woman who had a potion go very wrong. Her spirit has moved on, but her body remains. She had no family and died very recently. We haven't performed the ceremony to let her body pass on to the earth yet."

"Are you suggesting...?" I trailed off, not wanting to voice the possibility forming in my mind.

"Yes," he said softly. "I can petition the court to see if they will allow Winnie to use the fae's body instead of letting it pass on. However, the next court session isn't for a few weeks."

"Please, do whatever you can. I don't know if Winnie has that long."

He cupped my cheek. "I'll do everything within my power to expedite the court proceedings. I can't make any promises because the Elders are set in their traditions."

"Thank you, Uncle," I whispered, tears filling my eyes.

"Olivia," he said gently, reaching out to touch my hand. "Remember that we are all connected in this world, and the bonds of friendship and family are our greatest strength. No matter what happens, never forget that."

"I won't," I promised, squeezing his hand in return.

I returned from the Fae realm with strong emotions churning inside me. Hope, fear, and a sense of urgency tightened my chest as I thought about Winnie's fate hanging in the balance. As soon as my feet touched the living room floor, Ava stared at me expectantly, her eyes filled with concern.

"What did King Mitah say?" she asked.

"Okay, so good news and bad news." I tried to keep my tone light. "Good news is, there might be a solution." I told her about the fae woman who died. "The bad news is it could take a few weeks until we know anything for sure. Mitah will need to ask the court for permission to give the body to Winnie. Also, there's no known cure that the fae have."

Ava turned to the stairs. "Let's go fill Winnie and Alfred in. At least Alfred has the ability to tether Winnie's spirit to himself. That's an option if we need to use it. Or we could animate her."

I nodded. "It's a good plan."

Our only plan, because we needed to keep Winnie's ghost on earth until we got a body for her.

10
AVA

I SAT in a chair beside Winnie's bed, watching her sleep. Even in her sleep, I could sense her pain.

Alfred and I exchanged a worried glance before discussing our options in hushed tones. We had already considered tethering Winnie's spirit to Alfred using his necromancer powers, but we both knew that would only be a temporary solution. Having a ghost tethered to him for a lifetime would be draining to his powers and miserable for Winnie.

My healing powers were useless and bringing her back as a ghoul may or may not work in this body, since the healing didn't. We didn't know what the cancer would leave the body like. This was such a rare thing. We also had no idea if the original inhabitant of the body had done a spell to prevent animation. Many witches did.

"Isn't there *anything* else we can try?" I asked quietly, racking my brain for any magical loophole or ancient spell that might help.

"Unfortunately, we're running out of options," Alfred admitted. "But we'll keep searching. Maybe there's something we've overlooked. There's got to be something."

The sound of the front door opening and closing pulled me from my thoughts, and Rowan's and Zoey's voices echoed throughout the house. I glanced one last time at Winnie, who was dozing peacefully, and then made my way downstairs to greet them.

"Hey, you two," I said as I entered the living room, stopping short when I saw a massive house plant that now dominated our coffee table. "Wow. That's a lot of green."

"Isn't it great?" Zoey beamed and stroked one leaf. "We found it at this cool little nursery on the edge of town. We thought it'd be a pleasant addition to the place, you know, brighten it up a bit."

"Yeah. We just need to pick a good place for it," I said. It was nice, but geez, it was enormous. "How's your dad?" I asked Rowan.

"He's fine. One of the pride member's houses caught fire. They figured it out to some old wiring, but Dad's leading the repairs."

He'd gotten a phone call and had to get back to Louisiana pronto. Olivia had portaled him home yesterday.

The front door flew open, and Ian stormed in, looking surly, like he'd just gone ten rounds with an angry bear. He stopped abruptly when he saw us, his eyes flicking between the houseplant and the three of us.

"Uh, hey there, Ian," I said, taken aback by his expression. "Everything okay?"

He didn't respond, simply stared at the plant for a long

moment before wordlessly heading upstairs, leaving us all exchanging puzzled glances.

"Okay, what was that about?" Zoey raised an eyebrow.

"Who knows?" I shrugged, still a little uneasy. "Maybe he's just having a rough day."

"Maybe he's allergic to plants," Rowan suggested with a mischievous grin.

"Ha, yeah." I chuckled halfheartedly, though I couldn't shake the feeling that there was more to Ian's behavior than met the eye.

No sooner had Ian disappeared from sight than the plant decided it was high time for a little dance. Its vines extended in all directions, the leaves rustling like an agitated octopus on steroids.

Winston clearly wasn't amused by the plant's impromptu performance. He rattled his floorboards and opened and shut doors and cabinets in protest.

"Rowan, what the hell kind of—" Before I could finish my sentence, one of the plant's vines wrapped itself around Rowan, hoisting her into the air like some twisted version of a marionette. Her eyes bulged as the vine tightened around her throat, cutting off a scream.

"Rowan!" Zoey yelled, scrambling to help her cousin as I raced toward them.

"Get that thing off of her!" I clawed at the vine with my bare hands. It was like trying to untangle a garden hose made of steel. My powers wouldn't be of any use against a demented houseplant. I could maybe strike it with lightning, but that would almost definitely hurt all of us. Where the heck was Olivia when we needed her?

"Guys? What's going on?" Olivia asked, entering through the kitchen as if I'd summoned her to appear.

"Olivia, do something," I cried out, my nails digging into the vine as Rowan's face turned an alarming shade of purple.

"Right, got it," Olivia said, her eyes narrowing as she focused on the vines. She said a few words under her breath, and a shimmering wave of fae magic erupted from her fingertips, enveloping the plant. The vines shuddered and began to retract, releasing their death grip on Rowan.

"Got you," Zoey gasped, catching her cousin as she slumped to the floor, unconscious. I fell to my knees beside them, immediately channeling my healing energy into Rowan's bruised throat.

"Is she okay?" Olivia asked, concern etched on her face.

"Give me a moment." I flowed as much magic as I could into the poor tiger.

Finally, Rowan's breathing eased, and her eyelids fluttered open. "What happened?" she croaked, still dazed.

"Your new houseplant tried to strangle you." I tried not to sound as exasperated as I felt. "Next time, maybe we stick to something less, erm, murderous."

"Thanks." Rowan rubbed her throat as Zoey helped her to her feet.

"Seriously, though," Zoey said, eyeing the now-dormant plant warily. "Where did that come from? We just bought it at a regular nursery. I've gotten a ton of plants from there."

Olivia studied the plant. She touched its leaves with her fingers. "It's normal now. I mean, I don't feel *any* magic in it."

"Let's just hope this is the last surprise guest for a while." I cast one last wary glance at the innocent-looking houseplant before turning my attention back to Rowan.

"Rowan, are you sure you're okay?"

"Yeah." She coughed and croaked a bit, still touching her throat gingerly. "Just a little shaken, mostly."

"Let's get you back to the guest house." Zoey looped an arm around Rowan for support. "You could use some rest."

"Sounds like a plan," Rowan said weakly, and the girls headed toward the back door.

Once they were safely out of sight, I turned to Olivia with a raised eyebrow. "What the crap was that all about?"

"Spelled." She rubbed her temples as if trying to massage away a headache. "I felt a strong demonic energy when I stopped those vines."

I huffed, crossing my arms over my chest. "Just what we need, a demonic plant."

"Tell me about it," Olivia said with a sigh. "But when I reached out with my powers again, the energy was gone. It's almost as if someone, or something, was controlling it remotely."

"Remote control, demonic plant. Check that off our supernatural bingo." I shook my head, struggling to suppress a snort of laughter. "What's next? Possessed vacuum cleaners?"

"Let's not tempt fate." Olivia shivered. "We have enough on our plate already."

"True," I said. "Let's check on Winnie and figure out our next move."

"Right behind you," Olivia said.

Just as I was about to take the first step toward the stairs, a small corgi came trotting down, her ears perked up and tongue hanging out. "Roxie?" She belonged to Michelle's parents, which meant she slipped through the portal for a little visit.

"Looks like we have a visitor." I bent to pet the enthusiastic pup. "Hey there, little girl."

"Aw, she's adorable," Olivia cooed, joining me on the floor. "Isn't that Michelle's parents' dog?"

"Yep, that's their Roxie all right," I confirmed, scratching the dog behind her ears. With a happy wiggle of her butt, the corgi nuzzled into my hand, clearly enjoying the attention.

The corgi spotted Lucy and Lenore curled up together in the cat bed by the fireplace. Her eyes lit up, and she raced toward them, her stubby legs moving comically fast.

"Uh-oh," Olivia said, sharing a worried glance with me. "Lucy might not appreciate having her nap interrupted."

"Understatement of the century," I mumbled, watching with bated breath as the corgi skidded to a halt in front of the cat bed, her backside wagging furiously.

Lucy sucked in a deep breath, then screeched from her cat bed, eyes wide in terror as the corgi approached. "She's come to eat my baby!"

"Eat your baby?" I glanced at the tiny kitten nestled beside her, then back to the corgi, who seemed more interested in sniffing their fur than devouring anyone. "Lucy, I think you might be overreacting just a tad." I tried not to roll my eyes.

"Overreacting? This is no laughing matter, Ava. She's a ruthless predator, a heartless monster, a—"

"Did someone say monster?" Michelle appeared on the staircase, breathless and looking mildly concerned. When she spotted the corgi, her expression changed to one of surprise. "Oh, There you are, Roxie. You're a long way from home." She cocked her head. "And yet somehow very near.

"Michelle, this *beast* is trying to eat my baby," Lucy cried with all the dramatics, still clutching Lenore protectively.

"Beast?" Michelle echoed flatly, eyebrow raised.

I scooped up the corgi, who wiggled her body happily at the attention, then I handed her to Michelle.

Michelle cradled the dog like a baby and booped her nose. "She must've slipped into their portal closet when I wasn't looking. Sneaky little thing."

"Indeed." Olivia watched the exchange with amusement. "Fear not, Lucy. Your baby will be safe from the dreaded corgi menace."

"Menace is an understatement," Lucy said, still glaring daggers at the dog.

"Right, well, I'll just take him back to my parents' house then," Michelle said, turning to retreat upstairs.

"Good riddance," Lucy grumbled as the corgi disappeared from view. She nuzzled her kitten gently, whispering, "That mean old dog is gone, sweetheart. Mama won't let her hurt you."

The baby hadn't even woken up. "Crisis averted." I shook my head in disbelief at the absurdity of it all.

11
OLIVIA

THE MORNING SUN WAS A WARM, comforting hug as I walked over to the guest house to pick up Zoey and Rowan. It was like the universe telling me that everything would be okay. How thoughtful of the universe to give me a pep talk before my first attempt at teaching kitchen witchery.

I was substitute teaching at the academy today, and to say I was a bundle of nerves didn't quite cover it.

"Zoey, Rowan?" I poked my head through the door.

They were waiting for me. "Let's get this tour started," Zoey said with Rowan at her side.

Zoey had been accepted for fall classes at Rune Academy, and she couldn't wait to show her cousin around the academy.

"Okay, everyone," I said as we went up to the portal room. "I'll be subbing a kitchen witchery class today, so you're welcome to join me and learn something new." I paused for a moment, then added, "Or watch me fail spectacularly. Either way, it should be entertaining."

As we entered the classroom, nerves bubbled up inside me. Kitchen witchery was more Ava's thing, not mine. But Ava had turned down the offer to teach. She'd told me it wasn't much different from fae magic. Now, I was expected to teach these eager kids how to infuse magic into their baking. No pressure, right?

"Hi, hello." I did my best to sound confident in front of a room full of teenagers. "I'm Ms. Olivia, and I'm your sub. Today, we're going to bake muffins. But not just any muffins—magical muffins."

The students' eyes lit up with excitement, and I swallowed hard, hoping I wouldn't let them down.

"First, you'll need to choose a spell or intention you'd like to infuse into your muffins. It could be something simple, like bringing happiness or luck to the person who eats it, or something more complex, depending on your skill level." I glanced over at Zoey and Rowan, who exchanged excited whispers. As tigers, they couldn't infuse, but they could bake.

"Once you have your spell in mind, we'll start baking. As you add in the ingredients, focus on the magic you want to incorporate and visualize it swirling within the batter."

I walked around the room, giving guidance and answering questions while trying not to let my inexperience show. The kids seemed to be enjoying themselves, and I couldn't help a little pride when their faces lit up as they worked their magic into the muffins.

I clapped my hands together to get their attention. "Now that everyone's muffins are in the oven, we'll just have to wait and see how they turn out. Remember, practice makes perfect, so if your first attempt doesn't quite go as planned, don't get discouraged. You can try again."

As the smell of freshly baked muffins filled the air, I quizzed the kids on stuff from their last chapter in the Kitchen Witchery book, flipping pages and pulling stuff out at random.

When the timer went off, I stood. "It's taste-testing time. Let's see how your magical muffins turned out."

The students eagerly presented their creations, eyes widening as the spells hidden within took effect.

"Ms. Olivia, try mine first," said a girl with pigtails who proudly held up her blueberry muffin. I obliged, taking a bite and immediately experienced an explosion of flavor. It was like every single taste bud on my tongue had suddenly become extra sensitive. Wow, maybe magic really did make everything better.

"Whoa." I blinked, trying to regain my composure. "This is delicious. It's like the flavors burst inside my mouth, intensifying every ingredient. Great job, sweetie." The girl beamed at my praise, and I moved on, still savoring the lingering taste of the blueberries.

"Here, Ms. Olivia," said a boy who looked like he'd spent more time eating the batter than actually baking his muffin. I hesitated for a moment, then shrugged. Why not? Taking a bite, I braced myself for whatever spell awaited me.

Laughter bubbled up inside me, completely uncontrollable. I doubled over, tears streaming down my face as I tried to catch my breath. The classroom erupted into a chorus of giggles, the kids reveling in the pure joy of their magical mischief.

"Okay, okay," I managed between gasps of laughter. "That's definitely an A+ for execution." The boy grinned, clearly proud of himself.

My laughter finally subsided, and I wiped away the tears, mentally preparing myself for the next unpredictable concoction.

I approached the next student, a girl with wide eyes and a tight braid. She looked at me, her dark eyes sparkling with mischief. "You might not want to eat this one," she warned, clearly trying to stifle a giggle.

"Really?" I raised an eyebrow, intrigued by her caution. "Why is that?"

"Because it'll turn you into a chicken," she whispered conspiratorially, as if sharing a secret.

"Ah, I see." I pretended to stroke my chin thoughtfully, then leaned in closer and whispered back, "Well, in that case, I think I'll take this one home for my husband, Mr. Sam. He could use a good clucking." The classroom erupted in laughter, and even the girl couldn't help but join in. I winked at her and moved on to the next teen, who blushed under my scrutiny.

"What do we have here?" I tried to maintain some semblance of authority, despite the lingering traces of laughter in my voice. The boy hesitated before shyly offering me his muffin. It was a lovely shade of lilac, adorned with delicate frosting swirls.

"Give it a try," he urged, his voice barely above a whisper.

"Here goes nothing." I took a bite and braced myself for whatever magical effect was about to hit me. I chewed, swallowed, and waited. Nothing happened. At least, nothing I could immediately detect.

"Did I do something wrong?" the boy asked, disappointment clouding his face. And then, just like that, I had no idea who or where I was. Panic surged through me, and I glanced around the room, searching for clues.

"Uh, Miss Olivia?" the boy called out hesitantly, and my memory snapped back into place. "Are you okay?"

"Yes, I'm fine." I clutched at his station, still reeling from the brief moment of disorientation. "That was impressive." And completely terrifying. I swallowed hard and forced a smile. Then I told the class what happened. "His spell made me forget who I was for a few seconds. Very well done."

I'd have to look up what spell he used and file it away for a rainy day.

"Really?" He beamed, clearly relieved by my approval.

"Absolutely." I tried to shake off the lingering unease.

As I made my way around the room, tasting each magical muffin, I encountered a wide array of spells, from one that made my hair temporarily change color to another that caused me to speak in rhyme for a full minute. The students eagerly watched, thrilled with the chaos they'd created.

"All right, my little kitchen witches," I said with a grin as I surveyed the classroom. "I must say that I'm thoroughly impressed. You've all managed to not only create delicious muffins but also effectively weave magic into them. Bravo. You guys should give yourselves a pat on the back. I mean, who knew that magic-infused baking could be so... uh, transformative?" I chuckled, recalling the rollercoaster of sensations and emotions I'd experienced while tasting their creations.

A chorus of giggles echoed through the room, and the students exchanged amused glances.

"Does this mean we all get As?" one eager young witch piped up, her eyes hopeful.

"Indeed, it does." I nodded my head. "Each and every one of you has demonstrated exceptional creativity and skill today. So yes, congratulations, you've all earned yourselves an A for this class."

The room erupted into cheers and high-fives as the students celebrated their success. Their enthusiasm was infectious.

"Okay, okay." I raised my hands to quiet them down. "Let's not get too carried away. Remember, there's still plenty of learning to do in your next classes, so don't let this success go to your heads. It's time for us to clean up." I helped the kids pack up their muffins and clean their stations.

"Thank you, Ms. Olivia," they murmured as they began tidying up their workstations and gathering their belongings.

"Hey, don't thank me," I said with a wink. "You guys are the ones who put in all the hard work and made this class a memorable experience. Keep exploring your talents, and who knows what amazing things you'll accomplish?"

As the students filed out of the classroom, Zoey and Rowan going with them, chattering excitedly about their magical culinary adventures, a warm sense of accomplishment settled in my stomach. Sure, my taste buds may have gone on an unexpected journey today, but it was well worth it to witness the creativity, passion, and growth taking place right before my eyes.

12
AVA

"It's time for a friendly game of Clue." I organized the board game as Zoey, Rowan, Larry, Michelle, and Wallie gathered around the table. My gaze darted to the clock on the wall, waiting for Olivia to arrive so we could head to the coven meeting together.

"Ah, yes, because nothing says friendly like accusing each other of murder," Lucy said from her usual spot on the windowsill.

"Rowan did it in the library with the candlestick." Wallie laughed and pointed at Rowan before we even started the game.

"Nice try, Wallie. But first, we have to shuffle the cards." I chuckled at his eagerness.

As we dove into the game, Ian sat off to the side, watching us intently. The way he stared at Rowan made me uncomfortable, and I couldn't shake the feeling that something wasn't right.

"Colonel Mustard in the conservatory with the revolver."

Rowan's voice snapped me out of my thoughts as she made her guess.

"Wrong," Zoey responded playfully. "You'll never figure it out."

"Oh, yes I will, just you wait," Rowan said, her competitive streak showing.

"Hey Ian, why don't you join us?" I hoped to distract him from his creepy staring contest with Rowan.

"Uh, no thanks. I'm just enjoying watching the game." He twitched and forced a smile.

"Suit yourself." I narrowed my eyes at him. It was time for an intervention.

"Excuse me, everyone. I need to step outside for some fresh air." Staring at my brother-in-law, I flared my nostrils. "Ian, how's about you join me outside? Now." I grabbed his arm and dragged him out of the living room before he could protest.

"What's going on, Ava?" Ian looked offended once I got him on the back deck, the warm evening breeze lifting my hair.

"Cut the crap, Ian. I saw you staring at Rowan, and it's creeping me out. What's your deal?" I folded my arms across my chest. If he answered the wrong way, I was zapping him with a little lightning. He was a hunter. He could handle it.

He waved his hands in mock-supplication. "Staring? No, no, I was just watching the game."

"Really? Because it looked like you were trying to bore holes into her skull with your eyes." I glared and waited for him to explain that.

"Okay, fine, maybe I was staring a little." He rubbed the back of his neck awkwardly. "It's not what you think."

"Enlighten me, please." I didn't bother hiding how furious I was.

"Look, Ava, I'm sorry if it seemed creepy. I promise I won't do it again." He avoided my gaze. "Can we just go back inside?"

"Fine." It didn't appear I'd be getting any answers out of him. "But remember, I've got my eye on you."

"Understood." Ian nodded once, walked back into the house.

I turned to follow just as Olivia materialized in my kitchen. "Hey."

She grinned. "Hi. You ready to go?"

"Almost." I glanced back at the board game in progress, then turned to Ian. "Ian, you should probably head out. Now."

"Right," he mumbled, stuffing his hands in his pockets and heading for the front door without another word.

I pulled my phone from my back pocket and texted Wade.

You working tonight?

No, it's my night off. I'll be right up.

"Everything okay?" Olivia asked, concern furrowing her brow as we watched Ian leave.

Wade emerged from the basement. "Hang on," I murmured. I waited for him to join Olivia and me before explaining about Ian and his weirdness. "Wade, can you sit with the kids? Ian was watching Rowan like he wanted to strangle her, and it was creeping me out. I told Ian to leave, but I'd feel better if you were up here keeping an eye on things."

"Sure." Wade moved to the fridge where he had his own special stash of bagged blood. It was convenient for him to have some up here, as well as his apartment in the basement.

I grabbed the amulet from my office, then my car keys. "Guys, Olivia and I are heading to that coven meeting. We'll be back later."

"Have fun," Zoey called out, grinning mischievously as she moved her game piece.

We pulled up to Melody's house fifteen minutes later. The coven members were already gathered in Melody's cozy living room, murmuring amongst themselves. As we entered, the conversation died down and all eyes turned to us—or rather, the amulet I held in my hand.

"Thank you for coming, everyone," Melody said. "Ava has brought something for us to examine tonight."

I stepped forward, holding the amulet out for everyone to see. "I've been trying to destroy this thing, but so far, no luck."

Melody stepped closer, her gaze locked on the amulet. She reached out a hand, then hesitated, as if feeling an invisible barrier. "Ava, this amulet is tethered to you. It's giving off some seriously bad vibes. You need to find a way to get rid of it."

"Trust me, Melody, we tried. But nothing seems to work. We thought we'd ask the coven to see if anyone knew anything else." I'd hoped someone would tell me how to destroy it. The news about it being tethered to me was unnerving. "What do you mean, it's tethered to me?"

"I mean, it's drawing on your magic." She squinted. "I can't tell well enough to see if it's hurting you, but it can't be helping. It's too evil."

Olivia touched my arm. "I can't sense it at all."

"Nor can I." I stared at the amulet and tried to use my inner magic to visualize the tether, but it wouldn't come to me. "This thing is too stinking powerful."

I handed it off to the twins, Ben and Brandon. They examined it before passing it on to the next coven member. "I haven't seen anything like it," Ben said.

Brandon shook his head. "It feels old."

"The Viking necromancers had it." I told the coven all about the Vikings and how I'd killed them with my powers, which had not been my intention at the time. My lightning powers were harder to control when my emotions were high or my life or the life of a loved one was threatened.

When the last member, Leena, looked the amulet over, she handed it back to me. "Sorry, I've never seen it either."

"Thank you for looking into it." I carefully placed the amulet back into the small velvet pouch I'd brought it in.

"Of course, Ava," Melody said. "Just be careful until you can get rid of it, all right?"

"Believe me, I will," I promised.

She looked at the gathered coven. "Please, check your grimoires, family histories, and the like. If you think of any ideas, even remote ones, call Ava."

They murmured their agreement, then we stayed and enjoyed some food with the group, catching up. It was nice to have an evening away, have a glass of wine, and talk to my friends.

By the time we returned home, the kids had cleaned up the game and were nowhere in sight. Lucy and Snoozer were snuggled into one cat bed, with Lenore between them.

"Did you find a way to destroy that amulet?" Lucy asked without opening her eyes. Seriously, what was it with cats and their sixth sense?

"Unfortunately not." I sighed and put the amulet on the mantel. "No one had any ideas we haven't already tried."

"Maybe we should ask Luci for help," Olivia suggested.

"He's already looked at it, but we could ask him to take another look." I closed my eyes and summoned him. "Lucifer. I could use your help."

Lucifer appeared before us in his normal silent and kinda creepy way. "What's up, ladies?" he asked, his devilish grin as smug as ever.

"I'd like you to take another look at this amulet." I handed it to him.

When it touched his hand, he frowned. "When I looked at it before, it wasn't tethered to you. Have you been handling it?"

"Well, yeah. Liv and I have been trying to destroy it, but it just won't die."

"Can you try to destroy it?" Olivia asked.

"Let's see." Lucifer held the amulet in his palm. With a flash of hellfire, he attempted to incinerate the cursed thing. Surprise, surprise, the amulet remained unscathed.

"Interesting," Lucifer mused, his eyes narrowing. "This amulet is quite resilient."

"Tell us something we don't know," I said under my breath.

"I can't destroy it," Lucifer admitted, a hint of frustration in his voice. "But I can keep it in my collection until you find a way to get rid of it for good."

Lucifer took a deep breath, his eyes glowing with power. He raised a hand over the amulet, muttering an incantation under his breath. A sharp pain shot through my chest as the tether between the amulet and me broke.

"Ouch. That was intense." I rubbed my chest over my heart.

"Sorry about that." Lucifer didn't sound particularly apologetic. "The tether is broken now, but you mustn't touch the amulet again. It might reattach itself to you."

"Thanks for the warning." I was grateful for his help, despite his smug attitude. "And thank you for getting it off of me."

"Take care, ladies," Lucifer said, disappearing in another puff of smoke with the amulet safely tucked away.

13
OLIVIA

I HAD JUST WALKED into my kitchen when I spotted Lucy, her paw expertly prying open one of the upper cabinets.

It hadn't been the first time Lucy-Fur had come over. For whatever reason, she liked to visit on occasion. I really hadn't paid that much attention to why.

"No," I yelled. That was where I'd stashed the magic-laced muffin I'd brought home the other day. You know, the one that turned people into chickens. Of course, cats weren't known for their impeccable listening skills, so naturally, Lucy completely ignored me.

In a flash, Lucy thrust her head into the cabinet and emerged with the tainted muffin clenched in her little feline jaws. She tore off a huge chunk and swallowed it whole before I could even take a step toward her.

"Lucy, you furry little idiot!"

Before the words fully left my mouth, Lucy transformed right before my very eyes—from a fluffy white cat to a plump, squawking chicken. She let out an indignant cluck and bolted back through the still-open kitchen door. So much for a quiet morning at home.

"Great." I sighed. "Just what I needed today."

With no choice but to chase after the newly minted poultry version of Lucy, I sprinted out the door and followed the squawking chicken across the lawn, past the two new houses, around the pool, up the deck and into Ava's kitchen.

As I entered Ava's house, I found the place teeming with people. The kids were gathered around the kitchen table getting ready to eat, oblivious of the panicked chicken-cat hybrid frantically darting through the room. "Excuse me, pardon me." I wove around them in pursuit of Lucy.

"Olivia?" Ava called out in surprise. "What on earth are you doing here?" She stared at Lucy-etta in shock.

"Long story, but that chicken is Lucy." I puffed, pointing at the panicked bird. "She ate a prank muffin."

Ava's eyes widened in disbelief, and she bit her lip to keep from laughing. "Eggcellent." Together, laughing our butts off, we tried to corner Lucy without breaking any furniture.

"Olivia, remind me later to have a serious conversation about magic-laced baked goods and their proper storage," Ava said.

"Deal." I grunted, barely suppressing a laugh about the absurdity of the situation. "First, let's catch ourselves a chicken."

"Lucy ate a magic-laced muffin and turned into a chicken," Ava yelled out as we followed a screeching Lucy past Larry, Zoey, Rowan, Wallie, and Michelle. "We need to catch her."

"Wait, what?" Larry said, his eyebrows raised in confusion.

"Long story." I rolled my eyes. "Can you just help us catch Lucy?"

"Sure thing." Zoey joined our ragtag chase team, along with Larry, Wallie, and Rowan.

"I'm too large to run after a chicken, so I'll stay here and keep an eye on breakfast." Michelle settled back in the chair and forked up a big scoop of eggs. "Erm, sorry, Lucy!"

It was hard to chase a chicken when laughing this hard.

"Okay, everyone spread out," Ava said. "We have to corner her before she gets too far."

"Or before she lays an egg." The visual that statement brought to my mind made me stop and clutch the wall as I laughed.

The group collectively groaned at my bad joke. "Everyone's a comedi-hen," Wallie said, and then of course everyone laughed. The buttfaces.

"Come on, back to it," Ava yelled.

We chased Lucy through the house and eventually outside, where she darted around the yard like a feathered rocket.

"Got her," Larry cried triumphantly, finally scooping up the feathery, shrieking Lucy.

Just as I breathed a sigh of relief, Ava gasped and pointed toward the beach. "Uh, guys?" she said, her voice a mix of amusement and disbelief. "You might want to take a look at this."

Our gazes followed her finger, and we found ourselves staring down at Ian, who was dancing naked on the beach like a madman.

"Wow," Rowan said, shaking her head. "I knew Ian was a little off, but I didn't think he'd go full-on nudist dance party."

"Uh, should we do something?" Wallie asked, clearly uncomfortable with the situation. "That's just weird."

"Maybe someone should go down there and give him a towel or something." Zoey bit her lip, trying to suppress her laughter.

"More like a straitjacket," I said. "What is happening with this day? Clucking cats and nudist brothers-in-law?" He wasn't my brother-in-law, but we were all so close it kind of felt like it.

Ava closed her eyes and shook her head before turning away from the sight of Ian's wriggling member. "I'm never going to be able to burn that image from my memory, but Ian's not our problem right now," Ava said firmly. "Our focus is on getting Lucy back to normal."

"Agreed." My gaze flicked between Ian's naked gyrations and the chicken in Larry's arms. "But honestly, can this day get any stranger?"

"Olivia." Ava smirked, patting me on the shoulder. "In our world, there's always room for more weirdness."

She wasn't wrong.

Once inside, I plopped down on the couch. Ava and the rest stood around me, waiting for an explanation.

"Okay, so…" I tried to find the right words to explain the bizarre series of events. "I brought home a muffin laced with magic from the kitchen witchery class I taught. The plan was to let Sam eat it as a prank, but I forgot about it. Lucy managed to get her paws on it, and now we have a chicken instead of a cat." I looked at the poultry and realized she was glaring little chickeny daggers at me. "From the other muffins, the effects shouldn't have lasted this long, though."

"Wait, so the muffin turned her into a chicken?" Rowan asked, scratching her head.

I nodded. "And now we need to figure out how to turn her back."

"Any ideas?" Ava asked.

"Unfortunately, no." I sighed. "But we've dealt with weirder things before. We'll figure this out."

"Maybe there's something in one of my spell books." Ava headed toward her bookshelf.

As Ava searched through her collection of magical tomes, I recalled the days when our lives were simpler. No talking cats or magical mishaps. Even with all the chaos, I wouldn't trade our supernatural adventures for anything.

"Found it." Ava held up a dusty old book. "There's a spell in here to reverse animal transformations."

"Perfect," I said.

Ava read aloud from the book, her voice steady and confident as she chanted the words. A shimmering light enveloped Clucy-Fur, and within moments, our sassy feline friend was back to her normal self.

"Lucy," I cried out, scooping her up in my arms. She hissed at me, clearly not pleased with the whole ordeal.

"Unhand me, you fool." Lucy squirmed out of my grasp. "I need to find Lenore and recover from this traumatic experience."

"I really am sorry, Lucy," I said sheepishly, watching her strut away with her usual air of feline superiority. I exchanged a glance with Ava, who simply shrugged.

"Never a dull moment around here, huh?" I remarked, putting an arm around her shoulder.

"Wouldn't have it any other way." Ava smiled, leaning into me as we watched Lucy disappear down the hallway, her tail held high.

Later that afternoon, Sam came over, looking a little more frazzled than usual. He must've had another one of his psychic visions.

"Hey, honey," I greeted him as he walked through the door. "You okay?"

"You won't believe the vision I just had," he said, running a hand through his hair. "I saw Ava holding a swaddled baby, but I couldn't see the baby clearly."

"Really?" I raised an eyebrow, trying to suppress a grin.

Ava snorted. "Well, it's probably Baby Butt."

"Actually…" Sam hesitated. "I'm pretty sure it was Ava's baby. I don't know why, but I just had the strongest feeling."

Ava threw her head back and laughed. "Oh, really? You calling me fat, Sam? You saying I look pregnant?" She stood and turned sideways, rubbing her belly for emphasis, making us all chuckle.

"Uh, no, of course not." Sam held up both hands, his face turning an impressive shade of red. "I didn't mean it like that. I just...I don't know what it could mean."

"Relax, Sam." Ava patted his arm. "I'm not offended. But seriously, me with a baby?" She shook her head, still grinning. "No way."

As we continued to laugh off Sam's vision, my mind started racing. What if there was more to it? Maybe it wasn't literal, but something symbolic. Ava was half-necromancer, half-witch, and all-around magical badass. Could this vision be hinting at something else?

14
AVA

I JOLTED AWAKE, heart pounding as the sound of a scream tore through the night. Even Snoozer and Lucy were wide-eyed at the end of my bed, their fur standing on end. I said a few choice words under my breath because who doesn't love to be woken up in the middle of the night by a scream that could raise the dead? Then again, being half-necromancer, I could do just that on my own.

"Someone's screaming like they've seen a ghost," Lucy said, her snarky tone mirroring my thoughts. "Or worse."

"Great observation, Sher-cat." I scrambled out of bed.

The rest of the house was awake as well. Doors slammed and footsteps thundered down the stairs. Flinging the covers off me, I joined the frenzy, hoping there wasn't another paranormal catastrophe waiting for me downstairs.

As I reached the bottom of the stairs, I found Larry and Zoey at the backdoor. I joined them. Rowan and Ian were in the backyard fighting. Rowan looked weak, barely able to fight Ian off, while Ian screamed at the top of his lungs, "Why won't you die already?"

Terror coursed through me. What was Ian doing? How could he?

"Hey," I shouted as I stepped outside. "What's going on here?"

"Stay out of this, Ava," Rowan hissed, struggling to push Ian away.

"I will not stay out of it. This is my house!"

Ian's eyes were filled with a rage I'd never seen before.

"Seriously, Ian?" I said. Even as the words left my mouth, I sensed it.

This was not Ian. Not the Ian from a few weeks ago. Not the Ian I'd known for a while now.

As I stared at Rowan and Ian, it became clear that something deeper was going on here.

"Enough!" I shouted, my voice echoing through the night. My hand shot up, and with a flick of my wrist, a wave of magical energy erupted from my palm, separating Rowan and Ian like two magnets repelled by an invisible force as lightning cracked across the sky.

Sam and Olivia emerged from their house, their expressions a mixture of concern and annoyance. With his vampire strength, Sam flashed across the yard and easily subdued Ian.

Olivia caught up a minute later and dropped beside Rowan and Zoey. Zoey was checking Rowan over.

"Olivia, will you call Pearl?" I rubbed my temples. I didn't want to bother Drew, and Pearl needed to figure out what the heck was going on with her grandson. "We're going to need her help unraveling this mess."

She pulled out her phone and dialed the number. "Sure thing."

As I led Ian into my living room, followed by a sullen Rowan, the weight of the situation settled on my shoulders. The tension between them was almost suffocating, and I was going to get to the bottom of whatever their issues were.

"Listen." I folded my arms and leveled a stern gaze at the pair. "You two are going to start talking, and you're not leaving this room until we've figured this out. You've clearly got something against one another, and I want to know what it is."

"Good luck with that," Lucy said.

I looked down at her. "You're not helping. Go see if your kitten is okay."

The mention of her kitten had her scurrying from the room. She was a surprisingly devoted mama.

"Ian. Talk." Olivia glared at my brother-in-law as she pocketed her phone. "Why were you trying to kill Rowan?"

He just growled and glared at Rowan. "This is all her fault."

"Excuse me?" Rowan's eyes flashing with indignation. "You're the one who attacked me."

Before anyone could say anything else, a bright flash illuminated the room as Pearl Walker appeared via portal. She took one look at Ian and gasped. "*You*. How are you back?" Her eyes were wide with shock and disbelief.

"Uh, what?" I glanced around the room, trying to follow her gaze. "Who are you talking about?"

"Never mind that," Pearl snapped, her brows furrowing in worry. "Someone call Lucifer immediately."

Great, because this night wasn't confusing enough already.

Calling the ruler of Hell seemed to be a bit of an overreaction, but I summoned him just the same. "Luci?"

Pearl eyed me. "Does he not have a phone?"

I grinned. "He does. Summoning him annoys him."

Olivia shrugged. "It really doesn't bother him as much as he lets you think."

"Happy witching hour," Luci's smooth voice filled the room as he materialized beside me. "Ah Ferdinand, what are you doing here?"

"Who's Ferdinand?" Rowan asked, confusion etched on her face.

My face mirrored hers and everyone else's in the room.

"Wait, what?" I echoed, just as bewildered. Luci was looking right at Ian, but seemed to be addressing someone else entirely.

"HELLO, LUCIFER," Ian's voice rang out, but it wasn't Ian speaking. The tone, the inflection—it was completely different, as though another person had taken up residence in his body. Pearl's earlier panic made sense. Ian was possessed by someone named Ferdinand, and for some reason, he was back.

"Spill it." Luci had his King of Hell voice out. He meant business.

Ferdinand—or rather, Ian's body being controlled by Ferdinand—sighed and ran a hand through his hair. "You see, it all began when I was summoned to kill a tiger family. Because I was bound to the summoner, I couldn't refuse. I was instructed to eliminate 'the family,' but the summoner didn't specify *which* members of the family exactly." Ferdinand shrugged. "I took advantage of that ambiguity. I killed Zoey's parents, yes, but I couldn't bring myself to kill a child."

"Thanks, I guess." Zoey wrapped her arms around her middle.

Ferdinand bowed his Ian-head and clasped his hands together.

"You are most welcome. Instead," Ferdinand went on, "I found a dead tiger cub in India and left it beside Zoey's parents, hoping that would be enough to satisfy the summoner. By the time I realized Zoey had run off, she was long gone and impossible to find." He smiled wanly. "Impossible, irritable, whatever, I didn't look."

"But possessing Ian?" I pointed out, raising an eyebrow.

"He was the closest hunter," Ferdinand-Ian said. "Stationed near the tigers in north Louisiana. This time when I was summoned, I was much stronger. I didn't have to abide by her wishes, so I've been trying to discreetly kill her."

I gasped. "The plant."

"Yeah, among other things that failed spectacularly." Ferdinand-Ian crossed his arms. "I'm rusty. I poisoned her dinner, but then she barely ate. I put a venomous snake in her bed." He shrugged. "I have no idea what happened with that."

Rowan scoffed. "I live in Louisiana. You think I don't know to check my bed for snakes?"

Luci crossed his arms. "Who summoned you? Who's responsible for all this?"

Ferdinand hesitated for just a moment before pointing a steady Ian-finger at Rowan. The room collectively gasped, and shockwaves rolled through us all.

"Rowan?" Zoey choked out, her voice trembling with disbelief and hurt. "You're the reason my parents are dead? Why?"

Rowan just glared at us all.

"Zoey deserves answers," I insisted, my gaze locked on Rowan. "She deserves to know why her entire life was turned upside down."

Rowan glared at me, then Zoey. This wasn't at all the sweet young woman who'd arrived days ago wanting to reconnect with her long-lost cousin. "*My* father was meant to lead our pride. He was strong, wise, and fair. But he was cheated out of his rightful place, and your birth only served to solidify the usurper's hold on power."

"So, you thought killing my parents would...what? Magically make everything in your life better?" Zoey's voice cracked and tears welled up in her eyes. "Did you even care about the collateral damage you caused? Did you ever stop to think about how this would affect me?"

"Of course I did," Rowan shot back, her own eyes glistening with unshed tears. "You were supposed to die as well. Sacrifices have to be made for the greater good."

"Your version of the greater good is seriously warped" As much as I wanted to rip into Rowan some more, I forced myself to focus on the task at hand.

"Olivia, can you open a portal and bring Gerard here?" I hoped that Zoey's uncle could help us make sense of this mess. "We need to tell him what's happened."

"Of course." Olivia nodded, her eyes clouded with concern. She raised her hands, and a shimmering portal appeared in the middle of the room. A moment later, Gerard stepped through in his pajamas, looking disoriented.

"Wha—Ava? What's going on?" He took in the tense atmosphere. His eyes widened as they landed on Rowan cowering on the couch, and his expression grew dark. "What did she do?"

"Rowan summoned a demon to kill Zoey's parents," I explained, my voice heavy with disappointment. "She wanted you to be the alpha and believed sacrificing Zoey and her family would achieve that goal."

Gerard's face paled, and he looked at Rowan with disbelief and heartbreak. "Is this true?"

With a shrug, Rowan nodded. "And I would do it again."

Gerard put one hand on the back of the high-back chair. He was steadying himself, but probably didn't want to be too obvious about it. "You betrayed not only Zoey and me but the whole pride." His voice trembled with barely contained rage. "The punishment for killing an alpha without an official challenge is death."

"Father, you have to understand," Rowan pleaded, desperation etching her features. "It was for the greater good. Your rightful place was stolen from you."

"Greater good?" Gerard shook his head, tears glistening in his eyes. "There's nothing good in murdering innocent people and tearing families apart."

"Please, Father, I did it for us, for our family." Rowan sobbed, reaching out for him, but he moved away from her grasp.

"Enough," Gerard snapped, his voice choked with emotion. "As much as it pains me, I am duty-bound by pride law. I cannot make exceptions, even for my own daughter." He looked at me, anguish clear in his gaze. "Ava, I'm so sorry. I never imagined she’d do something like this."

"Neither did I." My heart ached for Gerard, who was losing his daughter, and for Zoey, whose world had been torn apart by someone she'd trusted.

"Is there anything we can do to help her at this point?" Olivia asked quietly, her voice barely audible over Rowan's sobs.

"Unfortunately, no," Gerard said with pain in his voice. "The law is clear, and we must abide by it."

"Zoey." Gerard turned toward my adopted daughter. "You're the rightful alpha. You should take your place."

"Me? An alpha?" Zoey shook her head. "No. Thanks, but I'll pass. I'm more of a 'tend to my plants and avoid responsibility' kind of gal."

"It is who you were born to be," Gerard insisted.

"Look, even if I wanted to, which I don't, I can't be an alpha." Zoey's gaze darted nervously toward me. She took a deep breath before continuing. "I can't form a bond to the pride because, well, I'm not alive."

Gerard studied Zoey. "What do you mean, you're not alive? Are you saying you're dead?"

Zoey looked sheepish, so I said, "More like undead." Then I looked at Rowan. "For someone who claims they're innocent, you sure do squirm a lot." With a flick of my wrist, I conjured magical handcuffs to hold her in place. The silver cuffs shimmered as they locked around her wrists.

"Is this really necessary, Ava?" Rowan asked, wincing as the cuffs tightened slightly.

"Let's call it an insurance policy." I gave her a mock grin. "Now, Zoey, why don't you and Gerard have your heart-to-heart?"

Zoey shot me a grateful glance before turning her attention back to her uncle. They started talking about her life after her parents died, how she'd actually died herself before I found her and brought her back to life—animated her. It wasn't easy listening to the pain in their voices, but she needed to get it out.

"Look, I didn't ask to be brought back, but I'm grateful Ava found me." Zoey had tears in her eyes. "She gave me a second chance at life and a family." Larry scooted closer, glaring at

Gerard. He'd been pretty quiet through all this, but anger simmered under the surface.

"Family is everything, kiddo." Gerard placed a comforting hand on her shoulder.

Pearl stepped next to me. "When Lucifer gets the demon out of Ian, I'll need Drew and Ian to go with Gerard to witness Rowan's punishment and confession."

I nodded with no idea what to say.

Pearl stepped down the hallway to call Drew to fill him in. She clearly didn't have the same problem bothering him during his investigation at the academy.

"Ferdinand, Ferdinand." Luci shook his head as he paced back and forth. "You should've known better than to let yourself be summoned and forced to kill someone. You should've contacted me immediately afterward, but instead, he took matters into his own hands. And you got summoned *again*."

Luci snapped his fingers, and a man appeared next to Ian, who slumped into the chair. The man, Ferdinand, I assumed, looked human, but at the same time didn't look human. The more I stared at him, the more I noticed. His eyes were a little too big. His nose flared out at the tip more than a human's would. His ears were pointed slightly and his lips super thin.

Ferdinand didn't make eye contact as he said, "Rowan summoned me again right before she arrived here. I had the strength to resist the summoning this time, but I chose not to. I wanted revenge for forcing me to kill an innocent family."

"And that's where I come in," Luci said. "To punish him."

I exchanged a glance with Olivia. This wasn't going to end well for Ferdinand, that much was clear.

Luci snapped his fingers, and just like that, Ferdinand transformed into a tiny black kitten.

"Seriously, Lucifer?" I stared at the little kitty. Ferdinand made an absolutely adorable feline. "You turned him into a cat."

Lucifer shrugged nonchalantly. "Well, he needs to be punished, doesn't he? I'll find a good family for him to live with for a hundred years or so."

"Of all the punishments in Hell, you chose this?" I gestured at the tiny black kitten cowering on the floor.

"Hey, don't underestimate the transformative power of being a helpless feline." A wicked grin spread across his face. "Besides, why are you all so surprised? It's the same thing we did with Lucy."

"Wait, what?" Olivia and I said at the same time while turning our gaze toward Lucy, who was perched on the windowsill, looking thoroughly unimpressed by the revelation. My mind raced, trying to piece together the implications of what Luci had just said.

Lucifer chuckled, rubbing the back of his neck sheepishly. "Maybe I forgot to fill you in on the backstory of that. Sorry."

"Could you be any more casual about dropping bombshells like that?" I made a mental note to have a long chat with Luci later. Meanwhile, the kitten huddled on the floor, looking utterly lost and terrified. A pang of sympathy for it tugged at my heart, even though it was once a demon who'd killed Zoey's parents.

I stared at Lucy, trying to wrap my head around the fact that she had once been a demon before her feline transformation. It explained *so* much.

Lucy, however, seemed completely unfazed by the bombshell Lucifer had just dropped on us. In fact, she appeared utterly bored with the whole situation as she sat there, licking her paw nonchalantly.

"Worry about yourselves, "she drawled as she hopped down. She looked at the kitten and sniffed. "I'm keeping him, but I don't like Ferdinand. His name is Poe." She snatched up the newly transformed black kitten by its scruff and sauntered out of the room, Lenore trotting along behind her like a loyal little minion.

"Did...did she just—" Olivia stammered, her eyes wide with disbelief.

"Apparently so." Looked like we had another kitten in the house. I just hoped Ferdinand, er, Poe, didn't talk like Lucy.

Snoozer, who'd been watching the entire scene unfold with his usual air of indifference, let out a heavy sigh, almost as if he were saying, "Here we go again."

With one last glance at us, he followed Lucy and the kittens out of the room.

15
AVA

"NOTHING LIKE A BIRTHDAY nap to make an old lady feel young again." I stretched and rolled out of bed. After fluffing my hair and washing my mouth out, I made my way down the stairs. Snoozer, Lucy, and their kittens trailed behind me.

"Old? You're practically a spring chicken compared to some of the witches we know." Lucy leaped off of the stairs, then growled. "Maybe not a chicken."

It took everything in me not to laugh. Lucy was still incredibly sensitive about her time as poultry. "Thanks, I guess." As I entered the living room, Zoey sat engaged in a conversation with Drew and Ian. Their faces were serious, and the tension hung thick in the air. So much for my relaxing birthday vibe.

"Hey, guys. What's going on?" Trying to sound casual. The last thing anyone needed right now was more drama. As soon as I really looked at Zoey's face, I knew the answer.

The guys had told her Rowan was gone.

"Oh, sweetie." I wanted to cry for her.

Zoey's eyes brimmed with tears, and the dam was about to burst. She choked out a sob, and my heart clenched at the raw emotion in her voice. "I feel so betrayed," she whispered, her voice cracking. "And I feel stupid for trusting her."

"Hey, no." I rushed over and pulled Zoey into my arms. Her body shook with sobs, and it took every ounce of self-control not to cry along with her. I stroked her hair gently, trying to find the right words to comfort her. "You can't blame yourself for this. Nobody could have predicted what Rowan did."

Zoey curled into me, drawing what little strength she could from my embrace. The room was silent, save for her muffled crying. Drew and Ian exchanged a somber look before quietly excusing themselves, leaving us to talk.

"Sometimes people let us down, Zoey." I tried to sound soothing. "But that doesn't mean you're stupid for caring about them. It just means they didn't deserve your love and trust."

We stayed like that for a while, Zoey's tears gradually subsiding as she allowed herself to be comforted. Zoey had been there for me, and I'd always promised to do the same for her.

My phone rang, and I awkwardly fished it out of my pocket while still holding Zoey. I met Larry's gaze for the first time since coming downstairs. He sat in the armchair next to the window, watching like he wasn't sure what to do. There really wasn't anything he could do. What Zoey was going through called for a mother daughter-moment. I was glad to be here for her.

"Hello," I said, answering the phone.

"Happy birthday!" Olivia laughed, then started singing to me.

Badly.

I put it on speaker, and it had the desired effect: it made Zoey chuckle. She sat up and wiped her eyes, then she held out her hand to Larry, who got up and moved to sit next to her.

"Thanks, Liv," I said.

"I was wondering if you could come over. I need your help with something."

"Sure. I'll be right over." I stood and headed out the back door to walk over to Olivia's house.

Olivia's kitchen had been transformed into a magical wonderland of baked goods and party balloons.

"Happy birthday." Sammie stood proudly next to a plate of cookies on the table. "I made these for you using magic."

"Wow, Sammie, these look amazing." I was unable to hide my delight. I just hoped those magical cookies didn't turn anyone into a chicken. Lucy still refused to talk about her adventure.

Zoey even managed a small smile at the display, and her spirits lifted ever so slightly.

"Go on, try one." Sammie bounced on his feet.

"Which one?" I feigned indecision even though I'd already picked out the scrumptious-looking cookie shaped like a witch's hat. As I took a bite, the rich chocolate flavor exploded in my mouth — it was easily the best cookie I'd ever tasted. "This is incredible, Sammie."

"Thanks." He beamed up at me.

Olivia picked up a cookie and waved it at Sammie. "Don't fill up on cookies. We're still going to Ava's for an early dinner."

"My house?" I asked. "I just got here."

Olivia grinned at me. Ah-hah. She'd just called me out of the house to set up something for my birthday. I'd have to pretend to be surprised.

An hour later, we headed back to Winston. When we stepped

through the back door, the sight that greeted us was nothing short of astonishing. My living room was *packed* with family and friends, all wearing huge smiles as they yelled in unison, "*Surprise!*"

I clasped my hands together in front of my face as happy tears sprang to my eyes. "Awe, you guys, this isn't necessary."

A split-second later, Michelle gasped. We turned to see her standing in a rapidly growing puddle of water, her eyes wide with shock.

"Um, surprise?" She squeaked, her voice more than a little sheepish. "My water broke."

Olivia's jaw dropped. "You're having Baby Butt right *now*?"

"Looks like it," Michelle said with a nervous laugh that turned into a moan as she clutched at her stomach. "Ohhhkay, that hurts!"

Wow, okay. This was definitely a first for my birthday. What a wonderful birthday gift if she even had it today. First-time babies often took forever to make their entrances. I waved my hands as I tried to figure out what we should do next. "We need to get you to your parents, pronto."

Olivia sprang into action. "Right. Birthing room. Got it. Zoey, can you grab some towels from the bathroom? Everyone else, let's clear a path for Michelle."

"Come on, Michelle." I wrapped an arm around her for support. "We're going to get you through this."

"Thanks, Ava." Her voice wavered, but she was determined. "And, uh, happy birthday?"

"Best birthday gift ever." The chaos of the moment only adds to the surreal beauty of the day.

"Everyone," I announced. "This party is officially canceled. Baby Butt has decided that today is the day."

Joy filled the room as everyone began to rush around cleaning up so I could deal with Michelle and Wallie.

We gathered our things and prepared to head over to Michelle's parents' house via the portal. She was doing a home birth because her aunt was a witch midwife. Baby Butt was too magical to be delivered in a normal hospital. I was planning to be there because I could heal. Hopefully, I wouldn't be needed.

"Let's just get there before Michelle gives birth on the living room floor," Olivia said as Michelle doubled over with a contraction.

"Agreed," I said, trying to keep from freaking out myself. Baby Butt’s power wrapped around Michelle and sent pulses of magic outward.

"Come on, Michelle," I said, trying to sound encouraging as we made our way up the stairs. "Just a few more steps and we'll be in the portal room."

"Easy for you to say," Michelle grumbled between gasps. She was gripping Wallie's arm so tightly her knuckles were turning white.

My son didn't complain. He simply supported her and rubbed her back, whispering words of comfort. "Almost there, sweetheart," Wallie told her, his voice strained but loving.

"Great, because I don't think this baby can wait much longer." Michelle's voice was laced with panic. She'd reached the end of her tolerance for pain.

"Deep breaths, Michelle." Olivia brought up the rear with the diaper bag and other supplies, although I knew for a fact Michelle’s parents were fully stocked with baby items.

"Deep breaths? Are you kidding me?" Michelle gasped, then

let out a sudden, gut-wrenching scream that made me freeze in my tracks.

"Michelle!" Wallie cried, his face a mask of worry and fear.

"Baby's coming now!" she shouted, her legs buckling beneath her.

I dropped to my knees without thinking and reached out just in time to catch the wriggling, slippery bundle that emerged from Michelle. Everyone in the vicinity lost their minds, yelling and scrambling. I kept calm and conjured a blanket, deftly wrapping my brand new baby granddaughter in it as Wallie and Michelle watched in shock.

Wallie picked Michelle up and carried her through the portal to her parents' house. I followed closely with my precious granddaughter in my arms. We moved very slowly, as the umbilical cord still had Michelle and Baby Butt attached to one another.

The moment we stepped through the portal, a wave of warmth and the scent of lavender embraced us. I glanced around at Michelle's parents' hallway before turning my attention back to the tiny miracle in my arms. She had a full head of dark hair and the most beautiful, delicate features I'd ever seen. Her eyes were closed, but I just *knew* they'd reveal themselves as a stunning shade of blue once they opened.

"Wallie, help Michelle get settled in her bedroom," I instructed, my voice soft but firm.

He nodded and carried her down the hall with me shuffling right with them. Once inside her room, Wallie laid her on the bed. Aunt Mandy bustled over, her experienced hands making quick work of the umbilical cord. She examined Michelle while the rest of us respectfully gave the baby all of our attention. Once she pronounced Michelle in tiptop shape, Mandy took

Baby Butt from me to do the same. She exchanged a few hushed words with Michelle as she laid the baby in Michelle's arms, who calmed under her care. I recognized it as a relaxing spell.

Wallie curled up beside Michelle and looked down at their daughter. "She's beautiful. I think it's time we tell them this little lady's name. What do you think?"

"Definitely," Michelle said, gazing lovingly at the baby. "Imogene Annette. Imogene after my grandmother and Annette after Yaya." Yaya's name had been Brenda Annette, so that was perfect.

"Imogene Annette," I repeated, rolling the name around in my mouth. "It's perfect."

As Aunt Mandy continued tending to Michelle and baby Imogene, Wallie sat by Michelle's side, showering her with love and affection. It warmed my heart to see them so happy, surrounded by family and magic. In this moment, everything felt right in the world.

"Congratulations, both of you," I told them, beaming at the new little family. "Imogene is absolutely beautiful, and she's lucky to have such wonderful parents."

Drew came in and wrapped his arms around me from behind. "She is beautiful."

I looked up at him, surprised. "Olivia called you?"

He squeezed me tight. "Of course."

I glanced at my bestie. "Thanks."

She just winked and left the room, leaving us to our family moment.

"Thank you, Ava," Michelle said, her eyes shining with gratitude. "We couldn't have done this without you. You've been there for us every step of the way, and we'll never forget it."

"Of course," I replied, a lump forming in my throat. "That's what family is for, isn't it?"

The atmosphere in the room was filled with love and warmth as Wallie and Michelle cradled their newborn daughter. Images of Clay, my late husband, flashed through my mind, and I felt a bittersweet tug in my chest.

"Clay would've been so proud," I whispered to them, my voice thick with emotion. "He'd be over the moon to see his grand-daughter."

"Thanks, Mom." Wallie gave me a watery smile. He knew better than anyone how much his father had wanted to be a grandpa, and it was a shame they didn't get to share this moment together.

"Your dad's spirit is definitely here with us," I assured him, smiling through my tears. "He's watching over all of you."

I moved closer to the new family and gently took Imogene Annette into my arms, marveling at the tiny bundle of life. Her little fingers curled around mine, and my chest filled with an intense surge of love for this child who had just entered our lives.

"Hi there, sweet girl," I cooed, brushing her soft, dark hair away from her forehead. "I'm your Grandma Ava, and I promise to always be here for you."

"Isn't she something?" Drew asked.

Wallie said, "That's your Grandpa Drew."

Drew's gaze jerked to my son. "Thank you," he whispered. "That's an honor."

Wallie gave Drew one of those silly guy nods, and I tried not to bawl, unable to take my eyes off Imogene. As I held her close, a powerful energy radiated from her small body. It was like nothing I'd ever experienced before, and I knew without a doubt that she was going to be someone extraordinary.

"Wow," I murmured, feeling the baby's power build, even as a newborn. "This little one has some serious magic in her. She's going to be a force to be reckoned with."

"Guess she takes after her grandmother," Michelle said, giving me a grateful smile.

Hopefully so much more.

16
AVA

I WAS SNUGGLING LITTLE IMOGENE, marveling at the perfect tiny human I held in my arms, when Luci made a grand entrance. The usual sarcastic remark that accompanied his appearance was notably absent. Instead, he looked like he'd just crawled out of a dumpster after being beaten up by a gang of supernatural thugs. His clothes were torn, his face was battered and bruised, and he had an alarming amount of dirt under his fingernails.

"Please, Ava," he croaked, desperation seeping through his voice. "I need your help."

"Wow, Luci." I was unable to resist the urge to add some snark. After all, what would the king of Hell need my help for? "You look like you lost a fight with a lawnmower."

"Ha ha, very funny." He glared at me, then winced as the action clearly caused him pain. "I'm tracking a monster across the remotest parts of the Highlands. It's one of the ones that escaped from Hell, and I could really use your assistance."

"Luci, I don't know if you've noticed, but we're kind of busy here with our own little miracle." I glanced down at Imogene, who'd started to doze off in my arms. "Can't this wait?"

"Normally, I wouldn't ask, but it's urgent." He hesitated, then added, "I don't actually need you to hunt the monster. I need your healing power. One of the few remaining ogres has been injured by this hellbeast, and I need you to heal it."

"An ogre?" I raised an eyebrow, already mentally preparing for the smell that would likely accompany such a creature. "You know, they aren't exactly known for their love of humans, right?"

"Trust me, I'm aware." Luci sighed. "But it's important. Please."

I glanced from Imogene to Luci, torn between the desire to help and the need to cuddle with my granddaughter while her mama was asleep.

"Fine, but we're doing this quickly, and then we're coming straight back here. Understood?"

"Absolutely." Luci nodded, relief flooding his features.

"Great. Let me give Imogene back to her daddy." I carried Baby Butt upstairs and through the portal. When I stepped into Michelle's bedroom at her parents', she was awake.

With one last snuggle and a whispered promise to return soon, I handed Imogene over to Michelle and followed Luci out the door, praying that I hadn't just made a terrible mistake.

I took a deep breath and glanced at Luci. "Okay, let's go."

"Thank you, Ava." He looked genuinely grateful. With a wave of his hand, a bright portal appeared in front of us.

We emerged on the other side to find ourselves in a remote clearing, surrounded by thick trees and the distant sound of rushing water.

"Where exactly are we?" I surveyed the area. Trust Luci to bring us to the middle of nowhere.

"Somewhere in the Scottish Highlands." He looked around as if trying to get his bearings. "The ogre should be close by."

"Great. Let's just hope she's not the 'I'll eat your bones for breakfast' type of ogre."

"Ah, there she is." Luci pointed toward a large figure lying a few yards away. As we approached, I braced myself for the worst. I mean, this was an ogre we were talking about. I expected something out of a bedtime story—huge, ugly, and terrifying.

When we got closer, she wasn't quite what I'd imagined. Sure, she was stocky and had greenish skin, but otherwise, she just looked like an ordinary woman.

Easing closer, I squatted beside her and placed my hand on her cold skin, hoping that maybe there was something I could do to help. Oh, no. "She's gone." What a strange sense of loss.

"Can you bring her back?" Luci asked, his tone almost desperate.

"I can try, but..." I trailed off at an unexpected flutter beneath my palm. Holy freaking crap. "The baby is alive."

"Baby? What baby?" Luci looked as surprised as I felt.

"Looks like your little scuffle with the ogre left more than just one casualty, Luci." My voice trembled as the reality of the situation sank in. "She was pregnant."

"Can you save the baby, then?" Luci's eyes were pleading, desperate. "Ogres are so rare."

"Let's hope so."

Okay, focus. I can save this baby.

I positioned my hands over the ogre's swollen belly. I just need to concentrate and...

Before I could even finish that thought, the ogre's belly convulsed, and with a sudden wet splort (yeah, I didn't know that was a word either), the baby shot out of its mother like a slimy cannonball.

"Whoa!" I managed to catch it mid-air. As the newborn squirmed in my arms, a burst of laughter escaped me. "That's the second baby I've caught today, and I don't want any more surprises like this."

"Is it okay?" Luci asked, his voice cracking with concern.

"Seems so." I wiped the goo off the baby ogre's face. "Congratulations, Luci, you're an honorary uncle."

"Very funny," Luci said, rolling his eyes, but they had relief in them, too.

The baby ogre opened its eyes for the first time, locking gazes with me. Also, for the second time today, I conjured a blanket to wrap him in.

There was something captivating about those deep green orbs, and a strange connection formed between us. This little one had no idea what kind of world awaited him, and neither did I, but at least we'd be navigating the chaos together.

Together it was because I was keeping this baby. At least until we found his family or… Good grief, what would I do with a baby ogre?

I cradled the baby protectively. "Let's get back home and figure out what to do next."

With a nod from Luci, we portaled back home.

We reappeared in my cozy living room. "Seriously though, no more catching babies for me, paranormal or otherwise."

"No more babies." Lucy gave the baby a very Lucy-ish glare. "You know, Ava, there are easier ways to expand the family."

"Tell me about it." I settled down on the couch with the baby ogre nestled in my arms. "But sometimes, life just has other plans."

I glanced down at the now sleeping baby ogre and said, "Welcome to the family, little one."

Drew walked into the living room and stopped mid-step. As a hunter, he'd no doubt sense that the bundle in my arms was not human. He glanced at the baby and a soft smile formed. Meeting my gaze, he said, "I take it we're keeping him?"

"Yes." I tilted my face up so Drew could kiss my lips. "Are you okay with being a dad to a baby ogre?"

"If anyone could raise a baby monster, it's us." Drew hugged me and the baby close.

What was one more member of this magical family, after all?

PREORDER the next installment of Witching After Forty, A Monstrous Midlife now!

If you want to know what murder Drew investigated, check out With a Wand in the Library.

If you want to know more about Ross the werewolf, read A Witching Babymoon.

READ AN EXCERPT FROM HUNTING IN THE MIDLIFE

Hunting in the Midlife is the first in a new spin off series featuring Blaire and Lily, Drew's sister.

Get your copy of Hunting in the Midlife Here

Here is the first chapter of Hunting in the Midlife.

Chapter 1

CHAPTER ONE: Blair

Lachlan James was my best friend and the father of my child. I loved him dearly, but if he didn't go away, I was going to neuter him.

"They're like a bunch of whiny pups," he said in an irritatingly petulant voice. He really didn't mean that, but he was the '*whiny pups'* alpha, so he had to deal with them. Well, technically, his beta, Reed, took care of pack issues and disagreements between packmates. That didn't stop Lach from coming to me to complain.

"Yeah, I can sympathize." Looking up from my laptop, I tried to give him *the* look. You know the one. The one that said he was being a brat and needed to get out of my office. Now.

I had work to do.

He didn't take the hint. Instead, he continued to complain about his pack's problems, which weren't really problems at all. Lach had been alpha for about five years now, and sometimes the peopling aspect of the job got to him. That's when he hid in my office and vented. Sometimes he pretended he worked there, and I took advantage of the free labor. It amused me that he was a born alpha and a darn good leader, yet he was an introvert.

He was one of those introverts who were quiet around people he didn't know and in large crowds, but he was playful and outgoing among friends and family.

I didn't mind him hiding out in my office at my antique store—My Junk, Your Trunk. Truly I didn't... usually. Today, my best friend was wearing on my last nerve. I wasn't sure why.

He turned to me and stared until I glanced up at him again. Then a slow, sexy smile formed. "You want to play hooky from our responsibilities today?"

I shook my head, knowing that we'd end up getting into some kind of trouble. We usually did. Like Bonnie and Clyde, only we didn't rob banks or kill people. And we weren't lovers. Not anymore.

Reaching over, I slapped the desk as I noticed something missing. The staple remover was gone from its usual spot. I certainly hadn't moved it. Narrowing my gaze as if that would help me see something that wasn't there, I shuffled some papers around, thinking it got shoved under them somehow. I needed to go through the monthly accounts receivable reports line-by-line to make sure everything was correct, and it was much easier if it wasn't stapled together.

I recently got a new printer/copier, and it was one of those fancy does-everything-but-wash-dishes-for-you types. When I printed out reports with several pages, it stapled them together. I hadn't yet figured out how to change that setting.

"Lachlan, did you move my staple remover?" I hadn't meant to cut him off mid-sentence, but that's exactly what I did. Rude. Oops.

He stared at me with his brows bunched so closely together they looked like a unibrow. "Why would I do that?"

My reply was simple and to the point, with an eye roll added in for good measure. "Because you thought it would be funny?"

He and our twenty-nine-year-old daughter were always moving stuff on me and playing all kinds of pranks. Wolves loved to be playful with their family and pack. They could also be fiercely protective. And territorial.

Lach reached across my desk and opened the middle drawer. Sure enough, there was my staple remover. It had been placed in a little nook of the drawer organizer, just big enough for it to fit. Technically, *technically*, that was where it was supposed to go. I used it often and didn't like getting it in and out of the drawer, so I kept it on my desk, on top of my inbox, which was almost constantly overflowing with papers.

He stared at me with amusement in his hazel eyes. His lips twisted as if holding back a smile, knowing I would get annoyed. Like that had ever stopped him before.

"It's not funny!" I wasn't really mad. He loved to play pranks on me, and I usually gave as good as I got. I couldn't pinpoint why I was so irritated today. Just one of those things that happened to us after fifty, which I'd just turned this past September. Random bouts of irritability and impatience.

Hello, midlife.

"Though I didn't put it there," he began in a perfectly reasonable voice. "That *is* where it goes, isn't it?"

I grumbled something unintelligible, and he smiled. He was always smiling. It was one of the many things I loved about him, just not at this moment.

"Always joking," I said as he walked out of my office toward the front of the store.

He laughed, not at all offended by my grumpy tone. That was Lach. Always up for a good time—in more ways than one. His inability to be too serious had been one of the main reasons we were still best friends after all these years, but never married, or mated, as shifters called it. We'd tried that once. Dating, not marriage. We'd celebrated a little too hard on my twenty-first birthday and slept together. We'd both woken up the next morning full of regrets and embarrassment. Promises of never doing the deed again were made. Our friendship was too important. Then six weeks later, a big fat plus sign on the pee stick.

But Lachlan was still a huge part of my life. Despite the lack of sexual interest between us, we made amazing co-parents. I would have never survived raising a shifter baby while being shunned as a hunter. I unofficially retired the day Meggan was born. Our daughter would be turning thirty next June and was the most amazing person, getting the best of both her parents.

We'd done something right in this life, at least.

Making my way to the front, I picked the mail up off of the counter and shuffled through the credit card offers and sales ads, and then went to pick up the letter opener. I liked to open my mail up here so I could toss the junk and my office wouldn't get cluttered with unopened mail. I kept my letter opener behind the counter, tucked in the corner.

It wasn't there.

Lachlan had been up to his old tricks again. I sighed and went back to my office to look in the drawer he'd put the staple remover in. Sure enough, there was the letter opener tucked away in the right side of the drawer.

Lach had a fondness for ghosts and mysteries, which was why he enjoyed playing pranks like this. He used to blame things on ghosts, but I knew better because I got hot flashes when ghosts were around. Don't ask. I don't know why.

It made me laugh despite my mood, and I couldn't wait to see what other pranks he had in store for me. Oh, wait. Yes, I could.

For now, I just needed to get my admin stuff done so I could focus on customers. Ignoring Lach as he sat in the chair behind the counter, pushing off with his feet and twirling in circles, I went to the front door and switched the sign from closed to open.

It was time to get this shop up and running. I would've wished for a slow morning so I could get the rest of my paperwork done, but I needed the business.

I didn't even make it back to the counter before the door chime went off, announcing my first customer. "Hello?" she called tentatively.

Turning, I realized I recognized her. Mrs. Flowers. She'd bought a decorative kettle the day before. Hopefully, she'd loved it and had come back for more. "Welcome back," I said warmly. "Please come in."

"Yes, hi. I need to return this kettle." She held a bag out in front of her like it was a ticking time bomb, and I couldn't help but wonder why, though I had a sneaking suspicion.

She opened the bag and pulled out the kettle, setting it gently on the counter in front of me, then backing away as it might blow at any moment.

"Is something wrong with it?" I frowned down at the thing and hated to ask. At the same time, I needed to know to confirm my suspicion.

"Oh, yes," she whispered. "I tried to boil tea in it last night, and it went absolutely crazy. As soon as it began boiling, it shot the hot water all over the kitchen, even in directions it shouldn't have been able to." She shuddered as if the memory of her experience would haunt her for the rest of her days. It just might. "We had to leave it until all of the water was empty from the pot, then clean up."

Oh, geez. I hoped she didn't ask for some sort of compensation. Studying her for injuries, I stretched out my hunter powers to see if I could pick up on ghostly activity. No hot flashes, which meant it didn't have a ghost hitching a ride. "I can't imagine why it would do that."

I kept my voice calm even though I absolutely *could* imagine why, but it wasn't like I could tell her that. It had to be cursed. I specialized in such objects, and it made me more than a little upset that one had slipped past me.

I glanced down at the kettle. It looked like any other, though it was strangely still warm even after sitting in the bag. "Did you want a refund or something else?"

"I'd like a different kettle if you have one," she said. "This one seems to be some sort of prank pot, but I can't figure out how. Maybe it was a part of a magician's set."

"I bet you're right," I said, tucking the kettle behind the counter and sliding it toward Lachlan. He grimaced but grabbed it and took it to the back room. "Go pick out any kettle and if it's more expensive, we'll do an even swap." I only had more expensive kettles, but not very much so. It'd be okay. I was lucky she hadn't been seriously injured.

Once I got her all settled and promised her this one was a nice, normal kettle, I hurried to the back room behind my office to check on Lachlan. I found him examining the kettle, turning it over in his hands, and tapping its sides like he might find clues inside.

He glanced at me. "I thought you could sense these things?"

I made a noise in my throat. "Usually, I do, but for some reason, I'm not picking anything up from this. Even now, knowing it is cursed."

That bothered me a lot. I might be a retired hunter, but I still had the magic in my blood. I was born with it. The magic made me stronger and a little faster, and I healed more easily than a normal human. That same power allowed me to sense paranormal beings and decipher which breed they were. My special ability was sensing cursed objects and ghosts. That was why I had opened My Junk, Your Trunk.

"Put it in the sink, please," I directed.

He nodded and lowered it into our basic utility-mop sink. I grabbed one of my many gallons of vinegar—a hunter's first line of defense against cursed objects—and dumped the whole gallon over the kettle.

It sat there like... well, like a kettle. There was no magic or smoke or anything. Not even a small scream of release.

"Rinse it off?" Lach asked.

I shrugged and dumped the vinegar out of the kettle, then turned the water on. The second the water hit the inside of the basin, the kettle began to shriek like a pig being chased by a pterodactyl. It could happen if the dinosaur shifters hadn't been run into hiding by the dragons like a thousand years ago.

I squealed as the water erupted from the end of the kettle's spout. Thankfully, it wasn't hot, but it was incredibly cold tap water. With another shriek, I turned the tap off and followed Lach out of the utility room, slamming the door behind me.

"Well," I huffed. "I'll be dropping that off with the hunters, ASAP."

Lach nodded and handed me a towel he grabbed from a nearby shelf. "I thought you were retired," he grumbled.

"Yeah." I mopped up my face. "Me, too."

Get your copy of Hunting in the Midlife Here

LIFE AFTER MAGIC WORLD

Life After Magic World

Math After Magic

New in 2023: Middle-Grade Fiction Set in the Life After Magic world! Now your kids can read hilarious adventures as well. Or you can. We won't judge. <3

Witching After Forty

A Ghoulish Midlife

Cookies For Satan

I'm With Cupid

A Cursed Midlife

Birthday Blunder

A Girlfriend For Mr. Snoozerton

A Haunting Midlife

An Animated Midlife

Faery Odd Mother

A Killer Midlife

A Grave Midlife
A Powerful Midlife
A Wedded Midlife
An Inherited Midlife
A Fiendish Midlife
A Witching Babymoon *(A FREE Witching After Forty book)*
A Normal Midlife
A Grand Midlife

Fanged After Forty (Paranormal Women's Fiction)
Volume 1 *(Books 1-3)*
Volume 2 *(Books 4-6)*
Bitten in the Midlife
Staked in the Midlife
Masquerading in the Midlife
Bonded in the Midlife
Dominating in the Midlife
Wanted in the Midlife
Sleighing in the Midlife
Awakened in the Midlife
Ransomed in the Midlife
Hoarding in the Midlife

Hunting After Forty
Midlife Hotspots
Midlife Sight
Midlife Accomplice

Godmother Training Academy
With the Wand in the Library

Wears Valley Witches

Volume 1

Next of Twin

Twinnin' Ain't Easy

Keep Your Twin Up

Clash of Twins

Twin Eater

OTHER HILARIOUS FICTION FROM L.A. AND LIA

Life After Magic World

Math After Magic

New in 2023: Middle-Grade Fiction Set in the Life After Magic world! Now your kids can read hilarious adventures as well. Or you can. We won't judge. <3

Witching After Forty

A Ghoulish Midlife

Cookies For Satan

I'm With Cupid

A Cursed Midlife

Birthday Blunder

A Girlfriend For Mr. Snoozerton

A Haunting Midlife

An Animated Midlife

Faery Odd Mother

A Killer Midlife

A Grave Midlife
A Powerful Midlife
A Wedded Midlife
An Inherited Midlife
A Fiendish Midlife
A Witching Babymoon (A FREE Witching After Forty book)
A Normal Midlife
A Grand Midlife

Fanged After Forty (Paranormal Women's Fiction)

Volume 1 (Books 1-3)
Volume 2 (Books 4-6)
Bitten in the Midlife
Staked in the Midlife
Masquerading in the Midlife
Bonded in the Midlife
Dominating in the Midlife
Wanted in the Midlife
Sleighing in the Midlife
Awakened in the Midlife
Ransomed in the Midlife
Hoarding in the Midlife

Hunting After Forty

Midlife Hotspots
Midlife Sight
Midlife Accomplice

Godmother Training Academy

With the Wand in the Library

Wears Valley Witches

Volume 1

Next of Twin

Twinnin' Ain't Easy

Keep Your Twin Up

Clash of Twins

Twin Eater

***

Packless in Seattle

The Midlife Prelude

The Midlife Shift

License to Midlife

Primetime of Life

COMPLETE SERIES

Series Boxed Set

Complete Series Volume 1

Complete Series Volume 2

Borrowed Time

Stolen Time

Just in Time

Hidden Time

Nick of Time

Howling Creek Paranormal Cozy Mysteries

Familiar Magic and a Dead Wolf

Magic Mishaps and Hidden Agendas

Magical Midlife in Mystic Hollow (Paranormal Women's Fiction)

Karma's Spell

Karma's Shift

Karma's Spirit

Karma's Sense

Karma's Stake

Karma's Source

Karma's Spice

Cornellis Island Paranormal Cozy Mysteries

COMPLETE SERIES

An Otterly Secret Scheme

An Otterly Ridiculous Riddle

An Otterly Laughable Lie

Midlife Magic Dating Service

Monsters Matchmaking

Trying the Trickster

Vetting the Vampire

Testing the Troll

Bellarose Cat Cafe

Secret Witches

Suspicious Wizards

Scheming Warlocks

Sisterhood of the Stones

COMPLETE SERIES

Citrine Wishes

Sapphire Omens

Onyx Interruptions

Wears Valley Witches

Volume 1

Next of Twin

Twinnin' Ain't Easy

Keep Your Twin Up

Clash of Twins

Twin Eater

Shifting Into Midlife

COMPLETE SERIES

Pack Bunco Night

Alpha Males and Other Shift

The Cat's Meow

Midlife Mage

Complete Series

Complete Series Special Edition

Unfazed

Unbowed

Unsaid

Uncaged

An Immortal Midlife

COMPLETE SERIES

Series Boxed Set

Fatal Forty

Fighting Forty

Finishing Forty

Immortal West

COMPLETE SERIES

Undead

Hybrid

Fae

The Meowing Medium

COMPLETE SERIES

Series Boxed Set

Secrets of the Specter

Gifts of the Ghost

Pleas of the Poltergeist

An Unseen Midlife

COMPLETE SERIES

Bloom In Blood

Dance In Night

Bask In Magic

Surrender In Dreams

The Firehouse Feline

COMPLETE SERIES

Series Boxed Set

Feline the Heat

Feline the Flames

Feline the Burn

Feline the Pressure

ABOUT LIA DAVIS

Lia Davis is the USA Today bestselling author of more than forty books, including her fan favorite Shifter of Ashwood Falls Series.

A lifelong fan of magic, mystery, romance and adventure, Lia's novels feature compassionate alpha heroes and strong leading ladies, plenty of heat, and happily-ever-afters.

Lia makes her home in Northeast Florida where she battles hurricanes and humidity like one of her heroines.

When she's not writing, she loves to spend time with her family, travel, read, enjoy nature, and spoil her kitties.

She also loves to hear from her readers. Send her a note at lia@authorliadavis.com!

Follow Lia on Social Media

Website: http://www.authorliadavis.com/

Newsletter: http://www.subscribepage.com/authorliadavis.newsletter

Facebook author fan page: https://www.facebook.com/novelsbylia/

Facebook Fan Club: https://www.facebook.com/groups/LiaDavisFanClub/

Twitter: https://twitter.com/novelsbylia
Instagram: https://www.instagram.com/authorliadavis/
BookBub: https://www.bookbub.com/authors/lia-davis
Pinterest: http://www.pinterest.com/liadavis35/
Goodreads: http://www.goodreads.com/author/show/5829989.
Lia_Davis

ABOUT L.A. BORUFF

L.A. (Lainie) Boruff lives in East Tennessee with her husband, three children, and an ever growing number of cats. She loves reading, watching TV, and procrastinating by browsing Facebook. L.A.'s passions include vampires, food, and listening to heavy metal music. She once won a Harry Potter trivia contest based on the books and lost one based on the movies. She has two bands on her bucket list that she still hasn't seen: AC/DC and Alice Cooper. Feel free to send tickets.

L.A.'s Facebook Group: https://www.facebook.com/groups/LABoruffCrew/

Follow L.A. on Bookbub if you like to know about new releases but don't like to be spammed: https://www.bookbub.com/profile/l-a-boruff

Made in the USA
Coppell, TX
12 October 2024